Shakespearean Detectives

SHAKESPEAREAN DETECTIVES

Edited by
MIKE ASHLEY

Carroll & Graf Publishers, Inc.
NEW YORK

Carroll & Graf Publishers, Inc.
19 West 21st Street
Suite 601
New York
NY 10010–6805

First published in the UK by Robinson Publishing Ltd 1998

First Carroll & Graf edition 1998

ISBN 0–7867–0596-5

Printed and bound in the United Kingdom

10 9 8 7 6 5 4 3 2 1

CONTENTS

ACKNOWLEDGEMENTS

The following stories are published for the first time in this anthology and are printed by permission of the authors and their respective agents.

A Man of Middle-Earth and *The Duke of Dark Corners* © 1998 by Gail-Nina Anderson; *The Name-Catcher's Tale* © 1998 by John T. Aquino; *The Chimes at Midnight* © 1998 by Cherith Baldry; *The Price of Virginity* © 1998 by Paul Barnett; *All is True* © 1998 by Stephen Baxter; *Master Eld, His Wayzgoose* © 1998 by Chaz Brenchley (printed by permission of the author and the author's agent, The Carol Smith Literary Agency); *Murder Most Foul* © 1998 by Richard Butler (printed by permission of the author and the author's agent, Dorian Literary Agency); *That Same Pit* © 1998 by Margaret Frazer; *Love's Labour's, Lost?* © 1998 by Peter T. Garratt; *The Fire that Burneth Here* © 1998 by Anne Gay; *A Gift for Killing* © 1998 by Susanna Gregory (printed by permission of the author and the author's agent, A.M. Heath & Co. Ltd); *Three Meetings and a Funeral* © 1998 by Lois Gresh and Robert Weinberg; *The Wine-Dark Cup* © 1998 by Claire Griffen; *Desdemona's Daughter* ©1998 by Edward D. Hoch; *A Good Report of the Worm* © 1998 by Tom Holt; *Love's Labour's Discover'd* © 1998 by Phyllis Ann Karr; *As Near to Lust as Flame to Smoke* © 1998 by Andy Lane; *As Strange a Maze as E'er Men Trod* © 1998 by David Langford; *Introduction* and *War Hath Made All Friends* © 1998 by Edward Marston; *Footsteps in the Snow* © 1998 by Amy Myers (printed by permission of the author and the author's agent, Dorian Literary Agency); *We Are for the Dark* © 1998 by Stan Nicholls; *Conspiracy Theory* © 1998 by Tina and Tony Rath; *Fortune's Other Steward* © 1998 by Mary Reed and Eric Mayer; *Stolen Affections* © 1998 by Lawrence Schimel and Jeffrey Marks; *Murdered by Love* © 1998 by Darrell Schweitzer (printed by permission of the author and the author's agent, Dorian Literary Agency); *Beneath Which Hour?* © 1998 by Peter Valentine Timlett; *A Kind of Wild Justice* © 1998 by Ron Tiner; *Methought You Saw a Serpent* © 1998 by Peter Tremayne (printed by permission of the author and the author's agent, A.M. Heath & Co. Ltd).

INTRODUCTION

Edward Marston

Like its predecessor, this anthology is inspired by Shakespeare's comedies, tragedies and histories. Characters and incidents are lifted from the plays and refashioned into whodunnits which stand on their own as mystery stories and, at the same time, throw new light on old dramas. This volume differs from *Shakespearean Whodunnits* in that it also includes stories which relate to unattributed plays, all of which have their supporters among scholars as the work – at least in part – of the Bard of Avon. These tales take us down less familiar paths and thereby help to deepen the mystery.

No writer has suffered more from the insidious effects of myth and hype than William Shakespeare. The first myth which must be dispelled is that we know almost nothing about him. In fact, we know far more about him than we do about any Elizabethan dramatist apart from Ben Jonson. Samuel Schoenbaum's definitive *William Shakespeare: A Documentary Life* lists all the documents relating to the playwright, and builds up a detailed picture of his life and times. Unfortunately, the portrait is largely one of Shakespeare the husband, the father, the country gentleman, the businessman and the litigant. What is lacking is material about his interior life as a creative artist.

The second and more pernicious myth is that this humble son of a Stratford glove-maker did not write the plays at all because he lacked the intelligence to do so. This is patent nonsense. John Shakespeare, his father, achieved a measure of civic renown, becoming, in turn, chamberlain, member of the town council, one of the fourteen aldermen privileged to wear the black cloth gown trimmed with fur and, in 1568, high bailiff, an office equivalent to a mayor.

His status gave his son automatic entry to King's New School in Stratford-upon-Avon, where the teachers were Oxford graduates and the educational standards were dauntingly high.

Hours were long and holidays infrequent. Learning was structured around Latin and pupils in the upper forms were forbidden to speak anything else. Roman drama was closely studied and it is no surprise that Shakespeare based *The Comedy of Errors* on a play he first encountered at school – *Menaechmi* by Plautus. A boy trained in the rigours of an Elizabethan classroom would be better versed in classical rhetoric and Roman literature than most holders of university degrees in classics today. Nor did Shakespeare's education end there. His capacity for learning was unlimited and he had ready access to books throughout his career.

When his father was high bailiff, one of his functions was to license performances in the town by visiting troupes, and Shakespeare was doubtless enthralled by the performances. He would almost certainly have travelled to nearby Coventry to witness the medieval mystery plays staged annually on Corpus Christi Day. These, too, would have left their mark on his imagination, and there are touches of Herod in more than one of his villains. Some years ago, in conjunction with the city's repertory company, I adapted the surviving Coventry Pageants for performance in the ruins of the old cathedral. Even in our own more cynical age, they proved to have enormous interest and theatrical appeal. To a God-fearing boy from Stratford in the sixteenth century, the full cycle of pageants must have been an overwhelming experience.

Shakespeare then was no country bumpkin who stumbled into the theatre by mistake. He was a gifted young man who discovered an affinity with drama at an early age and who devoted much of his adult life to it. Though he began as an actor, it is as a playwright that he achieved supremacy, serving his apprenticeship before spreading his wings as the resident poet with the Lord Chamberlain's Men (which later became the King's Men). Shakespeare was the only major dramatist of his day to have a stable relationship with a single company throughout his career, and the benefits were immense. While some of his rivals struggled to make a living, he retired to Stratford as a relatively wealthy man who made wise business investments.

Play-writing is a precarious existence in any era but it was especially fraught in the Elizabethan period. Though the demand for new plays was high, there were severe interruptions to theatrical life in London. The plague closed the theatres on many occasions and obliged companies to tour the provinces. Puritans and Privy Council looked with disapproval upon the profession and it suffered a further buffeting from the Master of the Revels whose office read and licensed every play before performance. Censorship was strict and those who flouted it could be imprisoned and tortured. Thomas Kyd, Ben Jonson and Thomas Nashe were gaoled, as were other writers whose work caused offence.

Collaboration was a normal part of the creative process and plays were often the work of more than one hand. Thomas Middleton made a telling contribution to *Timon of Athens* and Shakespeare worked with George Wilkins on *Pericles*. His collaborator on *Cardenio* and *All Is True* was John Fletcher, celebrated now for his lengthy partnership with Francis Beaumont though clearly attuned to Shakespeare's genius as well. Even such prickly individuals as Ben Jonson and John Marston saw the advantages of collaboration. Revision of another's play was also a useful source of income. Plagiarism, the sincerest form of collaboration, was an art perfected by many. One name on an Elizabethan drama is never a guarantee of sole authorship.

Among the plays in the Shakespearean Apocrypha are *A Yorkshire Tragedy, Arden of Faversham, Edward III* and *The London Prodigal*. The first three of these have generated stories for this anthology. It is highly unlikely that Shakespeare wrote any of them in their entirety but he may well have collaborated on one or more. A.D. Wraight, who has championed Christopher Marlowe's work for many years, has argued strongly that *Edward III* was written by Marlowe though its themes would have had equal appeal to his Stratford rival. We may never learn the truth but we can nevertheless enjoy some fruitful speculation.

My own story is based on *Edmund Ironside*, one of the most marginal of contenders for inclusion in the *Complete Works of William Shakespeare* and yet, in its own way, one of the most fascinating. Historically, Edmund Ironside reigned briefly in the early eleventh century before being decisively defeated by Canute who forced a partition of the kingdom. His subsequent death allowed Canute to take control of the whole realm. The story of Edmund Ironside's bravery would have been well-known to Elizabethan audiences and it is used in the play to make pertinent comments on the contemporaneous political situation. Its subtitle is:

> A true Chronicle History called
> *War hath made all friends.*

If Shakespeare did not write the whole play, he may yet have been a co-author whose contribution is seen most clearly in the striking imagery and the occasional flowering of the blank verse.

I had the good fortune to live in Warwickshire for thirty years, in close proximity to Stratford. I never missed a season, sometimes seeing an individual production a number of times. When the Royal Shakespeare Company launched its Swan theatre, built in the image of an Elizabethan playhouse, I was in the first-night audience to watch a rare performance of *The Two Noble Kinsmen*, another fruit of the collaboration between Shakespeare and Fletcher. The play, which reworks a plot already made famous by Chaucer in *The Knight's Tale*, has spawned one of the stories in this collection, and will continue to intrigue scholars as they try to assess the respective contributions of its co-authors.

Regular attendance at the Swan Theatre gave me an idea for a series of crime novels set in the world of the Elizabethan theatre. The mysteries feature Westfield's Men, one of the leading companies of the day, and the protagonist is Nicholas Bracewell whose position as book holder (or book keeper) involves far more than merely prompting, and exceeds the duties of a modern stage manager. The series not only gave me an opportunity to take an in-depth look at the most glorious period in our theatrical history, it also enabled me to build up a book by book picture of society in Elizabethan England. *The Queen's Head*, the first novel, came out in 1988 and celebrated the four hundredth anniversary of the Spanish Armada. Westfield's Men are still going strong in their tenth outing with *The Wanton Angel* in 1998.

Before I started the series, I made two promises to myself. I would not use Shakespeare, or any other Elizabethan dramatist, as a character in the books; and I would never steal a title from one of the Bard's plays. But my debt to Shakespeare and his contemporaries remains immense. The themes and conventions of Elizabethan drama provide me with my plots, and my characters strut their stuff in doublet and hose. Having worked with actors throughout most of my professional life, I have come to admire their sheer bravery in pursuing such a hazardous career, and I hear constant echoes of their complaints in the plight of their Elizabethan counterparts. Performance conditions may have changed radically but an actor is still a hostage to fortune, walking a tightrope between fame and ignominy.

The capability of Shakespeare is demonstrated to the full in this anthology. He has fired each one of us in quite different ways and sent us off on imaginary flights of fancy. Whether we are harrowed by *Troilus and Cressida* or beguiled by the magic of *The Tempest*, carousing with *Antony and Cleopatra* or sporting with *The Merry Wives of Windsor*, fretting over the publication of the *Sonnets* or straying unwittingly into the Gunpowder Plot, the results are the same. An intriguing whodunnit has been born and Shakespeare lives on.

We hope that you enjoy this large and varied collection of tales and that it will send you back with renewed interest to the plays which instigated them, and to the eternal mystery of the genius who created them.

Edmund Ironside 

WAR HATH MADE ALL FRIENDS

Edward Marston

There is no record of Edmund Ironside *ever having been performed. It was written in the late 1580s when William Shakespeare was still serving his apprenticeship as a playwright and is awash with the kind of material which engaged him during that period. Shakespeare would have been familiar with the legendary king from the pages of Holinshed, on whom he relied so heavily for historical source material. In* The Chronicles of England, *Edmund is remembered as the man who 'for his noble courage, strength of body and notable patience to suffer and endure all such hardness and pains as is requisite in a man of war was surnamed Ironside.' In short, an English hero.*

In its portrayal of national strife, the play anticipates the three parts of Henry VI, *while the character of Edricus foreshadows that of Warwick the Kingmaker, changing sides at crucial moments with devastating effect. Edricus, the fictional counterpart of Eadric Streona, Earl of Mercia, is the most interesting and well-drawn figure in the play, holding the balance between Edmund Ironside and his fierce Danish rival, Canute. In his long soliloquy, Edricus revels in his villainy and sounds at times uncannily like an early version of Richard III. For this reason he was an irresistible choice as the narrator of* War Hath Made All Friends.

After a close study of Edmund Ironside *more than one scholar has come to accept it as a discarded work by Shakespeare. It has been suggested that its political themes fell foul of the Master of the Revels. Those same themes reappear in* Titus Andronicus *along with a remarkably similar use of language and imagery. It is tempting to believe that Shakespeare simply shifted his story back in time to Ancient Rome to escape the hostility of the censor. Had they seen* Edmund Ironside, *an Elizabethan audience who gloried in the defeat of the Spanish Armada would have found special significance in the rhyming couplet delivered by a hostage who is cruelly mutilated at Canute's behest.*

> *We go thy cruel butchery to ring.*
> *Oh England, never trust a foreign king.*

The end justifies the means. That is my firm belief. Peace justifies war. Friendship justifies hostility. Survival justifies treachery. The pleasures of love justify the vilest act of seduction. And power – sheer, naked brutal, beautiful power – justifies any villainy which is used to attain it.

And I should know.

My name is Eadric and I am Ealdorman of Mercia, a title which I have held for almost a decade. I am one of the most powerful men in the kingdom, entrusted with the governance of all the lands between the Thames and the Humber. Everyone who dares to lay claim to the throne seeks my support. They call me Eadric Streona, curling their lip as they do so, but I bear that 'Streona' with a certain pride. It means that I am acquisitive, a quality sneered at by most people, yet one which they all share to a greater or lesser degree. What red-blooded man is not stirred by ambition? Who but a fool has no wish to acquire wealth and influence? Is not growth the most basic law of nature?

Because I am more ambitious than anyone else I have been more acquisitive, and that kind of success always breeds envy. Let them mock. Let them set me down as The Grabber. While they strike at me with a feeble taunt, Eadric Streona will go quietly on acquiring more property, more money, more friends, more status and much more power.

I will revel in my nickname and treat it as my prime acquisition.

Canute appreciates my worth. That is why he courted me above all other. With a man like me in his camp, his position was strengthened beyond measure. And so was mine for a time. Our armies were in Wessex when the first crisis arrived. Canute swept into the room, pulsing with fury and spitting his words out.

'Eadric!' he yelled.

'Yes, my Lord?'

'We have been betrayed!'

'By whom?'

'Leofric and Turkullus.'

'Ah!'

'The two earls have run back to Edmund to bleat their apologies like a pair of sheep. I trusted them, Eadric! I relied on their support.'

'That, perhaps, was a mistake.'

'A serious one.'

'Serious,' I agreed calmly, 'but by no means fatal. And better that they should defect now than on the battlefield where their treachery could inflict more harm. These are bleak tidings, my lord, but you have the means to punish their betrayal.'

'The hostages!'

'Yes, dread sovereign. It is always wise to extract pledges of loyalty in human form. Leofric and Turkullus each leave a favoured son in your keeping. The flight of the fathers means instant death for their progeny.'

'No,' said Canute, eyes blazing with revenge. 'Not death, Eadric. That would be too swift a release for them. I have other designs.' He clapped his hands and a guard came running. 'Take three men and fetch the sons of Leofric and Turkullus. Away!' The guard hurried off and Canute turned back to me. 'When those foul traitors left, they willingly sacrificed their sons to the sword. But I will betray their expectations as they betrayed me. The pretty boys will live as testaments of my anger.'

'Let them rather die,' I urged.

'Never!'

'But their fathers' villainy demands it. Anything less than summary execution would seem too light a sentence, my lord. They will say that Canute is weak and soft-hearted.'

'Not when they look at those two sons.'

'Dispatch them straight,' I argued with a persuasive hand on his shoulder. 'Send word to their fathers of the terrible consequences of their flight. It will shake their hearts. Kill them, my lord. Or let *me* send them to their graves. The situation demands it.'

Canute bristled. 'I make the decisions here!'

'Of course. But you did seek my counsel.'

'And you have given it Eadric.'

'Then let me give it once more.'

'No!' he snarled with a peremptory wave of his hand.

There was nothing more than I could do. I was not really pleading for execution because it was a more serious punishment. I wanted to spare two fine and handsome young men from the agonies which they would surely face. Long years of fighting against Danish warriors have made me well acquainted with their savagery. In the circumstances a quick death would be a form of blessing.

The prisoners were dragged in by the four guards. One look at Canute's expression told them what had happened, but they did not flinch. In times of war, even the most loved of sons is expendable. They understood that. They were prepared to meet their fate with a mixture of courage and resignation.

'Leofric and Turkullus are traitors!' roared Canute, drawing his sword. 'They have fled and left you behind to face my wrath. What kind of fathers would treat their sons with such contempt?'

'They made an honourable decision,' said one of the prisoners.

'We are ready to pay the price for it,' added his companion. 'Kill me first, my lord. I am not afraid to die.'

'You will be afraid to live when I have finished with you,' said Canute, seizing him by the arm. '*This* is the price a king exacts.'

His sword flashed and cut clean through the prisoner's wrist. A second vicious stroke claimed the other hand, but Canute's rage was still not appeased. Only when he had sliced off the captive's nose was he satisfied, leaving him drenched in blood as he turned to mutilate the other hostage with equal severity. I looked away from the punishment. Two young warriors would never bear arms again. Two handsome faces would be spurned by every woman for their grotesque ugliness. It would be a species of Hell for them.

'Take them away!' ordered Canute. 'Bind their wounds and turn them out. Let the world know what happens to those who desert me.'

Hiding their pain with great fortitude, the two hostages were hauled out by the guards. Canute wiped his blood-sheathed sword then gave me a grin of triumph.

'Was not that a more fitting penalty, Eadric?' he said.

'Yes, my lord,' I lied.

'Nobody will say that I am soft-hearted now.'

'Nobody.'

And I wondered how soon it would be before *I* betrayed him.

Edmund was not idle. Having secured the support of London, he moved into Wessex to try to restore its allegiance to the old dynasty. We met him first at Penselwood, then at Sherston, in indecisive skirmishes with losses on both sides. Edmund was a doughty soldier and more men flocked to his banner each day, inspired by his valour to attest their abiding hatred of the Danes. It was when he lifted the siege of London then parried our thrust into Mercia that I came to view his leadership with more than admiration. If any man could rout the Danes it was Edmund. So he proved. Canute launched another attack but our army was soundly beaten and forced to retreat to the Isle of Sheppey.

It was time for me to leave.

The name of Eadric still commanded enough respect for my messenger to be admitted to the royal presence. He handed over the letter which I had carefully composed and awaited a reply. Edmund read it slowly through. My words beguiled him. After reminding him that it was I who had helped to keep his father, King Ethelred, in power for so many years, I congratulated him on his feats on the battlefield and wished him success in driving the Danish menace forever from our shores. Imploring his forgiveness, I promised to pledge myself to his cause and renew my loyal service to his family.

Edmund Ironside, as he was now called, was visibly moved by the letter. Though his counsellors warned him that I could not be trusted, he knew the value of my support and overruled them. My unkempt and shabbily-dressed messenger cringed before him.

'Take this reply to your master,' said Edmund firmly. 'We do not wholly pardon his treachery but we will give him welcome if he cares to join our army. His life is safe.'

'Does he have your word on that, my lord?' asked the messenger.

'He does. Eadric will be treated with respect.'

'Then tell him so to his own face,' I said.

Pulling myself up to my full height and casting off the mean apparel of a messenger, I revealed myself as the author of the letter which he held in his hand. Edmund was both astonished and pleased, amazed at my cunning in gaining access to him and delighted that my betrayal of Canute was no ruse to lure him into ambush.

'Noble Eadric!' he said, spreading his arms wide. 'The King of England welcomes you back.'

'Thank you,' I replied, enjoying his embrace and the discomfort it caused his watching counsellors. 'But first attain your kingdom before you try to rule it. Canute still lives and danger is ever-present.'

'That danger has shrunk since Eadric came back into the fold.'

'I hoped that you would see it that way, my lord.'

'I do, my friend, I do.' He nodded eagerly then his face suddenly darkened. 'Why did you betray me?'

'I did not, Edmund.'

'You joined forces with the Danish army.'

'Only in order to learn their strength so that I could report it back to you. They had an English spy in their ranks and not a faithful ally.'

'Yet you fought against us.'

'With reluctance. And only to convince Canute.'

'You killed some of my men.'

'And lost an equal number of my own,' I reasoned. 'Few enough on both sides. War is bound to claim some victims. But I never led an attack, Edmund. I always held back in battle, waiting for the moment when I could follow my heart and ride with an English king once more.'

'So you shall, Eadric.'

'When?'

'When you have told me all you know about Canute's forces.'

'That can be done here and now, my lord.'

'Good,' he said with a smile. 'How large an army can he muster and how does he mean to deploy them? What are his weaknesses and how can we best exploit them? Turn messenger again, Eadric. Tell us the news. Help us to defeat our Danish foe.'

'Nothing would please me more.'

When I gave him the details he sought, the last traces of suspicion fled from his mind. I was accepted. Eadric Streona had lived up to his name once again. In a short space of time I had acquired a new king, a new command, a new security, a new set of hopes and instant repute as the man whose defection would bring about the ruin of the Danish army. I was, of course, too sage a politician to be lulled into complacency.

That night, I wrote to Canute to assure him of my loyalty. These are troubled times. A sensible man always keeps his options open.

The final battle came sooner than I expected and sooner than Canute would have desired. Sailing from Sheppey, his fleet anchored in the River Crouch and he led a raiding party ashore. Intelligencers reported his movements to Edmund who moved swiftly to cut him off. Loaded down with booty, Canute found himself hemmed in near Ashingdon. The only way for him to avoid battle and escape by land was to discard his spoils and abandon his fleet. He had little choice but to fight.

Edmund Ironside had mustered a large army with contingents from Wessex and East Anglia swelled by my own forces from Mercia, but his poorly trained levies would have been no match for seasoned Danish warriors in an equal contest. What gave him the slight advantage was superiority of numbers. Whom should I support? Edmund or Canute? An English king or a Danish usurper? The trick was to appear to favour both sides so that each would be grateful in the event of victory. As I lay in my tent on the eve of battle, I worked out how to pull the trick off.

Our army was camped on Ashingdon Hill, no more than a mile and half away from the enemy. They were in full view. When dawn came on that October morning in the year of Our Lord, a thousand and sixteen, we saw that Canute was assembling his forces on the hill at Canewdon. Edmund Ironside deployed our own army in three divisions with the Wessex contingents under his own command in the vanguard. On the left flank, Ulfcetel had charge of the East Angles while I led the Mercians on the right flank. Sheer weight of numbers told in our favour but I was not convinced that it would be decisive.

Edmund commenced battle by charging down the hill. We obeyed his signal to follow but geography was to have a critical influence. The gradient was much sharper on the left flank and Ulfcetel's men surged down it at a speed which we could not match on the right. I made virtue of a necessity, slowing our descent even more so that we could see how the battle fared before we engaged in it. Edmund and the men of Wessex clashed with the enemy first, then the East

Anglian contingents flung themselves upon the Danes. They fought with spirit but they lacked the ferocity of the marauders. Instinct had warned me to hold back and my decision was proved wise.

Seeing the gap on their left flank, the Danes immediately poured men into it so that they could attack the English from behind. Edmund and his army were suddenly engulfed. Both sides fought fiercely but the clear advantage now lay with the Danes. Since I have never believed in the needless waste of lives, I deemed it a prudent moment to depart from the field with my men. When the battle began, I was in the ranks of Edmund Ironside but I withdrew my support in order to yield the day to Canute. In effect, I fought on both sides and on neither. Whatever the outcome, I stood a chance of currying favour with the victor.

As I quit the field, however, I knew that the result was not in doubt. Canute would be triumphant and that would make him grateful to me. Outflanked and outnumbered, the English fought manfully until late in the afternoon but their cause was hopeless. Ulfcetel perished along with a large proportion of the English nobility, while the majority of Edmund's men were killed. It was a massacre. Edmund Ironside himself escaped with his life and his reputation for steadfastness, but he now had to negotiate from a position of weakness.

Shortly after the battle, he and his foe met at Deerhurst to agree to the partition of the realm. While Edmund was allowed to rule in Wessex, the north came under the direct control of King Canute. Since he now held sway over Mercia, it was to the latter that I naturally turned.

Canute received me with a mixture of suspicion and curiosity. We met on the bank of the Humber, an undisputed part of his kingdom now. I lapsed easily into the Danish tongue. It is always politic to learn the language of an invader. Honeyed words can often achieve more than armed conflict.

'I wondered when we would see you again,' began Canute warily. 'Where did you hide when you fled from the battlefield?'

'That was no flight,' I corrected with a smile. 'It was a carefully planned retreat to hand the advantage to you.'

'What I saw was a frightened man, scurrying for cover.'

'Then your eyes were blurred by the heat of battle, my lord.'

'You betrayed me, Eadric.'

'Only in order to serve you the better.'

'You joined Edmund's camp.'

'And sent immediate word that I was still your agent. I could help you best by knowing your enemy's inner counsels. To do that, I had to deceive you into believing that I was playing the traitor. It was only when Edmund heard of your rage at my supposed treachery that he took me fully to his bosom.'

'Whose side do you *really* favour?' he demanded.

'Yours, my lord. I always prefer to sup with a victor.'

'But my victory was not assured at Ashingdon.'

'It was when I held back,' I argued forcefully. 'Until then the issue was in doubt. You were heavily outnumbered. Had I fought for Edmund, he might now be wearing the English crown and you might have been driven out of the realm in disgrace. Think on that, my lord.'

He pondered. 'You were my spy?' he said at length. 'My loyal intelligencer? Is that what you are claiming?'

'The evidence was there on the battlefield.'

'But that battle need never have taken place if you had forewarned me of Edmund's movements. He took us unawares. Why did you not send word to me that he was pursuing us so closely?'

'There was no time, my lord.'

'No time or no inclination?'

'Report reached us that you were anchored in the River Crouch. That is all we knew. Edmund whipped us into action at once. How could I get a message to you when I was not sure of your exact position? I had to ride with the hounds before I could find their quarry.'

'Then you joined the attack on that quarry.'

'Seemingly.'

'You rode at the head of the Mercian army.'

'But kept them out of the battle.'

'Was that by design or cowardice?' he taunted.

'Design!' I retorted vehemently. 'A coward would not have fought alongside you as I have done with distinction. A coward would not have risked discovery by Edmund Ironside and certain death at his hands. A coward would not come to you now to pledge his loyalty when he could save his skin by going into exile. No!' I insisted, shaking with righteous indignation. 'Call me devious. Call me cunning. Call me anything that you choose. But do not name me as a coward my lord. Only a brave man could survive the dangers that I have courted.'

'Treachery involves a certain bravery,' he conceded.

'First and last, I was your man!'

'Prove it.'

'I have done so many times.'

'Then do so once more, Eadric.'

'If you wish, my lord.'

'Give me certain proof of your loyalty.'

'How?'

He bared his teeth in a wicked grin and I had my answer.

The surest way to learn the truth about a man is either to seduce his wife or bribe his doctor. I have used both methods with equal success in the past, and while I prefer the excitement of the former, it is the latter which often brings the greater reward. So it was with Edmund Ironside. Since his wife was beyond my reach, I had perforce to work through his doctor, and my money purchased far more than I could have hoped. A small, fussy man with an irritating habit of scratching his beard, the doctor was nevertheless an experienced physician who had nursed his wounded patient back to health after many battles.

He was privy to secrets denied even to a wife or a confessor.

'Edmund Ironside lies grievous sick,' he confided.

'From injuries sustained at Ashingdon?'

'No, my lord,' he said with a sigh. 'Though they have also taken their toll. He is in the grip of a strange malady and weakens by the hour.'

'Can you not recover him?'

'He may be beyond my skill.'

'Do I hear you aright?' I pressed, conscious of the significance of what he told me. 'Edmund Ironside is on his deathbed?'

'No, my lord,' he said quickly. 'I would never put it like that, and he has a will to live which is the best medicine of all. But he is patently unwell. His limbs ache, his throat is swollen and he has a fever that draws a river of sweat out of his body. And yet, when I least expect it, the fever gives way to a fit of shivering that is woeful to behold. You see my dilemma,' he added, scratching at his beard. 'As soon as I treat one set of symptoms, they are replaced by another. I am not sure if my remedies are curing the disease or feeding it.'

'Is he in pain, doctor?'

'Great pain.'

'It must weaken him.'

'So much so that I have to conceal the truth from his followers. Only his wife and his priest know the worst. Sickness is a cruel leveller, my lord. It has robbed Edmund of his Ironside.'

I was quick to see the personal advantages in the situation.

'Take me to him,' I ordered.

'I dare not, my lord!'

'Why?'

'It is more than my life is worth,' he protested. 'Your name is spoken with anger in the camp. You are reviled as an enemy. If I were to conduct Eadric Streona to the sick bed, I would be accused of treachery. I will not do it, my lord.'

'You will not have to, doctor.'

'I am relieved to hear you say that.'

'Yet I must see him.'

'It is impossible.'

'Only if I appear as Eadric Streona,' I reminded him. 'Were I to visit him in the guise of a fellow doctor, a learned physician whom you have consulted, then nobody would question my presence for a moment.'

'*I* would, my lord.'

'Your silence has already been bought.'

'No!' he exclaimed. 'You ask too much of me.'

'I ask nothing, my friend. What you hear is a demand.'

The doctor argued long and hard, scratching his beard with such vigour that I was surprised it remained attached to his chin. In the end, he capitulated. Having accepted my bribe, he was at my mercy. I merely had to proclaim him as my creature and Edmund's counsellors would have dismissed him at once and sought a fit punishment.

A gown and a hat turned me into a physician and I whitened my beard with chalk to add age and distinction. When the doctor was next sent for, he took me along as his assistant. We were admitted to the room where Edmund Ironside lay. Stretched out on his bed, he was streaming with perspiration and moaning quietly to himself as he constantly shifted his position. The doctor knelt beside him and conducted a thorough examination before bathing his face and neck with a wet cloth. Edmund consented to drink a cup of water but it took the two of us to hold him upright while he did so. Not for the first time, I was propping up a feeble King of England. It was almost as if his father Ethelred were still alive.

'Edmund,' I whispered. 'Can you hear me?'

'Do not bother him, my lord,' pleaded the doctor.

'Can he say nothing?'

'Not without effort. Make him speak and you torment him.'

'Let me ask but one question.'

'No, my lord.'

'Just one,' I said, leaning in close to the patient. 'You know my voice, Edmund, and you know my mind. Tell me this. Will you live?'

Defiance flickered briefly in his eyes before being washed away by a surge of pain. His whole body twitched in agony and the doctor took a long time to soothe him, throwing a glare of resentment over his shoulder at me as he did so. I ignored him. As I watched Edmund Ironside in agony on his bed, I was seeing history change before my eyes.

The patient eventually drifted off into a fitful slumber.

'He is in such discomfort,' sighed the doctor.

'Is there no way to ease his suffering?'

'None that I have not tried.'

'Do you have no kind remedy in your satchel?' I asked gently. 'Something that might put an end to his misery and allow him to quit this world with a degree of dignity?'

The doctor was shocked. 'My lord!' he spluttered.

'It is no more than I would ask for myself in a like predicament.'

'I have sworn to save lives, not to take them.'

'This life is already lost.'

'That is not true.'

'Look at him. Listen to that breathing. Smell that stink.'

'The fever may yet break.'

'And he will shiver to death instead. Show sympathy, man. Help him on his way to Heaven and you will be rewarded for your deed.'

'By execution!'

'Not if his death appears to be natural.'

'I will not do it, my lord,' he said querulously. 'I will not administer a draught to snuff out the flame of Edmund Ironside's life.'

'You do not have to do it,' I assured him.

'Then why do you badger me so?'

'Because I wish to help a dying man.'

'You help him best by leaving him in peace.'

'No,' I said, reaching for his satchel. 'I help him best by sending him to eternal peace. Find me the remedy in your satchel, doctor. You will not have to soil your conscience by administering it. As you see, I too, am a physician. Let me do the office.'

'That is tantamount to murder!'

'Is it?'

'I would sooner die myself than be party to this act.'

A doctor with scruples was the last thing I needed at such a crucial moment. When it came to murder, the fellow was obviously beyond bribery. Opening his satchel, I thrust it roughly at him.

'Will you take it upon yourself to deny Edmund Ironside an escape from his ordeal?'

Canute was in a joyful mood when we next met. Less than a month after the battle of Ashingdon, he was the unchallenged King of England. What his father, Sweyn Forkbeard, had only half-achieved, the son had now made secure. A Danish warrior sat firmly on the throne and a new form of Danegeld would be exacted from the whole country. It made Canute extremely grateful. He held a banquet in my honour.

'Eat your fill, Eadric,' he encouraged. 'You deserve it.'

'Thank you, my lord king.'

'The finest dishes have been prepared for you, my friend. You will eat nothing that will disagree with your stomach.'

He went off into a peal of laughter and I smiled tolerantly. An hour later, when he had feasted royally, he slipped a drunken arm around my shoulder and spoke in a hoarse whisper.

'How did you do it, Eadric?'

'Do what?' I asked, feigning ignorance.

'Prove your loyalty to me.'

'I have done that a hundred times.'.

'This was proof positive, man. Two kings cannot rule one realm. It is a perverse situation. You took steps to remedy it.'

'I took steps,' I admitted, 'but the remedy lay elsewhere.'

'Come, Eadric,' he coaxed. 'We are friends for life now. I will garland you with honours. For this duty to his sovereign, Eadric Streona will acquire more than ever before. Exult in your triumph.'

'I do, my lord.'

'And tell me how you did it.'

'With prayer.'

He blinked in disbelief. 'You *prayed* him to death?'

'I asked God to gather a suffering soul unto Him.'

'There was more to it than that, Eadric.'

'Possibly,' I said.

'Divulge. Share the secret with me.'

'There is no secret. Edmund Ironside died of natural causes.'

'With unnatural assistance from you.'

'What makes you think that?' I said artlessly.

'I *know* you, Eadric.'

'That is certainly true.'

'And you confessed that you bribed his doctor.'

'How else was I to get into Edmund's presence?'

'What physic did you administer?'

'None. I am no doctor.'

'But you found the medicine that cured his ills. What was it?'

'I told you. Prayer. Compounded with luck, hope and opportunity.'

'Opportunity to kill?'

'That did exist.'

'And you seized it with both hands.'

'They were closed in prayer.'

'Around the neck of Edmund Ironside.'

He went off into another peal of laughter, shaking with mirth and pounding me on the back with robust affection. Then he sat back and drained his cup before licking his lips with his tongue. King Canute regarded me shrewdly.

'Keep your secret,' he decided with chuckle. 'Only you and the doctor know the full truth.'

'Me, the doctor and God.'

'You rendered me great service, Eadric.'

'That is my sole aim in life.'

'On my behalf, you committed a murder.'

'But I did not.'

'I am no fool,' he said. 'When you went to his bedside, Edmund Ironside was still alive. By the time you left, he was dead.'

'A happy coincidence!'

'Why are you being so modest, Eadric?'

'It becomes me.'

Yet another burst of laughter rang through the hall. King Canute had settled on a version of events which suited him and nothing would alter his opinion. I was the killer, Edmund Ironside was the victim and this boisterous Dane was the beneficiary. I went along with the myth. It served my purpose and won back his indulgence. I could look forward to a long and comfortable life on my estates in Mercia. Had poor Edmund survived, it would not have been so. Bickering with Canute would inevitably have led to blows and more civil strife would have followed. I would have been forced once again to play one side off against the other. Myth was far more accommodating.

I would soon come to accept it myself.

Canute rose to his feet and dragged me upright beside him. He bellowed above the tumult then banged the table until the pandemonium subsided. Drunken warriors turned to listen to their king.

'We must drink a toast, my friends!' he announced. 'To the man in whose honour this banquet is held. The loyal servant who killed one king to make another secure. Raise your cups – to Eadric Streona!'

They drank, laughed, shouted, cheered and pounded their tables in wild approbation. There was no point whatsoever in telling them that I had no part in the death of Edmund Ironside. My notoriety went before me and it had now acquired an even darker hue. It was ironic. After a lifetime of lies and deception, I actually wanted to tell the truth for once.

But nobody would believe me.

Edmund Ironside died with mysterious swiftness in November, 1016. There were no suggestions of foul play at the time. Eadric Streona was welcomed into Canute's court once more, but the Danish king kept a close eye on him. Late in 1017, Canute had him murdered. One of the great villains of Saxon England met an appropriately treacherous end.

A GIFT FOR KILLING

Susanna Gregory

Whilst Edmund Ironside *is shifting into the Shakespearean canon,* The Reign of Edward III *has remained firmly rooted in the apocrypha as far back as 1760 when Edward Capell first suggested it might betray the hand of Shakespeare. The play was registered in 1596 and its true author remains unknown. Like other plays of this period it is probable that several playwrights had a part in shaping it, including Shakespeare. The play concentrates on Edward III's successful invasion of France, though as a sub-plot the play traces Edward's attempts to seduce the Countess of Salisbury. The following story uses that sub-plot as background as it takes us to the battlegrounds of France.*

Crécy, France: August 1346

With a bloodcurdling cry, Edward, Prince of Wales, spurred his horse towards the enemy, brandishing his broadsword above his head. The French soldiers, who had formed a tremulous line to block his advance, were more farmers than warriors, and their hasty training had not prepared them for the sight of a fully armoured English knight thundering towards them. One of them took one step backwards, and then fled, hurling his pike away as it threatened to tangle in his legs and trip him. Others followed, their howls of terror spreading panic among their compatriots, so that within moments Edward found himself charging into nothing but an empty glade strewn with abandoned weapons.

Next to him, Sir John Montagu reined in, eyes round with astonishment. 'Look at them, running like frightened rabbits! How does the French king hope to protect his realm with men like these?'

Edward was disgusted. 'This is my first battle. I expected more than to chase peasants!'

'The chroniclers will record this as a great English victory,' said the Earl of Salisbury, Montagu's older brother, wryly. 'Regardless that all we did was terrify a few yeomen.'

Edward felt uncomfortable in Salisbury's company, because there were rumours that Edward's father, King Edward III, had seduced Salisbury's wife. The countess was a beautiful woman and the king had a bad reputation with beautiful women. Edward suspected there was truth in the gossip, and avoided Salisbury when he could.

'Dressed in that armour, the chroniclers will declare you a hero whatever you do today,' said FitzSimon, Edward's standard-bearer. He eyed the prince's battle gear, gleaming bright gold in the sunlight, with undisguised envy.

Edward glanced at it proudly. 'My father and three of his most trusted barons gave this to me.'

'Well, you look magnificent,' said FitzSimon, with begrudging admiration. 'And we'll have it baptised in blood yet.'

'You're right,' said Montagu in sudden alarm. 'And it's going to be now. We spoke too soon about an easy victory – someone has rallied those soldiers, and they're coming back!'

With a roar, French foot-soldiers began to swarm through the trees, and the three young knights around the prince each lifted his lance in one hand and his shield in the other to meet them. Salisbury's warhorse, startled by the noise, reared and knocked the weapon from his brother's hand. There was a sharp crack as it splintered under heavy hooves.

'God's teeth!' exclaimed Montagu in horror. 'I'll have to fetch another.'

He hauled on the reins, urging his mount away from the attacking Frenchmen, while Edward risked a quick glance down at the lance. The thing was useless: its metal tip had broken off, reducing it to nothing more than a blunt-ended stave. A triumphant cheer rang out, and Edward realised the French had interpreted Montagu's manoeuvre as a retreat.

'Come back!' he yelled. 'They think we're running away.'

Montagu hesitated – no knight wanted to go into battle unarmed – but FitzSimon offered him his own, claiming it was easier to defend Edward's standard with a sword than a lance.

Montagu snatched it as the first of the attackers raced at him with daggers drawn. Close behind was a unit of French cavalry, and Edward recognised the Duc d'Alençon – one of a few who could inspire ill-trained, badly equipped farmhands to attack formidable English knights.

Steel clashed with steel as weapons met, and the air shivered with shouts and curses. More French cavalry arrived, and Edward found himself hard pressed, his gold armour serving to draw his enemies towards him. Salisbury fought like a demon, eyes flashing dangerously as he thrust and parried. His brother fought carefully and coldly, his face taut with concentration. FitzSimon was behind Edward, waving his standard and yelling at the top of his voice.

Alençon lunged at Edward with his sword. Instinctively, Edward raised his new shield to deflect the blow, confident that its superior craftsmanship would protect him. He was wrong. There was an ear-splitting clang, and he found himself clutching a handle while the rest of the shield dropped to the ground. For a moment, he did nothing but gape at it, and it was only Alençon's howl of savage delight that impelled him to duck and swing his sword at the Frenchman's stomach. Alençon's victory cry turned to one of agony, and Edward saw him topple from his saddle.

Alençon was not the only unhorsed knight. Montagu was also down. He feinted with his lance at the soldiers who surrounded him, his eyes wide with fear. Edward grabbed Alençon's destrier and tried to take it to him, but another French knight blocked his way.

While Edward and the Frenchman circled each other, Montagu fought his way towards Alençon's horse. He saw Edward's shield, and stooped to retrieve it, a stupid move that exposed his head to the Frenchman. The Frenchman immediately swung his morning star, a wicked spiked ball on a chain. Realising his mistake with horror, Montagu thrust Edward's shield upwards in an attempt to protect himself. There was a sharp crack and the shield disintegrated in Montagu's hands. The morning star continued its deadly journey and Montagu fell, his skull smashed like an egg inside his helmet.

With a yell of fury, Edward slashed and hacked at the Frenchman until he, too, lay lifeless on the ground. Edward snatched up the Frenchman's shield to replace his own, and fought on.

The battle continued until evening, and finally ended when it became too dark to see and the French king ordered his army to withdraw. Then, amid victorious cheers, King Edward of England filled a windmill with straw and set it alight to act as a beacon for his scattered troops. In small, exhausted bands, soldiers flocked towards it, celebrating what they were told was a rout with bean stews, cooked over campfires that twinkled across the dark countryside like stars.

The prince was elated by the victory and knew he had fought well, but he grieved for Montagu. He knelt next to the body until the glitter of gold caught his eye, and he saw his smashed shield.

His first instinct was to kick it, disgusted that it had broken so easily. But it had been a gift from Artois, a trusted friend of his father's, and he was loath to treat it dishonourably. Despite being French, Artois was England's ally, because he owned land the French king had confiscated. Edward's father had promised to win it back again, so Artois was inclined to be generous to Edward – hence the gift of a shield on the eve of his first battle.

Edward picked up the shattered wood. When he had been presented with his new panoply he had been proud beyond words, and had not deemed it necessary to inspect their quality. And, for the most part, his faith had been justified: the breastplate and helmet were dented, but had protected him well, while the lance had proved itself strong and reliable. Yet the shield, given by Artois, had disintegrated at the first blow.

Had Artois deliberately given him a defective shield? Edward examined it closely. It was simply made – a circle of wood covered by a sheet of metal, with a handle attached to the back. Like most knights' shields, it bore his personal emblem: it was coated with gilt and then painted with three red leopards.

He inspected the nails that had held the handle in place: they had been filed, so they would shear after a serious blow. He looked more closely still, recalling how the wood had splintered when Montagu had tried to protect himself. He swallowed hard when he saw the gilt-coating was a good deal more than mere decoration – it hid the fact that the shield was held together with glue, not proper joints. There was no question about it: the shield had been deliberately constructed to disintegrate the first time it was used in combat.

Later that night, Edward listened as other knights relived the battle, but found that any exultation he might have felt about the knightly way he had conducted himself was tempered by the knowledge that someone had tried to kill him. When FitzSimon asked what was wrong, Edward told him about the shield. The standard-bearer did not believe him, and Edward took him to his tent to show him the evidence.

'But this is dreadful!' said FitzSimon, aghast. 'Who would want to kill you?'

Edward smiled grimly. 'Other than the entire population of France, you mean? I suppose the person who springs immediately to mind is Artois – he gave me the shield.'

FitzSimon frowned. 'Rumour has it that Artois poisoned his aunt, because she owned estates he wanted for himself.'

Edward nodded. 'I've heard that, too – her murder was why he was exiled from France. But why would he want to kill me? The only way he'll get these estates back is if my father wins this war and gives them to him – something that won't happen if he's caught trying to have me murdered.'

'Artois is French. Perhaps there's a trace of patriotism left in him, and he wants England to lose this campaign.'

Edward sighed. 'Whoever made this shield knew what he was doing – the flaws are very cunningly concealed. Artois couldn't have done it himself, so he must have ordered someone else to do it. He's a clever man, and he'll never admit to plotting against me without evidence. If we want to catch him, we must find the person who made that shield.'

'Rhodri the Armourer was commissioned to make it. Your new equipment may have been a surprise to you, but the rest of us knew what the king and his friends were planning.'

'Well, then,' said Edward, rising to his feet. 'Let's talk to Rhodri.'

Rhodri had a portable workshop. Sharp orders and the hiss and clank of hot metal told Edward he was busy – welding broken armour and recasting weapons. The still night air rang with hammering and roaring flames, and stank of red hot iron and horses.

Rhodri, a heavily bearded man, was at the centre of it, cursing apprentices whose exhaustion resulted in inferior work, and berating others for slacking. When he saw Edward, he sighed impatiently.

'I'm busy,' he said. 'What do you want?'

'My shield,' said Edward, biting back anger at Rhodri's insolence – he would learn nothing by alienating the man. 'Did you make it, or did you delegate it to someone else?'

Rhodri met Edward's eyes defiantly. 'Why? D'you have a complaint?'

'I do,' said Edward coldly. 'The shield disintegrated the first time I tried to use it – it was constructed to be useless.'

Rhodri bristled. 'My shields are the best in England. If something was wrong with yours, then it happened after it left my workshop.'

Edward tried a different approach. 'When you made my shield, were you making others, too? Could a cheaper one have been substituted by mistake?'

Rhodri scowled. 'None of my shields are defective – no matter what they cost. And of course I was producing shields for people other than you – my services are in great demand on campaigns like this. Besides yours, I made one for Salisbury and one for his brother. I finished all three yesterday, and dispatched them accordingly.'

'Who commissioned mine?' asked Edward.

'That's no secret – Artois.'

'Did he pay you to make it with a flaw, so it would fly apart when I tried to use it?'

'D'you think I'd risk my reputation by making faulty equipment?' demanded Rhodri, outraged. 'This had nothing to do with me. Perhaps you should ask yourself whether you're ready to play with men's weapons, or whether you should've remained in the nursery!'

Edward's dagger was out of its scabbard when FitzSimon hauled him away. Rhodri, white-faced with anger, strode back to his work, leaving FitzSimon struggling with the furious prince.

'Rhodri's our best armourer,' FitzSimon reasoned breathlessly. 'He's a vital part of our campaign. Kill him, and you do France a favour.'

Edward tore himself from FitzSimon's grasp, and tried to bring his fury under control. Rhodri's foul temper was legendary, but even he usually balked at outright rudeness to the knights he served. Was there more to Rhodri's insults than a man worked to exhaustion by the demands of the campaign? Was he antagonising Edward to divert attention away from his role in producing the faulty shield?

After a while, Edward saw he was being watched by an unkempt fellow wearing a greasy jerkin – one of the men who gathered firewood for Rhodri's furnaces.

'I'm Will Woodman,' the man said. 'I've information for you, but I haven't eaten today, so my memory's dim.'

Edward flipped him a coin, and Woodman secreted it in his jerkin. 'You know why Rhodri evaded your questions? Well, it's because the king ordered him to make your armour himself, but he didn't – he let one of his minions do it because he was busy.'

'Why are you telling us this?' asked FitzSimon, openly hostile.

'Because Rhodri's a bad master, and mean with pay.'

'If Rhodri didn't make my armour, who did?' asked Edward.

'An apprentice called Torva,' said Woodman. 'He made three shields – yours, Salisbury's and Montagu's. But Torva won't be telling you anything. You see, he was murdered the same night Rhodri delivered the finished shields to their new owners.'

'We'll visit Artois today,' said Edward to FitzSimon the following morning. They sat in Edward's tent, a stuffy construction that smelled of warm grass and sweat.

FitzSimon nodded. 'We know Rhodri didn't make the armour, but the man who did – Torva – deliberately made it faulty, and then was murdered to ensure his silence.'

Edward sighed. 'It must have been Artois. I thought he was honest, but he's already poisoned an elderly aunt to get what he wants, and I'm naturally disinclined to trust a Frenchman fighting France for the English.'

'I suppose it's possible that Rhodri acted alone,' mused FitzSimon. 'And that Artois had nothing to do with it.'

'I've done nothing to harm Rhodri,' said Edward. 'Although I might, if we meet again.'

'He's Welsh and you're the Prince of Wales: not all Welshmen like being ruled by an English prince.'

Edward sighed. 'Perhaps you're right. Or maybe Torva took against me for some reason.'

FitzSimon shook his head. 'Then he'd still be alive. It's obvious

Torva was killed so that he wouldn't be able to tell anyone who commissioned faulty equipment for you.'

'So, both Artois and Rhodri have reasons for wanting me dead, and either could have arranged for a defective shield to be built,' said Edward. 'But which?'

'The intended victim might not be you at all,' said FitzSimon. 'Woodman said three shields were made – yours, Salisbury's and Montagu's. Perhaps the faulty one was given to you by mistake, and was really intended for Salisbury or his brother.'

'But the shields are different,' objected Edward. 'Mine's gold with red leopards; the Montagu coat of arms – on both Salisbury's and his brother's – is blue.'

'But they're only different after they've been decorated,' argued FitzSimon. 'Before they're painted, they look the same.'

A dreadful thought occurred to Edward, and he was unable to meet FitzSimon's eyes. 'Not Salisbury! You know the rumours – about my father and Salisbury's wife. You don't think my father . . .'

'. . . wants to kill Salisbury, so he can dally with Salisbury's wife?' finished FitzSimon. 'It's possible, I suppose. But then, perhaps Salisbury's brother was the intended victim.'

'Why him?' asked Edward. 'He'd no property to speak of, and was only a boy.'

'True. But he wasn't popular like Salisbury. He could be vindictive, and was always saying he thought our war with France was unjust.'

'So do many men,' said Edward. 'But that's no reason to kill them. What we need is solid evidence. Let's visit Artois.'

Artois was enjoying the sunshine, sitting outside his tent and eating raisin cakes supplied by the king himself. He smiled when Edward approached.

'Ah! England's brave young hero! I heard you fought brilliantly yesterday, and your gold armour served as an inspiration to every soldier on the field. Men will talk about this battle for years, and the Golden Prince will become a legend, like St George.'

Edward sat and helped himself to a cake. 'My armour served me well. The breastplate was hammered by French swords, but is only dented; my lance was strong; and my helmet saved me from more than one angry blow. Only the shield was defective.'

Artois seemed startled. 'What d'you mean? That shield cost me seven pounds – no mean sum for a man who's had his rightful inheritance stolen by the King of France.'

'First the handle came off, and then the wood shattered. In fact, Montagu was killed because it fell apart.'

'Montagu?' asked Artois. 'What was he doing with your shield? He had a new one of his own, as did his brother. I saw all three lined up when I went to inspect the one I commissioned for you – Rhodri's overwhelmed with orders for new equipment, and I wanted to make sure he hadn't exchanged quality for quantity.'

'And had he?' asked Edward.

Artois raised expressive eyebrows. 'I'm sorry the shield wasn't all you hoped for, Edward, but you've no cause to be ungrateful. I gave you a gift in good conscience, and it wasn't my fault it broke. Perhaps you were too rough with it.'

Edward gaped at him. 'It's a shield, Artois! It's meant to be treated roughly. But you haven't answered my question: what did you think of it when you saw it in Rhodri's workshop?'

Artois shrugged. 'The whole thing was covered in gilt, so I couldn't tell.'

'Rhodri didn't make it,' said Edward. 'It was made by an apprentice called Torva, who was stabbed the moment it was finished . . .'

'How dreadful,' said Artois, reaching for another cake.

'. . . which suggests someone didn't want him telling people he'd made my shield deliberately defective,' Edward concluded.

Artois tossed the cake away and turned to face Edward, his eyes hard and cold. 'I bought you a gift – an expensive gift – because I need to curry favour with your father if I'm ever to get my land back. I've no reason to harm you, and if I did, I'd be a little more circumspect than to have your death blamed on a shield I'd given you.'

He stood abruptly and left. Edward gazed after him. Had he arranged to kill the heir to England's throne to score a victory for France? Or had Rhodri made a shield to destroy a Prince of Wales who was not Welsh? Or was FitzSimon right, and the recipient of the shield was not meant to be Edward at all, but Salisbury or Montagu, and the shields had been confused before they had been painted? In which case, was the intended victim Salisbury, so that the king could continue to dally with his wife? Or was it Montagu, who held unpatriotic views about the war with France? Edward took another of Artois' cakes and went slowly back to his own tent.

Three days passed. Edward uncovered evidence that proved conclusively that Artois had poisoned his aunt, and spoke to witnesses prepared to swear that the king was indeed committing adultery with Salisbury's wife. Others informed him that Salisbury was aware of the situation, and was far from amused, but was powerless to prevent it. And there were also dark mutterings about the treachery of his brother Montagu, who had believed that England should not have invaded France.

'We need more facts,' said Edward, after an afternoon of unprofitable speculation with FitzSimon. 'Let's talk to Woodman again – see if he can tell us anything new.'

They walked to Rhodri's workshop, which was as noisy and hectic as it had been immediately after the battle. Piles of swords awaited sharpening, and knights fidgeted impatiently as new armour was fitted. Woodman was chopping logs, but abandoned his work when Edward nodded to him. They walked to a quiet spot behind some trees, away from prying eyes.

'What can you tell us about Torva?' Edward asked, slipping a coin into Will's dirt-encrusted hand. 'Did he leave a widow?'

'A brother,' said Woodman. 'Aelric works for Rhodri, too. Come. I'll take you to him.'

Aelric, like many who went campaigning in France, had brought his family with him. An older boy knelt near a fire and stirred something in a pot, while three girls played with an assortment of armour that awaited Aelric's attention. Aelric himself sat cross-legged in front of a breastplate, frowning as he concentrated on his work.

It did not escape Edward's notice that Aelric and his children wore new tunics. Moreover, the meal that bubbled in the pot was not just beans and whatever herbs could be gathered from the woods – the fare of most camp followers – but contained meat. Aelric, it seemed, had recently acquired some money.

Edward stepped forward and introduced himself, smiling as Aelric scrambled to his feet and effected a clumsy bow that his older children tried to emulate. The smallest girl, however, gazed at him with terrified eyes, as though he were a fiend from hell, not her future king. Edward glanced down and saw that Aelric had been painting the breastplate with a coat of arms.

'Is this your calling?' he asked. 'Decorating armour?'

Aelric nodded and gave a shy smile. 'I did yours. But not with paint – with best-quality gilt.'

Edward gestured at the man's smart tunic. 'Someone has recently paid you handsomely. Rhodri isn't a generous man, so I assume it was someone else?'

Aelric looked frightened, and for a moment, Edward thought he would not answer. But Aelric was a simple man, and Edward was the hero of Crécy – a man to be obeyed.

'My brother, Torva,' he whispered. 'I inherited his money. He was stabbed after . . .' His smallest child, the frightened one, began to cry quietly.

'After?' Edward prompted.

'After he delivered three finished shields to Rhodri.'

'And Torva was paid a special commission for one of the shields, wasn't he?' asked Edward softly. 'The one that was made imperfectly?'

Even if Aelric had been an accomplished liar, his children would have given him away. The one who had been sobbing suddenly increased the volume of her cries, while the others shuffled their feet in abject guilt.

Aelric nodded miserably. 'I told Torva to stay away from such commissions, but he wanted the money – he was saving to buy a cow, you see. And then he was stabbed.' His voice shook. 'I'm afraid I'll go the same way, if anyone sees me talking to you, and then what would happen to my children?'

'I'll see you come to no harm,' said Edward reassuringly. 'I'll have soldiers assigned to you until this is sorted out. So, tell me what you know.'

Aelric put his arms round his children protectively. 'Rhodri asked Torva to make three shields – for you, Salisbury and Montagu – because he was too busy to do it himself. Then, someone gave Torva five marks to make one of the shields imperfect – this person demanded it should break the moment it was used.'

'And who was this person?' asked Edward.

Aelric raised his voice to be heard over his weeping child. 'Torva didn't tell me, and I didn't ask. Then he gave me the three shields to decorate.'

'And mine was the defective shield?' asked Edward. 'The gilt one?'

'Oh, no!' exclaimed Aelric, appalled. 'I'd never have agreed to that – you'll be my king one day. No, the defective one was intended for one of the others. Torva gave me the shields, and told me not to mix them up. He put the defective one near the door, so that I'd know it.'

'So, you couldn't tell which one was which by looking?'

Aelric shrugged. 'I suppose I might, if I'd looked. But I'd only one night to decorate all three, so I just did my job. Rhodri would have skinned me alive if they'd been late.'

'So, who was to have the defective shield?' asked Edward. 'Salisbury or Montagu?'

'I don't know,' said Aelric. 'Because Salisbury and Montagu were brothers, they had the same coat of arms. Their shields were identical.'

'But you muddled them, didn't you,' said Edward. 'And the defective one was given to me.'

'No,' said Aelric, indignantly. 'I was careful about that. The other two had thick blue paint, but yours had gilt.'

The child's howls had reached the point where any further discussion was impossible. Edward knelt next to her and peered into her wet face.

'It was the children!' he whispered, as understanding dawned. 'I noticed they were playing with the armour waiting to be decorated when we arrived.'

FitzSimon snapped his fingers. 'Of course! The children must've played with the shields and mixed them up. Then, when Aelric came to decorate them, he didn't notice which one was defective, because he was slapping thick paint or gilt all over them by candle-light – he just told us he worked all night so that they'd be finished on time.'

Edward nodded, watching the stricken Aelric and his frightened brood. 'Having confused the shields, the children decided not to tell their father what had happened. They just put them back and hoped for the best.'

The terrified, guilty howls of the little girl told him that their reasoning was correct.

'Well,' said FitzSimon as they walked away. 'We can take Rhodri off our list of suspects. He clearly knew nothing about this.'

Edward nodded. 'And now we know the intended victim wasn't

me, it lets Artois out of the picture, too – he's no grudge against Salisbury or Montagu.'

'Not true. He might be seeking favour with your father by killing Salisbury – it's Salisbury's wife your father is courting, remember?'

Edward winced.

'I can think of one thing we can do,' said FitzSimon in the silence that followed. 'Do you remember how Salisbury's horse smashed his brother's lance just before the battle began? Well, if that lance is defective – and it broke very easily, if you recall – then we'll know for certain the intended victim was Montagu, not Salisbury. If Montagu's lance was flawed, then I'd say he was also the intended recipient of the defective shield.'

'You're right!' exclaimed Edward. 'We're stupid not to have thought of this before. Montagu's body is in his tent, waiting to be shipped to England. His armour will be with him. Let's go, and solve this once and for all.'

The sickly stench of decay and the buzz of flies pervaded Montagu's tent. Edward entered, trying to breathe through his mouth.

Montagu's body was shrouded, and his armour lay piled at his feet. Edward picked up the helmet. It was smashed, but few basinets could save their owners from morning stars, and he saw nothing that suggested Montagu's had been poorly made. With FitzSimon coughing and gagging behind him, he inspected the shield. It was identical to the one Artois had given him, except Montagu's was blue rather than gold. There were no flaws, and Edward saw it would have served him well. The lance, however, was not there.

'What are you doing?'

Edward whipped round, startled by the proximity of Salisbury's voice. He took one look at the black anger on the earl's face and decided to go on the offensive himself. 'Where's your brother's lance? Have you hidden it because you knew it was defective, and might prove someone wanted him dead?'

Salisbury paled. 'What are you talking about? His lance was shattered. You saw it yourself.'

'Was his belief that we shouldn't be fighting France embarrassing to you?' Edward continued. 'Did you have a defective shield and lance made for him, so that he'd die in battle?'

Salisbury's eyes blazed with anger. 'You don't know what you're saying! I was never ashamed of him!'

'Then who wanted him dead?' demanded Edward. He gripped Salisbury's shoulder as he tried to leave. 'You smashed his lance yourself when the French were almost on us. Did you murder your own brother?'

Salisbury shoved Edward away, and rushed from the tent. Edward darted after him, and, with FitzSimon's help, wrestled him to the ground. The earl spat and swore at his captors, behaving more like a stable-boy than a nobleman, but Edward saw tears glittering on his cheeks.

Eventually Salisbury quietened, and Edward became aware that they were not alone. Aelric and his children stood nearby, gazing open-mouthed at the spectacle of brawling knights. Salisbury muttered that he would not try to escape, and they scrambled to their feet, vainly trying to regain lost dignity.

The smallest child whispered in Aelric's ear. He nodded and addressed Edward. 'My daughter says it was him,' he said, pointing at Salisbury. 'He murdered Torva.'

Salisbury closed his eyes, his face as white as snow, while the child hid behind her father.

'She was frightened,' Aelric explained, kneeling to embrace her. 'She thought Torva was killed because she'd played with the shields and confused them. Later, she was out gathering sticks when she saw Torva's body – and Salisbury standing over it.'

'I didn't kill Torva,' said Salisbury wearily. 'He was dead – stabbed – when I found him. He must have fallen out with some other villain who makes flawed armour for a price.'

Edward's eyes narrowed. 'You know about these flawed shields and Torva's role in making them, do you?'

'As do you,' Salisbury flashed back. 'But *I'm* not accusing *you* of vile crimes because of it.'

'It isn't my brother who lies dead with his head smashed,' retorted Edward.

Salisbury was drawing breath to reply, when a polite cough made everyone look around. It was Artois, standing with Rhodri.

'I see you don't confine your accusations to just me, Edward,' he said laconically. 'Now Salisbury is the object of your venom.'

'I've evidence,' snapped Edward. 'There's a broken lance conveniently missing, and a witness to Torva's murder.'

Artois' smile was condescending. 'When you charged me with plotting to kill you, I began an investigation of my own – I'm already accused of murdering my aunt, and a man in my delicate position can't afford rumours that he also tried to dispatch the son of a king. Frankly, I didn't trust you to discover the truth – especially once I'd spoken to Rhodri here. You let his temper intimidate you, and consequently, you didn't learn all he knew.'

Edward glowered at Rhodri, who glared back defiantly. Artois gave Rhodri a look that made him shuffle uncomfortably.

'Well?' demanded Edward. 'What did you keep from me?'

Rhodri sighed. 'I was about to congratulate Torva for his work on the shields – I was busy, and hadn't the time to make them myself – when I saw him slink into the woods. I followed, and saw him meet a cloaked man, whom I heard asking whether a shield and lance had been made to "certain specifications". Torva said they had, and demanded payment. The cloaked man promptly stabbed him before hurrying away.'

'This cloaked man was Salisbury,' said Edward in triumph. 'This is nothing new!'

'Moments later,' Rhodri continued, 'Salisbury arrived. I saw him discover Torva's body, and I saw Aelric's daughter hiding in the bushes.'

'And did you see the face of this cloaked man?' asked Artois. His confident, superior expression suggested he already knew the answer.

'It was Montagu,' said Rhodri.

'No!' yelled Salisbury. 'My brother didn't . . . couldn't . . .'

'I lied to you,' said Rhodri, turning away from the spluttering Earl to address Edward. 'I lied and was insolent because I wanted to stay out of this. There are so many charges of treason bandied around these days, that honest men are safer keeping their mouths shut about what they know. But Artois said he'd hang me if I didn't tell you the truth now.'

'Is it the truth?' asked Edward.

Before he could answer, Salisbury stepped forward. 'It's the truth,' he said shakily. 'My brother killed Torva. I loved Montagu and don't want his reputation sullied – I want him remembered as a hero who died in battle. But he killed Torva because he ordered defective equipment and he wanted it kept a secret.'

'But why?' asked Edward, bewildered. 'Because his disapproval of the war meant he didn't want to slay Frenchmen?'

Salisbury shook his head. 'You still don't understand, despite the evidence staring you in the face. My brother was a coward: he didn't want to fight because he was afraid he'd be killed. He ordered defective equipment, so that he'd have an excuse to leave the field when it broke.'

Edward gazed at him, finally understanding. 'And you guessed this. You even let your horse tread on his lance, so that he could avoid the battle.'

Salisbury took a shuddering breath. 'I could feel his fear – he was terrified. I saw the relief in his eyes when I broke his lance, and then the despair when FitzSimon gave him another. And he was right to be afraid – he was killed in his first fight.'

'But he killed to save himself,' said Edward, unmoved. 'He killed Torva, so no one would know the lengths to which his cowardice led him.'

'And it was this cowardice that killed him,' said FitzSimon quietly. 'He died because he tried to protect himself with the very shield he ordered to be made weak. It could have killed Edward, but instead it killed him.'

Later that day, Edward and FitzSimon sat together, discussing the agreement they had made with Salisbury to keep secret Montagu's machinations. Montagu would be buried a hero; in return, Salisbury would turn a blind eye to the king's dalliance with his wife until the infatuation wore off – which it always did, eventually.

FitzSimon was inspecting the smashed shield. 'Without this thick gilt, you'd have noticed these defects.'

Edward nodded. 'I know, and it's put me off gold-coloured armour, I can tell you. From now on, I'll have no paint on my battle gear!'

'What about black?' suggested FitzSimon. 'You'll need some adornment, or you'll look unfinished. Plain black would look suitably princely, and yet still allow you to check for flaws.'

'True,' said Edward, musing. 'You'd better order me some then. What a shame – I'd like to have been remembered as the Golden Prince.'

Historical Note

The exact origin of Edward, Prince of Wales' nickname – the Black Prince – is not known, although it was probably not used in his lifetime. Many scholars believe it had something to do with his armour, although there are no contemporary accounts to say this was black.

Richard FitzSimon was Edward's standard-bearer at the battle of Crécy, and the Earl of Salisbury, Artois and Alençon fought there. Salisbury had a younger brother – John Montagu – although little is known about him. King Edward III had a flagrant affair with Salisbury's wife, and in this lies the origin of the Order of the Knights of the Garter (her garter).

The Second Part of Henry IV 

THE CHIMES AT MIDNIGHT

Cherith Baldry

One of the most popular characters created by Shakespeare was Sir John Falstaff, that rollicking, rumbustious, dissolute crony of young Prince Hal. In this guise he first appears in Shakespeare's Henry IV (Part 1). *He was believed to be based on an historical character, Sir John Oldcastle, who was sheriff of Herefordshire in 1406. He was apparently attached to the household of young Prince Henry but became a renegade in his final years in league with the Scots. He was captured and executed in 1417. As Oldcastle he had appeared in an earlier play, not by Shakespeare, called* The Famous Victories of Henry V (*c. 1586*) *which created his image as a likeable rogue. In the following story he shows his talents as a solver of crimes.*

Robin the page dug his spurs into the flank of the ambling, spavined brute that had carried him from London into Yorkshire, and would probably collapse, a bag of bones by the roadside, before the journey home was over. And good riddance. Through a mist of rain he gazed enviously at the troop ahead, the escort of Lord John of Lancaster and the Earl of Westmoreland, the victorious commanders, and wished he might be riding with them, well mounted, well armed, and covered in glory.

Instead, he was slogging along in their wake, his horse stumbling along a road churned to mud, last of the column, in company with his master Sir John Falstaff, Corporal Bardolph of the red nose and unquenchable thirst, and Falstaff's Gloucestershire stragglers, who might think themselves lucky that battle had never been joined at Gaultree Forest.

They were singing now, cheerfully and vilely off key, a soldier's song about a wench in every camp, though old Tom Wart was surely past wenching, while Francis Feeble and Simon Shadow were not come to it yet – if ever. Falstaff took a long pull from a leather bottle slung on his saddle bow, and joined in the song with a rumbling bass. Robin hunched himself into his cloak and tried to ignore the rain trickling down his neck.

Prince Hal himself had given Robin into Falstaff's service. If that was one of the merry prince's merry jests, Robin had had enough of it. Oh, there were times when he enjoyed the tricks and laughter, the nights drinking at the Boar's Head, but when he looked at Falstaff in the cold light of morning, what did he see? An old man, diseased, in debt, a self-confessed coward. A jovial man, a prince's favourite – but where was the honour in that, for Falstaff or his followers?

The rain drew off and sun broke through the clouds before they reached their lodging. From the top of a low hill, Robin saw Justice Shallow's estate spread out in front of him in a golden light, the trees of garden and orchard almost drowning the old house in a green wave.

'A pox on Lord John of Lancaster,' Falstaff grumbled as he set his horse down the slope. 'Has a cold liver and a colder heart. He cut the head off my prisoner, Colevile of the Dale, who would have paid me noble ransom. And now he thrusts him in here in Gloucestershire, just as I have Master Shallow ripe for the plucking. A paltry boy indeed. Has no more fire in his belly than would singe the wings off a gnat. His brother Hal is worth a million of him.'

Robin said nothing, but let his master grumble on as they approached Justice Shallow's manor. He gazed hungrily at John of Lancaster as he dismounted: lean, cool, his surcoat bright against steel grey armour. Westmoreland, too, older, more solid, more watchful, but still with that air of effortless authority.

Beside them, Falstaff was an untidy hulk. His scarlet cloak was faded, his leather jerkin cracked, his belt straining over his huge belly.

He stumped forward, ignoring the commanders, to clasp hands with Master Shallow as he came doddering out of the house at the head of his family and his servants.

Shallow was a wisp of a man, his twiggy hand lost in Falstaff's massive paw. He greeted his old friend warmly, only to fall into a palsy of bashfulness as Falstaff introduced the prince and Westmoreland.

'We'll stay but one night,' Lord John said carelessly, as Justice Shallow bowed and bobbed in front of him, tongue tripping over itself with welcomes. 'We ride post to London, to bring word of the victory. Sir John Falstaff –' he turned to the old man with a look of distaste – 'will probably honour your house for many days more.'

'And honour it is, indeed it is, Sir John,' Shallow babbled. 'We have heard the chimes at midnight, Sir John, that we have! When I was of Clement's Inn, and thou wert page to Sir Thomas Mowbray. Jesu, what mad fellows we were, thou and I and little John Doit of Staffordshire, and—'

'Master Shallow,' Lord John interrupted coolly, 'I shall need lodging for fifty men, and stabling for their horses.'

Shallow broke off, gaping. Senile old fool, Robin thought. Buried here in Gloucestershire, how could he know what it means to entertain a prince?

Lord John nodded to Westmorland, who said, 'Master Shallow, if you would but show me where my men can pitch their camp . . .'

Relieved, Shallow took his arm and led him off, calling for his servant Davy as he went.

'By cock and pie, if I do not ride with you,' Robin heard him prattling to Westmoreland. 'For I was once in London, and then was I called Mad Shallow. But you have not such cabbaleroes nor such bona-robas in these days as we had then. By the mass, there was no wench in all London to surpass Jane Nightwork, and she said to me . . .'

Robin saw Westmoreland's face set in polite boredom as he and the old justice disappeared around the corner of the house.

Master Shallow had ordered a table set up in the orchard arbour after dinner. A golden moon was rising as he escorted his kinsman Justice Silence, along with Falstaff and Lord John, to seats under the apple trees. Westmoreland had excused himself to go and see to the troops. The table was loaded with jugs of wine, and dishes of fruit and spiced cakes and sweetmeats. Robin poured wine for Falstaff, filched a handful of comfits, and prepared to be bored.

Master Silence was already well gone in drink, gazing into the distance with a smile on his face, and waving a finger in time to music that only he could hear. Now and then a snatch of song escaped him.

'*Fill the cup and let it come . . .*'

'Good neighbour Silence, drink,' Shallow urged him.

'Aye,' said Lord John. 'Let him drink himself asleep, and then Master Silence shall be silent indeed.'

Shallow laughed uncertainly. Robin thought he was beginning to realize that his noblest guest was less than charmed by his country hospitality.

'Nay, Lord John.' Falstaff was restored to good humour by the good dinner inside him and the tankard of sack in front of him. 'The god Apollo scorned not to come down from heaven and be a neat-herd. So may the true prince—'

'Peace, jobbernoul,' Lord John snapped. ''Tis not my brother you speak with now.'

'No true prince?' Falstaff cocked a brow, a glint in his eye. 'Then art thou a false knave, my lord, as the rebels at Gaultree knew well, before you lopped off their heads.'

Lord John turned on Falstaff with a look of fury, but before he could speak an outcry broke out at the far end of the orchard, nearest the house. A medley of raised voices, the words indistinguishable, until one voice rose above them and drew rapidly nearer.

'Master Shallow, oh, Master, Master—'

The servant Davy was running between the trees, arms outstretched, a look on his face as if a monster pursued him. He pounded to a halt and stood gasping in front of the table.

'Davy?' Master Shallow was on his feet. 'What is't, Davy?'

'Murder, your honour.' Davy gulped in air between every word. 'A dead man – shot – in the box-tree alley.'

Lord John had risen too. 'A man of mine?'

'No, m'lord. It's Wart. Thomas Wart. He lies there with an arrow in's back.'

Lord John seated himself, relaxing. Shallow looked helplessly from side to side, the wine dulling what wits he had. Falstaff was the first to speak.

'Bardolph, go and see.'

Bardolph saluted and ambled off, his ale mug still in his hand. Davy collapsed on the ground and sat with his head bent over his knees. He mumbled, 'I'd known him these two and forty year.'

Nothing could be heard except the gentle soughing of wind in the trees, and the droning voice of Silence. '*Come blow thy horn, hunter, And blow thy horn on high . . .*' The song limped on unregarded, until at last Robin saw Bardolph coming back.

Behind him, two soldiers were approaching through the trees, dragging a third man between them. Behind them came the Earl of Westmoreland, with a longbow in his hand. As they drew nearer Robin saw that the third man was Francis Feeble, the woman's tailor who had ridden with Falstaff to Gaultree. He was struggling ineffectually; the soldiers flung him down on his knees before the table.

'Here is your murderer, Master Shallow,' said Westmoreland.

Shallow's mouth worked, but no words came out.

'How know you this, my lord?' asked Falstaff.

'My men found him hiding in the box-tree alley,' Westmoreland replied. 'And there we found this bow.' He gestured with the bow in his hand. 'What more proof do you need?'

Falstaff fixed his eyes on Westmoreland; Robin suddenly thought how blue and piercing and young they looked in the reddened, wrinkled face. He snorted.

'I'd not hang a poulter's hare on such proof.' He leaned forward across the table. 'Francis Feeble. Look up at me, lad.'

Timidly, Feeble raised his head. He was a slender, pale man, who might have been any age, for all that Falstaff called him lad. His hair curled loosely round thin features. His eyes were huge with terror.

'Why did'st hide, lad?' Falstaff asked.

'I was afraid, Sir John.' Feeble's voice quivered, and he ended with a gasp that might have been a sob. 'I found Wart's body, and then I heard the soldiers, and . . .'

'And what did you there in the box-tree alley?' Lord John of Lancaster asked. He got up, strode round the table, and fastened a hand in Feeble's hair, wrenching his head back. 'Had you a quarrel with Wart? Did you choose that place to settle it?'

'We were drinking in the kitchen,' Davy said, from his place on the ground, his head still bowed. 'We drank to victory, and the king. There was no quarrel.'

'They're all in a tale.' Lord John thrust Feeble away from him. 'Hang him.'

Feeble broke into terrified weeping. 'Help me, Sir John! I swear before God—'

'Peace, boy.' Falstaff heaved himself to his feet, and stood with his hands planted flat on the table. 'Lord John, your justice is worth no more than a shotten mackerel.'

'You talk to me of justice, you old greasy tallow candle?'

'Aye, boy!' Falstaff took a pace towards him. Robin was reminded of a bear baiting he had once seen; how the bear, a brown ragbag slumbering at its tether, was suddenly transformed as the dogs attacked it into a roaring bulk, with swift, slashing claws. Then Falstaff relaxed into a good-humoured shrug. 'For any man in England may have a trial, be he the veriest villain that ever chewed with tooth. Here we have two justices –' He waved an arm to encompass the gibbering, appalled Shallow, and Silence still comfortably wreathed in wine fumes. 'And I shall make a third.' Ceremoniously, he took his seat again. 'Prisoner, how plead ye?'

'Thou? Thy guts are in thy brains!' Lord John broke into derisive laughter, and strolled away a few paces to stand beside Westmoreland. If Feeble made any reply to Falstaff's question, the laughter drowned it. Falstaff said,

'Davy, you drank together in the kitchen?'

Davy looked up at the sound of his voice.

'Aye, sir, as merry and friendly as you please.'

'And who left first?'

'Wart, sir, to go home to his daughter in the village. And Feeble a few minutes after.'

Falstaff mused, grunting, popped a sweetmeat into his mouth and chewed noisily. 'Bardolph?'

Bardolph stepped up and saluted. 'Sir?'

'Bardolph, you saw Wart's body? 'Twas the arrow killed him?'

'Aye, sir.'

'Where are the soldiers quartered?'

'In the home field, sir, t'other side of the house. And some few in the stables with the horses.'

'And from the kitchen to the box-tree alley, would Wart or Feeble pass the soldiers, or their weapons?'

Bardolph shook his head. Robin began to feel puzzled. At first he had thought Feeble must be guilty, in some drunken quarrel, though God knew the finicking Feeble was the last man to get drunk, or to lash out in anger if he was. But he could not have snatched up the bow in a moment's anger. Had he stolen it, hidden it in the box-tree alley ready for when Wart went home? Was he against all belief a cold murderer?

'Master Feeble.' Falstaff's voice interrupted Robin's speculations. 'On your feet, man. Grovel for no man, king's son though he be. Show the courage that took you to Gaultree, most valiant Feeble.'

To Robin's surprise, Francis Feeble struggled to his feet and stood with his head up. Falstaff swallowed a draught of sack, and wiped his mouth on his sleeve.

'Master Feeble, draw me this bow.'

Feeble stared. Lord John and Westmoreland exchanged a startled look, their amusement vanishing suddenly. Falstaff flapped a hand impatiently.

'Here, draw, draw.'

Nervously, Feeble took the bow from Westmoreland, as if he thought it was going to bite him. Robin saw with sudden enlightenment that he did not even know how to hold it. When he tried to draw it, the tough yew resisted, and he gave up, panting.

'And this skein of sleave silk, this winter cricket,' Falstaff said, 'put a good clothyard shaft into a man's back, in a poor light, with drink in him? An he did so, I'll creep into a hazel-nut with the Queen of the Fairies!'

'Then in God's name,' said Lord John, exasperated, 'if Feeble did not murder Wart, who did?'

'And why?' asked Davy. 'Tom Wart was an honest, God-fearing man. He never did no harm.'

Falstaff turned, and gave Justice Shallow a long, critical look. Shallow returned it, nervously, and groped for his cup. Davy, beginning to recover himself, got up and served more wine.

'If you look at Master Shallow,' Falstaff said, 'you see an old man, thin, white-haired, a cheese paring of a man . . . Never fear, honest Master Shallow,' he added, cutting off the justice's protest. 'I speak but for your good. But, my lord John, if you had looked at Wart, from behind and in this bats' light, what would you see?'

Lord John frowned. Speaking for the first time, Robin exclaimed, 'Someone killed Wart in mistake for Master Shallow!'

Shallow had gone white. Shakily, he gulped down his wine, and waved the cup at Davy to be refilled.

'Have you made enemies, Master Shallow?' Westmoreland asked. 'A man whose case went against him . . . ?'

Giddy with the wine, Shallow shook his head, and Davy answered for him.

'There's none, sir. He's a mild man, and a gentle.' He glanced at his master, and added, 'The knaves bring their cases to him, for he's easily cozened, sir.'

Shallow buried his nose in his cup. Robin thought he should be looking for his enemy, not blunting his fear with wine. Someone had killed Wart by mistake; how long would it be before he sent another shaft to strike his true quarry?

But by now Shallow was beyond reasoning. He took two apples from a bowl, and balanced them one in each hand, as if in a pair of scales. 'What could be more like? Handy dandy, which is the justice, which the . . .' He tried to juggle the apples from one hand to the other, dropped one of them and watched with drunken concentration as it rolled across the table and dropped into the grass. He giggled. 'Who could say which is which? Two apples, two old men, the two babes that Jane Nightwork exchanged when I was a mad lad at Clement's Inn, and . . .'

His voice trailed off as he realized that everyone was staring at him. Falstaff stopped with the tankard half way to his mouth, paused, and set it down gently on the table. Lord John never moved, even though Westmoreland grabbed him urgently by the shoulder. Very quietly, Falstaff said, 'Indeed, Master Shallow, you have heard the chimes at midnight. All of you, leave us.'

Davy and Bardolph glanced at each other, shrugged, and left. The two guards hauled at Francis Feeble, who struggled and said desperately, 'Sir John—'

'Peace, lad.' Falstaff waved him away. 'All shall be well.'

Robin had hoped that he might have been forgotten, in the shadows under the trees, but Falstaff jerked a thumb and said, 'Boy Robin, escort good Master Silence to his bed.'

Robin heaved the justice out of his seat, pointed him in the direction of the house, and pushed. Silence obliged by ambling off, song dribbling out of him like wine lees. '*When Arthur first in court, and was a worthy king . . .*'

Robin followed him until he could see his course set fair, then circled round and crept back towards the lamplight from the other direction. When he reached the shelter of a gnarled old apple tree, he could hear Falstaff again, but not see, so he swung up onto the lowest branch, and peered out through the leaves.

'When I was page to Sir Thomas Mowbray . . .' Falstaff leant across the table, eyes fixed on John of Lancaster. '. . . he called me to perform a service for John of Gaunt, that Gaunt would keep secret from his own household. He paid me to escort a gentlewoman into the stews of Eastcheap, and keep my mouth shut after. She carried a child, well swaddled, and a purse of gold. I took her to the Gilded Cock, and she bade me wait for her in the street. When she came out, she still bore the child, but not the purse.' He swivelled until his gaze took in Master Shallow, who was still giggling softly and drawing patterns in the spilt wine. 'Master Shallow, do you tell me now the child she fetched away was not the same child?'

Shallow belched. 'The Gilded Cock . . . the only place for a cup of sack, a dish of prunes, and Jane . . . ah, Jane Nightwork! She would never be having with me, Sir John.'

'Master Shallow.' Falstaff's voice would have put an edge on Toledo steel. 'Thou shalt have a bucket of sack, to soak thy venerable head like a haunch of salt beef, if thou dost not tell me what happened that night.'

The tone, if not the words, reached Shallow. He half rose, swayed, and slumped back into his seat.

'Sir John . . . sweet Sir John . . . In truth, I was there. She came – an old, fat gentlewoman – bearing a child. His head lolled, and his tongue, and his eyes were not set right in his head. Jane took him and gave the gentlewoman her own. He was a lusty lad . . .'

He gazed round blearily, and collapsed across the table in a drunken stupor. Falstaff drained his tankard and slammed it back on the table.

'John of Gaunt had been married seven year to my lady Blanche of Lancaster, and no heir to succeed him. So when his son was born an idiot, he changed him for another, who was strong and lusty, a son he could bring up as his heir. He knew not then, my good lords, that the boy would ever wear the crown. And so we learn that Harry King of England is no true born son, but the bastard of John of Gaunt by a whore out of Eastcheap.'

John of Lancaster laughed unconvincingly. His face was blanched in the moonlight. Westmoreland said, 'Repeat that, old man, and I'll hang your guts on every tree from here to London.'

'As you shot Wart in the box-tree alley?' Falstaff flung back at him. Westmoreland gaped. Falstaff went on, 'This poor silly gentleman –' he prodded Shallow, who was snoring gently – 'babbled to you of his days at Clement's Inn, as he babbled to any fool who would listen, and said something that told you he knew all. And so when you saw a white-haired, spindly old man tottering away down the box-tree alley, in the twilight, you shot him to close his mouth.'

Before Westmoreland could protest John of Lancaster had whirled to face him.

'Fool!' he said. 'Fool, to risk marring all. Who would believe an old dotard who has been pickling his brains here in Gloucestershire these fifty years?'

'Fool indeed,' said Falstaff. He looked round to call for more sack, realized no servants were in earshot, and rose to fetch the jug himself. Upending it over his tankard, he said, 'Fool, to shoot the wrong man. Knave, to lay the blame on another, too helpless to defend himself. My Lord John, how many more men must die to keep this secret?'

He drank, but stayed on his feet. Robin, stretched out above him on the apple bough, froze, regretting his curiosity. Men had lost their ears for less than this, or the heads those ears belonged to.

'You will not dare speak of it,' Lord John sneered. 'No man would believe you, either, you drink-sodden old villain.'

Falstaff skirted the table and paced forward towards Lord John and Westmoreland. Oddly, to Robin, he looked more like a soldier than he had done on the field at Gaultree with a sword in his hand.

'There's more,' he said softly. 'In these late wars, my lord, the rebels sent you a schedule of their grievances, which you swore to redress. But when their army was dispersed, you arrested them and executed them.'

Lord John flung his head up. 'I did not break my word! I promised them no safety for themselves. What I did promise, I will perform.'

Falstaff snorted. 'The letter of your promise, my lord. Not its spirit. You were ever cold, thinking before you speak. That promise of yours was right well spoken.'

'What do you mean?'

'And who were the chief of the rebels, my lord? Thomas Mowbray, grandson of the man who aided Gaunt so long ago, and Archbishop Scroop, who heard John of Gaunt's dying confession. What was in that schedule they sent you, my lord – sent by Westmoreland's hands? They wrote of their grievances, and asked for redress. Did they make a threat, that if they were not satisfied they would tell the truth about the king?'

'The archbishop anointed my father.' Lord John was blustering. 'Why would he do that if he knew he was not true born?'

'How could he not,' Falstaff countered, 'without breaking the seal of the confessional? He kept that secret, until he found another knew it, and he could speak at last.' He tugged down the hem of his jerkin, and folded his arms over his chest. 'You executed them to close their mouths, and to hide why you did it you executed others along with them – Hastings and that poor gurnet's head Coleville of the Dale. It was no execution, but murder, and you, Lord John of Lancaster, are a most royal murderer.'

Westmoreland gripped Lord John's arm. 'Kill him.'

'I cannot.' Lord John flung him off with a bitter curse. 'My brother loves the fat-witted old hog, and if he dies we will never stand his questioning.'

'And for love of your brother, my lord,' said Falstaff, 'I will be silent. But there is a price.'

Robin saw the two noble lords glance quickly at each other and then at Falstaff.

'You want gold?' Lord John sneered. 'You line your own purse with—'

'Be silent, boy.' Contempt rumbled in Falstaff's voice. 'The price is this. My lord of Westmoreland, one of your archers, misplacing his zeal, practised his skill in the box-tree alley as night was falling, and by mischance killed this harmless poor old man, this Wart. Go and report it so; send Francis Feeble about his business.'

Westmoreland did not move, until Lord John turned to him and snapped, 'Go. Do it.' Then he almost ran out of the orchard.

Falstaff swept Lord John a mocking, courtly bow.

'Our business is over, my lord of Lancaster. When you come to London, commend me to your grandmother Nightwork.'

Lord John took a step forward, hand raised as if he would strike Falstaff, but the blow never fell.

'And how long, old sot, before you spill it all out in your cups?'

Falstaff laughed. 'You know me not, Lord John. For what happened fifty years ago – I care for it no more than pullets' sperm in sack. But now, with the old king sick, where does England's best hope lie, if not in your brother – in my bonny Hal?'

'And your best hope,' Lord John spat at him. 'Your hope for power, to drag the laws of England into the mire, and set up the king's court in an alehouse.' Falstaff shrugged.

'A fat old man who let his knighthood sift through his fingers –' Lord John clenched his fist as if he tried to grasp at sand – 'for love of food and wenches and sack. And you are to be the mentor to a king?'

'Aye.' Falstaff drew himself up; he was tall as the Duke of Lancaster. 'A king who knows the alehouses and the stews of Eastcheap as well as he knows the chambers and corridors of Whitehall, my lord of Lancaster. A king who knows the drawers and the sewers and the ostlers, the silly hostesses, the poor poxy wenches who sell themselves because they have naught else to sell. The fat old men who love life too much to let it sift through their fingers –' he repeated Lord John's gesture – 'for the sake of honour that is no more than a word in the mouths of such as you. He knows them all, and he will be their king.'

The two men faced each other, until Lord John, a pale fury in his face, turned and stalked away through the whispering trees. Falstaff remained, staring after him.

'Come down, boy Robin,' he said, without turning to look up at the tree where his page was hidden. 'Fetch more sack. And speak not of this, or thee shalt hang higher than Salisbury weather-cock.'

Robin swung lightly down. He did not know what to say to the man who had stripped the paint from the face of honour so that he could not tell whether he would ever recognize it again. Instead he began tipping up the wine jugs on the table, looking for dregs to pour into Falstaff's mug. Falstaff stayed gazing into the trees where Lord John had vanished.

'Will you be such a king, sweet Hal?' he murmured. 'Or will you forget?'

He turned, and in the moonlight Robin saw that he was weeping.

A MAN OF MIDDLE-EARTH

Gail-Nina Anderson

Falstaff proved such a popular character that Shakespeare included him in a new play, apparently written at the request of Queen Elizabeth, The Merry Wives of Windsor *(1597). Although technically the play should take place in the early fifteenth century it is clearly set at Windsor in the Elizabethan period. But why should a few anachronisms spoil Shakespeare's plot. He used the play to make Falstaff the butt of a series of jokes and pranks. In the following story Gail-Nina Anderson looks behind those pranks to the secrets beneath.*

Though he knew he was bowing to the convention which demanded that all country landlords should be slow of wit and speech alike, Mine Host of the Garter Inn still could not resist raising a hand to scratch his balding pate and muttering, 'Well I never did!' as he regarded the blank space on the wall of the passageway.

The antlers that until yesterday had hung there scarcely seemed a prize worth the taking. Yet his pewter tankards remained untouched, his few prized items of glassware (reserved for guests of the highest rank only) still sat secure in the oaken wall-cabinet, and none of the brocaded hangings, bought second-hand from a London market, and proudly installed across the draughty doors on the upper landing only last month, had been so much as disturbed.

Whoever the thief was, they had contented themselves with a set of horns upon which it would have been difficult to fix any price at all. They'd been pretty cool about it too. There was no sign of tampering with the bolts on door or window, which meant that someone had simply sauntered in while the house was open, like any other paying customer, and walked off with their curious trophy, bold as you like.

And since the horns had been there last night (he could recall someone making the usual weak sallies about cuckolds, stags and all things pertaining to wifely infidelity and horned husbands) they must have been taken this morning. Not difficult, amid the bustle of sweeping floors, setting fires, drawing water, seeing to guests and greeting the occasional regular who happened to look in as they passed by. Not difficult, just odd.

Still, head scratching got him no closer to a solution, and he was forced to put the mystery aside by an insistent calling from the tap-room.

Even in the crisp morning sunshine, the atmosphere was beginning to get fuggy with the aroma of sweet wine warmed for breakfast, the fumes of that wretched tobacco, and a certain masculine tang of old sweat overlaid with a dab or two of rose-water or musk. The Landlord sighed.

Here in Windsor you grew accustomed to catering for all sorts, from the humblest itinerant beggar with a few coppers in his pocket to the highest in the land. The town was close to London, but decidedly not part of it. Similarly, it looked out towards the snug pastured and wooded acres of the southern counties, yet retained an air of urbanity. The periodic residence of the Royal Court at Windsor Castle provided a gloss and glamour, while their ardent hunting of the deer in park and forest reinforced the feeling that Windsor still owed its prosperity to woodland matters. Its most prosperous residents, like neighbours Page and Ford, were sturdy yeomen, but the money they invested in sound dwellings and solid acres came increasingly from the city businesses, trading, shipping and banking. Windsor sat between the old England and the new, changeless yet part of a modern world that reached out as far as the Indies and Americas. So you got used to all sorts. But still Sir John Falstaff stood alone.

'Mine Host, Ho there, good fellow – my very bones grow chilled for the want of burnt sack, and should the tallow of my belly once set hard, not all the fires of Hell will loosen it again to a benevolent flux or motion!'

Was that bawdy talk, wondered the Landlord, or the latest in courtly wit? When low-life and high-life mixed, as in the group before him, you could never be sure. He had known at a glance that Falstaff's cronies, Nym, Bardolph and the detestable braggadochio Pistol, were the sort of double-dyed rogues who would filch without a second thought and brag about it afterwards. Sir John, however, carried an air of grandeur which, like his incongruously fine clothes, might now be tattered and stained, but had once been the real thing. He was a wastrel but a wag, a tub of guts puffed up with his own importance but still a gentleman born. If he never quite admitted that he'd fallen on hard times, why, that was a sign of his good breeding. But if he once tried to rook the Landlord of a farthing . . .

Well, he couldn't. That was the other odd thing. Last night, before the theft of his antlers, the Landlord had already received evidence of an uninvited visitor, though whether it was the same one defied conjecture. When, at a late hour, he retired to his own modest chamber at the back of the house (kept prudently locked against just such light-fingered characters as were currently his guests) he had found a paper pushed under the door.

As with anyone who deals in the letting of rooms and the temporary privacy of stolen hours in strange chambers, he had been privy to the odd intrigue or two. So now he had assumed that his connivance was being discreetly sought for some secret assignation. It was part and parcel of a landlord's job, but still he tutted with disapproval as he stooped for the paper. Probably young Master Fenton, that sprig of the Court who was in town to woo pretty little Anne Page. It would scarcely be beyond the lad to request a private parlour or even a fast pair of horses to carry the girl off to a clandestine marriage in London. They made a seemly pair, but the Landlord, laboriously unwrapping the paper, had already decided he would have none of it. The lass was the pride of Windsor, fresh, comely and set fair for a goodly inheritance. It would break her mother's heart if she didn't make a fine marriage to Dr Caius, the fashionable French physician who had so profitably set up shop in Windsor. And her father had practically promised her to Master Slender, a country heir to old acres and an ancient name. Let the three of them fight it out, he'd take no sides.

But the paper once unfolded revealed not a petty bribe but a golden fee. Nothing to do with the desirable Anne and her allure of maidenhead and fortune together, it contained money enough to pay the fat knight's bill several times over, plus an ill-written message stating that this was precisely its purpose. Someone had paid Falstaff's bill in advance, and it certainly hadn't been Sir John himself. Far out at elbow, he'd already persuaded the Landlord to employ his fiery-nosed retainer Bardolph as a tapster to defray the costs of his stay. Had he been possessed of ready money it would surely have been flashed round the inn with the same pride he took in displaying his wit.

No, the Landlord could only conclude that person or persons unknown had taken it upon themselves to pay a bill which he had already anticipated might be troublesome to collect. And person or persons unknown had also stolen his antlers. And because he believed that, like Anne Page's suitors, things had a natural tendency to occur in threes, he was already anticipating a third mystery before the week was out.

While he mused, he had set Bardolph to serving his cronies from a great jug of wine while he went about spicing the brew warming over the fire. Whereas most local customers were content with the good ale he brewed himself, this crew demanded wine and affected connoisseurship of its quality. That didn't fool him. It was abundance that mattered to such as them. Hence his biggest vessels and most sturdy pewter tankards. He'd also put by some fine game birds, hung from hooks in the kitchen till their flesh was high-flavoured to the point of rankness, before he'd realised that food meant much less to this mob than a steady supply of the drink that inflamed them without quite inducing total intoxication.

He wouldn't waste on them the fine shoulder of venison he'd just acquired, via the services of his good friend Page, despite the fact that the deer in Windsor Forest were guarded round by the Fellows of the Walks to preserve the sport of shooting them for the gentry, the courtiers and even the monarch. Somehow Page, sturdy, reliable, open-countenanced Page, always quietly acquired the best of comforts for his well-ordered household, complete with bonny daughter, bright little son and cheerful, competent wife. At Mistress Page's table were served the best venison pasties in Windsor, and if no-one could remember who had shot the deer, it scarcely mattered. What was one fat buck more or less in so fertile a forest?

In fact, now he thought on it, the missing antlers had been a gift from Page, who laughingly said that such a trophy would make the humble Garter look like some lordling's country seat. Meanwhile, the aristocratic presence that currently graced his parlour was still audibly holding forth.

'Mirth, my lads, that's the manner of it. When you can raise a rosy smile to her sweet rosebud lips, you know you hold a woman's heart – not to mention her placket.'

The Landlord was not a man designed by nature for rollicking good humour, but if that was what was required he would, as a matter of professional pride, rollick with the best of them. Though he drew the line at the kind of belly-clutching, thigh-slapping merriment in which his scabby guests were even now indulging, he had evolved a wide, slow, gap-toothed grin which suggested enough beery good cheer to satisfy most bar-room requirements. He delivered it now, full power, together with what he hoped was a humorous crinkling up of the eyes and a deeply jolly shaking of the head in mock disbelief.

'Why Sir John, Cavaliero, Bully-boy – do you play the perfumed courtier yet, dazzling our Windsor maids with your fine wit and well-turned calves?'

'Not maids, Sirrah, but women. Full-blown and at the height, ha, of their mature charms.'

Anxious not to miss a jot of such inflammatory talk, the Host chose this moment to stride across to the table and swab at the inevitable spillage on its surface. Thank heavens it was plain deal. He was proud of his establishment, but eminently practical as to its management. As a visiting knight out of season, Falstaff might have the best painted chamber above stairs, but down here he sat in the tap-room with all corners.

'Potatoes, Mine Host, are your only fruit of Cupid. Let the skies rain potatoes, let sea-holly be candied and chestnuts sugared, and all the foods that inflame a lusty appetite be served up to a man and maid alike.'

Ye Gods, thought the Landlord, he means it! The old fool is here on matters of the heart, or at least the loins. Surely not another suitor for sweet Anne Page? More likely he was looking to an altogether earthier liaison with Mistress Quickly, currently the Doctor's housekeeper but generally known as the town midwife, layer out of corpses and dabbler in potions only to be spoken of amongst women. The most ubiquitous gossip in Windsor, she still managed to conceal something of her own background. The Landlord had long suspected her of a youth mis-spent in the stews of London before she brought her (undoubtedly entertaining and occasionally useful) knowledge of the world to this quieter location.

She had taken more than a thimble-full of Canary wine last night, and had been in deep conversation with Sir John. The compliments had flown between them like shuttlecocks, one to t'other. Though well-struck in years, she was sprightly enough to flirt, flutter and talk bawdy. If Falstaff regarded her as a conquest, however, his standards were scarcely high. Widows (giving her the benefit of the doubt, as no husband had been in evidence during her many years residence in Windsor) were notoriously easy prey.

'Older women, my boys! These are the continents to which you should launch your odyssey. Forget your green girls, lacking in wit because lacking in wooing. Give me a fine housewife who knows all the ways of the world and isn't averse to a little, hrrrufph, courtly gloss . . .'

Sir John preened himself, twirling a moustache and abstractedly stroking one fat, sturdy leg before thumping the empty tankard back on the table in unspoken demand for a refill.

'And they twist the purse-strings round their dainty fingers,' chimed in Pistol, leering over the back of his master's chair and engaging in the trick all his retainers shared of jostling aggressively for favour and attention.

Bullying bravos all of them, squabbling constantly, dividing their loyalties and creating endless petty intrigues. The phrase 'honour amongst thieves' certainly didn't have much meaning here. The Landlord let a passing speculation that one of them *must* have purloined his antlers distract him for a moment from the growing certainty that Falstaff was indeed smitten with Mistress Quickly (quite undeniably an older woman). But was she sufficiently responsive (or desperate) to have paid his bill for him? With coins, perhaps, filched from her master's coffers?

She had certainly been at the Garter the previous night, but who hadn't? News of such an entertaining oddity as Sir John spread quickly, and half the town had looked in to take a tankard, deliver a message or merely gawp at the exotic bird of passage (a super-larded goose, more like, surrounded by scabby dung-hill cockerels) perched on the best settle before the fire. Mistress Quickly had wooed him, Page had passed the time of day with his habitual good nature, Slender had twittered in awe of him. Fenton had ignored him entirely in favour of catching a glimpse of Anne Page when she came in with her jolly, laughing mother to carry her father and their country guests off to dinner. Now the Landlord recalled that Falstaff had gone off with them. Perhaps Page had become aware of the knight's lack of funds, taken pity on him, and covertly paid his bill. But if so, why the secrecy and the paper so clumsily scrawled that it looked as though the hand was being deliberately disguised? Why not make the gesture openly? Falstaff would certainly accept it as his due.

No, something was amiss. Years spent running an inn gave you a nose for trouble, and the Landlord could almost hear it twanging in the autumn air, like a lute-string pulled to snapping point. Something unpleasant was going to happen, and he didn't want any messy goings-on in his establishment.

Certainly, please God, not another sudden death. Some three years since, a visiting merchant had been taken with an apoplexy in a locked chamber to which momentarily (and inexplicably) the key could not be found. The ensuing fuss had been beyond belief. No, there was no need to anticipate extra excitement. The hum-drum everyday concerns of life provided more than enough diversion here in Windsor.

Dr Caius, for example, was as good as a play in his everlasting feud with the Welsh parson and schoolmaster, Evans. The two most learned men in the town, they none the less went at each other hammer and tongs whenever in company together for more than a couple of minutes. That their arguments were conducted on both sides in accents impenetrable to English ears only added to the general amusement. The Landlord had to admit that, so well-established was this long-running quarrel that even *he* had occasionally intervened to keep the momentum up. Could it be that one or other of the opponents had taken umbrage at his jolly notion of arranging a duel between them and then sending them off to stand in chilly fields at opposite ends of the town? The ploy had certainly cooled their anger without any danger of injury, but now he came to think about it, it might have wounded the volatile pride of either one of them. Might they have stolen away the antlers in revenge? If so, he supposed that the horns would rapidly reappear as part of some elaborate practical joke against himself. Heigh Ho – since he wasn't a married man, he would at least avoid any imputation that he deserved to wear the horns of the cuckold. It was slightly worrying to imagine in what other scenario his missing trophy might be made to play a role.

Other intrigues seemed to be brewing too, else why had Page's dour friend Ford virtually bribed him yesterday to hide his real identity from Sir John (as if it was likely to interest him in the first place) and to introduce him merely as Brook? At the time it had seemed like the prelude to some piece of Windsor home-grown wit, perhaps proving that the locals could hold their own against this tattered remnant of courtly days, but now the Landlord could no longer feel so sanguine. All around him he felt the press of other men's motives, impenetrably silly from where he was standing but ready to impinge on the orderliness of his daily routine. He crossed himself surreptitiously. The money wasn't fairy gold and the antlers had been taken by human hands – much more of this and he'd be imagining demons at the windows waiting to carry his less-than-saintly customers off to Hell-fire.

Sir John's deep, wine-rich voice suddenly penetrated his reverie, and he began to realise that things were rather more complicated than he had first thought.

'What was that you were saying, good Sir Knight?'

'Discretion, Landlord, discretion. I shall say no more, hrrumph, than that Mistress Ford hath a fine white throat and Mistress Page a sprightly step – and both of them fat purses and comfortable households to boot. And two such merry hinds surely deserve a merry buck in season . . .'

'They both have sturdy husbands too,' thought the landlord under his breath as he stooped to replenish tankards, pausing to give the table a cursory wipe with his apron in order not to miss a word of this self-congratulatory monologue. Surely nether of these cheerful matrons, the mainstays of Windsor society, could have lent a willing ear to Sir John's creaking flattery? Female nature was unfathomable to a mere man, of course. A plump, pretty woman approaching the middle age of life *might* conceivably look outside the stale familiarity of the marriage-bed for a little entertainment. Indeed, on those occasions when a heavily-veiled lady had discreetly flitted upstairs to join a waiting customer in a chamber paid for in advance, he had assumed the liaison to be of just such a kind. And if he had sometimes speculated as to identity, he was certainly too fond of his quiet life to let such thoughts pass his lips.

But not Mistresses Ford or Page! The best of friends and the jolliest of gossips, they could surely not have been seduced by the bombast of such a ton of lard. Alice Page's life centred round children, house and husband, and at the moment she had the added distraction of her daughter's proliferating suitors. But Falstaff *had* dined there. Had his silver tongue so gilded her self-esteem as to tip her down the primrose path? Ford's wife was another matter. Allied to a notoriously jealous and melancholy husband, she might have some excuse for straying to a warmer bed, but scarcely much opportunity.

Distracted by his own musings, it took the Landlord a moment to realise that Sir John had not only (with a little help from his bully-boys) made the wheezing ascent from the settle to his feet, but was also beginning to fuss as to his cloak and stick. Yes, the old boy was making a sortie onto the streets of Windsor at such a fresh hour of the morning as the Host would have laid hard money against. No wonder he had been down the stairs and imbibing his liquid breakfast so surprisingly early. It was all too easy to smell an assignation in this.

Not much given to the vice of swearing, the Landlord permitted himself a By-Our-Lady under his breath. This tasted of just the sort of trouble he most detested, but what could he do? He watched the knight bow with exaggerated courtliness to his fellows before leaving, and turned back to the work of the day with the forlorn hope that with such an early excursion from his frowsty bed, Falstaff had provided the third mystery he anticipated.

It was rather after the busiest time in the middle of the day, when custom came and went swiftly before starting the business of the afternoon, that Sir John re-appeared. Not that he actually showed himself in the public parlour, but the amount of noise and bustle apprised the Landlord that he must have slipped in the back door and covertly made his way to his room. Something was amiss, and while it was no surprise that quantities of burnt sack were soon ferried upstairs by Bardolph in order to effect a recovery, the demand for ewers of hot water and fresh towels was rather less expected.

Falstaff had emerged from his amorous encounter as something less than the hero of the hour, but while a lesser man might have hidden in shame, he was soon trumpeting his sorry adventure across the inn. An assignation with Mistress Ford, if you could believe it, with Mistress Page apparently thrown in as a side-dish. It would have been the saddest revelation of female iniquity, not to mention lack of taste, had the Landlord not been well accustomed to filtering truth out of the boasts, brags and ramblings of his customers.

'A most unlucky chance, my boys, a jest of blind Cupid for which the knave should be whipped like a schoolboy! That a husband might return so swiftly, and with such a wickedly suspicious mind. If ever I meet this neighbour Ford . . .'

But you have met him, thought the Landlord. Only he introduced himself as Master Brook, and I was part of the deception, and if we all come through this with whole skins I'll stop renting out rooms by the hour and turn tap-room preacher whenever there's bawdy talk about.

Though the details only emerged piecemeal, through the clamour of a surprisingly busy evening's custom, it became clear that the fat knight's lovemaking had begun as a triumph of warm welcoming and ended in disaster when he was bundled into a buck-basket of dirty linen destined for the laundry, and carried out of the house by two sturdy serving men under Ford's very nose. The disclosure that he had been carted all the way to the bleaching place at the edge of the river and tipped firmly into its waters rang a warning bell in the Landlord's mind. This was all too convenient and well-planned. It sounded like punishment or revenge, and he felt horribly sure that it must be connected with the advance paying of the bill. Had Ford set up the whole scene to try the virtue of his wife?

No, he would rather not consider where such a maze of deceit and fore-planning might lead, for here *was* Ford, going up to see Falstaff as bold as you like in the character of Brook, just as Mistress Quickly came down from his chamber with a broad smile on her face and began a merry conversation with the love-lorn Fenton. Page was nowhere to be seen, presumably entertaining Slender at home as his prospective son-in-law, but Evans and Dr Caius were to be observed in close, and apparently amiable, colloquy. If there was one thing worse than old feuds, it was new alliances. The landlord felt uncomfortably isolated as all around him familiar faces wore strange masks. This was worse than a court masque. An abstemious man by both preference and trade, he poured himself an unaccustomed tankard of his best sack, and settled down to watch events.

It was probably, he mused, a tribute to the strength of his wine that he had missed the events of the morning and was even now nursing a headache that threatened to split his brow asunder. He pushed aside the toasted ale that Bardolph (who had adapted to the role of tapster as a fish to its element) was proffering as the best cure for a hang-over, and tried to concentrate on the tale he was telling.

'. . . and so this time when Ford burst in, he was sure he'd find my master in the buck-basket, which he set to overturning, ranting his way through the household linen while half of Windsor looked on. A man might suspect his wife in private, but it's a mean trick to bring his friends to watch her discomfiture.'

'But Falstaff wasn't in the house?'

'Bless you, yes! Two cosy hussies with fat purses, and more than a ducking is needed to dampen *his* ardour. He was up in her chamber, disguising himself in women's clothes – though where they found any large enough . . .'

'The fat woman of Brainford, her niece is Ford's maid and her girth is as wide as the knight's. She goes round to gossip and affects to tell fortunes, and if Mistress Ford is silly enough to dabble in such rubbish, then perhaps she's daft enough to listen to your master's threadbare wooing.'

'Well she was certainly quick-witted when it came to getting him dressed up and hustled safely out of the house in full view of Ford and his cronies. He'd have got out without a scratch too, only how was she to know that her husband, riled up and in a fever of anger, had such a dislike of the old woman that he'd cudgel her – or rather Sir John – out of the house and down the street?'

How indeed, thought the Landlord, except that everyone in Windsor had heard Ford ranting about the fortune-telling old witch and the dangers of women playing such godless games. Someone was planning this, manipulating who would be where and when, and if their motives were fathomable at all, they certainly weren't fathomable to a man in his state. Bardolph's next words, however, were surprising enough to clear his fuddled head at a stroke.

'I meant to say – that little Welsh parson came back with the antlers he'd borrowed. Said to thank you for the loan, but they were too heavy and he'd found a lighter pair. He helped me put them back on the wall.'

Of course, there was a simple explanation for all this. In such a neat, comfortable town as Windsor events would *always* fit into a straightforward pattern if you just pushed them hard enough. No doubt Hugh Evans had been using the horns for some jolly pageant he was devising for the local schoolboys to perform next time the Court visited. Something involving antlers – Diana and Actaeon, perhaps? Some fluting lad appearing as the half-naked Goddess of the hunt was inflammatory stuff, but Evans' love of all things Classical might put it within the bounds of the possible. An antiquary to his fingertips, the parson would overlook even impropriety provided it came in sufficiently ancient garb.

No, let that particular mystery stay solved. It was Falstaff who continued to attract a myriad of little puzzles, and only by observing Falstaff would he ever get to the bottom of what was going on in Windsor.

Events, thought the Landlord, quite often got the better of even the most circumspect man. As you sat and scratched your head over a plan of action, someone wandered up, told you how to go about it and handed you a pocketful of clues. Not that Master Fenton was privy to everything, but he did have the confidence of Anne Page, not to mention the promise of her hand and heart. And of what worth were wise counselings not to get involved when Fenton was offering a possible key to such a niggling mystery?

Anne had been called in by her mother and Mistress Ford, in a state of high hilarity, to join in their revenge on the lustful Falstaff. Arranging to meet him privily in the woods, they would fright his lusts out of him by suddenly calling up a spine-chilling spectral manifestation of fairies and elves, woodland spirits of such eerie demeanour that the patchiness of their home-spun disguises would pass unnoticed. Even now Evans was draping his willing schoolboys in the green and white, red and black of the fairy folk. And Anne was to play her part too, as the Fairy Queen all in green. And what better chance for a romantic wedding to the eager Dr Caius than for her to slip away with her prospective bridegroom to be married then and there, even while the sounds of torch-lit mummery filled the forest?

Only five minutes later Anne, playing the dutiful daughter still, had been taken aside by her father and advised that, if she attended in the woods in a gown of *white*, she would be claimed by Slender, her country suitor, and whisked away for a night-time marriage with full paternal approval. So, witty girl that she was, and realising that this was destined to be her wedding night come what might, she had sent a message to Fenton. *He* must be the one to carry her off, and they would settle the consequences later. Only a little help in the matter of the priest was needed . . .

For a man with the Landlord's contacts, the finding of a willing priest and the provision of a little liquid refreshment to lubricate so oddly timed a ceremony had been simple. But he rejected Fenton's suggestion that he should stay and witness the wedding. If Falstaff was bidden to the woods, then only there were the mysteries to be solved.

Here in the Great Park, it must be admitted, things were beginning to look even less clear than hitherto. Trailing Falstaff had scarcely been difficult – you only had to follow the trails of his wheezing breath in the evening chill. As he passed Dr Caius's house Mistress Quickly had turned out briefly to greet him with great good humour and point him on his way to the Great Oak which was one of the landmarks of the park. And with the words 'Good hunting Herne!' she had handed him a shapeless bundle which was only unwrapped when his destination was reached. Hiding at a safe distance behind a tree and squinting by the uncertain light of a cloudy moon, the Landlord saw his prey shake out from Quickly's old cloak a set of antlers (considerably smaller than his own) and settle them atop his head.

Presumably to keep up his amorous spirits, Falstaff strutted at the foot of the oak declaiming words of fiery love in which he was now great Jove, now a slave of mischievous Cupid, now Herne the Hunter, ready to affright all who invaded his territory. Well, that explained the horns. Herne was a local bug-bear, the ghostly keeper of the woods invoked by mothers to scare their children from straying too far among the trees. Some said he was the ghost of a long-dead gamekeeper, but Evans insisted he had been one of the old gods, worshipped even before the Romans came. Either way, he was now Falstaff's disguise.

Why Falstaff needed a disguise at all, however, was a puzzle, the more so since half of Windsor seemed to know he was in the woods. As expected, the ladies Ford and Page slipped silently into view and greeted their ludicrous lover with exaggerated affection, but sprang swiftly back into the shadows as a rustling and chanting filled the air.

Despite himself, the Landlord felt the hairs on his neck bristle and rise at the sound. By the light of flickering torches a crowd of slithering, crawling, dancing shapes was revealed. Tattered draperies, smeared faces and strange movements combined to give a spectral effect, and he had to blink hard to dispel the sense that there really was something unearthly at work here. They circled the terrified knight, who had crouched at the foot of the oak for protection. Ford and Page were visible now on the edges of the group, smiling at the antics of the fairies. Surely the joke was getting out of hand?

Then it was all over as swiftly as it had begun. A shaggy, satyr-like figure had stepped forward and set his torch to Falstaff's horns, but no sooner had they taken fire then horns and disguises alike were whipped off and laughter filled the park. Evans, suddenly ridiculous in his furred leggings, was helping the knight to his feet while giggling schoolboys whooped and hollered on all sides. Ford and Page could be heard congratulating themselves on the wit and virtue of their wives, and good humour was clearly restored.

Now that the games were done the Landlord's habitual discretion triumphed over any further curiosity, and he decided on a swift, silent exit from the scene. Moving cautiously through the trees and back towards the comforts of the town, he froze as he heard voices from a small clearing. Mistress Quickly's laughter was unmistakable, and he recognised the ladies Ford and Page too, brushing leaves from their dresses and wrapping themselves in cloaks before they rejoined the merry crowd to walk home.

'So it was Fenton in the end, though you'd always favoured the Doctor.'

'Aye, and her father had favoured young Slender, but it matters little. I'm glad my daughter has sufficient wit to get her own way, just so long as she loses her maidenhead tonight. I love her as my life, but the time was right and if a little appeasement keeps the woods green, then things must be persuaded to happen in season.'

'But why didn't we finish it here and now, my dears? A man of Sir John's bulk might take an apoplexy from far less than a midnight jaunt, and were he found stretched out cold tomorrow morning who would be the wiser?'

'Think of the fuss last time! And besides, I've grown fond of his foolery. I knew as soon as I saw him looking at me that he was *my* knight, as ready as a fat trout to take the bait. I'd rather see him for the last time laughing and jolly at Page's table, than stricken at my feet like a hunted deer. I doubt it will take long anyway – he's old and the mark is upon him.'

'It seemed to take *us* long enough.' This was Quickly's more abrasive tones. 'When I was a girl I'm sure there was less to see to. Old Evans makes it as complicated as he can.'

'It's the threes that count. He dies as a man, a woman and a beast. And he dies by water, by fire and by . . .'

'What *is* the third way?'

'Does it matter? Say air if you like, the air that will rattle out of his throat as he breathes his last. Or earth, if you prefer. However we die, that's the element we all come to.'

The Landlord left them chattering and moved on, back to the warmth of the inn. Falstaff's party would leave tomorrow, and he must be ready with a cheerful farewell.

Pulling his cloak tighter round his body, he wondered how long it would be before news of Sir John's death filtered back to Windsor.

The Famous History of the Life of Henry VIII

ALL IS TRUE

Stephen Baxter

Two of the plays with which Shakespeare is associated have an odd relationship with each other. Early in his career Shakespeare appears to have contributed revisions to the play Sir Thomas More. *It was written some time between 1593 and 1595 but apparently was refused a licence and never produced, at least not during Elizabeth's reign. The play plotted the rise and fall of More and, curiously but not surprisingly, Henry VIII does not feature in it. Late in his career, in 1613, Shakespeare appears to have collaborated with John Fletcher on the play* All is True *later published as* The Famous History of the Life of King Henry the Eighth. *Here the playwrights were able to take rather more liberties, and looked in particular at the cunning of Thomas Wolsey. On this occasion Sir Thomas More didn't feature in the play. Stephen Baxter has used* All is True *as his starting point and brought in elements of* Sir Thomas More *to make a more complete study of one of the most significant events in British history.*

In the autumn of 1529 – with the downfall of Cardinal Wolsey still a shocking, recent memory – Sir Thomas More accepted an invitation to dine at the London home of Thomas Cromwell. And it was there that Cromwell first hinted to More that the destruction of Wolsey might not have been a Providential accident, as all of King Henry's Court believed, but the result of a deliberate act.

'. . . What if it were *not* an accident that Wolsey's private papers reached the king? Whoever perpetrated such a betrayal has killed Wolsey as surely as if he – or *she* – had driven a knife in the cardinal's belly. And now you have taken the cardinal's place as Lord Chancellor, Thomas. Perhaps it would pay you to meditate on this affair awhile . . .'

Cromwell was a stout, heavy-faced man with a hard mouth that turned down at the corners. He wore his wealth about his person: a gown trimmed with a black damask, rings with fine stones set in gold, about his neck a golden *Agnus Dei* with an engraving of Our Lady. Yet there were signs of Cromwell's humble origins, even here in his parlour, surrounded by his chests of treasure. More observed iron toasting-forks, rather crude, of which Cromwell was inordinately proud; it emerged that Cromwell himself had made these, as a lad in his father's smithy.

Cromwell had risen to become Wolsey's chief legal adviser. The cardinal's household had been the effective government of England, and Cromwell had rapidly accrued power.

Power which was now, More thought uneasily, about to be immeasurably increased.

'I admit I was surprised you accepted the lord chancellorship, More,' Cromwell had said. 'You are a man known for the purity of your conscience. You must know the king intends to progress his Great Matter of the divorce.'

Sir Thomas replied, 'I can support the king in his reform of the Church in England. I am no defender of gilded clerics. But – the king has agreed – I will not prosecute his divorce.'

'What a convenient thing a conscience is,' said Cromwell sourly.

'You would not say so, sir, if you possessed one.'

Cromwell laughed out loud at that. 'I foresee troubles ahead for you, More. *To Rome, sham*!'

More was puzzled. 'I do not understand—'

Cromwell waved a hand. 'I am no scholar, More, but I am a man who uses words. An anagram of your name. Rather apt – do you think so?'

More smiled thinly, and evenly asked after Wolsey's health.

'The cardinal is now at York,' said Cromwell smoothly. 'I have worked to restore his fortune. But I fear his health is already failing. His *accidental* downfall was a tragedy.'

More did not miss the emphasis.

Wolsey had been working to bring about a resolution to Henry's divorce from his queen, Katherine of Aragon, who had failed to bear him a son. Henry intended to marry Anne Bullen, a lady of the court he had met at a riotous – and carnal – celebration at Wolsey's palace at York Place some years before. Anne had been Henry's mistress ever since. Henry's intention was to have his marriage to Katherine annulled as sinful – for she was the widow of his brother Arthur – and, through the Legatine Court, Wolsey was working to convince Pope Clement of the justice of this case.

So Henry had thought. But then, suddenly, Wolsey was undone.

A folder of state papers handed to the king was found to include two of Wolsey's personal documents. One – intended for the pope – had set out Wolsey's secret intention to have Henry marry the sister-in-law of the French king. The other was a devastating inventory of Wolsey's personal wealth. The king was enraged at the betrayal, and Wolsey's destruction soon followed.

It had been an accident, or Providence. So the Court had believed. Now More wondered what was in Cromwell's cunning mind.

Cromwell sipped Flemish wine. 'Let me tell you the story of that fatal incident.

'Every morning, an hour or so after dawn, Wolsey would send a rider from York Place to Court with that day's papers of state. It was in that rider's packet that Wolsey's personal papers were carried to the king. The question, of course, is how they got there.

'Now I had spent the previous day working with the cardinal. That evening Wolsey hosted one of his notorious banquets. Mistress Bullen was there, playing her lute, which she had brought from her father's home. The wine flowed freely . . . Well. For myself, I did not attend the celebration. In fact I was away from York Place for the night.

'I returned the next morning with the day well advanced. All the guests, including Mistress Bullen, had departed, and the rider had already gone to the Court.

'I made for Wolsey's private office.' Cromwell rubbed his fleshy nose. 'I was surprised to find the cardinal there – drunk still and snoring in his chair, still regaled in the toga and wreath he liked to adopt for such occasions, somewhat stained with wine and meat juice. Evidently he had retired there with some dim intention of reviewing his papers. I disturbed Wolsey – he was a light sleeper with good hearing – and I apologised, ordered the cardinal's papers, and withdrew, leaving him to sleep further.

'The incriminating documents were taken from Wolsey's office. Now by the time *I* had gone to the office, the morning rider – with the documents – had already departed . . .'

And so, More thought with unwelcome cynicism, Cromwell had cleared himself of suspicion.

Cromwell went on, 'And since Wolsey himself was in his office – and any intruder would surely have disturbed him as I did – whoever was responsible must have taken the incriminating documents from the office *no later than the night before* – perhaps during the banquet – secreted them, and then hidden them in the rider's packet.'

More nodded. 'One of the banquet guests, perhaps. But which–'

'I cannot voice my suspicions. And, after all, Wolsey had many enemies; and the Court – as are all Courts – is full of deceit.' He laughed, and spoke with a peculiar emphasis. '*All is true. Strike out the liars, and what is left?* Think on that, More.'

More was puzzled by the remark, but said nothing.

Cromwell studied him. 'Perhaps you think all this suspicion is beneath you. You do not know what to make of me. Do you, More? I am of humble lineage—'

'So was Wolsey,' More retorted.

'Ah, but Wolsey was a churchman. And there lay the source of his power and wealth. I, on the other hand, rose to power by ability alone. And, in future, I will use that ability to translate the king's desires to reality. They call you *the man for all seasons*. But I am the man for the future, More. Do you not think so?'

More looked into Cromwell's eyes, and perceived there a moral emptiness which he found chilling.

More, though busy with the complex affairs of state, did not forget his conversation with Cromwell. And, the next spring, he took the opportunity to travel to York, where Wolsey, disgraced, had sought shelter at the bishopric.

At his own request Wolsey had been given a bare, monkish cell, with a small window looking to the eastern sun. He was withered, bent and suddenly old; when his greyed head turned to More, the Lord Chancellor saw that death was near.

More had never been a defender of Wolsey, but he had known the former cardinal as a hale, bluff, carnal man. And Wolsey's ambitions had reached beyond personal gain: he had tried, for example, to deflect England and France from war and towards a productive and peaceful competition. But all his life's projects had come to naught.

Wolsey seemed pathetically glad to greet More. His first questions were after Cromwell, whose star had continued to rise; this year he was to be sworn onto the Royal Council. 'Cromwell has stayed loyal to me, you know,' said Wolsey. 'Oh, Thomas, if I had served God as diligently I did my king, he would not have given me over in my grey hairs! . . .'

More sat with Wolsey for long hours; and at length, as the day declined towards evening, Wolsey's attention turned, without bitterness, to his own downfall.

'We had a fine evening, More,' he said, rheumy eyes glazed 'I don't expect you to appreciate such things – not to your taste—'

'It is a question of propriety,' More said gently.

Wolsey barked laughter. 'Perhaps. Mistress Anne – future queen, by God! – was there, playing that French lute of hers, just as she had the night I introduced her to the king . . .'

Wolsey said that before the celebration he had readied his state papers for transmission to the Court the next morning. After the banquet, late at night, Wolsey had made his way to his office with the dim intention of working a little. Once he had arrived there he recognised his own drunken state, and lay in his chair to sleep.

'In the morning I was first disturbed by gentle Cromwell,' he said.

'What time was it?'

'That office has no windows. But Cromwell told me it was mid-morning. I was still intoxicated, More! . . . But I remember how loudly the birds were singing. Odd, that . . . Cromwell covered me with a robe and, good-humoured, left me to sleep further.'

'You're sure Cromwell was the first to enter your office that morning?'

'Oh, yes. My hearing is very sharp. My sleep is light.'

'And he didn't disturb any papers?'

'He tidied my disorder a little. But the day's packet must already have gone by then; there was little to be done . . .'

Suddenly he grabbed More's arm. 'I hear their footsteps, you know,' he said.

'Whose footsteps?'

'The Devil and his familiars. I hear their soft footsteps – *plop, plop, plop* – all night, they torment me, banishing sleep. Or it may be some witchery by Anne Bullen herself. We have heard the rumours, seen that devilish sixth finger of hers. Or perhaps it is the Holy Maid of Kent. Perhaps she has cursed me like the king. Or perhaps it is an agent of Loyola. One of that Society of Jesus he threatens to found. Eh, More?'

'You are safe from mad nuns and Jesuits here, Wolsey,' said More; and he gently lifted Wolsey's hand away. But Wolsey looked to the window, at its slab of slate grey sky, and More saw madness in his eyes.

Before he went to his own quarters for the night More took a turn around the bishop's palace.

Walking around the grounds he counted windows until he found himself outside Wolsey's room. He heard the former cardinal's gentle snoring. He saw that a length of lead guttering ran just above Wolsey's window. More, though not usually given to athletic exertion, reached up and felt along the base of this guttering. He found a small hole in the lead, neat and circular. There was a round plug here, easy to detach. When he had lifted out the lead plug, stagnant water began to drip through the hole: *plop, plop, plop*.

He heard Wolsey, in his sleep, mutter and cry out.

Carefully More replaced the bung – the dripping stopped, and Wolsey calmed – and More walked off through the long grass, thoughtful.

By Christmas of 1531 Cromwell had become one of the inner ring of royal advisers, and was soon at the heart of the king's decision-making. And in 1532 Cromwell was the chief organising genius of the Supplication of the Ordinaries.

And Thomas More was, at last, forced into a crisis of conscience. More sympathised with many of the grievances laymen held against the clergy: ecclesiastical fees, tithes, the use of excommunication as a weapon in private disputes. And he knew that the king's personal resentment was sharpened by his difficulties with his own Great Matter. What More had not expected was a response as sharp as the Supplication, which clearly was intended to be the foundation of a new royal supremacy over church and state. King Henry would become the keeper of men's souls and consciences: a new God on Earth.

In May of 1532 the clergy submitted to Henry's demands, and Thomas More resigned. A year later – with Henry's divorce finalised by his new tame clergy – his new wife, Anne Bullen, was crowned Queen of England.

Sir Thomas – against the advice of his friends, who knew it would anger the king – refused to attend the coronation in any official capacity. But he mingled anonymously with the sullen crowds in the streets of London.

It was a day of blue skies and glittering sun. More saw the new queen sailing down the Thames amid a flotilla of barges, decked out in bunting and flags. Anne herself – heavily pregnant – looked undeniably beautiful, her long black hair clearly visible, that exotic whiff of Frenchness lingering about her.

But More recognised the queen's barge as that of poor, popular, discarded Katherine, with the old queen's cipher crudely hacked off and replaced by Anne's own.

Few caps were doffed, few cheers rang out. More walked on.

He thought over Cromwell's strange conversation about the downfall of Wolsey – the event which had, after all, led directly to this unholy coronation. Cromwell had hinted at the involvement of a lady. *Anne herself*, More realised, had motive enough to destroy the cardinal – if she knew about Wolsey's plan to marry Henry to the French duchess. Motive, yes – but had she had the *means*?

More recalled Cromwell's odd and chilling phrase: *All is true. Strike out the liars, and what is left*? Clearly Cromwell had intended some clue by this. But its meaning was too obscure for More to parse, man of letters or no . . .

But, More recalled, Cromwell was not so much a man of letters as *words*. Was it possible he had intended that sentence as some more literal puzzle, like the anagram on More's own name? *Strike out the liars* . . . And, immediately, More knew that Cromwell had indeed been accusing Anne Bullen.

But it was not easy to believe.

Bullen was known around Court as a wanton. Her chamber was a place of love-lyrics, music, dancing, tokens and sighs, of young men who came to garner the favour of a young and flirtatious woman. Whatever her faults, Anne Bullen was not secretive, More thought: not a schemer, not a secretor of damaging documents.

'. . . More! By God's wounds, what are you doing here?'

More recognised Sir Thomas Wyatt, a rakish poet and courtier – and, notoriously, an old lover of Anne's.

Wyatt – drunk, bitter and indiscreet – insisted on walking with More, and he boasted of the last time he had seen Anne. It had been at York Place on the night of the banquet which preceded Wolsey's downfall. '. . . Anne played her lute. Oh, she plays so prettily! And after, she let me escort her home – but she turned me away without so much as a kiss! – and that after an evening's dogged flirting . . . But I stayed as her father's guest, and the next morning I saw her, and she returned to her lute and played again . . .'

'The *same* lute?' demanded More.

Wyatt turned his thin, twisted face to him. 'What? Yes, of course the same instrument. It is her own; she brought it from France; she treasures it.'

'And you saw her take it from its case the next day?'

'I did. What is this questioning, Sir Thomas?'

'Please bear with me . . . *Did Anne tune her lute*, that morning, before she played to you?'

Wyatt frowned through his drunkenness. 'No,' he said, 'there was no need. That blessed lute was perfectly in tune with the instruments her ladies played.'

The wine flowed on, at the king's expense, and the revelry increased, bawdy and irreverent; and More was not sorry when Wyatt was swept away from him by the crowds.

After Anne's coronation – and the delivery of her child, the girl Elizabeth – Cromwell's great statutes continued to flow through the Reformation Parliament, and King Henry began to target the opponents of his revolution. A killing frost descended on England.

Elizabeth Barton, the hapless Holy Maid of Kent, was publicly humiliated and hanged. In the Eastertide of 1534 John Fisher, the pious Bishop of Rochester, was taken to the Tower.

As for Thomas More, his conscience would not allow him to swear to the supremacy of the King of England over the Roman Church. And so, a day after Fisher, More himself was summoned to the Tower.

In a dark, windowless cell in the Bell Tower – in filthy clothes, unable even to wash or shave – More waited out his fate. And the frost deepened.

As he strode about More's cell, Cromwell's black furs seemed to absorb the dim candlelight. 'I can tell you that a simple execution will suffice for you. This is royal mercy, More.'

More smiled. 'God forbid the king should use any more such mercy to any of my friends.'

'You are clever, More,' growled Cromwell. 'But your death is inevitable. It is the logic of our times.'

'It is your logic, Cromwell. You have organised this country into an image of the king's mind.'

'Whereas before—'

'It was an image of God's. Now we have only one God in England, Cromwell, and he is Henry.'

'No more cardinals for England, eh, More? No more bells and smells. Perhaps it is Providence—'

More allowed himself a laugh. 'There was nothing Providential about the incident that elevated *you*, Cromwell.'

Cromwell, facing the wall, stopped and stood still.

'I mean, of course,' said More, 'the destruction of Wolsey. Everything that has happened to debase England – and raise you – follows from that single point.'

'What do you know?'

More said patiently, 'Only what you told me yourself. *All is true. Strike out the liars, and what is left*?' More grabbed a paper and quill, and wrote out the phrase boldly.

ALL IS TRUE

'Now,' he said, 'I strike out LIARS –' His quill scratched the paper as he did so.

L T UE

'A simple anagram. LUTE. You wished me to believe that Mistress Bullen had somehow purloined the crucial papers, and smuggled them out of Wolsey's palace in the lute she played so prettily. To set me on that course of thinking you even teased me with an anagram of my own name!

'You are arrogant, Cromwell. Even though you had acquired so much power, you tried to consolidate further. You tried to have me falsely accuse the king's mistress, Anne Bullen, of betraying Wolsey. If I had done so, perhaps – you calculated – it would have led to my own destruction as well as Anne's.'

'*Falsely* accuse?'

'Oh, yes. You are a lawyer, sir, a man of words. But you know little of music.

'With those bulky papers crammed inside, the pitch of Mistress Bullen's lute would have been altered. *She would have had to retune it.* Yet I have the testimony of her lover – a very attentive witness – that no such retuning was required. So Mistress Bullen could *not* have committed this act of betrayal.'

Cromwell's voice was dangerously low. 'Then who?'

More sighed. '*You*, Cromwell. You went through the cardinal's manuscripts before the state papers were sent to the king. And you placed in the courier's packet the incriminating documents which would destroy Wolsey.'

'But that is impossible,' said Cromwell evenly. 'It is true I entered the cardinal's office that morning. But that was when the day was well advanced, long *after* the rider left for the Court with the papers of state. The cardinal himself is proof. If I had gone there earlier, I would have disturbed Wolsey. You have Wolsey's own testimony on the lateness of the hour—'

'But,' said More, 'the room was windowless; it was impossible for Wolsey to know what hour it was.'

'Then it is impossible to prove your allegation one way or the other—'

'*But the cardinal, drunk or not, was struck by the loudness of the birdsong*. Cromwell, have you never found a moment's peace to hear the birds? Their song is by far the loudest at dawn, for it carries best in the cool air of the morning – and at that hour the birds are laying claim to the territory they will exploit for the day; as they compete, the birds seek to shout down each other . . .

'Cromwell, you did not come to Wolsey's office late in the morning. *You came at dawn*, before the departure of the rider for the Court. And you came to extract the papers which would incriminate the cardinal, and place them in the packet to be carried by the rider.'

'Oh,' said Cromwell, 'this is all—'

'And you did not stop there. I visited Wolsey, at York. That wretched man suspected his sanity was being destroyed by witchcraft. It was not so. A simple leaking drain, a steady drip through the night . . . Mothers croon to their children to make them sleep, Cromwell; they know that sharp, regular noises disturb us, for they remind us of the wolves and other creatures of the night. That drip was loud enough and regular enough to make poor Wolsey – a man of light sleep and powerful hearing – imagine it was the tread of Satan, and drive him to madness.'

'I know nothing of this *dripping*.'

'There was a hole in the guttering, plugged by a bung of lead. Simple for a blacksmith's son to devise – or even manufacture yourself? – and to have some crony extract and replace each night. So, to ensure your grasp never faltered – even as you displayed your loyalty to the man – you tried to ensure Wolsey's rapid extinction.'

Cromwell paced for a time, then laughed. 'You have no proof of this. Plugs and lutes and the maundering of a dying old man. All is circumstantial.'

'That is so,' said More. 'But it is nevertheless true. Is it not, Cromwell?

'Perhaps, in the end, your own words have betrayed you. *All is true. Strike out the liars, and what is left*? You intended a misdirection, an anagram, a malicious word game. But, inadvertently, you spoke a deeper truth. For we are *all* liars, we mortals, however pious. Strike out the liars, and what is left is the burning truth of God, before which every man must submit.'

Cromwell growled. 'Not I, More. And not the men of the future.' And, his heavy black robe sweeping, he strode angrily to the cell door. 'Give my regards to the axe.'

The door slammed behind him.

'I will, Thomas,' said More, left alone. 'For the axe awaits you too.'

The candle guttered and died, leaving More in darkness.

The Two Noble Kinsmen 

MURDERED BY LOVE

Darrell Schweitzer

We now travel far back in time to ancient Greece. The Two Noble Kinsmen, *probably written in 1613, is ascribed as a collaboration between Shakespeare and John Fletcher. It is almost a companion piece to* A Midsummer Night's Dream, *being set at the time of Theseus, Duke of Athens, and drawing upon Chaucer's* The Knight's Tale. *The story is a romantic tragi-comedy, telling of two close friends, Palamon and Arcite, both of whom fall in love with Emilia, sister of Theseus's wife Hippolyta. The two friends become the bitterest enemies, and when one of them dies suspicion falls inevitably on the other. In the following story Darrell Schweitzer takes us beyond the tragic conclusion to the play to explore the motives and characters, and reveal what really happened.*

'Do you believe,' said the ancient man suddenly, as the fire burned low and the shadows drew on, 'that death has an echo? Do you believe it, boy?'

I didn't know what to say. I felt insulted. I was hardly a boy, approaching twenty, though maybe to so old a man I looked like one. I was a servant who fancied himself an apprentice; my master was the poet-philosopher Chosroes; I felt quite full of wisdom myself.

Yet to this ancient house-guest I could have been a fly on the wall or a doorknob, and he deigned to speak to me. Out of politeness, to avoid a bad report of myself, I responded civilly.

'Do you mean, sir, like an actual bell, that the ears can hear?'

(We philosophers must define our terms precisely.)

The ancient, a physician I had been told, leaned toward the fire. I crouched down to stir the embers. He dropped his cup, a cheap, earthen thing; but I caught it and saved it from shattering. He sat staring at me, his lips trembling, as if it were a struggle to speak. I put more wood on the fire and refilled his cup with wine.

(I thought to construct a pretty allegory out of the cup, the fire, and the shadows; but not now, not now.)

'The echo of death,' said the old man at last, 'is indeed Pluto's bell, ringing in Hades, for all of us, to summon our souls. Little more than a faint shivering of metal for most of us – but still we hear it – and, for the great, or in extraordinary cases, thundering out great peals which are heard down the years, even centuries, signifying a death which is not easily forgotten—'

'Even as comets blaze for the deaths of kings—'

He ignored my fine, stolen rhetoric and said, 'I'm going to tell you a story, boy.'

He didn't say why. I could have been that fly, that doorknob.

'It happened in Greece, a long time ago.'

'They say there are fairies in Greece.'

The old man waved his had impatiently to shut me up. 'And in Greece they say there are fairies in Scythia, and Scythia they say there are fairies in Hyperborea. But I only saw men there. There was much talk of gods and omens, but my tale is of men, and women, and of one woman in particular, in whose cries I heard the echo of death for the first time. Maybe she was the instrument of a god, but she was also mortal enough.'

'I was not much younger than you at the time' *(the old man began; how old he thought I was, I couldn't quite guess)*, 'though the thought of me as a boy seems as fantastic as any fairy story. But it was a long time ago. Theseus was Duke of Athens. He reigned there with Hippolyta, she who had been queen of the Amazons before Love – and her husband's army – conquered her.

In those days I was a person of low estate. I won't deny it. I was a *slave*, whose task it was to ride hither and thither across the countryside to deliver the potions of the physician Diomedes. Whatever the weather, or time of night, whatever humour I was in, I had to go forth when my master bade me. That this particular night was a foul one, that rain stung my face and I shivered in my flimsy *chiton*, that my bare legs and feet had gone numb clinging to the exhausted, terrified horse – none of these mattered, for the feelings of a slave do not matter, any more than do the feelings of a tool in the hands of a workman. You don't have time to feel. You merely *do*.

That I was cold and numb and not a very good horseman ultimately *did* matter. These things led me to disaster. Suddenly, lightning flashed. My horse reared up. I had a glimpse of an appalling apparition in the road – a dead woman walking, her grave wrappings streaming in the wind. Then I was tumbling head over heels, flying through the air. With the resilience of youth I landed unhurt, but was at once terrified, not of the apparition or of the lightning, but of the thought that the jars I was carrying could have been smashed, that my master's precious potions were lost, and I was in for a whipping to be sure.

I groped around in the dark for my satchel.

Lightning flashed again, and again I saw the shrouded woman. She was rummaging through the satchel, hurling this or that aside. I saw her open on intact jar, sniff the contents, and pour them out. Then she wept, and cried, "There is no death in them!"

Darkness closed in, and she was invisible.

In the darkness I heard her say, distinctly, "Palamon." Thunder crashed. I heard one more thing. She said, "Forever in love."

And it seemed that her voice lingered in the darkness for a long time, an echo, only slowly fading away.

I was alone in the rain and the cold, and I could only gather up the shards of the broken bottles, and the empty ones – for she had drained several. I made my way back to my master's house on foot and arrived in after dawn, covered from head to foot with mud. I expected the worst, and, sure enough, there was my master standing at his gate, striking his palm softly with a rod, pacing back and forth.

But he was a fair man. He let me explain myself first, and after I had done so, however incoherently, his manner changed all of the sudden, as if the sun had suddenly burst through a dark cloud; nay, as if a miracle had happened and a god had reached down and touched us both. That's how it seemed. I was on my knees. My master put his rod aside and raised me up. He embraced me fondly, muddy as I was, and called me, not by my slave name, Rider, but by my real name.

"Phraates," he said, "you are my oracle. You have provided the key ingredient, the clue, the solution to a problem which has sorely vexed me. For its solution I have been promised a rich reward. You too shall be rewarded. You have turned the key in the lock, and behold, the chamber is opened and the secret revealed."

I could only say, stupidly, "I have?"

The ancient Phraates, the house guest, paused in his narrative. Silently, he sipped from the cup I had saved from destruction. He sat back and closed his eyes. For a moment I thought he had actually gone to sleep. I sat on the floor before him – it would have been presumptuous to share his bench – and fidgeted impatiently, all the while thinking that if he never told me the rest of the story, I could make up the rest myself, a romance, which would bring me fame.

But then his eyes snapped open, and he seemed to be listening to something in the distance. I strained. I heard nothing but his own laboured breathing, him hissing between his teeth.

'In death,' he said, 'the gods often speak to us. By death, the living can be suddenly and irrevocably transformed, cast down, or raised up. So was I.'

(Phraates resumed his tale.)

'Probably to appease some god he embraced me, for he was the sort of man who sacrificed to Zeus before any great undertaking, to Hermes before he went on a land journey, to Poseidon before he went by sea, to Apollo when he sought learning, to Athena for the wisdom to understand what he had learned, to Aesculepius every day, because he was, after all, a physician. He did it then, probably, for some such obscure reason, though I will not say that he was without compassion, only that masters do not suddenly embrace their slaves like long-lost children any more than carpenters embrace a chisel – a wise master *takes care* of his slaves, even as a carpenter wraps his tools to protect them from rust, out of his own interest, and if the chisel could speak it would be glad for it – but I digress—

Master Diomedes summoned other servants, who hauled me off to the bath, then dressed me in finer clothes than I had ever had before, and tied on the first pair of shoes I had ever worn, and combed and trimmed my hair so I would look presentable, almost like a young gentleman—

I speculate that he did this on the instructions of some god, though I did not see any god, or hear any divine voice.

In any case, I was still a slave, but now my master's assistant, rather than just his delivery boy.

Phraates cleared his throat and paused again, seeming to organise his thoughts.

'We go through sudden changes,' he said. 'The wise man makes the best of them. If you're suddenly lifted up several steps of the ladder, keep on climbing. Don't ask too many questions. Keep your mouth shut'.

(He resumed his tale.)

'I had no time for sleep. I strained to keep awake and attentive as Master Diomedes and I raced through the countryside in his two-wheeled carriage, bouncing over the rough roads, hoofbeats and the wheels clattering.

Sometimes Diomedes had to shout as he explained the circumstances, somewhat.

"Lord Theseus summoned me," he said. "It is a matter important to the state. A noble warrior, a friend to the state –" (Bump! thwack! The master's head rebounded from the inside of the roof of the carriage.) ". . . pining away, a mysterious illness. I could find no cure, when it was so obvious. Why didn't I see it before? You have made it all clear to me, Phraates, and for that I am truly grateful."

"I thought that for once he truly was. That was another miracle. It was a time of signs and portents and miracles, if you believe in that sort of thing.

We rode. Diomedes told me something of the tale of Palamon, a great and noble warrior, a veritable Ares among men, perfect in courage and chivalry, but originally from Thebes and our country's enemy. (Or his country's. I, a slave, had come from elsewhere in my mother's womb, captive.) This Palamon and his cousin Arcite – also a mighty man of valour, and perfect in courtesy – fought against Athens in the recent war, and were captured.

Diomedes emphasised again and again that these two youths were flawless in every way, like sword-blades newly forged and polished by a master smith. But in prison they rusted, that is to say their souls corrupted.

"By love," said Diomedes. He spat the word. He, a man of reason, had little use for passion. He might propitiate Aphrodite, but only to get her to leave him alone.

By love were the two brothers undone. In prison, they both spied the beautiful Emilia. "Which one saw her first doesn't really matter, does it, Phraates?" said my master, "but to them it somehow mattered very much, and was the spark that ignited their deadly quarrel. So I suppose this *nothing* became everything."

Wearily I nodded my head. I meant to agree with him. I held my neck rigid, so I didn't nod again and fall asleep.

Once the two knights were wounded by love, it was all over between them. They struggled to remain true to their own heroic characters, adhering to all the outer forms, but each, basely, lusted after Emilia for himself (so Diomedes told it), for all she was sister to Queen Hippolyta and hardly a chattel. Did they *woo* her? Did they even let her know how their hearts were breaking for her? Did they ask if she had any feelings for *them?* Well, no. How could she?

"You'd think, Phraates," said my master, "that the sensible thing would have been for the two of them to confess their problem to the lady and let her decide which she would have, if either, but no—"

We hit another bump. I was nearly hurled from my seat. Diomedes caught hold of me and hauled me back into the speeding carriage, without slowing down. I wanted to ask why we were driving so fast, why my usually reserved master was suddenly in such a hurry, but I did not. Discretion is the better part of exhaustion.

Palamon and Arcite became madmen for love. Now each was the other's foe, unto death. It happened that Arcite was released from prison, and sent into exile, a generous sentence, you'd think, he being a foreigner anyway. If my mother had been exiled back to her own country, I'd never have been born a slave. But Arcite sneaked back in disguise. Meanwhile there was a veritable epidemic of lovers' lunacy. Cupid's arrows were falling like rain. The gaoler's daughter fell hopelessly in love with Palamon, again, it would seem for no reason, merely because she glimpsed him through the prison bars when she brought him his supper, or something like that. Such was her madness that she actually thought that Palamon loved *her*, and if only he could escape, the two of them could run off together. But she was a drab. What was she next to the incomparable Emilia (who was also the queen's sister, and rich)?

Nevertheless, she let Palamon out of jail, even though it put her own father's life at risk.

Palamon ran off, but without the daughter. He met Arcite in the forest. The two of them tried to settle their differences on the spot, but they made so much noise with their cries and their swords clashing that Duke Theseus's hunting party caught them in the act.

For their capital crimes (Palamon's escape and Arcite's violation of his parole), both could have been beheaded then and there, but Theseus was merciful (or perhaps crafty, or maybe bored and bemused), and he decreed that the two cousins, and assorted companions to assist them, should fight *to the death*, not in a sordid brawl, but in a proper contest.

Arcite won. Palamon wasn't killed though, and had to be led to the executioner's block. The axe was actually raised in the air when a messenger suddenly arrived, shouting, "Hold! Hold!" and bringing the incredible news that *Arcite was dying*.

He had capered about to celebrate his victory, and fallen from his horse. In a last act of breath-taking nobility, reaffirming the goodness of his character, he had surrendered his claim to Emilia, whom he bade Palamon marry.

That was the end of the official story, which is celebrated already in song and romance.

"But the truth, good Phraates," said my master, "may not be so neat. The blade left out to rust, may be a bit tarnished."

Blearily I said, "What happened to the gaoler's daughter . . . whatever her name was?"

"Her name does not matter, Phraates, but I see that I chose well to make you my assistant, for you go right to the heart of the matter. The daughter went spectacularly mad, traipsing around the country decked in flowers, singing mad songs. She tried to drown herself, but was rescued. I was called upon to supervise her cure. I did what I thought right. I instructed her own wooer, a lad of her own station who would be a proper husband to her, to call himself Palamon and come to her in the dark. The mad mind is easily deceived."

Somehow I doubted that, but I had enough sense not to argue medicine with the most learned physician in the land.

Instead I said, 'And what is the matter, that all this is the heart of?'

Now the carriage slowed. We were approaching a humble cottage. The door hung open, I could see. Chickens and sheep wandered in the yard.

"Again you are incisive, Phraates." Diomedes pulled on the reins. We approached the cottage cautiously. "The high matter of state, on which Duke Theseus consulted me again, is this: now *Palamon* is dying. He is now the Duke's valuable ally, and his brother-in-law, and he wastes away from some mysterious, draining sickness which even I cannot cure. Or could not until now, because I had overlooked the obvious cause and source."

"And what is that, Master?"

"You're tired, boy, or you'd know. It is that plague we call Love."

Now Diomedes brought the carriage to a halt. We two got out and walked to the cottage door. From within I could hear the sound of flies buzzing.

Inside was a dead man, sprawled over a table, his throat cut, his blood drained out into a bowl as if he were a sheep. But on the walls, in the murdered man's blood, someone had written: FALSE. FALSE. YOU ARE NOT PALAMON.

Diomedes sighed.

"It is one of love's casualties."

"Who is he?"

"The young man who was to become husband to the gaoler's daughter. Out here, far removed from the scene of her misfortunes I had hoped she would recover her reason, and live happily enough with the fellow."

"But the cure didn't work."

"No, Phraates, and now raging Love runs rampaging over the countryside. We must return to Athens."'

Ancient Phraates grabbed me by the wrist. He squeezed hard, with surprising strength.

'Have you ever been in love, boy?'

I had enjoyed my amours, and thought myself a gallant, but didn't care to discuss such things with this foul-breathed (for so he was) windbag (increasingly), so I lied: 'No, Sir, not really.'

He let wine dribble from his cup into his lap. He didn't seem to notice. 'Then you won't be unable to understand, boy, any more than I could at the time. I thought my master was a fool, to have overlooked the obvious. Only later did I understand the depth and profundity of his error, and only a deep thinker can even make such a profound mistake. He was right to despise love, but he should not have underestimated death. It was Pluto's bell, ringing, ringing, and the echo of it resonated out from Arcite's grave, and it drained away Palamon's life, and it made the gaoler's daughter mad—'

At this juncture an owl flew in through an upper window and hooted among the rafters. Another omen. A message from Athena, perhaps. We both ignored it.

(*The old man continued his tale.*)

'On the way back to Athens, Diomedes went on talking, but he let me doze off. He was talking to himself, explicating, reasoning, making excuses, rehearsing what he would say to Theseus, and, I think, to Pluto himself when he met him face to face and fought for the life of Palamon.

My master's manner was certainly changed. Where, before, he had been almost joyous that I had somehow provided the vital clue he needed – and the affair was still a muddle, as if I possessed the one tile that completed a mosaic, and I couldn't see what the picture was – now he was grim, his actions urgent.

He told me that Palamon was haunted unto death, by a spirit who came to him in his dreams, and whispered a secret so painful that nothing could make him tell it, even to his physician to save his life, or to Emilia his wife because she loved him (for so, incredibly, it seemed she did, smitten was she like all the rest by this plague of love).

Now, explained Diomedes, the cause of the malady was clear. The gaoler's daughter was mad again, or never cured. She had murdered her rightful husband as we had seen and gone rampaging after Palamon. To what end? To love him or to slay him?

But why had she been dressed as for the grave when I saw her on the road in the night?

Because she had so dressed herself, in her madness, explained Diomedes, and then, somehow, probably by her own hand, she had died, and it was her ghost I saw, and her ghost which haunted Palamon unto death, and now, at last it all made sense—

Only it didn't make sense. I was too weary to say more than "What if she's not–?" and I couldn't finish the thought, and I fell down in my weariness, my face in Diomedes's lap, and he held onto me, as a father holds his son, to prevent me from falling out of the carriage, and I flattered myself to think that he held me with genuine affection.

I dreamed I was locked in a tomb with the gaoler's daughter. She chased me around and round, her grave-wrappings streaming, as she screamed in agony of the beauties of love.

"What if she's not?" I said again, half awake.

My master was too distracted to ask, "Not what?"'

'I awoke toward evening. We were in the vicinity of Athens, on the grounds of a great estate. What followed was an interview with the illustrious Palamon. It was the only time I ever beheld that noble man. I do not jest or exaggerate. He was a noble man. Such a character is visible in the lines of a face, or in the way a man carries his body, Palamon was, on first sight, clearly a man of heroic cast; but he was also a haunted one, haggard and hollow, like a mighty fortress now falling into ruin, the bold lines of its battlements still obvious to all, but everything within crumbling to pieces.

We sat in his garden and the evening drew on. Bats and night birds flittered overhead. I sat a little apart from the two men, a table in my lap, pretending to take notes, as a learned physician's assistant properly should.

"Only when I am alone does the phantom come to me," said Palamon. "Whether I am asleep or awake, it comes. Somehow no one else ever sees it. But it comes, to whisper its horrible secret again and again – ask not, good Diomedes; you know it is a secret I must take to the grave with me to guild the tatters of my honour, and give the impression that I died a whole man. If others are with me and it does not come, still I am haunted by the knowledge that it is out there, that it can never rest because of what it has told me."

"I think I can lay it to rest," said Diomedes.

"I can only hope," said Palamon, "though I am without hope."

"But tell me the secret, and I can lay that to rest too."

"I would fall on my sword first."

Realising there was no purpose in continuing such talk, my master turned to conversation to other matters, to pleasantries, to heroic tales of war, to the various other deeds Palamon and his dead brother

Arcite had done, many of which had not been anywhere recorded or celebrated. I took careful notes then, fascinated, thinking this either material for some grand romance, or a treatise on madness.

Thus we filled the time. Hours past. It was fully night. Now, quickly, my master made a sacrifice to Hekate, goddess of witches, darkness, and of graves; and another to Athena, for protection, and yet a third to Diana for purity.

I shivered a little, though not from cold, as the two of us drew off a distance and hid behind some bushes, while Palamon rested on his couch. My master held a lantern, carefully covered, so no light could escape.

We did not have long to wait. I saw something white moving between some trees, near the wall of the estate.

"Master!" I whispered.

"Hush! Silence! The spirit comes!"

The spirit came, hideous in its aspect, though in the form of a maiden; trailing smoke, seeming to smoulder from within; its bones rattled as it came, and it held aloft a skull, which glowed like a lantern.

The spirit circled Palamon's couch, once, twice, thrice. I could smell the fumes of its burning, like tar.

And the spirit spoke, saying, "Palamon, Palamon, I have come again from your brother Arcite to reproach you and to say that you are not an honourable man, who have stolen what you could not win—"

Then Diomedes stood up and shouted, "Spirit! Speak not!" He uncovered his lantern, filling the yard with light.

The spirit turned, astonished as any living miscreant would be, and it backed away a little bit as Diomedes and I approached. My master held up his hands. He began the rite of exorcism, commanding the spirit into silence, but instead it began to sing in a high, sweet voice. Its words were complete nonsense:

She is dead and gone, my lord,
She is dead and gone.
Let grow the apple and the grape,
But pluck the bitter pear.

"Spirit! I command you to be silent!"

"But I am a mad spirit, My Lord, and cannot be silent."

That was when I was certain. I saw, by the light of the lantern, that the apparition's legs were bruised. Her bare feet were bleeding, as I imagined they might be from climbing the stone wall that surrounded the garden.

I repeated my own enigmatic utterance from before.

"Master! What if she's not?"

"Not *what* boy? Not *what?*"

For an instant Diomedes was furious, but before he had time to react further I had flung myself onto the supposed ghost and wrestled it to the ground. It was solid enough. It wriggled in my grasp. I burned myself from the coals embedded in its clothing, but I didn't let go.

In an instant Palamon had lighted another lantern, and he and Diomedes stood over the fallen ghost, and all was revealed.

I held the gaoler's daughter in my arms. Still she fought. I couldn't get my hand over her mouth to silence her in time, and thus she was able to cry out for all to hear (and at the commotion some others of the household leaned out of windows and heard).

"Palamon! False lover! I loved you with all my heart. I risked everything for you! You spurned me! You cast me aside like an old shoe! Therefore I tell you again, Palamon, that Arcite did not die by any accident! I *know* how it was done. Someone, some agent of yours, maybe, someone who loved you and would do anything for you, slipped the poison into his drink before the battle. But he was too strong. The poison took too long to act. Then he defeated you, because he was the better man, but then he grew wobbly in the saddle afterwards, and fell and broke his head. You are not the victor! You are not the hero! No god has granted you any reprieve! You are a thief of love!"

"And you, poor girl," said Palamon slowly, "are love's assassin. I do not blame you. I blame love, who has slain all these good people."

I thought I heard something else just then, faint and far-away, a deep-voiced bell, tolling.

'The rest is too appalling to tell in much detail. What I finally did say, once I had the girl firmly in my grasp was, "Master! I meant to say, *what if she is not dead?*"

Indeed she was not dead. Her shroud and bones were all mummery. She had soaked the shroud in a resin which retarded the coals, giving the effect of slow smouldering. There was a candle inside the skull.

Diomedes shook his head. "For once, good Phraates, you have missed the mark. You should have asked, *what if she is not mad?* She is not mad. She never was. Driven by passions and impossible longings, yes, but never deprived of her reason. Therefore I could not cure her. With her trailing flowers and mad songs, she was *so* conspicuous. But she could put off such things, and change her aspect, and move about all but invisibly, and seem just another drab. I don't doubt that she poisoned Arcite, mingling with the servants unnoticed."

The girl hissed and snarled like an alley cat. I held her tightly. Then she wept. Then she began to sing again.

"Master," I said, "I think it possible that she has *become* mad, now that it's all over."

Diomedes sighed. "If so, then we must cure her."

I hadn't noticed that Palamon had slipped away. Now there was a scream from within the house. I saw then, that he was gone. A woman came out into the garden, sobbing, telling us that Lord Palamon had fallen on his sword, and was dead.

The girl in my arms sang a slow, sad song in praise of Love.

'We didn't get to cure the girl. Lord Theseus had her walled up, and therefore, as in my dream, she was buried alive and left to scream.

The Duke sat in judgement before Diomedes and myself. Hippolyta was there, and Emilia, shrouded in mourning.

"I cannot bring myself to believe," said Theseus, "that the Lord Palamon could have been in any way a party to this murder. He was a man of true honour."

"Nor do I believe it, dread Lord," said Diomedes. "It was the girl alone."

"Nevertheless, for fear of scandal, Palamon took his own life."

"It was an honourable thing, if regrettable."

"And his memory must remain honoured. No suspicion of any taint must ever be voiced. You, physician, have performed your duties as best you can, and you shall be paid for them. You are a citizen of repute, and I trust your silence. But I think that, for caution's sake, we ought to have your slave killed. He knows too much. Fear not, I shall add an extra sum to your fee to cover the expense."

At that moment, all time seemed to stop. I felt only abject, helpless dread. I looked at my master, searching his face for some sign of humanity, some indication that I was more than a *thing* to be cast aside when I was no longer useful. Certainly I trembled. Maybe I even began to weep. It was useless to say anything, so I remained silent.

Diomedes looked to me. I could see him weighing the various factors in his mind. Then he turned to Theseus.

I tell you I thought nothing of love then, but I heard Pluto's bell quite clearly.

"You are mistaken, Lord," Diomedes said. He put his arm around me and drew me to him. "This is not a slave. This is Phraates, my assistant and my apprentice and my adopted son."

And still I heard it.'

Old Phraates let out a rude noise, half a grunt, half a snore. His cup rolled about in his lap, staining his robe. Then he shook his head and seemed to come back to himself.

'Well? What do you think of that? *I've told no one this story until now, until everybody else in it was safely dead these many years. So why do you think I told it to you, huh?'*

I was amazed, but, as I have said, full of myself, and I proceeded to explicate the old man's tale, arranging the parts neatly for moral edification, showing how each god intervened in the lives of the characters: here Ares, in the war; Aphrodite in the intrigues of love; Artemis for the purity of that love; Zeus, bored and bemused, who moves all men about like game pieces on a board. By all of them, arbitrarily, are our lives governed. I went on at some length in this vein, until the old man spat angrily and hurled his cup against the hearth.

'Shut up! Shut up! Listen! I told you the story because it means nothing. I could have told it to a doorknob and it wouldn't have made any difference. Life and love and politics and wars, all mean nothing. That was what I learned, from that adventure, and over the years. All of us hear death's bell, when it is time, and we may have our comforts and our friendships before then, but in the end nothing else matters. My master Diomedes was a good man, but a fool. He thought it was love. No, it was the echo of death, so powerful that Arcite heard it, then the gaoler's daughter, then Palamon. It resonates still. Hark! Listen! Listen!'

He held up his hand. I listened. There was only silence in the hall, but for the occasional snapping of the embers.

It was only after a long time, by the glassiness of his eye, that I could tell that the old man had died, right there, frozen in that position.

Before I went to summon Chosroes, I swept up the pieces of the broken cup. I noticed that, though it was cheap ware for casual use, there had been a design painted on it, that of two warriors locked in battle while a lady looked on. But now the picture was just a pile of fragments and could never be put back together.

That was my pretty allegory. Thus I explicated.

THE WINE-DARK CUP

Claire Griffen

We stay in ancient Greece for our next story, set at the time of the Trojan War when the Greeks, led by Agamemnon, besieged Troy for ten years, seeking to reclaim Helen, wife of Menelaus, who had been abducted by Paris. Shakespeare used Homer's Iliad *as his source for* Troilus and Cressida *(c.1602), and the play starts at much the same point, with Achilles having killed the Trojan Hector in revenge for the death of his friend Patroclus. Also woven into the play is the love affair of the Grecian Cressida for the Trojan Troilus whom she deserts for the Greek Diomedes. In this story Claire Griffen weaves all these threads together and then seeks to unravel them to solve the mystery of who really killed Patroclus.*

In its ninth year, the Trojan War was legend from the Greek isles to the Hellespont, from Egypt to Ethiopia. There's no need for me to relate the cause; it's well-known to even my youngest great-great-grandson how Paris, Priam's son, eloped with Helen, the wife of the Spartan king, and how this sordid scandal was ennobled by the gathering of the Greek kings and the launching of a thousand ships.

There are many tales that I have lived to tell you, for I, Nestor, King of Pylos, am the oldest man in the known world, having gone adventuring with Theseus and Laomedon, Hector's grandsire. Sometimes as I doze before the fire Prometheus breathes on the ashes of long-dead heroes and I recall how Theseus fought those hybrid beasts the Centaurs, half-man, half-horse.

But it's of the Trojan War I've come to tell. The minstrels still sing of that tragic triangle Patroclus–Achilles–Hector, but there was another – Troilus–Cressida–Diomedes and sometimes the two become ravelled in my mind and I have to speak to set the tale straight. Were Thersites here *he*'d jog my memory. I wonder what became of him, that impudent rogue with his crooked body and satyr's face, whose riddle unmasked a murderer in our midst.

I recall a time, and a place where the wine-dark sea lapped the Trojan shore. Our ships were drawn up on the beach, the beaks of their prows starkly piercing the starless night. Ashes drifted across the sands from the ships burnt by the Trojans and there was a reek of charred timber in the air.

Thersites came to the door of my hut and craved admittance. A slave brought me his name. I was sitting on a carved chair I had plundered from Thebe with a crimson-dyed sheepskin across my knees. I was an old man even then though I still went out to fight.

'Thersites, that rapscallion! Have I the will to put up with his insolence? Why not? He might lift my spirits.'

I was drinking wine sprinkled with cheese and barley-meal, my favourite refreshment, and I ordered a cup for my unexpected guest. He did not come straight to me to do me honour, but stared with unabashed curiosity at all that made me comfortable, brought from home or plundered from neighbouring towns, animal skins and purple-dyed linen, tripods and copper cauldrons, vats of wine and silver goblets.

'My lord,' he bowed as low as his crook-back would allow. 'I greet you with respect.'

I laughed at that. 'A month ago you described me as a mouldy piece of mouth-gnawed cheese and told your masters my wits had been motheaten while their grandsires were still in the womb. Have I grown young and witty that you give me respect?'

'I bring you a riddle. I can't take it to Achilles for he howls at Patroclus's bier like a man being flayed alive and I can't take it to Hector for he lies dead and mangled in the yard.'

I glared at him. 'What mischief are you at?'

'Hear my riddle and judge.'

He warmed his hands at the brazier. I studied him by the glow of the coals. It was a cruel, crafty face, but there was a certain intelligence in the slitted eyes and a wry humour in the thick-lipped mouth. I fancied myself a shrewd judge of men. There was a gravity under the villain's boldness that made me take him seriously.

'Ask your riddle then.'

'*Who killed Patroclus?*'

Before the twelve ships from Ithaca, was the meeting-place of the Greek kings. There they assembled in answer to my summons. Most came reluctantly; the past three days of fighting had been long and arduous, all were weary and some bore wounds. Exhaustion blunted their curiosity, there was only resentment that I had dragged them from their beds or supper tables.

I saw Great Ajax seize Thersites by the scruff of his neck as he tried to sidle past. 'What's the old dotard called an emergency council for? The River Scamander's choked with Trojan dead and our enemies are bawling their eyes out over Hector. What more can the old man want?'

'Were you dragged away from your supper?' retorted Thersites. 'Why do I ask? I can tell from your swinish breath you've had your snout in the trough.'

Ajax cuffed him. 'Bitch-wolf's whelp! Take yourself off. This is a council for kings.'

I found it necessary to intervene. 'Gently, good Ajax. Thersites is here under my protection.'

'So you've found a new master, you lice-ridden cur, someone else to steal from, spy on and lie to.' Ajax gave him a shake and let him go.

'I never lie, great prince, as I'll prove when I say your horse has twice your brain which makes it a half-wit.' He capered away with his lopsided gait before Ajax could retaliate.

I glanced about the circle of kings and princes, some torchlit, others in shadow. High King Agamemnon had put on his regalia for the meeting, a gold-embroidered talaris and a purple himation. On his black hair he wore a gold diadem. He had a hard face, I thought, high-nosed, sensual-lipped, a Greek beard that left his lip clean-shaven, and eyes as cold as agate. Beside him sat his brother, tawny-haired Menelaus, husband of the faithless Helen.

Misery loves company 'tis said. If true, our wounded sat together, red-haired Ulysses with a bloody rag tied around his thigh, Diomedes the Argive still limping from the arrow Paris had shot through his foot.

Ajax preferred to stand leaning against his spear. With his shaggy hair and beard and the animal skin he wore with claws and tail still attached, he looked like one of those hybrid beasts, half-man, half-lion.

One other stood among us, the prophet Calchas who had abandoned his fellow-Trojans and come over to our side because he'd had a vision the Greeks would win. I'd always been disappointed as a boy that men of such calling didn't have eyes that flashed lightning. Calchas was a very ordinary man. I noted he wore a chlamys of dark blue, the colour of mourning.

All eyes were on me, waiting for me to speak. Since I had called the council, it was my duty to open the discussion.

'Thank you for the respect you've shown me in attending this meeting. Many have praised my wisdom. Others no doubt call me a garrulous old fool. I'll try to be brief. The years that have given me wisdom have also given me compassion. It grieves me that Hector's shade must wail forever outside Hades because he lies unshriven.'

A low growl rumbled through the assembly.

'Is that what this is about?' demanded Menelaus. 'I was at the Scaean Gate, indeed I was one who fought for Patroclus's body. Hector intended to place his head on a pike above the city walls and throw his body to the dogs. Let Hector lie unshriven.'

'Ay,' agreed Ajax. 'I saw him strip the armour, Achilles's armour, from Patroclus and put it on himself. He flaunted it before Achilles. Good for my kinsman that he knew the chink in his own armour and breached Hector through the gullet. That was a sight to see.'

'It's not of Hector that I wish to speak,' I said, quickly, 'not yet. 'Tis of Patroclus. Thersites has a riddle.'

'What!' shouted Ajax. 'That misbegotten mongrel? That scab I long to scratch?'

'I beg you all to remember he is under my protection.'

At my nod, Thersites limped into the centre of the square. Despite his deformity and low estate, there was nothing servile in his manner. He glanced at each face in turn with a sly smile.

'My question is simple, my lords. Only one among us knows the answer, but will he tell? *Who killed Patroclus?*'

The kings to a man were struck dumb. I could see that they thought my wits had at last gone a wool-gathering, if I could give credence to this fellow's buffoonery.

'Is that it?' Ajax got out. 'You monstrous sham! Hector killed Patroclus.'

'No, my wet-witted lord. Hector merely finished him off. Patroclus was already dead on his feet when Hector ran him through.' Thersites called softly into the shadows. 'Automedon, stand forth.'

A short, stocky, sullen-faced fellow came into the torchlight. We all knew Automedon, Achilles's charioteer. He had driven Patroclus on that fateful day.

'Tell this assembly what you told me of Patroclus's encounter with Hector.'

'That was for your ears only, Thersites.'

'Now it's common knowledge.'

Automedon shrugged and began reluctantly; his narrative gaining fervour as he made the tale live. 'The battle was going badly for the Greeks, but still Achilles would not fight because of his quarrel with Agamemnon,' here he stole a nervous glance at the High King. 'But he allowed Patroclus to borrow his armour and lead out the Myrmidons. Patroclus was filled with a flame, he fought as never before, he killed kings and the sons of kings and his career brought him to the Scaean Gate where Hector stood. As he shouted his challenge and sprang from the chariot, it seemed that Apollo punished him for his arrogance. He staggered in his gait, cried out that he was blind and foamed at the mouth. Seizing the moment, Hector ran forward and transfixed him with his spear.' He fell silent, trembling at the memory.

There was a brief silence.

'Could he have had a seizure?' suggested Menelaus. 'I've seen men seized with a fit fall down and foam at the mouth.'

Thersites shook his head. 'Patroclus had a favourite hound. It was a merriment among us that it lapped wine. Before he drove away, Patroclus drank a battle cup and flung the lees into the yard. The hound licked them up from the dirt. I found it later, twitching, its mouth flecked with foam.'

There was an even longer silence. Agamemnon worked his mouth as if he tasted wormwood. He reached for a wine cup from his slave. The slave was clumsy and the wine splashed on the king's tunic in ominous stain.

'Poison.' Only Diomedes was brave enough to state the obvious. 'And Thersites accuses one of us.'

'Your brain's as twisted as your back' growled Ulysses. 'What does it profit you to make this mischief?'

Thersites screwed up his eyes. 'Only the truth.'

'Truth!' snorted Ajax. 'You fork-fanged snake!'

'Of course I could take my tale to Achilles. You all saw what a fine slaughter he made among his enemies today. Shall I let him loose among his friends?'

That gave the others pause. We had all been witness to Achilles's frenzy of grief. None of us wanted to give him further cause for rage.

'I think we should conduct this enquiry among ourselves,' said Agamemnon, judiciously.

Thersites showed his yellow teeth in a rodent smile. 'I thought you'd come to that decision, great king.'

'What trick do you have up your sleeve?' demanded Ulysses. 'We all know you for a rascal and a spy, sneaking from tent to tent to listen and watch. What dirty rag are you going to drag out to shake in our faces?'

'I'll begin with you, O *king* of tricks. Do you recall the night the Trojans came to our camp to arrange the one-day truce for both sides to burn their dead? Who was it who took Prince Troilus to the tent where Cressida dwells that he might see her trysting with Diomedes? Hadn't she told us she was pledged to Troilus? Was *that* not an act of mischief to make Diomedes the Trojan's enemy? I thought he was your friend.'

Ulysses squirmed under the Argive's cool stare. 'I wanted to deal Troilus a hurt, to let him see that Troy could be won by the Greeks as easily as Trojan Cressida had been won by Argive Diomedes. So what if Troilus sought him out on the battlefield? Diomedes is the better man. One swipe of his sword, one son less for Priam.'

'Remember how Hector spoke long with Achilles that night of the truce,' mused Menelaus. 'They exchanged courtesies and challenges, why not gifts?'

'Would Hector bring an amphora of wine like a common merchant?' scoffed Diomedes. I could see he was still smouldering with the revelation of Ulysses's betrayal.

'Hector was too honourable a man for such a scurvy deed,' I objected. 'Poison is a womanish trick.'

'What you don't know about human nature, good king, would choke the Scamander,' returned Thersites, and I had to swallow that since I wanted to get at the truth.

'But Hector feared Achilles,' Ajax reminded us. 'He fled from him today along the city walls 'til Achilles overtook him. What a sight! Shouldn't we give thanks to whoever killed Patroclus? It brought Achilles back to the fighting and sealed Hector's doom.'

'Do you still believe Achilles held back from the war because of his quarrel with Agamemnon?' sneered Thersites. 'Nothing so high and mighty. The vain fool was in love with Polyxena.'

'Priam's daughter!' Agamemnon was outraged.

'Oh, yes, he loved an illusion glimpsed from afar on the topless towers of Ilium. He might as well love his own reflection in the Scamander for all the joy it gets him. Troilus brought Achilles a message from Polyxena on the night of the truce, begging him to be true and kill no more of her kinsmen. Maybe Troilus didn't fancy Achilles as a brother-in-law.'

'Are we assuming now that Achilles was the intended victim?' demanded Ulysses.

'All theories need thrashing,' said Thersites, silkily. 'I haven't finished with *you* yet, O king of that flea-bitten rock in the sea called Ithaca.

'Agamemnon wanted a victory to fling in Achilles's face. He ordered the Greeks to march past Achilles's compound, a royal thumbing of the nose, a *we can win without you* taunt. Now *that* I call a sight! I climbed onto the prow of a ship to watch them. First the kings in their battle-chariots thundered by, the crests on their helmets rippling in the wind. The war-horses, scenting their destiny, trumpeted shrill reply to the distant horns of the Trojans. Then went the warriors, the sun gilding the heads of their death-dealing spears. Their armour flashed like a field of flames . . .'

'Enough!' I begged, afraid the kings would become impatient. 'Would you rival Orpheus as a poet? Tell us why you accuse Ulysses.'

'When that king of a fly-speck drove past our compound he mocked Achilles and Patroclus and said, "I have the right medicine for your pride. Drink it and be humbled."'

'And you garnered something sinister from *that*,' scoffed Ulysses. 'I meant we would rub his nose in the glorious victory that we planned.'

'But it didn't work out that way, did it? The Trojans rubbed *your* nose in it,' said Thersites, pertly.

Ulysses scowled. 'They laugh on the other side of their faces now.'

But Thersites went on, 'That same night you and Ajax were sent as ambassadors from Agamemnon to beg Achilles to take up arms for only the ramparts lay between the Trojans and the sea and the Greeks were hard-pressed.

'Shall I paint the scene for you, as vivid as a mural on a palace wall? Achilles was playing his lyre and singing a lay of ancient heroes. Patroclus lounged listening and playing with the ears of his hound, Automedon was slicing meat from the chine of a pig for our supper. You were made welcome and took meat and wine and bread with us before you began your plea. It was plain to see why you'd been chosen by the council. Your words were sweet with honey, smooth with oil. You begged Achilles to pity his friends who would be dead or dying on the morrow, you described the glory it would bring him were he the one to kill Hector.

'Achilles was breathing hard through the mouth. There was in his look an eroticism as if he'd been making love. "I was born to die young, but I am owed some honour for it. Why should I throw my life away for Agamemnon and his lovesick brother and all you other pirates. I'd sooner sail away and live a long inglorious life than lift one finger to help you plunder Troy." '

'I'm sure you recall the quarrel that followed; both you and your mutton-headed colleague were full of sound and fury. Ajax scorned you for grovelling to Achilles's vanity. Patroclus reminded you, Ulysses, that your grandfather was a thief. And what was your answer to that, O king of a dung-heap? "Never remind a man of his ancestors unless it's to praise them. You are no longer my friend, Patroclus." '

Ulysses darted a quick, wary glance around the circle of faces turned to him. 'The next time I saw Patroclus he was dead, but not by my hand.'

'You could easily have smuggled in the poisoned wine under your himation and, when you saw your arguments were in vain, slipped it out onto the table.'

'That would imply I didn't care who drank it – Patroclus, Achilles, Automedon or the hound. Or even you, you foul-mouthed miscreant. I'd like to put the sweet taste of poison on your tongue. As for revenge, I'd rather take up the cestus against Patroclus for my family honour.'

'It's true you had just cause to resent Patroclus,' murmured Agamemnon, who had never liked Ulysses. In fact, there were few men he liked or who liked him. But at the moment his dislike was centred on the red-headed Ithacan.

'So did you have just cause.' Thersites turned suddenly on the High King. 'You felt stripped of your dignity when Patroclus mocked you. He had you sized to the very inch. I wish he'd bequeathed *me* his gift of mimicry.'

Agamemnon hid his chagrin with a cold smile. 'I've not had contact with Patroclus for a month.'

Thersites returned his smile. 'Ah, but your charioteer has. There's a brotherhood among charioteers. He visited Automedon to keep him up-to-date with the war news. He likewise could have smuggled in an amphora of wine and left it on the table. You are the sort of man, High King, who would send an assassin in the dead of night.'

I gasped at his audacity. Ajax sprang forward to launch his spear, but Agamemnon held up a restraining hand without removing his gaze from Thersites's face.

'For no other reason than that Patroclus aped me? *You*'ve insulted many men, rat-catcher, yet stand un-murdered.'

'I'm only a down-at-the-heels drudge men can thrash, and do. Patroclus was the Prince of Opus, made for love and war, and above all he had the protection of Achilles, *the greatest of the Greeks*.'

Agamemnon's eyes were like flint, but he said nothing.

'My brother would not stoop so low,' defended Menelaus.

'Would you, *cuckold*?' taunted Thersites.

The Spartan's face turned the colour of his hair. He reached for his dagger. Thersites cowered away, but continued his defiant attack.

'Do I speak an untruth? Doesn't every man here know you're a cuckold? "His horns are gilded by Greek blood. What an army of us die while Paris nightly spears the Spartan queen."

I'm quoting Patroclus, Menelaus. What a turn of phrase that man had!'

The Spartan sank back in his chair. 'There were times I longed to seize him by the throat and squeeze the breath through his sneering mouth.'

'Ah, yes, murder has many hand-maidens. Hate, lust, greed, betrayal, jealousy, *vengeance*.' Thersites turned his body in the direction of the Prince of Salamis. 'When *you* quarreled with Patroclus in the tamarisk grove four mornings ago you told him he lived on borrowed time. Remember that moment, Great Ajax, when you tried to wrest a kiss from Cressida and Patroclus stood in her defence.'

Ajax darted a quick glance at Diomedes and shook his fist at Thersites. 'Give me the chance to knock you into a better shape.'

'I'd have a better chance knocking sense into your thick head,' retorted Thersites.

'If you spied on us you know the rest.'

'I recall your words. "In such a Sylvan glade as this could not Great Pan chase a nymph and catch her?" Where did Ajax learn such poetry? He must have hired Ulysses to tutor him. The usual way Ajax woos a woman is to jump on her like a lustful he-goat.'

'Get to the nut of the quarrel,' growled Ajax.

'You reminded Patroclus of the time he had fled to the protection of King Peleus, Achilles's father. And the reason he sought sanctuary? He'd killed a boy in a quarrel over a dice-game. The boy's family had never got justice for it.'

'You dig old dirt, Ajax,' I intervened. 'Patroclus was a boy himself then and the death an accident.'

'Nemesis has a way of catching up with those who owe her,' muttered Ajax.

'Will anyone here own to being that dead boy's kinsman?' called Agamemnon. I thought there was an edge of relief to his tone that the focus had been shifted to another motive.

But he was met only with silence. Diomedes, shifting his pierced foot painfully, leaned back in his chair so that his face fell into shadow.

Thersites continued his prosecution. 'May I offer my poor self as another reason for Ajax to hate the Opian? When I was in the service of this brute he thrashed me mercilessly. Patroclus caught him at it one day and took me from him into his own service.'

'And glad to be rid of you I was,' snarled Ajax. 'You tormented me worse than any Fury. Nestor's welcome to you.'

Diomedes leaned forward into the play of light. 'Has Thersites no tale to tell of Nestor?'

There was an angry murmur among the other kings, but I held up my hand for silence. 'The youth is right. No man is immune to suspicion. What have you to say of me, Thersites?'

The little man spoke gently; for a moment he looked human. 'Good old king, out of your mouth have you involved yourself. *You* were kinsman to that boy, for you've knowledge of the crime. Ajax knows about it because his father was Peleus's brother and Patroclus's deed was common knowledge in that family. Who else here knows of it?'

Again, a silence.

I felt compelled to speak. 'Yes, it's true I was uncle to that slain boy, brother to his mother, but I held no resentment against Patroclus. No blood-price, no blood spilled could bring the boy back to life.'

'You shared a drink with Patroclus on that last day. Wine sprinkled with cheese and barley meal.'

'Again, true. He came to my hut to enquire for news of the battle; things were going badly. But he only swallowed a mouthful, only lingered a moment. He had something else on his mind.'

'Or some*one* else.' Thersites gave another twist of his body. 'It's no use, Diomedes, diverting attention to good Nestor. I've left you 'til last and for good reason. Tell us of the day you brought Cressida out of Troy? Cressida, daughter of Calchas the soothsayer, Calchas the *traitor*, who read in the entrails of some pig that we Greeks will win the war. He begged Agamemnon to exchange Cressida for some prisoners he held that he as a fond father might have her by his side. And on the day of the truce, you, Diomedes, went in and got her.'

'What of it?' growled Diomedes. 'Everyone here knows I was the emissary.'

'By the time you had her back to the Greek camp you were all calf's-eyes for her and she for you despite her promise to Troilus. All the Greeks crowded around for a kiss when she arrived, Menelaus, Ulysses and the rest. She played the demure maiden and refused you, but still let you think she was accessible. Patroclus drank in every contour, every feature of her like a man dying of thirst. I knew then he'd soon be asking me to act as go-between.'

'Go-between!' shouted Diomedes. 'Pimp!'

'If you say so,' murmured Thersites. 'You know your lady best.'

Diomedes was incensed. 'I'll feed that scabrous tongue of yours to my dogs.'

'From Troilus to Diomedes in a single night,' Thersites continued, remorselessly. 'Why not to Patroclus? Didn't that put a taste of poison in your mouth, young King of Argos?'

'Where is your proof to any of these allegations?' demanded Agamemnon. 'Fables. Half-truths. Slanders. That's all you've thrown at us. Give us one sound fragment of evidence that points the finger at one who stands before you.'

Diomedes ignored him and addressed Thersites in a voice that trembled. 'Were I mad with jealousy would I not strike at the heart? I who have made so many widows of women of Troy. Ask *them* if I used poison.'

'Ah, yes, poison is a tricky business.' Thersites seemed determined to turn the knife in the Argive's wound. 'How well I remember Patroclus and Cressida gazing at each other in the tamarisk grove after Ajax had slouched away, Patroclus drinking in her beauty which has been compared with Helen's, though one is akin to ebony and the other touched by gold. She drinking in his admiration. "So Patroclus is a reputed murderer," she said sweetly. "As Cressida is a traitor's daughter," he replied. "My father is also a prophet," she retorted. "I wonder what odds he would give my life," he said, laughing. Well, he got his answer.' Thersites peered about the circle. 'Why doesn't Calchas speak? Why stand silent while your daughter is maligned?' He ran his eye over the prophet, who despite the coolness of the evening began to sweat. 'I see you wear mourning. For Patroclus? Or for Hector? Let's have your daughter here. She might know the answer.'

'My daughter knows nothing . . .' stammered the prophet. Even in the warm torchlight I could see he had lost colour; his face had a clammy pallor.

'Nothing of what?' taunted Thersites. 'Nothing of prophecy? I've heard it said she's another Cassandra. But 'twas you, Calchas, who promised Agamemnon a great victory on the day before Patroclus died. Tell us, Calchas, what did the omens tell you of Patroclus's death?'

'Nothing.' The soothsayer looked both surprised and sullen at being interrogated by such a scoundrel. He glanced at Agamemnon for help, but the High King gave him not a whit.

'Because, of course, if you'd had a vision you'd have warned Achilles. Achilles, who befriended you at Aulis and gave you his house to live in. What of your other prophecies? "The Trojans will win if Troilus reaches the age of twenty. The war cannot be won without Achilles and the Myrmidons. The ships could not sail from Aulis without the sacrifice of Agamemnon's daughter Iphigenia." But nothing of Patroclus, or was he another sacrifice? What more do you crave to make men believe you're more than a blood-hungry mountebank?'

'Speak up, Calchas,' growled Diomedes. 'No surer way to bring Patroclus to your tent for a friendly cup of wine than the lure of your daughter's beauty.'

'*No*.' In his agitation the soothsayer lost control of his strength and sank to his knees. 'I had no hand in his death, I swear.'

'Do you swear by the gods?' asked Thersites in that silken tone that made my skin crawl. 'By your daughter's life? Or by her honour?'

Calchas hung his head, his shoulders heaving.

'Let Cressida stand forth. Let's see what men vie and die for.'

Her white talaris, falling in graceful folds, could not disguise the line of her legs as she walked nor the shape of her breasts. On wrists and ankles she wore pearl-eyed serpents. Her black hair was divided in three braids bound at the ends with gold. She had doe eyes in a sun-warmed face and was enough to stir the blood of any man, even one as old as I thought myself to be.

I longed to go to her and take her hand as courtesy dictated, but some intangible shield lay between us. I did not recognize it then for what it was, though I did later.

'I'll say whatever my lords want me to say,' she said in her sweet voice.

'Of course you will,' Thersites replied. 'And you'll love whoever fortune favours.'

She smiled almost demurely. 'It is my nature.'

'Will you sit on the High King's lap and tickle his beard?'

She giggled softly and stole a provocative glance at Agamemnon.

'Of course you will,' smirked Thersites, 'but it won't save you from a charge of murder.'

She gave a violent start. Diomedes sprang from his chair, smothering a cry as he trod on his injured foot.

Thersites smiled maliciously. 'I flit about as nimbly as a crow, lady. I spy – and I fly. If I saw Ulysses take Troilus to your tent to watch your tryst with Diomedes, I also saw Troilus steal back to treat with you and I knew then you had never left Troy. Let us come to that fateful day Achilles sent Patroclus to enquire after the battle. The Trojans had breached the wall and fired two of the ships. He went first to Nestor's tent and then to yours to enquire for your safety. You begged him to take up arms against your own kinsmen. That should have given me warning. I am too much the cynic; I cease to be amazed at the rascalities of lovers. He returned promises for your pleas. He drank in your beauty. And your poison. You pressed the amphora into his hands and bade him drink a pledge to you before he rode into battle. I thought it a sweet folly – until I saw the hound.'

Cressida's face had lost all its sweetness, had frozen into a mask as vindictive as any harpy's or any Gorgon's wreathed in snakes. She spoke. 'Calchas is not the only prophet out of Ilium. I, the daughter and grand-daughter of seers can also foresee. To Troilus will fall the glory of slaying Achilles.'

A movement like a wave rolled through the assembly.

'For that you let yourself be thought a wanton,' pursued Thersites. 'It made it so much easier to deal with Patroclus, didn't it? You had to be sure he wouldn't return alive or your ambition would be thwarted. 'Twas Cressida killed Patroclus. It was not predestined, but premeditated. And all for nought. If Troilus was at the Scaean Gate today his arrow missed its mark.'

She made a smile that made my blood run cold. I knew then what had lain between us was the aura of evil. 'The war has not yet run its course.'

Again there was a movement through the council, this time a shuffling of feet, a release of tension and a secondary tautening of sinews for action.

'What are we to do with this scheming, murdering girl?' demanded Ajax.

The young King of Argos sent a darkling look about the assembly. I did not know until then he could be vicious. But then he felt he had been made a fool before all the company.

'In Achilles's compound are twelve Trojan youths captured today in battle. On the morrow Achilles will cut their throats and throw them on Patroclus's funeral pyre. Let one youth be ransomed by his family and Cressida take his place.'

'That's too harsh,' I protested. 'Let her be returned to Troy.'

'Back to the arms of her lover to tell him what she's seen of our defences?' scoffed Ulysses. 'You are too merciful, good old king. To the Trojans. You'd have our doom.'

'I know a better punishment.' Thersites gave his grotesque, lopsided caper that made him seem like a being from the Underworld. 'Wasn't Aphrodite in all her beauty given to Vulcan, the hideous blacksmith? Give Cressida to Thersites.'

The girl recoiled, almost falling in her shock. 'No! I will drown myself in the sea.'

'The council will confer on her fate,' pronounced Agamemnon gravely.

'Do we tell Achilles of her infamy?' Ulysses looked from face to face.

'Perhaps after the funeral games when he is more at peace,' I counselled. 'Hector's body must be released to his family.'

'And you, Thersites shall be rewarded for your part in this.' Agamemnon turned a malignant eye on my servant. No doubt he was thinking that Thersites had enjoyed making the great kings squirm under suspicion when all the time he had known the true culprit's identity.

Well, as even the youngest descendant who sits at my feet can recount, Troy fell and there was as much woe to the victors as to the vanquished. In the event Achilles slew Troilus and Achilles was slain by Paris. Paris died from a poisoned arrow and Menelaus got Helen back, for all the joy it brought him. Agamemnon was murdered on his return to Mycenae by his vengeful wife and her lover. Diomedes went home to find his kingdom usurped and it took Ulysses ten years of fighting prevailing winds and hardships to reach Ithaca.

And Cressida? I cannot recall her fate. Nor for the life of me, not for the span of my hundred years, can I recall what became of Thersites.

But I do remember the pale dawn as we left the council and stood in the prow of one of my ships to gaze across the field of red and yellow flowers to the topless towers of Ilium and the burial mounds of long-dead kings.

'See the ancient oak and the fig tree,' I pointed out. ' 'Tis said the gods perch on their branches in the guise of vultures to watch men fight.'

Thersites scoffed.

'Do you mock the gods?' I asked, severely.

'Shouldn't I thumb my nose at whoever fashioned me – this cruel joke of manhood? It's better to mock than to hate or cry.' He smiled whimsically.

'Patroclus who was beautiful lies dead and I unwittingly acted as a pimp for Death. Did I name Cressida before the kings from a sense of guilt? No, I did it because Patroclus made me laugh. I shall miss that.'

He looked across the plain at the ancient oak and the fig tree. 'You must be right and vultures are gods. They make a fine feasting of our mortal dreams.'

THE FIRE THAT BURNETH HERE

Anne Gay

For his poem The Rape of Lucrece, *written in 1593, Shakespeare turned to the legends surrounding the fall of the kings of Rome in 509*BC*, and the establishment of the Roman republic under the first two joint consuls, Lucius Junius Brutus and Tarquinius Collatinus (or Collatine as Shakespeare calls him). The event that led to the fall of the tyrant Tarquinius Superbus was his son's rape of Lucretia, the wife of Collatinus. Shamed by this outrage, Lucretia stabs herself to death. Brutus was able to raise a rebel army and march on Rome, and that is the point at which our next story begins.*

'Claudia! Claudia? Where are you?'

My desperation echoed from the stony scrub above the stream but that was the only answer I received. The heat of noon shimmered in the little valley. Even the crickets had fallen silent. Panic drummed in my ears. I called again, and a raven flapped up through a crippled willow, cawing its anger at being disturbed.

My heart clenched; my blood felt dense and black like the shadows as I slithered down the slope away from the makeshift camp. The bird of ill-omen flew from left to right against the pitiless stare of the sky: sinister. All at once I knew what I would find.

From above Collatine yelled, 'Valerian! Leave her! We have to get to Rome!' My patron's words snagged on the tangle of misshapen trees, excuse for me not to heed him. And up there amongst the soldiers there was a sudden burst of talk. Even in the breathless air I couldn't quite hear what he said to me next. It sounded like, 'What's one more slave at a time like this?' But surely when his own wife's blood-stained body was yet unburied he could not be so callous? He shouted again: 'Valerian! Come on! The king marches to meet us!'

The fate of kings was nothing to me then, not when I could not find my love. Slave? My Claudia? No! Not when I almost had her purchase-price and she had my soul. She would never leave me willingly. It was the one truth I clung to in a world of alarums and upheaval.

Ignoring Collatine, I clambered down to the willow that blocked the stream. Trapped against its trunk was a sodden heap of blackened leaves. Above it a cloud of bluebottles thrummed in a giddy dance and the choking air was heavy with decay. I crawled out along the wrinkled bark, forcing my way unsteadily through the net of branches. The tree shifted under my weight or I might never have seen—

Her hand. My Claudia's hand unseen by the man who had lain her in her hasty grave. Her body lay half in the water, half on the fetid mud. For a moment I could not bear to touch her for fear that my fear was true.

Trembling, I pushed aside the stinking leaves that clogged her mouth and nose, but I was right. She would never breathe again. The trails of slugs mirrored tears of grief upon her face and her blood had pooled crimson on her breast. While I had drowsed in the noon-tide heat she had died a lonely, frightened death.

'Valerian!' Collatine's shout seemed to come from a different world. A ghost myself in this strange reality where Claudia was no more, I lifted my darling and staggered back up the slope to my lord at the camp.

Men shouting in the sweltering heat of afternoon. Horses snorting and trampling sun-bleached grass. The clatter of swords on greaves, the rattle of javelins as men swung up around the litter that held the cause of all this uproar: Collatine's late wife, Lucrece.

As I bore my grisly burden into their midst, a silence grew as though

Claudia's death had planted it and I had nourished it with my unheeding tears. The stillness stretched until it encompassed everything. Collatine, pale already, turned whiter still. At the outskirts of the camp, the peasants stooped motionless under ancient olive-trees. Each looked at his neighbour askance and suspicion spread a web of silent poison.

But movement shattered the bubble of quiet. The drapes of the litter fluttered aside, and Lucrece's friend the Lady Priscilla said, 'Hurry! What's all the delay?' At the same moment Brutus stepped out from behind the carved wooden bier and spoke up. 'What's toward?'

Then he saw my beloved lifeless in my arms. Casting one glance back at Priscilla where she reclined beside the swathed body of Lucrece, he turned to focus his burning gaze on me. The air crackled with the lightning sheathed in his regard. 'You are one of Collatine's clients, are you not, sir knight?'

I nodded.

'Do you know at whose hands this woman came to die?'

Twice I tried to speak before my tongue found words. 'No, Lord Brutus. But I swear by all the gods that I shall not rest until her murder is avenged.'

'She must have wandered from the camp and met with thieves,' Brutus said. Around him men relaxed their vigilance. Why not, when each now had his alibi? But I wondered how many thieves would dare approach an armed band the size of ours, not half a day's walk from Rome. The tension lessened. Now he strove to weave it again to his design.

His look speared me. 'Your vengeance must wait. Lucrece has first claim. Did you not swear an oath this morning for vengeance against her despoiler?'

Reluctantly I nodded. The mud was cracking on my darling's throat where the sun pitilessly baked it. 'Then do not,' Brutus declaimed, 'forswear yourself to your Lady and your Lord. Think first of the people of Rome! They must know what Prince Tarquin has done.'

Now he turned to the crowd – the knights and soldiers who, like me, had ridden with him from Collatine's house; the farmers and peasants who had run out along the road to see what caused the clamour.

'Look well, you Romans! Another murder almost at the city's gates while the king plays at war! And this noble knight' – he sought, but could not find my name – 'will lay aside his vengeance for the honour of our race! Come with us! We are bound for Rome, to show the people what the Proud King's son has wrought.' He flung a hand to point dramatically at the litter, and Priscilla pulled back the veils to show Lucrece's martyred corpse. 'Gaze upon her proud beauty in cruel death. This is what Prince Tarquin has done – defiled a lady, raped her at knife-point, tortured her with threats. Only this morning she was yet living. Each of these knights' – he fixed us all with his hideous stare – 'heard her tell of her agony. If she did not lie with Prince Tarquin in her own marriage-bed, he would rape and slay her and place beside her the corpse of a naked slave. Her line and noble Collatine's would be forever dishonoured!'

They had heard it all, this crowd, piecemeal along the road, and some in excitement, others implacable or maudlin with pity, the throng had come along. But for them the best part of the drama lay ahead in escape from their daily woes. Brutus stoked them well.

'See her pale loveliness! Her body fouled, this noble matron summoned us to avenge her. How she wept in grief and despair! It tore our minds. For love of her husband she could not stand the disgrace. When we had sworn our pledge, she plunged her dagger into her breast to lave dishonour away in her heart's blood. We ride to the forum to show all of Rome what manner of scum rule in the land. Will you stand idly by while princes rape and ravage? While brother must laugh as brother's life and lands are taken?'

I heard someone beside me whisper on garlic-laden breath, 'He speaks of what the king has done to him!'

And Brutus rode us roughshod on the steed of his oratory: 'Romans, have you not heard? The king has had word of his son's infamy. Even now he rides with his army to stop us telling the tale. Prove now, brave men, that truth is a stronger weapon than a spear! Let us bring down the Proud King and his sons! Let us have done with the evil of the Tarquins for ever more! For the glory of Rome, are you with us?'

How they cheered! The olive-grove rang with their shouts so that the horses stamped and reared and everyone gave acclaim: 'Lead us, Brutus!' 'With you we'll bring down the tyrants!'

His eyes glowed golden in the sun until they seemed not flesh but coals of Hades. Exaltation posed him like some statue, the target for every gaze. Until that morning, he would have got barely a glance. I could not believe it.

Brutus, the king's nephew, the king's fool, the butt of all his jokes.

Long had he hidden behind the disguise of Dullard, laughing when the king robbed his brother of house and wealth and life, laughing still when his own property was stripped and part-restored. But when he saw Lucrece's blood-soaked corpse there was that light in his eye as though madness seethed in the cauldron of his skull. Yet he was the only one who had a plan that might not fail.

This time he did not come apart and laugh madly at disaster. This time, with the sun polishing his close-cropped curls, he spoke loud so that all could hear: each knight and soldier and every sweating peasant in the glade. 'Then quick, lads! The king himself is coming to head us off! Tarquinius Superbus and his sons are bringing the army from Ardea. Why stay to meet him when we might spill Roman blood? What better revenge than to lock him out of his own city? Come help us to throw down the tyrants!'

They left me. In ones and twos, then tens and twenties, they shouldered past me. I tried to shelter my poor love's body but in their haste they all but trod us underfoot. As the bier threatened to knock me aside I felt Priscilla's hatred though I had done nothing to deserve it.

Then my patron Collatine pushed his war-horse through the departing crowd. He too had lost his beloved; from him at least I expected some word of sympathy or kindness.

He reined in and stared down with cold eyes. 'She was only a slave, Valerian. My wife's slave.'

'But she was a princess in her own land!'

'They all say that. But now she is a slave, and a dead slave at that. Leave her. You have a duty to me, Valerian, and to your mistress Lucrece. Are you a coward? Or will you make good your vow?'

My arm jerked as I went for my dagger but I could not seize it and yet hold my love. Patron or not, no man called me a coward with impunity. A monumental anger besieged me; the deserted grove shimmered in the amber air of the afternoon as though a storm were overhead. With Claudia in my embrace, all I could do was say through clenched teeth, 'I am no coward, Collatine. But Claudia and I have loved each other in secret until I could win her price in battle. I cannot leave her now. I will lay her in the first temple I come to, and stand with you against the king.'

A flush of anger darkened his features. I thought he would say more but he swallowed back his words. I could not understand his rage, but he nodded curtly and kicked his horse into a gallop so hard I heard the thud of his heels in the poor beast's ribs. Never would I have treated a horse so.

How hard it was to lift poor Claudia to my saddle! Only this morning she had climbed up eagerly, snuggling against me as I held her tight. 'If only' circled in my mind. If only we had not stopped for a nooning! If only our poor horses had not been so weary with the long ride from the siege at Ardea. If only the town had fallen so that I might already have bought her manumission.

If only . . .

But I could not believe in some passing gang of thieves. It had to have been some one of our own party. But why? And in the name of all the gods, who? As I laid her in the cool of a shrine near the city, I could not believe that such a gentle spirit would have harmed anyone. My oath to avenge her was hard as stone and hot as fire in my heart.

It was late in the summer afternoon when the city wall stood out above us on the hills. Its shade was welcome. I heard the guards cry out in panic and the towering gates began to swing closed at the sight of so many men.

Collatine, impassioned now, showed them the blood-drenched body of his wife. They were legend, the hero Collatine and his chaste bride. And there stood the imperious Priscilla, weeping piteously. I waited, but Collatine never once mentioned the murder of my beloved.

Still, he had his effect. The gates opened wider, and we rode into a dazzle of sunshine, the peasants running to keep up. Clamouring, jostling, the populace all but carried us along the broad streets leading to the heart of the city. All along the way Brutus spread the tale from horseback. Out of the stews at either side swarmed the plebs, reeking of cheap cooking and cheaper wine, tanners with their charnel stench, fullers streaked with white, even the cut-purses, ready to throw down the system that held them in poverty. In the low place between the Capitoline and Quirinal hills the crush was frightening. As the people poured into the forum on the reclaimed marsh the new temples pressed them in. An atmosphere of hatred rose as though to darken the clean skies.

With sight of poor Lucrece to goad their feelings, Brutus's oratory built them to a pitch of rage that would have challenged a forest-fire. Even I, walled up inside my grief, felt outside me the tides and currents of emotion.

Someone yelled, 'The king is in sight! Old Tarquinius Superbus himself, marching down on us.'

Dismay swirled through the crowd, unleashing dread of the tyrant. The edges of the throng unravelled as people ran to hide.

'Attack us?' Brutus showed no trace of the Dullard now. His laughter echoed from the colonnades, a frightful sound that stilled the commotion. 'How can his makeshift force take this great city? Half his officers are here with us. Collatine! Close the gates! The king and his lecherous sons will find himself beaten if he dares to storm us. You, Publius! Fetch cauldrons of boiling water to the wall.' And so, with brisk command, he carried the crowd with him.

Lucrece's body had done its work. Collatine abandoned it to Priscilla's tender mercies. When I looked again, it had gone.

I stood my turn upon the walls as the soldiery hurled insults and ordure down at the king. Superbus roared defiance but a volley of arrows turned him back. At last he stood bewildered, shaking his head like an old, defeated bull. The shadows were long now, the sky crimson with grief for my dead love. Farewell to the last day that she had lived. Finally the once-king wheeled about and rode away from the gates, his sons trailing after him in humiliation and defeat.

Brutus stood his troops down. All around the city, people cheered and lit bonfires to celebrate in the stifling night. Myself, I had a duty to perform, a place to ready for my poor dead love. In this heat, it were best if she were interred by the morrow. All of my wealth I had put into fitting myself and my mount for war but with the siege dragging on I had nothing back in prize-money. A fitting tomb was beyond my meagre purse and, reluctantly, I would have to approach my patron.

At last I found Collatine private with Brutus. Someone had told me where to find them in the fine house which long before had been Brutus's own. I wondered what had happened to the king's favourite who had so briefly owned it. As I approached down the mosaicked corridor I heard triumphant laughter, hastily smothered when I threw open the door.

Collatine's face could not hide its joy. It was still visible through the tawdry rags of sorrow he tried to assume. I saw equally well that he was uncomfortable with my presence. He sought to disguise his fluster with arrogance. 'What is it?' he snapped.

'Sir, I come to beg a favour. I have no tomb ready, and my Claudia was your wife's own slave. May I have permission to lay her with the Lady Lucrece?'

A slight shrug that almost cast him off-balance. He was well gone in wine. 'She may as well. See to it in the morning, Valerian.' His back turned in a curt gesture of dismissal but I coughed gently.

'Well?'

'Sir, please could you tell me where the Lady Lucrece is to be laid?'

'Our family mausoleum. You will find it at the end of the Corso, just this side of the gate. Now go, and leave me to my sorrow.'

His sorrow, as he called it, burst out ill-masked by ribaldry as I left. I could not understand it. Only this morning he had been white-faced and grim. How could he now be so casual about his wife who had died defiled? As for myself, I felt as though the heart had been ripped from my body. Harpies of misery raged out of the darkness at me. I could not rest.

The graveyard, when I found it, was an uncanny place. Clouded moonlight drifted shadows over rank grass and a fool sobbed wildly, running between the tombs when he heard my step. Well did I know that the displaced lived here among the dead, but the man's affliction harrowed me.

I held a blazing torch to read the inscriptions as I groped my way along. Faint winds disturbed the rustling trees so I could not hear if anyone else were by. A place between my shoulders felt the press of unseen eyes, but who was there other than the fool and myself?

When I found the mausoleum, it stood open. I thought of robbers and corpse-defilers. Eldritch shrieks sounded underground. The night was hot, yet I shivered.

Holding the torch higher, I drew my dagger and felt my way down the steps. Though I am a soldier, I have seen strange things . . .

Trapped underground, the heat was suffocating, moist and noisome with the memories of mortal flesh. I walked softly through the mirk though no-one could have heard my footsteps above that hideous wail. My skin crawled. To either side of me were coffins and half-mummified corpses racked on shelves. And I had thought to bury my love in this unclean place? Almost, I turned back, but I had to know what was making that awful sound. At the end of a passage, I turned a corner and saw a light ahead.

Priscilla! She kept throwing her arms over Lucrece, crying bitterly, 'What have I done?' Little had I thought there would be anyone here. Surely Lucrece's funeral would be a grand affair? Why was she not lying in state in some holy place? And why was Priscilla with her?

Her weeping was dreadful, a desecration of the ground where I had thought to lay my darling. Priscilla began to pound at Lucrece's breast. Though I had never liked the woman, chivalry urged me to comfort her extravagant distress.

I propped the torch in a bracket. Moved forward.

And stopped. From Lucrece's mouth mewled a cry. It ripped through my mind, a hideous groan. But surely no earthly creature could make such a sound? It held me paralyzed as Lucrece's blood-caked arm swung weakly aloft to fall across Priscilla's shoulders.

Swiftly Priscilla bent to kiss Lucrece's mouth. The corpse that should have been stiff was soft and pliable, writhing in a sensual agony beneath Priscilla's questing hands.

But I had watched Lucrece stab herself! Only that morning the blood had flowed crimson, rivering faster than . . . than anyone I had ever known die upon a battlefield. The dagger had clattered on the tiles. And Brutus – Brutus? – had held it until we swore our oaths on its dripping blade, then I hadn't seen it again until Priscilla snatched it from my grasp.

Now it was on a shelf beside their lamp. Unnoticed by the clutching lovers, I reached around and caught it up.

But they had spotted me. With a cry Lucrece pointed, head lolling, marble-eyed, and Priscilla rolled clear. 'What are you doing here?' she shrieked, and came round to shield Lucrece from view. 'Get out, you filthy man!' Her fingers hooked like claws. 'And give me back that dagger!'

Lucrece let out a curse too earthy for any ghost.

That was the key. I stepped back, fingering the blood-caked iron, but nothing was amiss. The edges were sharp enough.

Sharp enough for murder. Priscilla took out a dagger of her own.

'You!' I blurted. 'You killed her!'

Wilfully she misunderstood me. 'No! See now, here she is,

recovered!' Then she added, low and threatening, 'And what you have seen, you'll pay for.'

She came at me then like a madwoman, hand held high, the down-thrust blade gleaming in the lamp-light.

They teach us better in the army. I stepped under her arm, my hand scything at her elbow so that the blow she intended went astray. Her knife clattered on Lucrece's bier. With my dagger pricking at her throat I gritted, 'Tell me then why you killed my Claudia.'

She laughed. 'Her? Why should I kill her?'

Lucrece, then? At noon she had been motionless in her litter.

Her curtained litter. What might not have been concealed behind those veils?

But she must have been drugged. Even now she could scarcely sit, let alone commit murder. No, not Lucrece.

Yet dimly the pattern was coming to me.

Lucrece whispered through her throat full of tomb-dust, 'Kill him or *he*'ll kill us.'

'Not me, lady,' I said. 'I would never hurt a woman.'

They laughed, both of them. Shoving Priscilla so that her limbs tangled in her lover's, I backed away in disgust. Their lust meant nothing to me, but their lies! The hurt done to a good man! Pity for Collatine flooded through me. No wonder he had boasted of his wife's chastity. Their bed must have been cold indeed if he had nothing else to vaunt.

Already they were recovering. I hurled the bloody dagger from me and pelted up the stairs.

The sultry, languid breeze outdoors was a balm. Yet I heard Priscilla's footsteps echoing from the tomb, and hid behind a tree. A fury of ancient days, she burst out of the mausoleum. Racing along the path to the postern-gate, my huntress plunged off towards the city.

I let her go. Whom could she tell? Not a soul without betraying her guilt and Lucrece's. The whole city would lynch her if they knew. I was a fool to throw away the dagger, though, and if I'd tried, I could have found the pig's bladder filled with blood that must have made the 'suicide' so real, indeed so overdone.

Still, their outrageous plot was finished. I could not mourn the passing of the kings after all their bloody deeds, but did they have to rely on trickery? It left a foul taste.

And the only death had been my darling's, an innocent witness, perhaps, to their deception. With no money to my name, I had to find somewhere clean to bury her. And how could I face Lucrece's husband in the morning when I knew he'd been betrayed?

Storm-clouds flew overhead and the first winds of autumn skirled through the branches. Quietly I walked back under the lowering walls, the dark trees alive on my right. My head was bowed in thoughts of misery, though within the city revellers caroused by crackling bonfires. I could smell the char from here. And the fool screeched somewhere beyond the rustling leaves.

What I did not hear was the killer who launched herself at me. A bright line of fire seared through my ribs, pinning my arm to my side. Her weight threw me to the ground. By chance she had landed with her stomach on my shoulder and the fall had winded her. I rolled aside, dizzy with pain and blood-loss. When I came swaying to my knees I peered through the shifting starlight.

But it was neither Priscilla nor Lucrece. Instead I was face to face with Collatine.

Relief welled up in me. 'My lord! Are you all right? There's nothing to fear. It is I, Valerian.'

The hero, my patron, drew another blade. Unbelieving, I lurched to my feet and kicked the dagger from his hand. Drunk as he was he could not stop me, though he tried. We wrestled back and forth, me with my arm still trapped against my body by his knife.

All the time he panted in wine-sodden breaths, 'No witnesses. There must be no witnesses.'

I hurled him backwards, heard his head crack on a rock. Dazed, he stared up at me.

'It was you!' I said. 'Tarquin never raped your wife. It was just a tale so—'

But that didn't work. He could never show his face again if Lucrece was still alive.

With blood oozing from a gash on his temple, Collatine said, 'Was. Was raped. Didn't think Tarquin would really do it but he did. Now she's free and I'm free. Rome's free. But I never touched your slut. Got to kill you.'

On a broken stone a footstep slurred. I whirled but no-one stood there. Instead a shadow stepped forward beside Collatine. Mocking, urbane, the Dullard said, 'Very true, dear boy,' and in his hand was a sword. I'd seen him clown with it before the king but he wasn't clowning now. He lunged and I scrambled back towards the sheltering trees.

This time he heard it too. The slap of sandalled feet.

Around us were the dregs of the city – the halt, the crooked and the penniless. A tense silence thrummed in the breeze.

A man, his rags covering his face, stepped within the circle and said, 'You can't kill us all. You have your city, Brutus. What can this man tell that threatens you?'

Brutus let the tip of his sword fall. 'Another time, then.'

The man in rags gestured, and three men cocked their bows. 'No, *lord consul*. Leave him alive. All of us have what we want, except him. Collatine's wife is free with her adored. The hero can choose a more willing bride and still keep Lucrece's dowry. And we are free of the tyranny of kings. Who knows? You may even grant us plebs a vote. But this man lives since you sacrificed his love to make us free.'

Brutus, co-consul, ruling where he had been despised. I had it now: 'You killed her, didn't you?'

He shrugged, then bared his breast theatrically. 'So have your revenge and plunge the city into anarchy!'

Fire raged through me, an incandescent lust to slay my lover's killer. The hilt of my dagger burned its imprint on my palm.

But he was right. Even for Claudia I could not cause such slaughter. I couldn't even afford to bury her with the honour she deserved. I was bound by my helplessness.

Not quite. The lord of thieves said, 'Give him your arm-rings, Brutus. And Collatine, your purse. That's right. Now the rings from your fingers.'

What could two men do against so many? In hatred they hurled their wealth down on the grass.

'Now, Brutus, and you, O noble Collatine,' said the faceless man in rags, 'if you remember what you have seen, there are a thousand in this city to wipe your memory clean. Begone.'

They left, but the homeless did not go far. I could feel their silent solidarity. They knew it was for their sake among others' that I stood now forsworn. Alone and bleeding, I stooped to pick up the price of my love's fine tomb from the gems and gold amongst the tussocks.

My heart burned within me at my treachery to my love. As I staggered away from Rome towards the roadside shrine, the fool wept for me in the night.

AS NEAR TO LUST AS FLAME TO SMOKE

Andrew Lane

We have now moved forward just over three hundred years to the time of Antiochus III, king of Syria. Pericles, heir to the kingdom of Tyre, is in Syria, at Antioch, where he seeks the hand of Antiochus's daughter, but he fails to answer a riddle set by the king. Afraid of Antiochus, Pericles departs, but is shipwrecked. The following story is set after Pericles's departure and before his fate is known, and traces the events that follow in Syria.

When first performed in 1608, Pericles *was one of the most successful plays of its day, but the original version no longer survives. It may originally have been written by George Wilkins and either completed or revised by Shakespeare.*

I am no viper, yet I feed
On mother's flesh which did me breed;
I sought a husband, in which labour
I found that kindness in a father.
He's father, son and husband mild,
I mother, wife, and yet his child.

How they may be, and yet in two,
As you will live, resolve it you.

The expanding ball of flame carried the fragile chariot up with it, tumbling it in mid-air and flinging its passengers off like a bucking stallion. A wheel came loose and spun lazily away from the twisted mass of metal, while burning leather thongs and fragments of wood rained down upon the plain, trailing ribbons of smoke behind them.

Only moments before, Lord Thaliard had watched as a cloud of dust approached the low foothills where he was camped. The cloud had soon resolved itself into a group of chariots, one leading the others by several hundred yards. In its prow King Antiochus the Third, Son of Seleucus and undisputed King of Syria, had been whipping his horses onward, his robes billowing in the wind and the sun glinting off the jewels of his crown. The chariots of his elite guards had been left hundreds of yards behind as the king showed off his legendary horsemanship, head thrown back and laughing as he rode. Behind him, a veiled figure wound one hand around his waist. Her dark hair streamed in the wind of the chariot's frantic passage, and Thaliard's heart beat faster as he recognised Thea, Antiochus's daughter.

For a moment, as he stood there on the hillside watching the chariots approach, Thaliard had wondered how he was going to explain the failure of his mission. Pericles, Prince of Tyre, still lived. Antiochus would not be pleased. And that meant Thea would not be pleased.

And then the fire came, erupting from the midst of the dust, lifting the chariot up toward the heavens like an offering to the Gods.

Thaliard watched, horrified, as Antiochus and Thea fell screaming from the wreckage. The King thrashed his arms and legs wildly as he plummeted, while Thea's robes and hair were an eye-searing inferno of flame. Thaliard could not turn away: his fingernails dug into the palms of his hands and his scalp seemed to crawl as they both hit the ground and bounced, coming to rest near the dismembered bodies of their horses. Even at that distance Thaliard could see that their bodies were bent double and twisted. Greasy smoke rose from Thea's blackened remains.

Fragments of chariot continued to rain down on them for several moments longer.

'Great Rimmon protect us,' Eucaerus, Thaliard's most trusted lieutenant, whispered from beside him. His face was ashen, the scar he had gained during his time as a spy in Greece livid against his skin. The flames gilded his greying hair with scarlet. 'The wrath of the Gods has fallen upon him for his sins!'

'What sins?' Thaliard snapped.

'I meant –' Eucaerus stopped. Thaliard would have turned to look at him, but his attention was distracted by what was happening down on the plain, where Antiochus's guards had caught up with the scattered wreckage. They stayed in their chariots, keeping their distance from the body of their king and gazing fearfully up to the encampment on the hillside. They were waiting for direction, and Thaliard knew that it was him they were looking to. He had been Antiochus's favourite, after all, his trusted right hand.

'Bring the bodies here,' he said without turning. 'And send a messenger to Antioch with the news.' He heard Eucaerus turn to leave, and added, 'And have the priesthood sacrifice three goats to Rimmon to ease the path of their souls.'

Without moving from his position he watched as the bodies – or what was left of them – were carefully gathered up in silken sheets and carried away with fear and reverence. Once the plain was deserted, Thaliard turned his back on it and strode toward the camp. He had left it in the hills while he undertook his mission in Tyre. When he had arrived back, unsuccessful, he had dispatched Eucaerus to Antioch as a messenger, expecting to be summoned immediately back to court, but Eucaerus had returned to say that the king and his daughter would arrive within the hour. The largest tent had been immediately set aside for a feast. Now it acted as a temporary resting place for their bodies.

Entering, Thaliard dismissed the soldiers and priests. Grypus, High Priest of the House of Rimmon, approached him as the rest left. His ornate robes, scarlet embroidered with gold thread, brushed the ground as he walked. 'A tragedy,' he murmured, his voice stern and deep. 'There must be mourning across the land.'

'It will be so ordered,' Thaliard said. Grypus hesitated for a moment, and Thaliard turned to meet his questioning gaze. 'Yes?'

'It would be . . . unfortunate . . . if the apotheosis of King Antiochus were to lead to a struggle for power in the land. A firm hand is required.'

'Apotheosis?'

Grypus shrugged. 'The Gods are powerful and capricious. What would be more natural than for them to recognise those same qualities in Antiochus and wish for him to become one of them?'

'And Thea?'

Grypus's face twisted, as if he had bitten into something sour. 'King Antiochus will require a . . . companion in heaven.'

'One might have expected the Gods to provide such a man as him with a woman who could fulfil his more physical desires,' Thaliard snapped, suppressing a sudden rush of grief and anger, 'rather than take his daughter from our midst to serve his needs.'

'Perhaps,' Grypus said quietly, 'the Gods know more than we do.'

Ignoring Grypus's cryptic words, Thaliard thought for a moment. The priest was a practical man. His explanation was a convenient one, and it would calm the populace more than the suggestion that the Gods had been displeased with Antiochus's actions. Gazing into Grypus's eyes he could tell that the priest believed it as little as he did. 'Very well,' he said, 'Antiochus is now with the Gods. What of Syria?'

'There are . . . factions . . . who might wish to take the throne themselves.'

'Antiochus's only son died years ago,' Thaliard said quietly, 'and three of his daughters are already married to rulers of other lands who have no interest in Syria. Thea, of course, isn't married. The riddle has always prevented that.'

'There are others,' Grypus said. 'There are always others. His brother, Philopator, was named co-regent during his campaigns in India. Philopator is an ambitious man.'

'So am I.' Thaliard looked away. 'I appreciate your honesty. Don't worry: Rimmon will decide.'

When Grypus had followed the rest of the priests and servants out of the tent, Thaliard approached the first of the two shrouded tables that were now acting as biers, and carefully lifted the sodden material.

The sour smell of blood was nothing new to him. He was an assassin and a soldier. He had bathed in blood, waded through it, seen it stream from bodies like wine pouring from a ripped wineskin. Blood did not frighten him. But this . . .

In death as well as in life King Antiochus had demanded more than any other man. One death was not enough for him, and so he had to have three. His body had been rent as if by the cuts of a thousand knives, then his skin scorched and cracked by the mystical fire that had destroyed his chariot, and then he had been broken by the fall so that his limbs were twisted into grotesque shapes. His eyes, mercifully, were closed, but his lips were still curved into the grin Thaliard had seen on his face just before the fire had blossomed around him.

'My king,' Thaliard murmured softly, 'Rimmon grant me the wisdom and the power to rule as mercifully and justly as you have done.'

Bending forward, he gently kissed Antiochus upon his bloody lips, then pulled the material back to cover his face.

He hesitated before approaching the second table. The material covering Thea's body was greasy and soot-stained, rather than bloodied, and the stench of cooked meat that rose from it was almost overpowering. Whatever power had visited Antiochus, it had dwelled longer with his daughter.

That soft, peach-fuzzed skin. Those pale blue eyes. The knowing half-smile on those lips . . .

He reached out and pulled the sheet off before he could change his mind.

Thea's body looked more like a carcass cooked for a banquet than it did a woman. Her pale, smooth skin was now brown, blackened in places, and slick with fat; her body was shrunken and the tendons of her arms and neck stood out clearly. Fragments of burned silk were embossed against her body. Her face—

Great Rimmon: her face was just a charred shape, bereft of features and coated with half-melted clumps of hair. Thaliard felt his stomach heave and took a deep breath, quelling it. This was not the time. Later, perhaps, in the privacy of his own tent, but not now, not here, where so many invisible eyes would be watching him, weighing his bearing and his actions.

Before he had left for Tyre, he had told her how much he loved her. She had laughed, and said that he had to solve her father's riddle first like everyone else. He had taken his life into his hands then and kissed her, roughly, pinning her arms behind her back, but she hadn't resisted. As he had left her, Thaliard had smiled to himself, expecting some coaching on the answer to the riddle when it came time for him to answer it. He would need the coaching: failure to answer the riddle didn't just mean failure to win Thea's hand – it meant a painful and ignominious death.

But the death hadn't been his.

He started to cast the sheet back over her remains, and paused. Something was wrong. There was a smell: sweet and heavy on the air. A smell that reminded him of the Temple of Rimmon. He bent closer to the body and, ignoring as best he could the smell of cooked meat, he sniffed.

It was stronger now: the same smell as the oil that they burned in the temple on ceremonial days. Frankincense, the priests called it. Had the bodies been prepared for burial already? There hadn't been time, he was sure of it. Perhaps Thea had used something similar as a perfume, or in her bath; but no, the smell was far too strong. Before the fire it would have been overpowering, and Thea had always disdained excess.

Something was amiss. He could feel it tugging at his mind. Frankincense burned easily, he had seen that in the temple, and Thea's body was burned to a far greater extent than her father's. Heaven-sent fire was one thing – the Gods could not be questioned or brought to account for the things they did – but this was a different matter. The Gods did not need human help with their fiery thunderbolts.

He straightened up, keeping his face expressionless for the benefit of whatever observers were hidden behind the walls of the tent. Quickly, he crossed back to the bier upon which Antiochus lay and pulled the sheet away. It was the king, there could be no doubt about that, but when Thaliard looked at his face he did not see a grin of superiority any more: he saw a grimace of fear. A knowledge of impending death.

He bent closer and sniffed, but could smell no frankincense. That was even stranger: why should Thea, but not her father, be covered in the oil? That was the reason her body was more burned than his, but it didn't make any sense.

Oil. Oil that the priests used. Oil that caught fire easily and could not be put out. 'Powerful and capricious', Grypus had said, and Grypus was the High Priest. Had there been a power struggle of some sort between Temple and State that Thaliard had been unaware of? Had *Grypus*, rather than the Gods he served, caused Antiochus's death?

How could he? Frankincense burned, but not by itself. It had to be set alight by something, and there had been no sign that either Antiochus or Thea had done so in the chariot. Letting the sheet fall, Thaliard turned and strode out of the room.

Gods could not be questioned. But men could.

Eucaerus's tent was his first destination. The two guards came to attention with a clank of armour as Thaliard approached. By the time he entered the tent, his lieutenant was gazing expectantly at the opening. Eucaerus had been removing his breastplate, and something about his position, and the swaying material that separated the front of the tent from the sleeping quarters at the back, told Thaliard that he had not been alone.

'My Lord?' His voice still held a trace of a Greek accent. He had developed it during the years he had lived there and spied on the Greeks for Antiochus.

'Eucaerus, I need your assistance. When you rode to Antioch, did you see Thea?'

'I did, my Lord.'

'And how did she seem to you?'

He smiled, and his lined face seemed to soften slightly. 'She seemed even more beautiful than I remembered, my Lord.'

'Was she wearing perfume?'

Eucaerus frowned. 'My Lord?'

'Was Thea wearing perfume?'

'Not that I could detect, my Lord,' Eucaerus replied stiffly.

Thaliard scowled. 'And how was Antiochus?'

'As dynamic and forceful as ever.'

'Neither of them were worried? Concerned? Fearful?'

Eucaerus shook his head. 'No, my Lord.'

'And what of Antiochus's brother, Philopator? Did you see him?'

'I understand he is away from Antioch at the moment.'

The suspicion of Grypus that Thaliard had been nurturing suddenly shifted toward Philopator. How convenient that he was absent, just when his brother had been killed. Philopator's brief reign as regent during Antiochus's campaign in India had been lax, and his distraction had allowed the economy to slide. Antiochus had been forced to take strict measures to recover the country's prosperity upon his return. Was he now building an army? Was he preparing to take the throne of Syria for himself?

Philopator or Grypus. Either way, his course was clear. He had to get back to the court and protect the country.

'Eucaerus, prepare to strike camp. We must return to Antioch as soon as possible.'

'As my lord instructs.'

Outside the tent the sun was just touching the horizon, and the sky was layered with crimson and purple clouds. Thaliard tried to lose himself in the sight, to let himself melt into the landscape and still the ceaseless circling of his thoughts, but it was no use. All he saw when he looked at the sunset was the blossoming fire on the plain.

His thoughts ran wildly, like a chariot in the hands of an inexperienced driver. What had caused the ball of fire? More puzzling still: why had it been necessary for Thea's body to be more badly burned than her father's? The grimace on his face, whether pain or pleasure, could still be seen, but Thea's features were unrecognizable.

Unrecognizable. Thaliard held the word in his mind, turning it like a dark jewel, examining it for flaws. Unrecognisable. Almost as if by design . . .

His arrival at his own tent broke his chain of thoughts. There were four guards in front of it, rather than the usual two, and their breastplates were freshly polished. He seemed to be slipping into the role of king without conscious effort. Those around him treated him as king, he gave orders like a king, what was a coronation but a validation of something indefinable that had already occurred?

There was someone waiting for him in his tent: a bulky figure wearing a tunic of fine cloth and a purple cloak.

'Lord Philopator!' Thaliard kneeled. The soldiers outside – how could he have been so arrogant? They weren't for him at all, they were Philopator's personal bodyguards.

'Lord Thaliard – please, rise.' Philopator waved a vague hand, and Thaliard stood.

'You honour my humble camp with—'

'Let us save time by abandoning the formalities,' Philopator said. Thaliard glanced up. Philopator's fleshy lips were curled into a half-smile, but Thaliard sensed another expression lurking behind his face, one he could not quite make out. 'I had travelled to Antioch to see my brother when I heard he had ridden out to greet you. I followed, only to find . . .' His hand waved toward the plain. 'I could ask what your plans are, Thaliard, but I suspect I might not believe your answer. The penalties of having been involved in too many court intrigues: everything becomes intrigue after a while and all answers are assumed to be lies. Equally, you could ask me my plans, but you have no reason to believe my answer any more than I would believe yours.'

'Then where does that leave us?' Thaliard asked.

Philopator shrugged. 'For what it is worth, let me volunteer some information. You may choose to believe it or not.' He looked away, toward where the plain lay beyond the confines of the tent. 'I have no desire to rule Syria. I tried it once, when Antiochus was campaigning in India, and I found I had no talent for it. Being a regent sapped my time and energy for no reward that I could not obtain by other means. And besides – the risks are too great for my liking.' He turned back, and the hidden expression had broken through his half-smile: an earnest, almost begging look. 'Should you wish to become king, Thaliard, I will not stand in your way. More than that: I will pledge myself to you.'

Thaliard felt a hysterical laugh bubbling up within his breast, and suppressed it ruthlessly. The future of Syria could well rest upon what was said in this tent. 'Events are moving too fast for us, Lord Philopator. We should discuss this later when . . .' He meant to say, 'When the blood on King Antiochus's body isn't still wet,' but he just trailed off instead.

Philopator nodded. 'My offer stands for as long as it takes you to make a decision.' The half-smile returned to his lips. 'If I return to Antioch, would you trust me not to take the throne before you arrive?'

Thaliard shrugged slightly, as Philopator had done earlier. 'I haven't said that it matters to me if you do,' he replied.

'Of course not,' Philopator said. He turned to leave, but Thaliard reached a hand out to stop him.

'You said that the risks of being king were too great for your liking. What did you mean?'

'You're an assassin, Lord Thaliard. You should know.'

Thaliard turned to look Philopator in the eye, and what he saw was his real expression – not the half-smile, not the earnest begging, but fear. Raw fear.

'I didn't kill King Antiochus,' Thaliard whispered.

'Of course not,' Philopator said again.

'How could I? That fire – how could any human agency cause it?'

'That presents no great mystery.' Philopator shrugged. 'Greek Fire, they call it. The Greeks aren't telling what it is made of, but it burns like the very flames of hell and it cannot be put out, not by water anyway. My brother sent many spies to Greece to try and discover what it was, but they came back with very little information – or so he said. It's a substance like wax that they keep beneath oil, in vases. When they take it out into air it ignites immediately. Or so I have heard.' He smiled his little half-smile. 'I have never been to Greece.'

Like sunrise across a previously unseen landscape, Thaliard suddenly became aware of something so obvious that he could not see how he could have missed it. 'No,' he murmured, 'but I know someone who has.' He rushed out of his tent, past the doubled set of guards, leaving Philopator standing open-mouthed. By the time he was half-way to Eucaerus's tent he knew what he would find. Eucaerus's guards tried to stop him, but he pushed past them and threw the flap open. He wasn't surprised to see that his lieutenant was gone. Turning, he ran back toward his own tent. Philopator was just leaving, and Thaliard almost knocked him off his feet.

'Lord Thaliard, what—?'

'No time.' Thaliard glanced around. Rough woven rugs covered the floor, along with more comfortable silk cushions. It would take him too long to search them all. There had to be another way.

He kicked a cushion out of the way in frustration. He didn't know how long he had, but if he was right then it could only be a matter of minutes. The cushion sailed through the air and hit a pile in one corner of the tent. They scattered, revealing a stretch of woven flooring that seemed darker than the rest.

Thaliard strode over to the corner and bent down to touch the flooring. His fingers came away sticky. Oil. He knocked the rest of the cushions away to reveal a rough clay vase. It sat in a puddle of oil that was leaking from a small hole in its base. Traces of tallow around the hole indicated to Thaliard that neither the hole nor the leakage were an accident.

The oil only just covered a large, irregular block of wax inside the vase. Another few minutes and the wax would have been exposed to the air. Quickly he scraped the remnants of the tallow back across the hole in its base, sealing the oil in.

Straightening, Thaliard look at Philopator's sweating face. He still wasn't sure. The frankincense pointed to Grypus and the Greek Fire to the vanished Eucaerus, but the vase could have been hidden in his tent by Philopator. He had to narrow it down! 'My Lord,' he snapped, 'your life is in danger. It is imperative that you stay in this camp tonight and let my forces guard you.'

Philopator shrugged. 'Very well, Thaliard, if you think it wise.'

'This tent is the finest one I have. I insist you rest here for the night. I will sleep elsewhere.'

'Whatever you suggest.'

Thaliard took a few steps away from the vase and toward the flap of the tent. Philopator's gaze followed him – bewildered, but not panicked – and didn't flicker once toward the vase in its puddle of oil.

That settled it. Philopator knew nothing of the vase or its contents. A crimson wave of fury swept over Thaliard. Picking up the vase he moved toward the tent flap, being careful not to slosh the oil inside the vase too much. He didn't know how much – or how little – exposure to air the substance within required before it ignited.

'Thaliard, I don't understand!' Philopator's plaintive voice cried from inside the tent.

Knowing he had to get rid of the vase as soon as possible, he rushed downhill toward the edges of the camp. The sky was the colour of an old bruise, and the horses were whinnying, as if they smelled something on the wind. A stone turned under his foot and he almost dropped the vase. Oil spilled over his hand, sticky and warm.

Too warm.

He glanced over his shoulder. The camp was clustered behind him, the horses directly ahead, pastured on the gradual slope at the base of the hill. If he threw the vase now the camp would be safe but it might fall among the horses, and they were worth more to Syria than his soldiers were. He took a deep breath, then jogged on. Once he got past the horses he could throw it down on to the plain with impunity.

If he got beyond the horses.

Voices made him hesitate. Two figures were buckling horses to a chariot on the pasture to one side of the path. Distracted, his foot turned on a stone and again the vase almost fell from his grasp. The clatter of pebbles attracted the attention of the figures, and the largest of them turned. In the meagre light of the fast-fading sky, Thaliard could just make out the features of his most trusted lieutenant.

'Eucaerus!' he shouted, 'Stop where you are!'

'Don't try to interfere!' Eucaerus shouted. 'We're not trying to take the throne. We just want a life for ourselves. A peaceful life.'

Thaliard looked toward the second, smaller, figure. He couldn't see her face, but he knew who she was. Who she had to be. 'Why, Thea?' he asked simply.

She turned, and her face was just a shadow. 'Because you could never have let me go, Thaliard,' she said. 'Because you had to believe I was dead before you would stop looking for me, and Eucaerus and I could find happiness together.'

'Thea, I—'

'You what?' she interrupted. 'You loved me? Like my father loved me, Thaliard?'

The confrontation seemed to have taken a sudden turn into unfamiliar territory. 'He was your *father*,' Thaliard said, frowning, 'of course he loved you. That's no reason to kill him.'

'You don't understand,' she said quietly. 'Nobody understands. It was the answer to the riddle. It was in plain sight, right in front of the world, and my father enjoyed the fact that only he and I ever knew. Another secret we shared.'

Thaliard felt a sudden, sick realisation weighing heavily in his heart. Remembering Grypus's words, he wondered how many other people had guessed. 'What about Pericles?' he asked.

'Pericles was the only other person ever to solve the riddle, so my father sent you to kill him.'

'I failed.'

'It doesn't matter.' Thaliard could see the glint of tears on her cheeks. 'I had grown accustomed to the . . . to the things my father and I did . . . the things he forced me to do . . . but seeing the contempt on Pericles's face when he understood the answer to the riddle made me suddenly wake up and realise what I had become . . . what had been done to me. Pericles has gone, and it doesn't matter whether he is alive or dead – I've had my revenge on Antiochus now. I made him ride in that chariot, strapped to the reins with the means of his death in a vase between his feet. Eucaerus helped me – he and the few members of my father's guard who were more loyal to Eucaerus than to him.

And I almost had my revenge on you, for wanting to do the same to me as my father did. Make me an object. Own me.'

'An object? Like the slave – I presume it was a slave – you drenched in frankincense and put on the chariot in your place? Did she deserve what happened to her, just because she had the same build and the same colour hair as you?'

Thea shrugged. 'That's what slaves are for: to serve without question, and to give their lives if we need them.'

Thaliard turned back to his lieutenant. His friend. 'Don't you see what she's doing, Eucaerus? She's just using you because of your popularity with the guards, and your knowledge of Greek Fire. What was it all for? She's replaced her father with you: a man the same age as he was. How long will *you* last after you've ceased being useful?'

Eucaerus snarled and took a step toward Thaliard. Thaliard braced himself, but Thea laid a hand on Eucaerus's arm. 'Leave him,' she said, 'he's not important.'

That, more than anything, was what cut Thaliard. Not the betrayal by the lieutenant he trusted, not the betrayal by the woman he had loved, but the casual dismissal.

Eucaerus nodded, and vaulted into the back of the chariot. Extending a hand to Thea, he pulled her up. He glanced back at Thaliard and said: 'Don't try to follow us. We have more of the Greek Fire, and we're not afraid to throw it out of the chariot behind us if we're chased.'

He flicked the reins. The horses trotted off, and he flicked the reins again to speed them up. Thea slid an arm around his waist to steady herself. Turning, she waved sardonically at Thaliard.

As if he were in a trance, Thaliard lifted his hand to wave back.

And realised he was still holding the oil-filled vase.

The chariot speeded up as the gradual slope of the hill gave way to the level plain, and Eucaerus forced the horses to a gallop. Thaliard swung the vase behind his back. The hot oil spilled across his fingers, burning them. The weight of the vase dragged his arm forward, and he added his strength to it, boosting it higher. As it reached the top of its arc he could see the silvery meniscus of the oil, with the peak of the wax beneath emerging from it like an island from the sea. He let go, and watched with a curious lack of feeling as the vase flew up, tumbling and spilling its oil, before falling toward the retreating chariot and hitting it just behind where Thea was standing.

The oil splashed silver against the night, and for a moment Thaliard could see the dark mass of the wax splatter against her legs.

The expanding ball of flame carried the fragile chariot up with it, tumbling it in mid-air and flinging its passengers off like a bucking stallion. A wheel came loose and spun lazily away from the twisted mass of metal while burning leather thongs and fragments of wood rained down upon the plain, trailing ribbons of smoke behind them.

Thaliard took a deep breath as the remains of the chariot, the horses, Eucaerus and Thea rained down around him. 'As your king,' he murmured, 'I condemn you as traitors, regicides and murderers, and I sentence you to death.'

He turned and began the long walk back to his tent, already planning an explanation for the priests to pass on to the people.

To *his* people.

STOLEN AFFECTIONS

Lawrence Schimel and Jeffrey Marks

The Comedy of Errors, *which was first performed in 1593, is set at about the same time as* Pericles. *It starts out as a tragedy, though the improbability of the events soon twists it into a comedy. To reveal too much about the play, however, will also reveal too much about the following story. Suffice it to say that it is set in Ephesus, where Egeon of Syracuse has come in search of his sons and has been arrested because of the rivalry between Ephesus and Syracuse. The two sons have long been separated and do not know each other. One of them, Antipholus of Ephesus, is married but finds himself debarred from his house. Now let the story take over.*

'You must help me, I am going mad with worry. Why is he doing this to me?' Adriana paced exasperatedly across the room, throwing himself down beside her sister on the plush divan.

'Tell me, truthfully, have I grown so old and ugly like a withered flower, that he now casts his affections on some younger beauty?'

'You are wrong,' Luciana insisted. 'I am sure that he favours no other than yourself.'

'Then why does he stay from me so long?' Unable to contain herself, Adriana leapt up and crossed to the window again, to look for Antipholus. 'Where is he so late into the night? Why does he make promises to see me, his lawful wife, and then does not show? Even for his own supper, he does not return! No, I am sure of it, he has taken a mistress. And I would pay any sum of money to find out who she is!'

Adriana rushed back to her sister's side and sat beside her again. 'Help me in this,' she begged. She took a gold ring from her finger, and presented it to her sister. 'Here, I will give you this if you will help me discover the truth of this matter. Please, help me.'

Luciana folded her sister's fingers to cover the proffered valuable. 'I will not take your gold, sister, though I will help you, if only to see you calm again. Your love, and to prove Antipholus's true and steadfast love for you, will be payment enough.'

Adriana threw her arms about her sister, weeping with a mixture of joy and frustration. 'Thank you,' she whispered into Luciana's hair. 'I will not rest until I know the truth.'

Luciana walked among the stalls, hardly noticing what she looked at. She was deep in thought, and often thought best wandering here in the market, where her mind would suddenly find inspiration amid the jumble of colours and objects and sounds, by noticing some random item which was the key. She never knew in advance what it would be, but invariably, by letting the problem mull itself over in her mind as she browsed, an end of the solution would unravel itself from the mess and she'd be able to pluck it free, then trace it back and undo the tangle.

She would look for evidence that Antipholus was having some affair with another woman, and once she had proven that there was absolutely none to be found, she could tell her sister that her fears were simply the insecurities that come from spending too much time indoors alone. Adriana should take up some hobby, to while away the hours when her husband is busy with his work and other friends.

Wandering through the market, Luciana listened to see if she might overhear any idle gossip or speculation about Antipholus, if anyone else thought he was acting out of character. Luciana was sure that Antipholus was above suspicion in this; he was the model of a loyal husband, good to his wife, and good on his word. She could not imagine that he would betray so solemn a vow as marriage, why the—

Her thoughts were interrupted suddenly by the presence of Antipholus himself, striding toward her with his manservant Dromio.

Luciana felt quite unprepared, for though she was at that very moment thinking about him and looking for clues and evidence about his life, she had not meant to confront him directly so soon, merely to follow in the wake of his passing like the white crests behind a ship.

As Antipholus approached, his face broke into a broad grin. He was quite a handsome man, Luciana thought, noticing his dimples and the barest graze of razor's edge. Oh to be that blade! It would be no wonder if other women fancied him. Why, were he not already married to her own sister, Luciana might be tempted herself!

Antipholus stopped before her, and gave a deep courtly bow. Luciana noticed that Dromio looked distraught and perhaps a bit exasperated as he stood behind his master.

Straightening, Antipholus declared, 'Fair maiden, how is it that I've not seen you before?'

Luciana was rendered speechless for a moment by this ridiculous question. Was he mocking her? Or had he gone completely mad? 'But you have, Antipholus,' she at last answered. 'Many times.'

He looked stunned, as if he'd bitten into a bread and found it contained an unexpected filling. 'How is it you know my name? What is this witchcraft?'

Dromio flung his arms in a grand gesture as he stepped forward. 'This is your sister-in-law, master, the lovely Luciana.'

Antipholus looked blankly at his manservant. 'That would mean I was married, and yet my eyes are set for only one woman.' He stared at Luciana, raptly. 'But you are right, Dromio: she is lovely.'

This curious display troubled Luciana greatly. If Antipholus was willing to play court to her – his sister-in-law – in this brazen fashion, to so totally cast aside his beloved wife Adriana, who even now waited for his return, why should it be implausible for him to also be pursuing – or have captured – some other woman as well? Luciana feared that perhaps her sister had been right in her surmises about her husband's wandering affections.

'Good sir,' Luciana declared, 'where are your manners? Don't you know who you are?'

He took her hand in his and caressed her fingers as he spoke. She noticed the remains of a cut on his finger. It had not been there that morning. 'I am Antipholus, my lady, and it is my great pleasure to meet you.'

Luciana caught a glimpse of gold through a hole in Antipholus's pocket. It was odd, Luciana thought, that Adriana had not yet attended to that; she usually took greater pains with his attire, but perhaps the strain of her believing him unfaithful distracted her.

Luciana put her hand on her brother-in-law's arm and smiled. But her heart sunk as she realised the glint of gold she'd seen was a chain of links. Adriana had not mentioned his commissioning this for her; what other woman could it be for? Though smiling still, so as not to betray her knowledge or actions, Luciana's heart sunk further with this proof of his inconstancy. And determined to obtain the proof, with a deft motion, the chain was hers and tucked safely within her pocket, while Antipholus, oblivious, gazed at her.

Dromio tugged at his master's sleeve, pulling him away. 'We are late to our appointment, Sirrah, we must away.'

Antipholus let himself be led away, but not without looking over his shoulder to where Luciana stood, frozen in body as her mind raced with thought and speculation. He smiled broadly at her, and blew a kiss to her, before disappearing with Dromio behind the bulk of a nearby building.

Luciana found herself unable to move, shocked by the proof of her senses. She had indeed just heard, with her own ears, such words as were tantamount to an outright confession of adultery. She had as well this proof of gold – and moreover recalled that, as Antipholus had held her hand, she had felt no wedding band pressed against her skin. Which could mean only one thing: he had removed it so as to court and seduce some other woman, who was ignorant of the fact that he had already mortgaged his affections and affairs to Luciana's sister.

With a sinking heart, Luciana went to inform her sister of this sad news.

'Pray sister,' Adriana begged, 'what have you found?'

Antipholus planned mischief, of that Luciana was certain, but of what sort she did not yet know. 'It is too soon to tell,' she began.

Adriana's eyes brimmed with tears. 'I can tell from your eyes that you know more. What is so wrong that you think it better to lie to me?'

Luciana embraced her sister. 'You know I cannot lie to you.' She had never been able to keep a secret from her sister. 'I mean you no harm, I assure you. I just cannot make sense of what I've learned today, there's something more I've overlooked that will solve the conflicting facts. I do not know how Antipholus could do the things he's done.'

'Tell me what you know!' Adriana wailed. Sniffles came from both sisters now. 'Who is she? Who is this demon in a dress?'

'I know not, but your husband was too charming to me today in the market. He professed love to me as Dromio looked on.'

Adriana patted her sister's hand. 'Antipholus has always thought of you as I do. Certainly he has not the ill-breeding to have eyes for my own blood. But tell me who it is that has stolen his affections?'

'I know not, but I am sad to say I think you may be right. I pleaded for you when he paid his court. But that love I begged for you, he begged of me.' She reached into her pocket and pulled forth the necklace.'He bore this.'

Adriana wailed. Plainly it was for some other woman, for she knew nothing of it. 'The miscreant! That vile deformed decrepit man! Oh, how I hate him! I wish never to see his ugly, vicious self again!'

'Yes,' Luciana said, 'who would miss the company of one such as that? We are well rid of him.'

Adriana wailed again. 'Oh, but sister, I still love him, even though he be unfaithful. What shall I do?'

Luciana took her sister's hand. 'Fear not, dear sister, I shall not rest yet. I will learn her name and we shall both hate her with fervour.'

Luciana went out again into the marketplace. But this time it seemed a cacophony of loud sounds and visual distractions, and held no insights to her troubles.

She watched a fool on a corner juggling three identical balls at once. And as she watched, a careless passerby, heedless of who was in his path, jostled the fool, sending his juggling awry. That moment – the look on the fool's face when he knew that his three balls would fall, no matter what he did to try to keep them in the air – was how Luciana felt with her current conundrum. No matter how she tried to keep the answers from indicting Antipholus, every new evidence pointed to the same conclusion. But still she felt that it could not be so, that there was some vital information she yet lacked. She could not fathom what it might be, however, and perhaps Adriana was right, and the only piece missing from her puzzle was the name of the woman who had stolen Antipholus's affections.

The fool retrieved his three small orbs and resumed his caper. Luciana dropped a coin in his cup, wishing she could find balance as easily. She needed calm, some place quiet where she could think and sort out the troubling information she'd collected thus far.

She watched the arc of one of the juggler's balls as it flew into the air. But her gaze did not pause at the zenith of the ball's journey; her vision carried up and up, until she saw the spire of the abbey tower rising above the marketplace, and suddenly Luciana knew where to go. She made her way to the abbey steps and rapped on the heavy door, and soon the doors were opened – by the Abbess herself!

'Beg pardon, Lady,' Luciana said, bowing before the Lady Abbess. 'I had not meant to disturb you. I had thought one of your servants would attend the door.'

'There is no task too humble for this body to perform. What troubles you, daughter?'

'Some questions plague my mind, Lady, and I had hoped to sit within the quiet of your courtyard, that I might sort them out within the peace and stillness of your sanctuary.'

'Be welcomed then,' the Abbess said, and moved aside to let Luciana enter.

As the heavy door closed, Luciana felt that it shut out all the chaos of the outside world. And even the world within herself seemed stilled, quieted. The problem of Antipholus still waited to be solved, but it no longer preyed upon her soul as heavily as it had a moment ago, outside the Abbey's walls, in her frantic search for information.

The two women moved through the silent halls, making hardly any sound but the rustling of their passing, the soft tread of their feet and the shifting of their clothes, fabric against fabric. They passed out into the courtyard, and sat together on a bench overlooking an intricate patchwork of herbs and flowers.

Luciana felt embarrassed that she had so disturbed the Abbess from contemplation by her selfish interruption, seeking peace of mind, but she was grateful for the older woman's presence. They sat without speaking for a long time, and Luciana let the stillness settle within her. At last she asked a question.

'Lady, what is the heart capable of?'

The question seemed to hang on the air, and Luciana considered what it was she had asked. It had not been the question she thought she was looking for, but she realised it was the fundamental question that had plagued her. Could Antipholus have betrayed Adriana's love?

And what of Luciana's own heart, the emotions she had felt when Antipholus had courted her so openly in the market – and her head had felt dizzy with a pleasant sensation that alarmed her. She dearly loved her sister, Adriana, so how could she commit this treachery, to feel these emotions for Antipholus, even if they were never acted upon? Because to feel them was the first step to acting on them, and Luciana doubted the power of the human heart, if she herself could feel such turncoat emotions.

'The human heart,' the Lady Abbess said, with a faraway look on her face, 'is our greatest pleasure and our deepest pain. It is a tender creature, delicate as the petals of a flower. Yet it is also as barricaded as a fortress, sealed against attack. The heart is not an easy thing to understand, nor is it easy to be true to one's heart.'

Luciana thought of this courtyard, the heart of the fortress that was the abbey, quiet and still, a sanctuary from the world. And within this small square heart, was the unfurling petals of the rose, the heart of the garden they sat in.

'Sometimes,' the Lady Abbess continued, 'the heart can do braver things than we ever believed we were capable of. Sometimes we will make sacrifices for the heart that should be impossible to withstand.

'Once, in my life before this abbey, I had been mother to two sons, the most beautiful boys in the world. But that is how the mother's heart always sees her children; she would do anything for them. No sacrifice is too great. None.'

Luciana entered the marketplace again, her soul quieted by the Lady Abbess's advice, by the stillness of that courtyard, which she now carried in her own troubled heart. With new resolve, she set about the task at hand of finding where Antipholus's true affections lay – with his lawful wife or, as evidence seemed to indicate, with some new woman who had ensnared him in this betrayal.

A hoary merchant tried to capture her fancy with a new scarf. As if a swatch of cloth could solve this riddle!

Still, the man distracted Luciana from moving on so fast. The bright crimson colour of his cloth reminded her of the painted lips of the women of ill repute whom men could frequent – for a price. Could it be that Antipholus sought comfort there?

Distasteful as thoughts of those women were to her, Luciana could not help but hope that it was indeed so. For surely Antipholus could not be paying court to some young noblewoman, which would create, were it discovered, incredible scandal and much shame for her sister Adriana. If he had simply lost his heart to some tart he visited to slake his thirst, why it was expected of men to have lusts that one woman alone could not satisfy . . .

Luciana worried, after his earlier brazen behaviour with her, that he had somehow taken leave of his senses. He might very well be causing scandal for Adriana with some unsuspecting noblewoman – though how a noblewoman of Ephesus could not have heard of him and his marriage, she did not know. Perhaps some young lady visiting Ephesus from elsewhere . . .

She hardly knew what she would tell her sister. With a heavy heart, she resolved to visit first a certain quarter, to discover if Antipholus had recently visited there. Luciana grimaced with the irony of it all, when she found herself hoping that she'd learn that he had, a far preferable truth to any of her other speculations.

Luciana chose a scarf from the merchant, but something far more drab and sedate in colour.

'The other colour suits you better,' the merchant said as he accepted her coin. 'A fiery red, bright as blood. And there'll be blood tonight, mark my words.'

'What is to happen tonight?'

'A hanging. A merchant from Syracuse they discovered here, snooping around.'

'What was his crime?' Luciana asked.

'I just told you! From Syracuse he was, come to sell his wares illegally no doubt. Or else to judge the market here.'

'Did he not know the law?'

'Bah! He claims he was seeking his sons, torn from his breast when they were but infants. A pitiful story, to be sure – conconcted to save his neck! But pity will not cancel duty. The law is the law; my cousin was one of those wrongly hung in Syracuse that started this. Our Duke is an honourable man; he'll see to it that justice is carried out.'

'Yes,' Luciana agreed, 'the Duke is an honourable man.'

She took her new scarf, wound the cloth about her face and torso to disguise herself. She hurried through the streets, almost as quickly as Antipholus and Dromio had disappeared earlier. Where had they been off to with such haste, she wondered?

The streets seemed crowded as she rushed, and glimpsed from the corner of her eye – she dared not stare at anyone directly, lest they recognise her – everyone looked identical, as if the world were filled with only one man multiplied many many times, like reflections in the facets of a beaten copper dish.

Luciana wondered what she would ask when she arrived at her destination. She could not simply—

She stopped short, and from behind someone pushed against her, not having expected her to pause so suddenly. She meant to murmur an apology, but could not find her voice. She felt again like that fool she'd seen earlier, in that moment when he knew all his balls would fall.

There before her, yet again, was Antipholus!

Luciana wondered, briefly, if he were the one following her, and nervously glanced about, looking for a safe haven where she could hurry to and hide. She wanted to be back in the safe heart of the Abbey, that still, quiet courtyard.

Antipholus had not seen her, she realised, or if he had, did not recognise her beneath the dark green scarf. He looked like a man possessed, and she was startled to note how the shadow of a beard had grown in the brief hour since she had seen him last. He entered the Porpentine and disappeared from her sight. Was this the appointment he was in such a hurry to keep? She hurried toward the bar, wishing she could follow him inside to spy upon his actions. But she dared not risk her own reputation, for her disguise would not hold up to such close scrutiny as she could expect within, as a solitary woman.

Still, she moved close by to the windows and strained to hear his dialogue from within.

'Where is the gold I gave in charge to thee?' Antipholus's voice boomed like the horn announcing an incoming ship.

Luciana slipped her hand inside her pocket to finger the gold links.

'To me, sir?' came Dromio's meek reply. 'Why you gave no gold to me.'

Luciana flinched, expecting the blows she knew would come. But she heard no more over the din of a cart passing on the street behind her. She looked about, nervous that she looked conspicuous loitering in this fashion beneath their window.

'I shall go to visit a wench of excellent discourse,' came Antipholus's unmistakable tones.

Luciana paled, and hurried away lest she be noticed when he emerged.

The journey back to a more respectable part of town led Luciana near the docks. She walked briskly, wishing to leave behind the tang of brine and acrid stench of rotting fish, but did not hurry so much that she drew attention to herself by her speed.

Much to her surprise, she saw Dromio crossing the path ahead of her, heading toward the water. How could he have already got here so quickly, she wondered, when she had had a head start on the journey? How queer that both Dromio and Antipholus should be so many places all at once, as if the city streets for them could be traversed much more rapidly than for other folk, as if they knew some secret maze of shortcuts from place to place to always wind up ahead of her.

Feeling that her sleuthing up until now had not resulted in much concrete evidence, Luciana followed Dromio, hoping to find some concrete proof to tell to Adriana. As she trailed behind him, she noticed he bore bruises she had not seen before, and guessed that Antipholus had indeed beaten him for losing or spending the gold, in that moment when she had not been able to hear their conversation.

Dromio made directly for the docks and stepped on board a ship. Luciana stayed by the buildings and waited for him to alight again, her mind racing through imagined possibilities. She wished that she might have followed him more directly, but the burden of her sex prevented her from entering certain places, and besides, a ship was a dead end where she would be trapped and too easily discovered.

At last, Dromio came down from the gangplank and headed back toward the centre of town. Just as he passed before her, Luciana stepped forward. 'Dromio!' she cried, as if this were a chance occurrence. 'What a surprise to find you here!'

'Fair lady, how do you know me?' He met her gaze directly, with no look of recognition.

How could this be that two grown men had so taken leave of

their senses? Perhaps Antipholus had not forsaken Adriana, and was simply mad. Was this a contagion that infected them both? Were they possessed by spirits, and their true selves displaced?

Calmly, Luciana replied, 'I've known you lo these many years, faithful servant.'

'Oh, that you were my mistress! That I would not be beaten so.' He showed the bruises Luciana had noted earlier.

'What do you here at the docks, Dromio? In search of fresh fish for dinner?'

'We'll have plenty of fish, my lady, plucked right from the sea. We sail tonight. Ephesus is a strange place and we wish to stay here no longer. Perhaps Syracuse will hold better luck for us.'

He sounded, Luciana thought, as if he had not spent his entire life here in Ephesus, and she wondered again how a man could so totally lose his identity to this sickness or dread spirit.

'Good day, lady, I must be to my master, lest he beat me for the delay.'

Dromio passed her and moved down the street, leaving her standing there, rooted to the spot by the knowledge she had learned: Antipholus planned to leave Ephesus tonight.

She must find her sister at once!

Luciana was interrupted by a voice that called her name. Antipholus again, who hurried to match his stride to hers. Once more she felt that eerie sensation that he must be following her actions, to cross her path so often.

'Fair maiden,' Antipholus said, 'we meet again.'

Luciana regarded him coolly, noting how he had shaved his stubble again before his remarkably quick meeting with the 'wench of excellent discourse.' Could he have slaked his lust in such a short time and still managed to find her here so quickly?

Or had he meant Luciana when he made that remark?

'Indeed we do,' she replied, with no visible emotion, 'as kin should.' She would remind him of his proper place as her brother-in-law.

'As kin, my lady? Oh, that that was so.'

'It is, I assure, you, Antipholus.'

'If we are to be so bold, might I call you fair Luciana?'

Luciana stepped back, fearful that this malady that afflicted these men might be contagious even to her. Though so far it seemed only to addle their weaker male wits. His eyes seemed clear, and his brow was not red with fever, but clearly he was not a man of healthy mind, no matter how hale and attractive his body looked.

'You may as you always have,' Luciana said, in hopes that he would suddenly remember and act in a more proper fashion.

Instead, he took a step toward her. 'It does seem as if I've known you for quite some time, dear lady, when I am only newly arrived in Ephesus. How is that?'

Luciana took a step away from him. 'Perhaps it is because we have indeed known each other that long.'

'But not quite so well. It is thyself; mine own self's better part. Mine eye's clear eye, my dear heart's dearer heart.' His hand brushed hers, but she recoiled from him and his statements, knowing it was wrong for him to pursue her, even if he were gripped by fever or spirits as he so obviously must be to act in this fashion.

Antipholus continued, seemingly unnoticing of her reticence he was so blinded by his own love. 'Thee will I love and with thee lead my life. Thou hast no husband yet, nor I no wife.'

Luciana blanched at his bold disavowal of his marriage to her sister. 'Good sir, you overstep yourself,' she said, and turning her back on him, left him where he stood.

'O, woe is me!' Adriana wailed, at the news Luciana relayed of Antipholus's intention to fly from Ephesus that very night. Adriana paced again, crossed back to her perch at the window, hoping to espy her wayward husband. She turned back to Luciana. 'I pray you, sister, find out who has stolen him from my arms? With what vixen does he now elope for Syracuse?'

'I will not rest, my sister,' Luciana said.

A commotion outside drew their attention. 'Justice, Duke!' a voice cried.

'Look,' Adriana cried, 'there is the villain now!'

Luciana crossed to stand behind her sister. Antipholus was being held by an officer. Beside them stood a gold merchant, and before them all the Duke himself, with his entourage.

'What has he done now?' Adriana wailed, and rushed off to save her beloved husband, forgetting his betrayal for the moment because he was in need of her aid.

Luciana followed her sister out into the street more calmly, thinking over the day's confusing events in her head. Antipholus looked haggard and distressed; the shadow of his beard had thickened into scruff. How curious this sudden speed by which his beard grew and disappeared; perhaps it was some side effect of the sickness that now gripped him?

Or could it be, Luciana wondered, that there were two of them, one clean shaven, the other as he stood before them now.

Luciana suddenly began to pay attention to what they were saying.

'I never received a chain from you,' Antipholus stated.

A different merchant spoke forth. 'But you told me outright in the market that you had indeed received a chain from Angelo.'

Luciana stepped forward. 'Is this the chain of which you speak?'

All attention focused on her, somewhat surprised by her speaking forth into this matter of men.

'That's it!' Angelo cried. 'My handiwork is evident,' he said, smugly.

'I never saw it in my life,' Antipholus said.

'A lie! I gave it you this afternoon!'

'No,' Luciana corrected. 'You gave it to Antipholus, but not to this man.'

'What foolery is this?' the Duke said.

'I beg your patience, my Duke,' Luciana explained, 'but it seems that there be not one but two Antipholuses in Ephesus: this one before us, and another, his exact likeness, save for a few small differences. I had this chain from him this afternoon. Angelo gave the other Antipholus the chain, yet wrongly expects payment from this one.'

'But then, where is this other Antipholus you claim?' the Duke asked. 'Who if he exists, owes this merchant for what he had received of him.'

At that moment, a second Dromio entered the street. All jaws dropped when they saw Dromio standing in two places at once.

'Now all our eyes deceive us!' one of the merchants cried.

'What ho, impostor!' Dromio cried at his double. 'What do you there? Give me back myself!' Each Dromio flew at the other to wrestle and fight. The officer abandoned Antipholus to draw them apart.

'Mayhap Luciana's tale is sooth,' Antipholus said slowly, his mind trying to comprehend what was going on, 'and somewhere in Ephesus

I have a twin like this, who has stolen my name and who knows what else!'

'I do not think he means you harm,' Luciana said. 'I have spoken with you both this afternoon and so I know the most about his character.'

'And what part have you in this curious affair?' the Duke asked.

'I?' Luciana said. 'I have none, except to prove the love—'

Her answer was interrupted.

'O most radiant one!' a voice cried from behind their crowd, and all turned to look at a second Antipholus who, as if summoned by his name, called to Luciana. The crowd drew back and the two Antipholuses confronted one another.

The officer stepped between them, to prevent another fight. But both Antipholuses simply marvelled at one another. ''Tis like the mirror come to life.'

'You see,' Luciana continued, hoping to explain things before more complications esued, 'I merely set out this afternoon to prove that Antipholus had been steadfast and true, as is his nature, to my dear sister Adriana.'

'Who dared doubt me?' Antipholus interjected, but was ignored, except for Adriana stepping to his side and putting an arm about him.

'Myself began to doubt as well when this Antipholus paid me court, but knew that the other Antipholus would never be untrue. I thought some demon had possessed his soul and corrupted him, thinking he'd removed his wedding ring as if to pretend he had no wife and thereby claim some other woman's affections.

'But as I wandered through the town all day, looking to prove that there was no mistress, I realised that there were these strange irreconcilable differences between the times I saw Antipholus, one after the other and back again. First it was their behaviour: one man recognised me, the other did not. This Antipholus has a scar on his hands, which the other does not. This one is clean shaven, while the other is not. And this Antipholus wears his wedding ring, which if he removes it –' Luciana took Antipholus's hand from Adriana's waist and demonstrated – 'will have a pale band beneath to prove his many faithful years of love.'

Luciana turned again. 'This Antipholus, who bore no ring, neither had no mark – which I noticed when he paid me court.'

'Sweet lady,' Antipholus said, 'does this mean your earlier reservations were for your sister's sake?'

'Indeed, sir, as any woman would do for her sister,' Luciana replied, slipping her hands into his. 'But now I can profess my true feelings.' They smiled at one another, and onlookers felt as if they watched two mated swans, in love for life.

'But how came these twins to be?' The Duke interrupted.

'It is a long, sad story,' Luciana said, letting her hand fall from Antipholus's to face the Duke, 'but one which will, I hope, have a happy ending. But there is one who can tell it better than I. Where is the merchant of Syracuse sentenced this morning to hang by the moon's first light?'

'What involvement has he in this?' the Duke inquired. 'We were on our way to see that his execution be carried out, as the law requires, though we spared him all the day through to help his fortune.'

'Merchant from Syracuse?' one of the Antipholus twins asked, but was ignored.

'He has a tale to tell,' Luciana continued, 'that could melt the stoniest heart.'

'I have heard it once, already,' the Duke said, 'and it is right pitiful. Fetch the man hither,' he instructed one of his officers.

'Dromio,' Luciano said to one of the pair of Dromios, not certain if it was the Dromio who knew her well or the one who did not, 'go thou to fetch the Lady Abbess here, as well; there is some news I must tell her that concerns her. Tell her it is of great import, she must come herself.'

'Tell her the Duke commands her presence as well,' the Duke himself added. Before correcting himself. 'No, tell her the Duke requests her presence, and urges her to come. For if this maid says it is of some import, after the proofs she has laid before us these minutes past, I am wont to believe she speaks sooth!'

Dromio left, and the remaining crowds marvelled at the twin Antipholuses yet again.

Adriana let go of her Antipholus and hugged her sister. 'I am so glad you were right,' she whispered in Luciana's hair.

The officer returned with the prisoner.

'Father, what has happened?' one Antipholus cried, and rushed to hug the older man.

'Oh, my son,' Egeon wept, 'how I have searched for you, fearing I had lost you as I once lost your brother.'

Their reunion was a poignant sight. Tears threatened even the Duke. 'Sir, it is as you said before, and glad I am you've found your son in time. Found, in fact, more than you'd dared hope, for you've found them both.'

The other Antipholus approached with awe. 'O blessed day, that I discover, a father in addition to a brother!'

'Will thou,' the Duke asked of the twins Antipholus, not sure which of the pair was the one he knew, the husband of Adriana and good citizen of Ephesus, 'pay the coins required by law to mortgage the life of this merchant of Syracuse, who otherwise must die with the failing light.'

'Gladly will I pay that sum, and twice again,' Antipholus said, his voice growing louder with emotion. 'As many times as need be, I'll pay to ransom my long-lost father's freedom.' He, too, embraced the older man to his bosom.

Dromio returned with the Lady Abbess behind him. Luciana took a deep breath to begin explaining, once again, all the complications that had taken place and been revealed, but there was no need.

Egeon looked up and whispered, 'Aemelia?'

The Lady Abbess began to weep, to see her husband and her two sons, whom she'd believed lost, alive and before her once again, after so many years.

There were many tears of joy shed all around, and anyone who heard the tale soon cried that all had been saved and spared, and found happiness.

'And what of you,' the Duke asked Luciana, 'what boon do you seek, having solved this pretty riddle?'

Luciana slipped her hand into that of her Antipholus. 'I have all that I desire, now,' she said.

'Then you shall marry him,' the Duke declared, 'and I shall give thee one thousand coins, the same sum as was paid for this man's life, for your dowery.'

Luciana looked into her Antipholus's eyes and smiled. She felt a trembling in her heart, but it was not the agitation she had earlier felt; now, there was no room for agitation. Her heart was like a quiet courtyard filled with light and herbs, peace and stillness; there was no room for worries or doubts, for her heart was too full with love.

THREE MEETINGS AND A FUNERAL

Lois Gresh & Robert Weinberg

Although I included a story based on Julius Caesar *(1599) in the first volume, there is plenty of material to be found in this play to make it worth revisiting. The events around the assassination of Caesar are well known, but always worth reconsidering through fresh eyes, such as those of the soothsayer.*

Half asleep. Too much wine. The ground was hard for a man of sixty, but the leaves were soft on his face, almost like the touch of a woman – Julia, his second wife – and Lucillus wanted to feel those leaves, sleep with them, pretend for just a few minutes more . . .

Why stagger back to his room in the commoner's quarter of Rome? Nothing awaited him *there*.

Here, he had the stars. And beyond the stars were the gods. It was *appropriate* that Rome's soothsayer slept with the gods.

'Tomorrow, the city celebrates Caesar's triumph over Pompey.'

Were the gods talking to him?

Lucillus sat, sweeping the leaves off his face. He'd been having trouble hearing for well over twenty years. He pulled his soldier's cloak more tightly around his body.

'Caesar leaves Rome on the 18th for Gaul.'

Again. Lucillus was certain that he heard the words. But the gods never really talked to him. Because Lucillus wasn't really a soothsayer. He was just an old soldier swindled out of his pension by his third wife, Domitia. He told fortunes, he was a magnificent showman, and all of Rome thought he spoke directly to the gods, and yet . . .

He didn't.

'The arrangements have been made?' The voice was high-pitched, perhaps that of a young man or woman. Not the voice of an Immortal. But rather, the voice of a Roman citizen.

Lucillus shifted his weight and leaned slightly so he could peer between the bushes. For a soothsayer, information was critical.

Two people stood beneath the trees less than ten feet away. They wore hooded robes that veiled them in anonymity, dark blots in the moonlight. Lucillus couldn't even tell if they were male or female. Lovers, perhaps, meeting for a midnight rendezvous. Or wealthy landowners, making a bargain.

'All is ready. Hopefully, one other will join us tomorrow. It matters little. Caesar dies before the week ends.'

Caesar dies?

Lucillus felt his eyes grow wide. His arms went rigid, his skin tingled.

Who was this person who dared to pronounce death for Caesar? The words were fuzzy and low: a product of Lucillus' poor hearing. It was tough being so old, making his living as essentially nothing more than an eavesdropper.

'There can be no delay.' The first speaker, voice faltering slightly.

'Don't worry. With his guards dismissed, Caesar stands unprotected. Seeking to impress the mob with his lack of fear, he's made himself an easy victim. Our plans are set.'

'I hope it works. Otherwise . . .'

'Remain calm. Freedom is only days away.'

The two patches of darkness touched briefly. Then, they were gone. Leaving Lucillus alone and very frightened.

Death. Conspirators plotted against Julius Caesar. Unless he was warned, the hero of Rome was doomed. But how? How could humble Lucillus, a penniless soothsayer, warn great Caesar?

Years in the legion had made Lucillus a realist. Rome's prefects would demand proof of the conspiracy before they would alert Caesar. Lucillus had none. Just an overheard conversation between two people he couldn't identify. He possessed neither details of the plot nor the names of those involved. The prefects would never believe such a tale. Worse, others might.

Those conspiring against the Tribune would know he spoke the truth. No doubt they numbered among the rich and powerful of Rome. Treachery belonged to the upper class. Senators, perhaps, or members of Caesar's inner circle of friends. Cautious men, unwilling to take any chances, they'd make sure Lucillus was silenced. He'd disappear, and their plot would remain secret.

Grasping his staff, Lucillus rose shakily to his feet. Walking to the spot where the two had stood, Lucillus searched the ground for some clue about their identities. As expected, he found nothing. He had no facts, no faces, no proof. Only the words he'd overheard. 'Caesar dies.'

Still, Lucillus refused to admit defeat. He had served under Caesar in Gaul. The Tribune was a great man. He had done much good for Rome and promised to do much more. Allowing him to perish beneath assassins' knives was unthinkable. There had to be some way to warn Caesar of his peril and not pay dearly for the effort.

What if Lucillus warned the Tribune directly? In a manner not easily ignored?

For years, whispers among the legions had proclaimed Caesar superstitious. The Tribune believed in portents and signs, and he often consulted with oracles about upcoming campaigns. It seemed unlikely that seizing control of Rome had changed his beliefs. Caesar might heed the words of Lucillus the soothsayer.

The next morning, Lucillus put on his finest white tunic and set off to find Caesar. In Rome, the rich and powerful wore togas, while ordinary citizens and commoners dressed in robes and tunics. Whatever their station, all wore white.

Locating Caesar wasn't difficult. The Tribune, surrounded by a great crowd, was making his way slowly towards the marketplace. At Caesar's side strode his dearest friend, Marc Antony. Close behind came Cassius, Casca, Decius, Cicero, Brutus, and many other noble citizens. Off to the side walked Caesar's wife, the haughty and aristocratic Calpurnia.

As Lucillus made his way closer to Caesar, he heard the Tribune say something about his wife to Marc Antony. Whatever the reply, it was drowned out in the flourish of trumpets. For a moment, the crowd fell silent. Sensing his opportunity, Lucillus spoke.

'Caesar!' he cried, his voice shrill with emotion.

'Ha. Who calls?' asked the Tribune.

'Bid every noise be still,' demanded Casca. 'Peace yet again!'

'Who is in the press that calls on me?' asked Caesar. 'I hear a tongue, shriller than all the music, cry "Caesar!" Speak; Caesar is turn'd to hear.'

Lucillus trembled. If he revealed too much, his life was forfeit. Yet this was his one chance to warn Caesar of peril. In a clear voice, Lucillus spoke.

'Beware the Ides of March.'

Caesar frowned. 'What man is that?'

'A soothsayer bids you beware the Ides of March,' said Brutus.

'Set him before me; let me see his face.'

'Fellow,' said Casca, looking straight at Lucillus, 'come from the throng; look upon Caesar.'

Casca's eyes were cold and hard, filled with suspicion. Lucillus wondered if perhaps he'd been one of the two last night. Or Cassius? Or even the noble Brutus? Lucillus had no clues. Still, just as he didn't know them, the two who plotted Caesar's death didn't know Lucillus. To the conspirators, his words came directly from the gods. They had no reason to suspect otherwise.

'What say'st though to me now?' asked Caesar, staring at Lucillus. 'Speak once again.'

'Beware the Ides of March.'

Caesar scowled, obviously not liking what he heard. Then, after a few seconds, he laughed. 'He's a dreamer,' declared the Tribune. 'Let us leave him: pass.'

Turning, Caesar once again set off for the market. Antony, Calpurnia, and the rest followed. Caught up in the sweep of the crowd, Lucillus had no choice but to join the mob. Better, he felt, to be among the crowd than alone and at the whims of Caesar's enemies.

Thus, from the centre of the throng in the marketplace, Lucillus witnessed Marc Antony offer Caesar a golden crown three times. Saw Caesar push the crown away with the back of his hand three times.

Listened to the crowd roar its approval of his actions. Observed the naked hatred on Casca's face. Heard Cicero say something to a friend in Greek.

After Caesar and the other noble citizens departed, Lucillus listened to the commoners speak. Despite his rejection of the crown, the Tribune seemed to have fooled very few. The crowd knew he had ambitions.

'Tomorrow Caesar appears before the Senate,' declared one man.

'They're sure to offer him the crown,' said a second.

'He'll resist, but somehow I expect they'll convince him it's for the good of Rome,' said a third.

They all laughed.

Now Lucillus understood why Caesar had found his warning so distasteful. The Tribune expected to be crowned emperor of Rome on the Ides of March. In Caesar's thoughts, the following day promised greatness, not danger. His ego was greater than even his fear of the supernatural.

Lucillus needed hard facts to convince Caesar that a secret cabal threatened his life. He had only one possible hope. Tonight, he would return to the same grove where he had slept previously. And pray that the two conspirators returned for another rendezvous.

Thunder roared in the sky and lightning flashed. A storm threatened as clouds cast a mantle over the moon. Yet no rain fell.

The grove was black, the only illumination a brief flash of lightning. Lucillus huddled beneath his cloak, hiding behind the bushes.

They arrived in darkness. One flash of lightning showed the spot between the trees empty. The second blast, a moment later, revealed two cloaked figures embracing beneath the arching branches. Lucillus had little doubt this pair was the same he had seen last night. Their first words confirmed his suspicions.

'How goes the plans?' asked the slighter of the two, the one Lucillus thought to be a woman.

'Well,' said the other. 'Tonight, they meet . . .'

The rest of the words were drowned out by a roar of thunder. The impending storm made eavesdropping difficult. Especially with the poor hearing of a sixty-year-old man. If he wanted to hear more clearly, Lucillus would have to move closer.

There was another thick clump of bushes only five feet from the pair. If he was careful, he could crawl there on his belly unobserved. It was risky, but he had to take the chance.

Drawing his dark cloak around him, Lucillus flattened himself on the ground. Years of service on the frontier fighting barbarians had taught him stealth. Moving without a sound, Lucillus wiggled across the bare earth towards the nearby shrubs. The two were talking again, but he paid them no attention. A good soldier concentrated on one objective at a time. Dividing your attention could be deadly.

Lightning flared just as he pulled himself behind the bushes. The edge of his cloak flapped for an instant in the white light. Someone gasped.

'What's wrong?' asked the second conspirator, his voice sharp, as Lucillus' blood turned to ice.

'Nothing,' said the other. From this close, Lucillus knew for sure the speaker was a woman. 'I thought something moved. But, nothing's there.'

'This storm has you seeing shadows,' said the male conspirator.

'Caesar claims such weather foretells change.'

'Caesar sees omens in everything,' said the man. His voice, though muffled by his cloak, sounded familiar. But Lucillus couldn't tell for sure. 'He's filled with superstitions. Are you sure he suspects nothing?'

'He thinks only of the crown,' said the woman. 'His ambitions make him blind. He's a fool.'

'No different from all the rest. They think we share their concerns for the Republic. That we joined their plot for the glory of Rome. Idealists. They believe once Caesar's dead, the Senate will once again lead.'

'They'll learn their lesson soon enough,' replied the woman. 'Now, I must go and prepare for tomorrow.'

They embraced again and then were gone. Leaving Lucillus baffled, still not sure who they were. He still had no evidence for the Tribune, no proof of a conspiracy. Unless fate intervened, Caesar was a dead man.

It was morning. The bright sun gave no hint of the storm the night before. Lucillus, surrounded by a crowd, stood in the street outside the Senate waiting for Caesar. Today, voices whispered, Caesar would be crowned emperor. Lucillus said nothing. A wrong word could get Lucillus killed.

Down the street came Caesar. With him walked Casca, Brutus, Antony, Publius and the others. Doubtless, some among them were plotters. But which ones?

Caesar nodded at Lucillus. 'The Ides of March are come,' the Tribune declared.

'Ay, Caesar,' answered Lucillus, not sure what to answer. 'But not gone.'

Before Lucillus could say more, a man pushed his way forward from the crowd, waved a paper, and cried, 'Hail, Caesar! Read this schedule.'

Caught by surprise, Caesar stepped back. Immediately, one of the nobles accompanying him moved close.

'Trebonius doth desire you to o'er-read, at your best leisure,' declared the noble, pulling a scroll from his toga, 'this his humble suit.'

'O Caesar, read mine first,' said the man from the crowd. 'For mine's a suit that touches Caesar nearer; read it, great Caesar.'

'What touches us ourself shall be last served,' answered Caesar.

'Delay not, Caesar,' urged the stranger, pressing his note at the Tribune. 'Read it instantly.'

'What, is the fellow mad?' said Caesar, scowling.

Lucillus wondered what secrets the note contained. What made it so important? But Caesar seemed unconcerned.

'Sirrah,' said Publius, 'give place,' as the Tribune turned and made for the Senate.

'What, urge you your petitions in the street?' said Cassius. 'Come to the Capitol.'

The crowd followed Caesar. As before, Lucillus allowed himself to be pulled along by the rabble. Perhaps closer to the Senate, there'd be another chance to warn Caesar of his peril.

The man with the petition was gone, melted away into the streets. Who was the man? Had he also sought to warn Caesar of the conspiracy? It seemed unlikely, yet life was filled with odd coincidences.

Ahead, Caesar was talking to several of the noble citizens. Lucillus spotted Brutus, Casca, and Cassius among those nearest to the Tribune. But Marc Antony, Caesar's closest friend and supporter, was nowhere to be seen. Lucillus trembled, sensing disaster.

'Speak, hands, for me!' cried Casca suddenly.

Knives flashed in the sunlight. Lucillus gasped in horror as dagger after dagger plunged into Caesar's body. Blood spurted onto the streets of Rome. The Tribune collapsed to the ground, dead.

'Liberty! Freedom!' cried one of the assassins. 'Tyranny is dead! Run hence, proclaim, cry it about the streets.'

The crowd ran, screaming not in celebration but in blind panic. Blood and death belonged in the arena, not in the streets. If Caesar could be killed so easily, was anyone safe?

Lucillus, distraught and bitter, ran with them. Though the conspirators proclaimed their noble motives, they might not look favourably on one who had tried to warn Caesar. Best that he keep off the streets until order was restored. Only then would he know if it was safe for him to remain in Rome. Or if he should flee for his life.

The rest of the morning passed in a blur. The streets of Rome stayed deserted, as citizens and commoners kept to their homes and wondered what would happen next, now that great Caesar was dead. What was the murderers' plan?

In his small apartment, Lucillus wondered if the conspirators *had* a plan. He remembered the words he heard amidst the thunder and lightning. Did the killers actually expect the Roman Senate to once again take command of the empire? Could grown men be so foolish, so easily fooled? Lucillus suspected the worst.

By mid-afternoon, word filtered through the commoners' section that Caesar's funeral would be held late in the day, in the marketplace. The noble Brutus was going to speak. As was Marc Antony. An odd match. Though he still feared for his safety, Lucillus knew he had to attend.

The marketplace was crowded with citizens. Lucillus stayed to the rear of the crowd. No one seemed to pay him special attention, but he was taking no chances. One hand held his dagger ready beneath his tunic.

Brutus spoke first. His speech was intelligent and thoughtful, detailing how he loved Caesar, but how he loved Rome more. Again, Lucillus remembered the words spoken last night in the grove. How the cloaked figures laughed at the idealism of the other conspirators. Without question, Brutus numbered among those who had been called fools. For all of his noble thoughts, Brutus was no politician.

Marc Antony brought the body of Caesar, still clad in the

blood-stained toga, to the market. The grim spectacle served as a vivid reminder of the conspirators' violence. According to Antony's words, he came to bury Caesar, not to praise him. But, notorious as a gamer and an athlete, Antony was also an orator.

Brutus had appealed to the honour of the people. Antony addressed stronger, baser emotions. He spoke to their anger, their greed. Mysteriously, he produced Caesar's will, proclaiming he had found it in his closet. Told the crowd he could not read it, that the terms would inflame them against Caesar's murderers. Then let the mob persuade him otherwise.

The results were exactly as Antony predicted. By nightfall, Brutus and Casca and the rest of the conspirators had fled the city. The Senators trembled in their homes. And bands of angry citizens roamed the street.

Lucillus knew he should remain in his room. That, with Caesar dead, there was no justice for the two he had overheard plotting. Yet, despite all of his fears, all of his suspicions, the darkness once more led him to the grove at the edge of the city. Where he waited and waited for the two cloaked figures to appear.

Long hours passed and no one came. Finally, Lucillus was forced to conclude that the plotters no longer had any reason to meet in secret. Vague suspicions crystallised into certainties, guiding his uneasy footsteps. The path led to the home of Julius Caesar. Where, in the rear garden, away from the sounds of mourning, he spied the same pair from the previous nights. This time, they sat close together on a bench, whispering, drinking from a wine flask.

'The storm made Caesar afraid.' The woman's voice was soft and slurred from wine. Yet, in the quiet of the night, Lucillus recognised her. It was Calpurnia, once Caesar's wife. Now his widow. 'Knowing my husband well, I begged him not to go to the Senate. To stay with me, even if doing so would make him appear a coward.' She laughed. 'I knew his vanity would force him to do just the opposite.'

The man shifted Calpurnia's hood to expose her ear, then leaned until his lips brushed her hair. His voice was low, and thick with drink. 'Like Brutus, he trusted the wrong people. And paid the price for his folly.' A familiar voice, but still . . . Lucillus could not be *sure*.

'We lose much with the false will,' said Calpurnia, 'but in return, the city is ours for the looting. The crowd names you king.'

The other figure laughed, embraced Caesar's widow passionately.

The hood of his cloak fell back, revealing his fair features in the moonlight. Sadly, Lucillus nodded, his worst fears confirmed. Turning away, he made his way silently out of the garden. Honour had deserted Rome.

Brutus had betrayed Caesar for noble reasons. The two in the garden had plotted entirely for power and riches. Though neither had ever touched steel, Caesar's true murderers were Calpurnia, the Tribune's wife – and her lover, Marc Antony, Caesar's closest friend.

A GOOD REPORT OF THE WORM

Tom Holt

Antony and Cleopatra *(1607) is in many ways a sequel to* Julius Caesar, *though is generally more highly regarded. Shakespeare was able to contrast the different Roman and Egyptian cultures and portray Antony torn between duty and love. In the play we meet Enobarbus, Antony's loyal general. Historically he was Lucius Domitius Ahenobarbus. He had sided with Brutus and Cassius after Caesar's murder before transferring his allegiance to Antony. He urged Antony to fight Octavian's forces in land, but instead Antony fought at sea, off Actium, and was ignominiously defeated. Ahenobarbus blamed Antony for the defeat and changed sides again for Octavian, but died soon afterwards. In the play, Antony had sought to regain Ahenobarbus's loyalty and had returned all of his treasure. Ahenobarbus dies of a broken heart. In the following story Tom Holt is not convinced with the broken-heart verdict and looks again at the death of Ahenobarbus.*

> Clown: Truly, I have him. But I would
> not be a party that should desire you to
> touch him, for his biting is immortal; those
> that do die of it do seldom or never recover.
> *Antony & Cleopatra*; Act V, Scene 2

I looked down at the thing in the box and wrinkled my nose.

'That's a dead body,' I said. 'I've seen ever so many of them over the years. What the hell has it got to do with me?'

I looked at it again, and noticed something I'd never been close enough to see before. His hair was dyed, or bleached; at any rate, the bronze-red colour stopped a brooch-pin's width from the roots. It figured; if your family name is Ahenobarbus, which means Bronzebeard in Latin, and you have the misfortune to come into the world with boring old black hair like everyone else, there must be a temptation to do something about it. Nevertheless; the great, the universally-respected Ahenobarbus had been walking around all these years with a lie on his head. That intrigued me.

The tribune drew the sheet back over the shrivelled face. 'He died on our watch,' he said, looking past me. 'There's got to be an investigation. And you're not exactly rushed off your feet.'

I wasn't having that. 'Come on,' I said, 'that's not my job and you know it. I'm not even army, I'm a civilian secretary.'

'Doesn't matter,' the tribune replied. 'Under certain circumstances, I'm authorized to delegate military functions to appropriate civilian personnel; even,' he added, stifling a yawn with the back of his hand, 'uppity Greek clerks, if there's no-one else available. You're it. He's all yours. I want a report in three days' time, so I can close the file. Don't be difficult,' he added, as I opened my mouth to object. 'See it from my point of view. We've just won the war, we're taking possession of a third of the known world here; I need my soldiers to do proper military things, not fool about writing reports. Help me out, will you? I'll do you a favour some day, I promise.'

I caught sight of a toe sticking up where the cloth had been pulled forward; it looked ridiculous. 'Why does there have to be an investigation anyway?' I asked. 'He was Antony's chief of staff, a rebel. If we're doing formal investigations on dead rebels now, we'll be at it for the rest of our lives. I don't know if you've noticed, but everywhere you look is knee deep in them; possibly,' I added, 'as a result of the big battle.'

The tribune sighed. 'Because he defected to us before the end, technically he's one of ours,' he said. 'Look, all you've got to do is examine the body—'

'No thanks,' I said, moving away a step or two. 'He's been dead for days. You examine him.'

He grinned at me. 'Ah,' he said, 'but this is Egypt, remember. In Egypt, they embalm anything that moves – well, anything that doesn't move, you know what I mean. You leave your dinner to go outside and take a leak, chances are you'll come back and find some so-and-so's whipped the innards out of your cold roast duck and marinaded it in frankincense.' He jerked his head towards the thing in the box. 'Believe me, he'll still be fresh as a daisy when you're a bundle of bones and hair. Wonderful country, this.'

'All right,' I said. 'I examine the body and write a report. That's it?'

He nodded. 'And you'd better interview the guards who found the body, just for the record. Won't take you five minutes, and that'll be the job done.'

I thought of the last time I'd seen Domitius Ahenobarbus – does that make it sound like I knew the man personally? Sorry, badly phrased; I didn't. But I had seen him appear in public, at Mark Antony's right hand, two steps back, always the model lieutenant, or henchman, or whatever you want to call him. Back then, of course, Antony was Us rather than Them, one of the Triple Pillars who were re-establishing truth, justice and the Roman way after Julius Caesar's murder, and so Ahenobarbus had been Us too. I remember hearing somewhere that he'd chosen the wrong side in the war against Brutus and Cassius, but he'd made a remarkable recovery after that, finding his way onto Antony's staff and gradually becoming indispensable, which must have taken some doing. Everybody I'd spoke to who'd actually met him said he was a good man, a regular guy, on good terms with everybody. Certainly what I'd seen of him at Misenum, at Pompey's camp, seemed to bear out the general impression; I remember noticing him laughing and chattering with Agrippa and Maecenas, at a time when it was pretty obvious that they were soon going to be Us, while Ahenobarbus would inevitably be Them. I remember, too, hearing that he'd defected to our side after the sea-battle and thinking just a bit less of him after that; just another big false face behind a smile, I said to myself, and thought no more of it. And now here he was, sun-dried and gutted and steeped in tanning fluid and stuffed with lavender and rosemary like a scented cushion not eighteen inches from my nose, and there I was, still a poxy little clerk and still alive. Looked at from that angle, writing a report so that they'd be cleared to bury his body seemed the least I could do.

'Right,' I said, muffling my nose in the hem of my tunic, 'let's get this over with. Ready?'

'Ready,' the boy replied unhappily. He looked even greener than I did, which made me feel better. Nothing like seeing somebody even more pathetic than you are for bolstering the ailing self-image.

'Then here goes.' I pulled back the sheet, revealing the naked body. 'Report on the corpse of Lucius Domitius Ahenobarbus. There are no obvious marks of violence to be seen on the body, likewise no discoloration or distortion of the face that would suggest death by poisoning or witchcraft. I conclude therefore that he died a natural death. Have you got all that?'

'Almost,' the boy replied, his head down over his tablets. 'I got as far as "*violence*".'

'Oh for pity's sake—' I stopped short. I'd seen something I hadn't noticed before; two little puncture marks just above his right wrist. They were very faint, only visible because of the way the skin had shrunk. I knew what they meant, from personal experience; I was bitten by a snake when I was seven years old, and nearly died.

'Sorry,' the boy said. 'What came after "violence"?'

'What?' Snakebite, I thought. There is a lot of it about at the moment, but I never knew it was catching. 'Oh yes, no obvious marks of violence to be seen on the body . . .'

Well, it was eminently possible. All manner of important people seemed to be getting bitten by snakes these days, and you didn't have to be Aristotle to draw the conclusion that even Important People In History can die as a result. On the other hand, if I wanted to put down snakebite as the cause of death, I'd have to find some corroborative evidence; detailed questioning of the guards who found the body, or something like that. Could I be bothered? Apparently – and much to my own surprise – I could.

They were perfectly representative examples of the Roman soldier, those two; a big, broad, cow-eyed lump of a veteran and a little lad, no more than sixteen, with long bony arms and red knuckles. The old man did all the talking, and whenever the kid tried to say anything, he'd shut him up without even looking round. They told me their names and I had my boy write them down, but I can't remember what they were.

'We were on sentry duty,' the veteran said, 'middle of the third watch, and he came up the middle road of the camp, walking kind of slow.'

'Like he was drunk,' ventured the kid.

'Be quiet, you. Yeah, like he was drunk, or someone'd bashed him on the head. Well, we had to challenge him, so we did, and he said his name, Lucius Domitius Ahenobarbus. Obviously we knew who he was, but we didn't say nothing.'

'Not our place to say anything,' said the kid.

'Shut up,' said the veteran, before he'd finished. 'Anyway, he stood there for a minute, like he was trying to think where he was, then he asked us the way to the admiral's quarters. Well, we weren't going to tell him that, but we had to say something, so we said—'

'Just a minute,' I interrupted. 'The admiral? You mean Agrippa.'

'Yes, sir. That's what he said, actually, he said Agrippa, not the admiral. Anyhow, we said we didn't know, and he sort of shrugged his shoulders and said something about how he wasn't feeling too good and wanted to sit down for a bit. So he wandered off about ten paces and sat down and just, like, stayed there, looking up at the stars. Then,' continued the veteran, 'he fell over, or rather he sort of slumped over, and when we went to have a look, there he was, dead.'

I thought about that for a moment. 'How long was he sitting there before he fell over?' I said. 'Almost at once?'

The veteran shook his head. 'More like half an hour, maybe a full hour; you lose track of time, sir, on a long sentry shift.'

'I see. And did he say anything while he was sitting there?'

'Not that I can remember, sir. Sorry.'

So it could have been snakebite; it can work that way, depending on the sort of snake that bites you, whether you're young and fit or old and frail, that sort of thing. I had enough for my report now, no need to go scratching around for more details. Instead, I went to his tent and spoke to his servant.

'All this ought to go to his son, of course,' the old man said. He lifted the lid of one of the enormous cedarwood chests that took up most of the space in the tent; it was full of silver coin. 'But I don't suppose it will; they'll confiscate it because of where it came from. You heard about that, I suppose?'

I nodded. Everybody had heard how, when Antony found out that Ahenobarbus had betrayed him and gone over to Octavian, he'd made a point of sending his personal fortune after him. A magnificent gesture, everybody said, and typically fatuous.

I dipped my hand into the chest – well, could you resist the temptation to bury your hand up to the wrist in silver coins, just to see what it feels like? – and glanced at what I'd trawled up. There was something odd there. I let the coins fall back.

'Tell me,' I said. 'Have you seen any snakes around here lately?'

He shook his head. 'Don't think so. But it's funny you should say that, because he got bit by a snake.'

I looked up. 'Really? When?'

'Oh, a few days before he died, two or three. Funny thing to happen; he was in the town, wandering round the market square, and he stopped at this stall. He was after figs, I think; anyway, the man was serving someone else, so he lifted the lid off a jar and this snake came out and bit him.'

'You don't say.'

'Oh yes. Well, it frightened the life out of him, you can bet, but the man only laughed and said it was all right, it was a pet snake – you know, for doing conjuring tricks and stuff with; they milk the poison out of them every day, so if they bite it doesn't matter. Anyway, he was so relieved he forgot about being angry. Gave the man a gold piece, in fact.'

'I see,' I said, as something uncomfortable fell into place in my mind. 'In that case, I'll trouble you to open up those other chests.'

It served me right, of course. If I'd left well alone, I could have written in my report that I'd found signs of snakebite on the body, and allowed whoever read it (would anybody actually read my report, I wondered? No reason why anybody should, so long as a report was actually written and put on file) to draw their own conclusions. Now I'd have to postulate a second snake (this time a snake with real poison); and what about the time difference? Would the print of a snakebite still be visible three days later? I reckoned it would, if there was even just a trace of poison left in the snake's mouth to inflame the skin and stop the puncture-marks closing, but of course that's just my guess. I can't remember how long the marks stayed when I was bitten. Fine witness I'd make.

I went to see Agrippa. Now, because Agrippa is the admiral of the fleet, victor of the decisive battle of Actium and right-hand man to Octavian himself, and I'm just a Greek clerk, I didn't see Agrippa himself, just his secretary; which was, of course, the way I preferred it.

'Loads of times,' the secretary repeated. 'Thick as thieves at one time, before all the trouble blew up. If Octavian and Antony'd been on anything as like good terms, we wouldn't have had the damn war. Stupid, stupid war,' he added, draining the last knockings of the jug into his cup. I signalled to the girl for another.

'It's always the way,' I said. I had no idea what I was agreeing with, but he didn't seem to notice. 'And what about afterwards?' I asked. 'After he left Antony and joined up with us. That meant they could be friends again.'

He shook his head. 'Not a bit of it. Never came round to see us, and he never went round there; and that's Agrippa for you, no loyalty. Wouldn't risk his standing with the big chief to go and see an old friend fallen on hard times. Always been like that, he has. Always the main chance with him, and the hell with people. Not like your Ahenobarbus,' he added. 'Now whatever else he was, he was always good as his word, wouldn't let down a pal. All sorts of things he did for Agrippa back when they were on good terms, and a fat lot of good it did him.'

I frowned. 'I wouldn't have said Ahenobarbus was your actual paragon of loyalty,' I said. 'He changed sides as often as a coin changes hands.'

He waved his hands vaguely. 'Don't you believe it,' he said. 'Sure, he left Brutus and joined Antony; but he only joined Brutus in the first place because Octavius Caesar put his name on the death-lists after Julius was killed, and that was because of his family, see. His family were involved in the plot, Lucius Domitius wasn't. And then Antony got Octavius to pardon him, so he dumped Brutus and joined Antony. Loyalty, you see, to the man who'd helped him.'

'Quite,' I said. 'And then he dumped Antony for the man who'd wanted him executed in the first place.'

He frowned. 'Well, anyway,' he said. 'He was all right, Ahenobarbus. It's a pity Agrippa didn't have the common decency to see him, after he'd written him letters and all.'

None of this was helping me get my report written; nevertheless, after a bad night's sleep I went to see a friend of mine in the staff office and asked to see the report on Cleopatra.

'Sure,' he said. 'What on earth do you want to see that for?'

I shrugged. 'I just need to check some details about snakebite,' I replied. 'I don't know a lot about it, and then I figured there may be something in the report, since that's what she died of.'

'Oh. Well, be my guest.' He opened the box and pulled out a long brass cylinder. 'There's a bit in there that might help you,' he said. 'But if you want to know about snakebite, what you need to do is read a book about it.'

'Really. Always assuming,' I added, 'that there's someone with so much time on his hands that he'd write a whole book about snakebite.'

He smiled. 'Aratus the astronomer,' he replied. 'The name of the book, oddly enough, is *Aratus On Snakebite*. And if you go and see the Ephesian doctor and ask him nicely, he might just let you borrow his copy.'

I read the report on Cleopatra anyway; then I called on the Ephesian doctor, who wasn't happy about lending me the book but perked up considerably when I offered to buy it. For the record, it's a very boring book. Trust me.

It took me a long time to track down the next person I needed to talk to, and that was odd in itself. Usually, in my experience, market traders are a gregarious bunch; they're all good buddies and know each other's business, always ready and willing to gossip about their fellow men. Not, apparently, in this town. Rather than give up, I went back to the camp and nagged the tribune into lending me a platoon of soldiers.

'What the hell do you need soldiers for?' he asked.

'Do you want your report or don't you?'

'You do whatever you like,' he replied. 'Just don't kill any civilians if you can possibly help it. We're officially the good guys now.'

'I'll bear that in mind,' I said.

I selected a stallholder at random, had him arrested and brought to a spare tent in the camp that nobody was using. He was utterly terrified by the time I showed up to question him, and delightfully helpful and forthcoming. As a result, I was able to go back to the market and find the man I'd originally been looking for; a dealer in dates and dried figs, who also did conjuring tricks.

'I gather you've got a tame snake,' I said.

He looked at me. 'No,' he said.

'Let me rephrase that,' I said. 'Until recently you had a tame snake; then you lent it to somebody and it met with an accident.'

He carried on looking at me. 'Why are you asking me this?' he said.

'It's all right,' I assured him. 'Just tell me one thing and I'll leave you alone. I saw a snake act once, years ago now; the man played a flute and the snake came out of its basket, up a rope and down the other end. Did yours do that?'

He nodded.

'That's fine.' I'd got what I wanted, but I decided to try out something else, just to see what happened. 'It must be hard,' I said, 'losing your best customer.'

He shrugged. 'No great loss,' he said. 'Sure, there was the prestige; but I prefer customers who actually pay the bill.'

After that I wandered round the market for a while, just talking to people.

'Well?' the tribune asked.

I sat down and dumped my satchel on the floor. 'I haven't written it,' I said. He didn't like that. 'Oh come on, Philocleon,' he said. 'I ask you to do one simple thing, one little favour to me personally, and you can't be bothered.'

I shook my head. 'I don't think you really need a report,' I said. 'Just close the file and to hell with it. After all, what's one more dead rebel among so many? We won, didn't we?'

'That's beside the point,' he replied sternly. 'I've got the corpse of a Roman senator cluttering up my supply tent, and I can't dispose of it without a report. All I want is a few lines on a roll of paper and then I can get on with doing my job. Is that so much to ask? Of a friend?'

'Please yourself,' I said. 'I just thought, if I explained to you why I really don't think you need a report, you might change your mind.'

He looked at me for a long time. 'How long have we known each other?' he said.

'Four years,' I replied. 'Though I wouldn't say we've ever been close.'

'Get on with it,' he said.

I sat forward on the uncomfortable little standard-issue folding stool. 'You told me earlier,' I said, 'we're officially the good guys now, right?'

He nodded. 'It's a valuable province. We get enough grain from Egypt every year to feed the whole City. Now, if we roll the dice the right way, we'll get it all for free. So; orders are, we're the good guys.'

I nodded. 'Which is going to mean a lot of work,' I said, 'bearing in mind how popular Cleopatra was; with the unwashed multitude, I mean.'

'She was a Ptolemy, and they've been running the place since Alexander's time; hell, they founded this city. Yes, she was popular. What's that go to do with anything?'

'Nothing,' I said, 'just checking my facts. Actually, I spent an hour or so taking a random sample of opinion on the matter down in the market-place – people'll tell a Greek things they won't tell to a Roman – and yes, it's extremely important that public opinion's handled right, especially since Cleopatra's dead.'

'She'd always have been trouble,' he replied. 'I still don't see the relevance.'

'All right.' I fished in my sleeve and took out my purse, from which I extracted a coin.

'Stolen goods,' I said. 'I stole it from Ahenobarbus' money chest.'

The tribune didn't say anything.

'All right,' I went on, 'I'll trouble you to tell me what's on the coin.'

He frowned, puzzled. 'What, you mean the pictures and stuff? If you like. On one side we've got the head of Venus, and on the other there's a man holding what looks like a statue, and the name Caesar. What of it?'

'You tell me.'

'It's one of Julius Caesar's coins,' he said. 'Which makes it, what, eighteen or nineteen years old?'

'Thank you. Now look at these.' I dropped two silver coins on the table in front of him. 'These I got in my change the other day. Tell me about them.'

He scratched his head, then looked at the coins. 'Well, the one with a galley on's one of Antony's wartime issue,' he said. 'Millions of 'em there must be, floating about in these parts. And the other one – well, look who we have here. Quite a flattering portrait and there's his name, Lucius Domitius Ahenobarbus.'

I nodded. 'One of the perks of being paymaster general is getting your name on the money. I asked around; there's only a few hundred thousand of these, compared with gods alone know how many of the galley coins. But around here they're common enough. Except in one place.'

'Really? Where?'

'Ahenobarbus's money-chests,' I replied. 'All the coins in there were old Roman issues, minted in Rome. Does that strike you as odd? Here's a man who's spent quite a few years in the East with Antony, held important jobs and made important money out here, after leaving Rome under a cloud and defecting to the enemy in the middle of a war—'

'Brutus's war, you mean?'

'That's right. I don't suppose he had much opportunity to bring along chests and chests full of silver coin; I think all his money must have been accumulated here, in the East. But all the coins in his money chests are City mint. Doesn't that seem odd to you?'

'Well, yes,' he said. 'But I don't see—'

'You can tell where money comes from just by looking at it,' I went on. 'They're all silver denarii, standard weight, standard fineness, but our money's got our designs on it and their money's got theirs. So,' I continued, 'if someone looked under the mattress of one of our loyal commanders – Agrippa, for argument's sake – and found hundreds and thousands of little silver galleys and portraits of Lucius Domitius Ahenobarbus, not to mention that dinky one with Antony, Cleopatra and the kids, though that's quite rare; that might make it hard for our loyal general to explain how he came by so much enemy coin, don't you think?'

He held up his hand. 'I can see what you're getting at,' he said. 'Well, I'd have to be thick as a brick not to. You're trying to tell me he didn't really defect, Antony sent him here to pretend to defect, and all the money was for bribing potential traitors; it was all City money so it wouldn't give the game away. And then someone found out, so they killed him.'

'Not quite,' I said. 'Suppose this potential traitor was Agrippa – I've got no evidence beyond the fact that they were friends before the bust-up between Octavian and Antony. Ahenobarbus wrote letters to Agrippa after he defected but never went to see him, and Agrippa's servant thinks he's a treacherous little rat who'll go where the advantage lies and the hell with anything else. But suppose Agrippa was the traitor, and suppose someone else – Maecenas or Dolabella, one of the big men on the general staff – suspected something.'

The tribune drew his finger across his throat. I nodded.

'But there's no proof,' I said, 'apart from the money; and what you can't prove had better stay unsaid, so let's forget all about that, shall we? Well?'

He nodded. 'I agree,' he said.

'Right, I won't put *that* in my report. So what's left? Let's see. How about cause of death?'

'That needs to go in, certainly.'

I sighed. 'The problem is,' I said, 'I don't know what he died of. All I know is what he didn't die of, which isn't the same thing at all.'

'You'd better explain that,' he said.

'He didn't die of snakebite,' I replied. 'Which is odd,' I went on, 'because he was bitten by a snake only a few days before he died. What's odder still is that he was bitten by a snake that went on to bite someone who quite definitely died, in a highly public, not to say dramatic manner. Now that really is odd, don't you think?'

The tribune was sitting very still.

'To go back to what we were talking about earlier,' I said. 'It really is very convenient for us that Cleopatra killed herself – well, the snake killed her, but you know what I mean – because if she hadn't she could have been a real pain in the neck, given how popular she is with her devoted subjects. Of course, if she hadn't killed herself we'd have had to get rid of her somehow, but we wouldn't dare do it openly for fear of bringing the house down round our ears, so to speak. We'd have had to be crafty; for instance, we'd have found the man who supplied figs to the royal household – quite a character; he also used to do conjuring tricks for her late majesty, I gather, with his tame performing snake – and get him to dose a batch of figs with poison. Incidentally, don't you think it was touching the way Cleopatra's two ladies-in-waiting chose to die with her? I thought that was an inspiring show of loyalty, in a world where there's treachery everywhere you look. Of course, they'd have died anyway if we fed the royal household a bushel of poisoned figs, but it wouldn't make nearly such a good story.'

'I don't think I want to hear any more of this,' he said.

'Tough,' I replied, 'because you started it. Of course, in any clever scheme, such as you'd need if you were murdering Cleopatra, there'll always be loose ends, and the mark of a good murderer is tidying them up. Like, for example, a man gets bitten by a snake that is in fact a pet and harmless; then the snake goes on to bite the queen and kill her. Loose end. You'd want to make sure that loose end got cleared up.'

The tribune stood up suddenly. 'All right,' he said. 'But what's all this got to do with the money, and Agrippa?'

I shrugged. 'I don't know,' I said. 'I think it's probably a coincidence. It was seeing that money that made me think something was strange about all this, but I don't think it's anything to do with the snake and the basket of figs.' I smiled. 'If you like,' I went on, 'I can carry on investigating, and you never know, I might turn up the missing clue that makes some sense out of it. For all I know, Antony might have been involved in this notional plot to kill Cleopatra – it'd be the only way for him to get off the hook; she's dead, he blames her, Octavius forgives him and lets him go into a cosy exile somewhere warm and far away; who else could he trust with a mission like that apart from his most loyal follower? It's a hare-brained idea, of course, like challenging Octavius to single combat; but people do all sorts of crazy things when they're desperate. In that case, they'd have tried to get Agrippa, Ahenobarbus' old chum, to act as go-between, and since Agrippa's such a nasty piece of work he'd have to be well paid. It's lame, I know,' I said, 'but it's the best I can do without further investigation. Now, you just say the word and I'll be on to it like a dog on a snake; after all, we both want this report to be a good one, don't we?'

The tribune looked at me, long and hard. He looked ten years older than he had the previous morning. Served him right.

'Report?' he said. 'What report would that be?'

'Sorry,' I said. 'I thought you wanted me to write a report.'

'Who, you? Nah, you're just a Greek clerk.' He smiled, very tightly. 'Writing reports is strictly for the military.'

A KIND OF WILD JUSTICE

Ron Tiner

With this story we move forward in time to that group of plays which are almost contemporary with Shakespeare's own period. In the first anthology I included a story by Kim Newman which reflected on the illusory deceptions played in Twelfth Night *(c. 1601). The following story takes a deeper look at some of the background machinations within the play, and in particular at the aftermath of the practical joke played by Sir Toby Belch on the upstart steward Malvolio.*

It was the evening of the last day of March. Spring was approaching and at last the weather was turning warmer.

Maria lay in bed clutching the letter in her hand, and thought over the events of recent days. Naked under the woollen cover, she felt the effects of its touch upon her skin more keenly even than usual; the weight of it draped heavily across her body seemed particularly sensuous tonight as she lay there in the darkness with the distant sounds of late carousing filtering through the leaded window. She turned her head to the left and reached out to touch the empty place where her husband should be: should be, but as usual, was not. His voice was doubtless prominent within the cacophony that presently emanated from the premises of the wineseller at the other end of the street.

At first she had been enormously flattered when Sir Toby had proposed marriage. She, a mere housekeeper, would be greatly elevated by such a match, for even though he was what common folk liked to call decayed gentry, he was well connected. And such a man! Rumbustious and forthright, he could match wits with the best – aye and fight the best too. Here, she had thought, was a man who could quench the fire between her thighs and fill the empty longing in her belly.

It was after the great trick they had played on Malvolio and they were both in high spirits. And deep in their cups as well, she remembered with a tight smile. She had been almost as drunk as he was and they had laughed and danced and sung bawdy songs late into the night. God's breath, how they had laughed at the image of the pompous fool, so viciously cross-gartered that he walked stiff-legged and was in danger of cutting off the blood supply to his feet. And, red-faced with the strain of it, he had maintained a smile so painful that his eyes had turned bloodshot.

'Why, Malvolio,' the mistress had exclaimed in her snooty, cut-glass voice, 'what ails thee, man?'

Maria grinned to herself once more at the memory, but there was bitterness in it. The stupid bugger! Served him right, she thought. But it was no good; she could not escape the nagging suspicion that it was her part in the affair that had driven him to suicide. She had gone too far, turning the jest into a callous, malignant trick. When he had later tried to face them with an angry and contemptuous reproof, she and her friends had laughed scornfully and followed him out of the tavern, chanting, 'Smile, now, Malvolio. Don't forget your garters.'

He had run out onto the clifftop with the cat-calling crowd in pursuit, turning at the edge to hold his hands out like upturned claws and screaming like a tormented animal. Then he turned and threw himself headlong into the sea. Two weeks later, they learned, his mutilated body was washed ashore fifty miles away in Caspia.

She thrust these unpleasant reminiscences from her mind, but those which flowed in to replace them were not much more pleasing.

Her expectations regarding her new husband had been disappointed. She had mistakenly seen his rowdiness as an expression of virility and expected the rollicking fun to continue when they got home and went to bed. His roaring laughter and his unbridled licentious talk put him at the centre of all the fun in the tavern, but once away from the throng, he was hardly capable of maintaining his body in an upright posture, and his male gristle was likewise unable to stand.

She was thirty years old and certainly no virgin. She knew what to expect of a husband and knew the taste of it, too. But now she wanted more than tastings; she wanted a child. Sometimes there seemed to be a great hole of longing between her legs and up into her belly that would need a barge to fill it.

She tucked the letter under her pillow, then ran the palms of her hands down her body and, with fingers spread, softly into her pubic hair, remembering as she did so her first lover, her cousin Horatio, and that gentle summer half a lifetime ago. His freckled face and unruly ginger hair came back clearly to her mind as she recalled how, one day, he had come to her with his saucy eyes shining. Horatio, with his reckless japes and boundless energy had taken her maidenhead, and they returned to their favourite haunt every day that summer to enjoy each other.

They were discovered of course. Maria, refusing to show contrition, was sent away to service in the house of the Lady Olivia. Poor Horatio was sent to sea and was lost, presumed drowned, within the year.

Her second lover was Danilo, who was for a time Lady Olivia's steward, Malvolio's immediate predecessor. He took a liking to Maria and they regularly had quick, stand-up couplings on the stairs and in the pantry when the family were at meals. But that came to an abrupt end, too, when he was discovered selling one of the silver spoons from the sideboard to a travelling pedlar. After spending two days in the stocks, he too was sent to do service in the Queen's navy.

Malvolio was his replacement and that was why she had hated him so vehemently. She needed her carnal thirst to be regularly quenched and he had nothing but a shrivelled pisspipe between his legs. That paltry, prancing apology for a man. That posturing nincompoop. That bollockless popinjay. She was glad he was dead.

The extended denial of her bodily wants vexed her and she became mean-spirited and snappish. Sir Toby was the only one who offered something of an outlet for her frustration with the sadistic pranks he liked to play on his drinking companions. The most regular butt of these jokes was Sir Andrew Aguecheek, despite the fact that it was he who invariably paid the landlord at the end of the night. Sir Toby found he could enlist Maria's willing aid in these spiteful enterprises, and she could always be relied upon to write the necessary letters in such a way that a little extra cruelty was added to the jest.

And then, to her astonishment, during their celebrations following the joke they played on Malvolio, he asked her to marry him. Drunk as she was, she was not so far into her cups that she could not recognise the chance of a lifetime. What a stroke of luck! She called the priest in immediately, before he had time to sober up and change his mind. And now they had their own bedroom in the great house.

But the carnal delights she so desperately wanted were still denied her. Sir Toby was a randy-mouthed libertine while he held a tankard in his hand, but at home he was an ill-tempered, flatulent bully by day and a useless, snoring hulk by night. He tried only once to do his husbandly duty and that was on their disastrous wedding night. Dismayed as she was by the massive hairy belly that was revealed when he took off his clothes, it was when he tried to mount her, and the weight of him nearly crushed the life from her small body, that she was first truly revolted by him. And then he couldn't perform. He strained, he belched, he farted, he fell asleep and snored like a brewery all night long. The filthy, pot-gutted bastard.

Since then her revulsion had grown and she had become increasingly shrewish. Her snappish remarks and cutting rejoinders had in those few weeks grown more hate-filled and poisonous. Any show of vulgarity from him brought forth a vitriolic stream of abuse from her that sent him slamming out of the house cursing all womankind.

And then the foreigners had come.

And with them the dark-eyed and dangerous man whose letter she now took again from under her pillow.

She held it against her face and breathed in the scent of it. She could detect the mouthwatering musky smell of him, faintly discernable: the reckless aroma of Carlito.

She clenched her teeth and sucked in her breath with a hiss. Her body quivered with the sexual excitement that remembrance of their last meeting brought with it. She ran her free hand over her breast and downwards; a fingertip dipped briefly into her navel, then down again into the soft, silky curls and on under. Her knees parted.

'Carlito,' she whispered, as her hand quivered like a newly hatched butterfly and her fingers began a rhythmic, secret caress.

They came, they said, from a great island in the south of Italy. A land called Sicilia, where the summers were hot and the winters mild. And the wine they made there was the finest in the world, they said; rich, and red, and full-bodied.

The family arrived quietly one freezing night in early March, in a great ox-cart, which contained all their belongings and a number of big barrels of wine. They established themselves in the tithe barn that had stood unused since the monasteries were destroyed decades before.

Late in the morning, Sir Toby, nursing his usual hangover, was trudging morosely down the street, muttering curses upon the sharp-tongued termagant who had driven him out of doors. His head ached and his guts were churning ominously. He needed a drink.

He came upon a bull-necked man in his fifties fixing a notice board above the door of the barn and his spirits lifted.

Nasteroni, it read, *Purveyor of Fine Sicilian Wines*

'Good morrow to you, neighbour,' he called out.

The man gave the pegs that secured the sign a last thwack with his mallet and jumped down from the tub on which he was standing to hold out a massive, hairy hand.

'Giancarlo Nasteroni at your service, sir.'

'Sir Toby Belch.'

'You're a gentleman, then!' The foreigner was evidently impressed. It was very gratifying. 'Come in and taste my wine, sir.'

Sir Toby was feeling better already as he allowed himself to be ushered over the threshold. Inside, a substantial area had been furnished with benches and a couple of large trestle tables. Two great lengths of sackcloth formed a curtain which hung from a beam across the entire width of the place closing off the rest of the barn's interior.

'Cherubina!'

A hefty, middle-aged woman with iron-grey hair came scuttling towards them from behind the curtain. 'This is Sir Toby Belch.'

Signora Nasteroni was evidently also fooled by his title. They probably assumed he was rich, he thought, as pewter pots containing generous measures of dark red liquid were quickly set out. Well, they wouldn't find out the truth until after he'd had at least one drink.

But he was astonished to find that the price required for this generous measure of restorative fluid was so paltry that he would be able to finance an entire week's guzzling on the few pence he had in his purse.

He took a couple of good swallows and leaned his back against the wall.

'Ah! Hair o' the dog! Never fails.'

He smacked his lips and sucked a stray drop from his moustache. The couple stood before him, smiling broadly, displaying matching sets of discoloured teeth.

'You like my wine, eh?' the swarthy patriarch asked proudly. 'You will wish to come to my winehouse every day.'

He and his wife simultaneously picked up their tankards and regarded him across the rim as they drank.

'And now you must meet my children.' He turned towards the curtain and roared 'Carlito! Alessia!'

The other two members of the Nasteroni family were introduced: their daughter was fat and comely and twenty summers old, her olive skin as smooth as fine porcelain. Her brother was a little older, with dark eyes and unruly black hair.

'I drink to the health of the famous Sir Toby.' he said.

They all drank, and then began politely to enquire about Sir Toby's family. No children? Ah, he would soon be populating the countryside hereabouts with his progeny, they were sure. Why, his wife of but six weeks or so was probably, at this very moment, wondering about the increased size of her belly.

They placed a capacious jug on the table, for which they took a single coin without even looking at it. It was evident that, in their strange country, it was not considered polite to be seen to be interested in money. He refilled his tankard to the brim and the little company got noisier and more good-humoured.

When more customers came in, the two women bustled away to serve them but each time, Sir Toby was gratified to notice, they returned to his table as soon as they were done.

He was the centre of attention. They kept topping up his tankard to overflowing each time he put it down and he became more and more loquacious and grandiloquent. The family's enthusiastic appreciation of his jokes and stories spurred him on to increasing exaggeration of his exploits.

When he told them a fictionalised version of the humiliation of Malvolio, omitting the tragic final outcome, they were sitting in a circle around him. They all stood up and roared with laughter as they clashed their tankards together above his head and drank his health for the umpteenth time.

It was one of the happiest moments of his life.

And the wine continued to flow just as freely in the days that followed. The price was so ridiculously low because their own currency had become almost worthless, and foreign gold now had a specially high value in their country.

From that first day, he and Sir Andrew spent almost every waking hour at the wineseller's and, night after night, wove their way home down the main street singing lustily and receiving more than the occasional swearing reproof from upstairs windows.

And then he took to staying the whole night there. In the early afternoon of the following day Maria, viciously ill-tempered, came down to the winehouse carrying a rolling pin. She strode in, but failed to see her husband, who had slipped to the floor and lay hidden under one of the tables.

She could hear low voices in conversation somewhere beyond the curtain. She walked between the tables, pulled it aside and went through. Beyond, in the vast, shadowy interior of the barn, bulging wineskins hung from the massive oak beams that supported the roof. A few barrels stood along one wall.

The four members of the Nasteroni family were kneeling on the floor doing something to some skins which were laid out there. They all turned as she entered, regarding her with obvious hostility. Her anger evaporated, and she nervously attempted to explain her intrusion.

'I . . . I was looking for my husband.'

They looked at each other and a slow smile spread across the faces of the parents. The signora said:

'The wife of the famous Sir Toby.' It was not a question and their meeting obviously pleased her very much.

Maria gave a little nod. The two men stood up and came towards her, smiling, and looking hard at her. They were strongly built and considerably taller than she was. She felt small and vulnerable. She trembled a little and, as she did so, the rolling pin dropped from her grasp. The sudden noise of it hitting the floor broke the tension and the whole family laughed heartily.

'Come,' said the older man in a big, warm voice, 'we will show you how to make a wineskin the Sicilian way.'

The family set to, chatting desultorily in a language Maria did not understand. They laughed quite a lot, obviously happy in this work that the whole family shared. They laid out two skins, roughly square in shape and the two women sewed them together down the sides to form a bag while the men cut more leather into long strips. These strips were attached to the bottom corners of the bag, so that when the skin was suspended from an iron hook set in one of the low beams, they hung down like broad tapes, two at each corner. The sewn edges were soaked with wine so that the leather would swell and close the tiny holes made by the needles, thus rendering the bag waterproof.

They all sat down to drink while the leather was being soaked. When this skin was filled with wine, they said, they would have to go out to the tannery to buy more leather. They needed two special wineskins now, they said. One small one and one big one. They all laughed at that; a contented, happy family. Maria felt a pang of envy.

Dusk was approaching by this time. The men brought a barrel over to the new wineskin and its contents were carefully poured into the skin, which bulged and stretched as it filled. The women held it steady, checking constantly for any sign of a leak.

As they put down the half-empty barrel, Alessia explained how the strips of leather must now be quickly bound around the full skin to prevent the weight of the wine from causing the leather to stretch too much and split. Each of the four now took one strip and began binding it diagonally across and round the wineskin, to form a lattice pattern. Tightly laced like this, the skin was now firm and strong; diamond-shaped bulges showed how the wet leather had stretched. The top was securely bound and the ends tied with a special knot.

They stood back to admire their handiwork. Signor Nasteroni must now go to see the tanner, while the women bustled off to wash tankards and prepare for the evening's work. A significant look passed between the young man and his mother before she passed out of sight through the curtain.

Maria and Carlito were left alone.

He went across and picked up the rolling pin she had dropped earlier. Standing in front of her, he held it between thumb and forefinger, dangling it before her eyes. He evidently found their situation very amusing.

'Is it a weapon, or did you come to cook for me?' His smile mocked her; his teeth looked surprisingly white in the gathering gloom. He was standing very close to her and she could smell the sweat on him.

'Maria!' He pronounced her name as though tasting it, rolling the 'r' along his tongue: 'Ma-ri-a.' He whispered it this time. 'She has an Italian name. Did she come to find an Italian lover?' His voice was soft, but far from gentle. There was a quiet menace in it that excited her. He tossed the object away into the shadows.

She swallowed hard and tried to speak but no sound came out. His dark eyes seemed to strip her naked. The nearness of his body was frightening, but she did not want to run away.

'Carlito has a weapon also.' He placed his palm against the top of his chest, right in front of her face and moved it slowly down the front of his body. She felt mesmerized, forced to follow it with her eyes, down, down to his groin, then up again to his belt to lift out a dagger with a long, slim blade.

'Does Maria know what this is?' Their bodies were so close now that her breasts were almost touching his midriff, a few inches above his waist. His voice was still little more than a whisper. 'It's a stiletto.'

He held it no more than two inches from her face, chuckling quietly. The blade glinted in the dim light.

'And does she know what I'm going to do with it?' He took her hand and held it as, slowly and precisely, he slit the sleeve of her dress right up to the shoulder. The cloth gave way as though melted by the keenness of the knife's edge. Then he raised her arm, exposing the little patch of dark hair in her armpit. As the blade touched her skin a delicious tremor of fear jolted through her.

With the same slow deliberation, he shaved the soft bush away in one delicious movement. The sound it made was like the throaty hiss of a venomous snake.

'You know what we are going to do?'

'N . . .' Trembling and breathless, she still could hardly speak. She gave a little shake of her head.

'No?' His dark, dangerous eyes held hers captive.

He placed the point of the stiletto under the lowest button of her bodice.

'For a Sicilian, it is an art. First there is the promise.' He gave a little jerk and the button flicked up in an arc over his head to land with a tiny skittering sound several feet behind him. The point moved up to the next button.

'Then there is the enticement.' The second small button followed the first.

'Then the play.' A third button soared away from her.

'Then the revelation.' Another button.

'And then, of course . . .' When he flicked the top button away her bodice fell open, baring her bosom. He clamped the blade between his teeth and inserted both his hands, caressing the outer curve of her breasts with his palms while his thumbs teased her nipples. Her knees turned to water and his hands moved expertly under her arms to support her.

Lifting her easily, he carried her like a baby over to a large bed of hay in the corner.

Maria lay now holding the letter against her face. She ran its words through in her mind. '*Your Carlito wants you tonight. Our time is now. Come to me at midnight.*'

The bell had chimed the eleventh hour long ago. It must be time, surely. The letter had dropped in at her window soon after darkness fell, just as she had lit the candle. Since that moment she had waited in a fever of excitement. Her body felt like a ripe fruit longing to be plucked. Her skin seemed to have become so sensitive that she could not bear to have her clothes on. She wanted only the touch of *his* hands. She had stood naked, holding the letter between her breasts, trembling with longing. Then she had become a little chilled and got into bed.

But what did that special, secret part of the letter mean?

'*Remember R*' it said.

And then followed that special code that signified to her the intense process of his lovemaking.

First there must be the promise
Then must come the enticement
Then the play
Then the revelation
And then . . .
Come tonight and know it all

The hours they had spent on that bed of hay were a long waking dream of sensual delight to her. She could not think of one fragment of it leading to another in preordained steps.

And what was R? Probably some strange-sounding Sicilian word she had never heard spoken, she supposed. But what could the last mystery be? Could he know of more carnal pleasures than she? Of course he could. He had proved that already. Her whole body shook in anticipation of sensual delights as yet untasted.

She dressed herself with trembling hands, tucked the precious letter lovingly into her cleavage and stole quietly down the stairs and out into the chill night air.

Down the street she ran, keeping to the darkest of the moonshadows as the bell sounded twelve.

Carlito was waiting at the small rear door of the barn. He took her hand and pulled her inside.

'She is here,' he called loudly. In the centre of the candlelit interior, was a table at which sat Sir Toby and Sir Andrew surrounded by the Nasteroni family. A fire was burning in the hearth, but all the wineskins and barrels had been removed and so had the long curtain. The place was virtually empty.

Her husband looked mildly surprised to see her, but he seemed far less drunk than she would have expected at this time of night.

'Come and drink with us,' shouted the fat matriarch cordially.

Maria was too surprised to do anything but comply. Carlito was directly behind her, forcing her forward towards the group. A cup of the rich, red wine was placed in her hand and she drank a deep draft to steady herself.

Giancarlo Nasteroni addressed Sir Andrew.

'Now, sir, it is time you paid the true price for my wine.' All cordiality had vanished from his manner: there was menace in it now. 'I know that this fat fool cannot pay me.'

Sir Andrew looked puzzled and stood up unsteadily, facing him.

'I don't think . . .' He got no further. With sudden appalling violence, the Sicilian spun him on his heels and cut his throat with one brutal slash, sending a bloody fountain gushing out across the floor.

Maria tried to scream, but Carlito's hand covered her mouth and she was held fast. She watched in horror as the foppishly dressed body crumpled to the floor, gurgling and twitching in a welter of gore, and his murderer calmly cut the purse from his belt.

Sir Toby leapt to his feet, but he too was grabbed and held silent. The women picked up two ready-prepared wineskins, one small one and one big one, and the struggling pair were thrust inside them. The leather strips were bound in criss-cross pattern and tied tightly round their throats, so that they were unable to make a sound and struggled for every breath. They were then suspended from the iron hooks.

The family stood back respectfully as the patriarch called out, 'You can reveal yourself now, cousin.'

Maria saw a thin man in a hooded cloak enter at the far end of the room. He held a long knobbed cane almost as tall as himself and he leaned heavily on it as he limped painfully down the length of the barn towards them.

He stood for several long minutes in a near-crouching posture in front of them, using the cane almost as a crutch. She could hear the heavy rasping of his breath.

Then he drew back the hood and she saw that it was Malvolio.

But it was a Malvolio drastically altered. A livid scar disfigured his face, running down his forehead and then diagonally across the empty pit where once his left eye had been. Another scar, seeping horribly, left his mouth sagging open at one side, revealing broken teeth.

'Yes,' he hissed bitterly, 'you thought me dead and gone from your disgusting lives. But I survived the plunge from the clifftop. The pain itself made me want to live long enough to share with you the torment you had visited on me.

'It was I who sent the message from Caspia telling of the discovery of my broken body. But I did not say there was no life left in it. I let you assume that.'

He hobbled back and forth before them, then stood still again.

'I am Nasteroni on my mother's side,' he went on, 'and for a Sicilian, revenge is an artform. We like to do it with style.

'First there is the promise. I made this to you in plain terms on the day you offended me. "I shall be revenged on the whole pack of you,"' I said for all to hear.

'Then must come the enticement. You must fall into our hands and put yourself at our disposal willingly, which you have done. Then there is the play, what we sometimes call the sting. And after this the revelation, for it is only fitting that you should know the author of your demise. And then, of course, must come death, for if you take away my good name you do something that makes me a pauper, yet enriches you not a jot. It is the meanest of all crimes.

'The last drink you were given contained a potion that will cause a rictus in the features which will make your teeth clamp tightly together and your lips to shrink back in a ghastly grimace. The wineskins in which you are encased are wet, but in this warmth they will soon dry and in doing so, will shrink and throttle you.

'Tomorrow is the first day of April; the feast of all fools. I have engineered that the Lady Olivia shall be the one to discover you. I shall be interested to know how she reacts when she sees you before her.

'Smiling.'

'And cross-gartered right up to your necks.'

THE DUKE OF DARK CORNERS

Gail-Nina Anderson

Measure for Measure *(1604) is a rather dark comedy and one where you wish Shakespeare had taken more time to explore the situations he develops rather than wrapping it up all rather quickly with elements of farce. The Duke of Vienna has left his puritanical deputy, Angelo, in charge. Although Angelo outlaws treachery he finds himself victim to his own lust when he encounters Isabella, a novice in a convent, and sister of Claudio, whom Angelo has imprisoned. Needless to say no one likes Angelo, who continues to act like a tyrant until the Duke returns. Although condemned to death he is spared. But what happens after the play ends? Read on . . .*

The Duke of Vienna sighed deeply. He was better on calculation than spontaneity, and unforeseen circumstances left him feeling uncomfortably twitchy. His much-vaunted wisdom derived from an ability to weigh up situations and predict outcomes, preferably from a safe distance, and at the moment there was no distance at all between his princely person and something decidedly unpleasant in the flower-bed.

At his side the gardener coughed discreetly. If he was waiting for words of incisive command, thought the duke, then he might as well wander off and mulch a fruit-tree or two, since what he wanted at the moment was time alone to collect his thoughts.

'How long has he been like this?' he heard his own voice saying, proving that the habit of authority is a hard one to break.

'He came out here to take the air just after breaking his fast, your Honour. An hour or so ago. Her ladyship sent a page to remind him of your visit, and the boy discovered him dead. We left him as he was found, thinking you'd want to . . .'

The voice trailed off and the Duke finished the sentence himself. 'Inspect the body?'

In truth it was the last thing he wanted to do. When he awoke that morning his utmost desire had been to stay in bed beside his sleek young Duchess, and he heartily wished he'd done so. But there were affairs of state to discuss, and he had already arranged this semi-official visit to Angelo, his semi-official advisor. And now the man lay dead in front of him.

Concerning that fact, at least, there could be no doubt. The rictus of sudden death was all too apparent on the familiar features at his feet, and it was difficult to entertain the hope that this had been a natural occurrence. The circumstances didn't have the tact to resemble the approved demise of a court official, found worn out to parchment pallor amongst his papers, like old Escalus, or popping off in the middle of a banquet, hand clutched to heart, from a surfeit of rich food and richer wines.

Angelo had just been approaching the cool middle of life, when men of his spare, dry constitution look fit to go on forever. And out here in the scented spring air of the garden wasn't the place for sudden death. Clearly something had gone disastrously wrong – one glance at the suffused blackness of the corpse revealed that – and he was expected to wave a staff of office and sort out the mess. He sighed again. He knew his enemies viewed him as calculating, devious and downright Machiavellian, but right now he simply felt tired.

'Could be bees, your Eminence,' said the grubby little man by his side, whose attitude of awe-struck respect was rapidly deteriorating into an unwelcome camaraderie. 'Some folks take most peculiar to a bee-sting, and puff up like a bladder filled with . . .'

The Duke swallowed hard on the return of his breakfast and clutched at the proffered straw.

'Have you noticed any bees around this flower-bed?'

'Remarkable few for the time of year – and of course he isn't so much puffed, now I look at him, as strangulated. I disremember one time when I assisted the hang-man to string up a friend of mine, and the minute the rope tightened he went just such a colour as Lord Angelo there.'

The Duke felt a spasm of pure annoyance threaten his composure. No wonder the puny little wretch didn't look like a gardener – he was more like a pimp, a cut-purse or a tapster from the stews. This was obviously one of Angelo's many lame ducks, a down-and-out plucked from the vice-ridden back alleys of Vienna and given honest work in the large, bustling household he had gathered around him. Publicly bound to applaud such charitable gestures, the Duke never the less had a basic distrust of all low-life types, with their rabbiting tongues and lack of decorum. That Angelo tolerated and nurtured them was, he considered, an act of penitence out of all proportion to the man's own, single, slip from grace.

And there was the rub, of course, and the nub too. That Angelo insisted on living (admittedly well-lapped in luxury) on the outskirts of the city, that he never showed his face at Court, that he would proffer his valuable advice on policy and protocol in a private capacity only, directly into the Duke's ear, were all the results of that one wretched misadventure the previous year. Pray God that his death wasn't another thread in the same sticky web.

'Of course, your Honour, if bees aren't in consideration then we hang fire, as you might say, between an Act of God and an act of man. There's many a death carries the wrong label, but what Justice loses, Discretion may win, begging your Grace's wisdom. No bees, but there are the stings of enemies, and he must still have plenty of those since . . .'

His mouth was open to continue, and only a strong sense of his own dignity prevented the Duke from clapping his hand across it to enforce silence.

'Enough, my man. That's all forgotten.'

'No it's not.'

'Officially the matter is closed.'

'Closed's not forgotten. Best story in years, a tale for a winter's night in a cosy tavern. What greasy monk could invent a better one? Jack-in-office (begging your Lordship's pardon) gets his comeuppance. Blackmail, lechery and a pretty nun to boot.'

The fellow had been leaning on his spade, gossiping conspiratorially as he might have spoken to his own equal in tavern or brothel, but at these words the Duke's face changed to such a mask of anger that the little man straightened up automatically. Assuming a more respectful posture he began to edge away, biting his bubbling tongue. The nun shouldn't have been mentioned, though honestly she was the best bit of the story.

'Enough speculation,' barked the Duke, and turned to the anxious attendants waiting at a discreet distance behind him.

'You may carry Lord Angelo into the chapel and let the physician examine him before the women lay him out. This is a sad mishap, but the ways of mortality are many and a simple explanation will doubtless be found. Meanwhile I must proffer condolences to his wife.'

Widow, he corrected himself under his breath. The Lady Mariana had wasted her youth and beauty in fruitless virginity, waiting for Angelo the reluctant fiancé to finally claim her. Last year had precipitated her into longed-for wifehood and now she was already a widow. He hoped her calm, phlegmatic temperament and famed patience would support her through this new tragedy, because quite frankly, an hysterical woman was all he needed right now.

Leaving a knot of activity round the corpse, the Duke strode along well-tended paths back to the Grange. It was, of course, partly his own fault. A twelve-month ago, without any previous test of the man's mettle, he had left Angelo in charge of the entire city, trusting to his icy logic to enforce some harsh legislation. The intention was to stamp out vice, crime and all moral laxity. With hindsight, of course, it was simply a recipe for disaster. Angelo had laid about him with an even-handed justice which was as impolitic as it was morally admirable. Closing down brothels was one thing, but enforcing the death penalty for a little aristocratic dalliance was entirely another. When young Claudio had been condemned for fornication, even the pimps and whores being dragged to gaol had stood aghast that he should share their fate. And when Claudio's sister Isabella, a novice nun of unimpeachable purity (the Duke ran the attractive phrase through his mind) had pleaded for her brother's life, Angelo the puritan had so far forgotten himself as to try and debauch the maid.

This was the worst sin of all for one in authority – public harshness and private indulgence. No, the Duke corrected himself, the worst sin was being found out. But he had had to uncover Angelo's lapse, in order to set all right. Claudio was reprieved, Angelo was forgiven, and the Duke was back at the pinnacle of Machiavellian probity. Then there were the happy endings, to bring a glow to the hearts of an adoring populace. (Damn that gardener!) Claudio married his fecund, penitent mistress, the Duke raised the peerless Isabella from cloister to court by making her his Duchess, and Angelo had been safely wedded to patient, long-suffering Mariana.

It had seemed so appropriate, to pluck this quiet, shadowy woman out from her tedious years of vigil in the Grange, from the endless hours of pious longing and equally pious embroidery, and to finally match her to Angelo. And now the wretched man . . . oh, it didn't bear thinking about. Pray God that Mariana could control her grief, that an easy explanation could be found, and most of all that any fresh scandal could be firmly quashed.

The Duke was in the process of making a mental note to tell Angelo, charity or no charity, to dismiss his garrulous gardener at once in the interests of discretion, before he recollected that his counsellor was now beyond discretion and authority alike. Such admirable traits were all too vulnerable, and only vile rumour seemed to go on unchecked.

As he entered Angelo and Mariana's ancient, stone-built house the Duke was struck, not for the first time, by its air of comfort and plenty. Who would have thought that on marriage, the dour and self-denying Angelo would have taken such pleasure in his domestic circumstances? On his rather public retirement from public life the man had eagerly embraced the role of Lord of the Manor, complete with loyal (if slightly tarnished) servants, gentle wife, tapestried chambers, well-nurtured gardens and an enviable atmosphere of orderly well-being. And from here he had continued, in the most discreet manner possible, to advise his ruler and to accept the informal advocacy of anyone needing a word spoken in the right place. He had adapted to such politic indirectness in the same spirit as he had taken to home pleasures and well-upholstered surroundings, though in the midst of all he had always looked the puritan still.

The Duke could envisage him now, upright and black-clad, smiling his thin smile, expounding some abstruse (but always apposite) piece of legal lore, yet letting his thin fingers stray the while over a jewelled casket or brocaded cushion. The senses, held so long in check, had definitely been awakened. Pray God there was no embarrassing lapse waiting to be uncovered.

At the entrance to the long gallery a gaggle of serving women, some already red-eyed with weeping, made way for him with a flurry of curtseys. It was easy to spot those older ones, still clad in Mariana's preferred livery of grey, whose service pre-dated her marriage and the transformation of the dusty, neglected house of enforced virginity into the generous marital home. Two or three younger women, though still dressed with a neatness becoming to their station, were obviously later additions. One in particular, despite tightly braided hair and decorous downward glance, looked fit to be a beauty. The Duke only became aware he was staring at her when she raised her eyes to meet his and he noticed the rosy blush that mantled her cheeks. Given Angelo's new-found social conscience, he mused, this slip of Eve's flesh was as likely to be a reformed whore as a modest maiden, and he groaned inwardly as he brushed past her. Angelo had proven once that man's natural inclination to sin will burst through any plastering of virtue, and now the possible implications were too messy to contemplate. A less dutiful wife than Mariana . . .

By now he had been announced at the door to her private chamber, and felt himself growing tongue-tied with anticipation. One glance, however, told him that his fears were unfounded. Mariana, clad in brocades rich in texture but still of her habitual, self-effacing grey in colour, had clearly been weeping, but greeted him with quiet dignity.

'So soon a widow, my Lord, so briefly a wife. You have seen the body?'

The Duke nodded, relieved to let her take charge. Even so, the directness of her next comment took him by surprise.

'Bees, the gardener surmises, and certainly there were many buzzing around when last I spoke to my husband in the garden. When I spoke to him for the last time.'

She sank gracefully onto the padded settle, and for the first time the Duke noticed her page, crouched at her feet in an attitude of sympathetic misery. The boy, notable equally for his russet curls and angelic voice, had been a comfort through the dull hours of Mariana's empty betrothal, and was now almost too old to be a lady's page. His discovery of the body must have distressed him, but the Duke was surprised to note just how dark were the shadows around the lad's eyes. His full lips carried a look of bruised innocence far more disconcerting than mere tears, and there was a new look of self-consciousness to his beauty.

'He had become very, very close to my husband,' said Mariana, stroking his hair with a gesture of maternal fondness as the page suppressed a sob.

Simultaneously, the Duke suppressed an idea too black to be entertained.

'Perhaps a word in private?'

At a nod from Mariana the boy scuttled away, clearly relieved to be freed from the Ducal gaze. With the automatic gesture of ingrained habit, Mariana picked up the length of half-embroidered silk at which she had been stitching. It was black, but lavishly relieved with a cross and lilies worked in tones of dull silver. Even as it attracted her visitor's attention, she crumpled it between slender white palms and put it to one side.

'I meant it for a chasuble, suitable for a funeral mass or times of mourning. I little knew how seemly that would come to seem.'

The Duke found himself reaching across to pat her hand, in the best paternal gesture he could manage. At close quarters her face looked pinched and meagre. Had she ever been beautiful, he wondered? And how pleased had Angelo been to take her for his wife? The cool tones of her voice brought him back to the matter in hand.

'There are no problems, I assume? I may arrange the funeral?'

A long pause.

'The bees?'

The Duke found himself momentarily lost. Should he let it go? Condone a verdict of natural death? As if to fill the awkward pause he let his gaze stray round the room. There was ample evidence on the cushions and fire-screen of Mariana's eternal embroidery, but the large tapestries covering the wall betokened professional manufacture and looked to be French. There were vases of fine Venetian glass on the table, and from a perch in the corner a tiny monkey chattered incongruously. Mariana smiled wanly towards this exotic pet, then intercepted the Duke's gaze.

'Presents, from those in need of advice, or advancement, or a personal audience with your Grace. My husband's influence at Court seemed only to grow after he had quitted the place. A man who knew everything but no longer sought to advance his own career. So there were many gifts, and they amused him. He had developed a taste for fine things.'

Even as the word 'bribes' entered his mind, the Duke firmly rejected it. Every courtier accepted offerings of this kind when his star was in the ascendant, or handed them out where they would do most good when he had a suit to advance or a cause to plead.

Something in the tone of Mariana's voice, however, suggested that the subject suddenly carried more than conversational interest. Without thinking, the Duke lowered his own speech into tones of well-practised concern.

'My dear – surely you harbour no suspicions?'

'Rich gifts wax poor when givers wax unkind,' she quoted, as though she hoped for a moment that the proverb would answer his question. 'I suppose that the gifts *were* all from friends, but it's so easy to make enemies. One false step.'

The Duke's thoughts wandered unbidden to the page's bruised eyelids, darkened with experience, but his attention snapped back with the lady's next words, hesitantly though they were uttered.

'Only this morning there were gloves, fine perfumed Italian gloves sent from the Court. He put them on at once, but the civet made his hands itch.'

She was looking hard into his face now, with an uncharacteristic directness, and despite a sinking sensation deep in his stomach, he couldn't avoid taking up her challenge.

'A pretty conceit, but he always did have sensitive skin. Who would have sent such a costly toy?'

Her eyes were already cast down again, and for the first time during the interview, she looked to be on the verge of weeping.

'The gift was anonymous, but my lord laughed when it arrived and spoke almost gaily of an old score being amicably settled. He was so light-hearted so very short a time ago.'

The tears began in earnest now, and the Duke had no qualms about leaving the grieving widow to the ministrations of her women. He needed to think, to bring into play his renowned caution and (however reluctantly) to view the body. As he left the main house and walked along the path to the adjacent private chapel, he noted the unappealing gardener already busy re-ordering the flower-bed where Angelo had died.

The page knelt beside him, gathering up fallen blooms. One suspicion was as bad as another, and he somehow doubted that a sight of the body would bring any peace of mind.

Inside the dimly lighted chapel the air struck chill. Angelo, already washed, was being decently shrouded in fine linen, and the Duke was pleased to note the presence of the household physician.

'A sorry, sorry business, your Grace. I never attended a sadder. So swiftly death can strike, even in man's prime.'

The Duke moved to the makeshift bier and, trying to suppress a strong natural repugnance, twitched gingerly at the fabric covering his councillor's face. The skin was still blotched, the complexion horribly dark.

'Were there any . . . abrasions on the body?'

'Oh no, my Lord, nothing like a wound. His fingers are red,' (the doctor indicated Angelo's hands, crossed on his chest) 'but that's from inflammation, not blood spilled.'

A moment's respectful silence hung heavy in the air, before the doctor took his courage in his hands and spoke again.

'In truth, sir, I think he choked, though there was no food in his mouth. Something seems to have swelled inside, and the air passages contracted. I've seen such effects before, coming on for no good reason and catching a man unawares. A violent apoplexy, perhaps?'

The question was a pure formality. A useful fiction, no doubt, but nothing less apoplectic than Angelo's spare frame and measured manner could be imagined, and he had by all accounts been quietly relaxed on the morning of his death.

Noting the Duke's discomfiture, the doctor stepped forward with a sideways glance to check that no-one was within hearing distance, and cleared his throat nervously.

'Your Grace, some poisons might do this to a man, swifter than the words that describe them. There are subtle concoctions brewed in Italy with the which, one hears, all the machinations of the Papal Court are now thoroughly laced. Men there carry amethysts with them, to purify their wine and neutralise all noxious poisons . . .'

This so closely echoed the Duke's own thoughts that he started involuntarily, frightening the doctor out of his conspiratorial attitude. They looked at each other across Angelo's corpse. The silence was like lead.

'Bees?'

A long glance, and the decision had been taken.

'A text-book case, your Grace, once the suggestion has been made. All the ancient authors aver that while to most of humanity a bee-sting is no more than a pin prick on a sunny day, to some poor souls it means instant death. The poison enters their system, thickens the blood, and chokes the vital passages whereby life is sustained. It would have been extremely quick.'

'A tragedy none the less. The city can ill bear such a loss.'

The doctor nodded in agreement, and again covered Angelo's face. There was no need to say more. Those used to policy know that when a verdict has become official, all clues will inevitably support it, until any other explanation becomes unthinkable. Angelo disturbing the insects as he reached to touch a flower, his attempts to brush them away and the stings on his hands, inflaming at once to furious redness – all this was now as a picture painted, fixed and visible in the mind's eye.

Perhaps he had sucked at his burning fingers, then clasped at his own throat as it swelled from inside? Not a pretty scene, but a mercifully harmless one. Except, of course, for Angelo.

Relieved as ever that loose ends could be so neatly tied, the Duke permitted himself the luxury of a swift exit. There were affairs of state to see to, and Mariana's household would want to be fully occupied with funeral arrangements. Besides, beyond a formal, condolent farewell to his hostess, his task here was finished.

Mariana, calm again, rose from her embroidery to greet him. He noticed a skein of gold thread already being stitched onto the sombre silk, and its yellow glow against the black reminded him of the bees, now confirmed to be notably early and unfortunately active this year. It was only as she rustled into a curtsey of farewell that he noticed too a thickening of her waist, a new fullness of her slight figure. So in one way, despite all that had happened, the marriage had been a success. It was well. A babe would make her widowhood sweeter by far more than her comfortless virginal vigil could ever have been.

As soon as the Duke had gone, Mariana sat down again, leaning back gratefully onto the plump cushions. No sense in tiring herself on this difficult day, with the funeral still to oversee. All had gone better than she had hoped, and she permitted herself a silent smile. Too soon yet for laughter, music and all the elegant indulgence that her position would assure her, but she could afford to wait. She'd had so many years of practice. Besides, she had always accepted that there would be some months in solemn black to endure, enlivened though they would be by this satisfying swelling of her belly.

Through the casement she could see her page, still looking dazed by the morning's events. A great shame, but she thought the boy was losing his looks as he entered manhood. He, at least, would be as pleased as she that Angelo was dead, though if he continued to look troubled by unwelcome knowledge . . . well, a small sacrifice might have to be made in the cause of security.

Without thinking, she resumed her needlework. The years of solitude, pacing dingy corridors just to keep her feet moving, stitching endlessly just to give her hands employment, would not pass away all at once. Today had seen at last, however, the fulfillment of dark, secret vows uttered so long ago within the corrosive bitterness of her own soul, and she felt strangely calm. This taking of control was a good thing. And she smiled again at the memory of her own inventiveness. As if her lamented lord's own half-dark, half-light life hadn't provided enough bewildering false clues, the matter of the gloves had been a stroke of pure inspiration on her part. So lucky she had noticed the fine pair on the Duke's own hands and recollected that they had once been mentioned as a courtly gift from his brother-in-law Claudio, a man whose dislike of Angelo had never been disguised. No wonder the Duke had grabbed with such unseemly haste at the first safely inoffensive cause of death that could be conjured up.

Looking down at the length of rich fabric in her lap, she clucked with annoyance. The sunburst of gold had never been part of the design, but she had begun stitching it as soon as she noticed the tell-tale spots of bright orange pollen staining the black silk, her fingers moving with feverish haste to cover the marks. She should never have carried it into the garden with her when she dusted Angelo's favourite blossoms with the delicate Italian poison she had taken such pains to procure. She knew that Angelo would have to touch, to stroke, to bury his face in the perfumed petals like a bee intoxicated with honey-promising sweetness.

Permitting herself a sigh for her spoiled needlework, she wondered whether the panel might yet be adapted instead into an altar-cloth for her chapel. Not that she planned to spend as much time there as hitherto. Letting the fabric fall, she ran her fingertips over the jewel-encrusted casket that held her silks, and made a soft cooing noise to set the monkey chattering in response. Pretty beast, pretty things, so much to enjoy. She clasped her long, white hands appreciatively round the fullness of her stomach. Mother-to-be, with a rich household all her own. So many years as Angelo's abandoned fiancée, wasting youth and beauty in hopeless tears. She had always known that one day she would be Angelo's wife, but for some considerable time now it had seemed to her that to be Angelo's widow would be best of all.

LOVE'S LABOUR'S DISCOVER'D

Phyllis Ann Karr

Love's Labour's Lost *(c.1594) is a comedy based on a simple but rather absurd premise. Ferdinand, King of Navarre, and his lords Berowne, Dumain and Longaville, have banned women from entering the court, though find themselves in something of a pickle when the King of France's daughter arrives with an all-female embassy. The Princess has arrived to resolve the position regarding Aquitaine, which was granted to Navarre as surety against a loan that the King of France received from Navarre to help him finance his wars. France claims to have repaid half the loan but Ferdinand knows nothing about it. The resolution of this issue is overlooked in the rest of the play, but not so in the following story.*

What a rage Don Adriano flew into, the day he saw sweet Jaquenetta strolling in the king's park with Costard the clown! Anyone would have thought my fat old master some fighting cock cheated of his hopes for a hen and dashed with a bowl of slops besides – for Don Adriano had eyes for Jaquenetta himself, and all the world, or as much of it as had ever met him, called Costard a fool. Though all the world, and I along with it, had been fooled in that, perhaps by Costard's great size combined with his soft bearing. For we expect giants to be fierce and, when they are not, suspect them of silliness instead.

Yet at the time, sharing the world's opinion, I twitted my raging old knight, 'If the silly hen insists on a stroll with the capon, why should not the gallant cock cast about elsewhere?'

'Capon?' cried my master. 'Who dost thou call "capon?" Nay – no arguments now – run and fetch me the constable to apprehend those two! Quickly, boy! Make haste!'

'As swift as lead, sir!' I replied, choosing not the best moment to tease him, for he turned purple and, seizing me by both my arms, gritted into my face,' As swift as lead, sirrah! AS SWIFT AS LEAD?'

'As swift as lead fired from a gun, master!' I explained, and so won a laugh – not a large one, because of his anger over Jaquenetta – and my freedom to run his errand for him.

What law had sweet Jaquenetta broken with Costard? Why, simply to be seen within a mile of the king's court. Jaquenetta was female, as all the countryside had good cause to know, and our young King Ferdinand had made up his royal mind to inaugurate his reign with three years' hard study, as if thereby he could make of himself a second Solomon; and, during these three years, no woman was to come within a mile of him and his chosen fellow students, lest she distract them from their deep and noble scholarship. Indeed, I had thought on first hearing the proclamation, the monarch that would attempt to rule under such self-imposed conditions sorely needed all the wisdom he could borrow from any source; but when I observed as much to my master, Don Adriano had bade me be still, for he himself was in some loose measure associated with the king's oath . . . although I'd wager his conscience would not have proved so nice had he himself been the man strolling with Jaquenetta in the king's park! Since Don Adriano's connection with the royal court of Navarre was by long standing rather than birth, he might even have found some exemption through which to wriggle his bulk by dint of his Spanish blood.

When I returned with old Antony Dull the constable, we found my master already recording the offence in an angry epistle, which he stayed to finish even while waving Dull on to arrest the offenders. In good-natured regard of Dull's doddering years, the guilty pair permitted themselves to be apprehended, even though Costard could have pushed him down with one finger and Jaquenetta skipped away like a squirrel from a tortoise.

Jabbing the rolled and sealed letter in Costard's direction, my master ordered the constable, 'Deliver me this base minnow – this small unlettered soul – to His Grace King Ferdinand, along with this missive detailing in full his obscene and preposterous crime. As for the weaker vessel, I will guard her here myself.'

'Please you, sir,' said Jaquenetta, 'send me along with them to see the king.'

'Sweet child of our grandmother Eve,' Don Adriano replied, 'they have declared as penalty for any female who comes within a mile of court, that she shall lose her tongue! Abide here in my keeping, and I promise you I will prevent it from coming to that.'

So she abided, but poutingly; and she disappeared into Don Adriano's house as soon as she could find the excuse, leaving my master alone with me beneath the trees.

'What sign is it, boy, when a man of great spirit waxes melancholy? For by this you may know the greatness of my spirit: that I scorn to sigh,' said my master, gazing after Jaquenetta with a sigh that the bellows might envy. 'Comfort me, tadpole,' he went on. 'What great men have been in love?'

'Hercules, master,' I supplied him. 'And Samson, who carried the town gates on his back like a porter. And Sir Hector the champion of Troy.'

'Hector!' Don Adriano belched forth another lusty sigh. 'Ah, the sweet war-man, and all his great deeds done for love of his wife and tiny son.'

'Andromache, as she was called,' said I. 'And their child, I think I have heard, was named poor Astyanax, that the Greeks slew in sacrifice.'

'O, well-educated infant!' Don Adriano fondled my head as if forgetting that I was no 'canine,' as he often called hounds and dogs. I did not like it, but I endured it for the sake of the entertaining scraps I might pick up from his rich table of melancholic reminiscence. After a moment, he resumed, 'Sweet boy, is there not a ballad concerning a king and a beggar?'

'The world was surely guilty of such a ballad,' I prompted him, 'some years ago.'

'Some years ago,' he repeated slowly. 'When we were still in our green salad days . . . and yet not so very many years ago, for all that. It was at the Duke Alençon's brave castle . . . Two beauteous heirs had His Grace of Alençon. Two sweet blossoms sprung from the same gallant stock. The Lady Katharine still barely more than a bud, but Elinor her sister – ah, the Lady Elinor was a flower full-blown! Yet she died, sweet lady! Died for love, that same month thy own father, my poor juvenile, and I passed there with certain members of the late king's court, His present Majesty's sire . . . All, all three are dead and rotten – good King Charles of Navarre, the brave Lord Rousillon, and Elinor the fair sweet heir of Alençon. When they breathed, they were brave souls! . . . Boy, sing me some sad song.'

So I learned no more at that time, but sang him songs and riddled him riddles until Constable Dull returned with his hand on what passed for Costard's collar.

'Sir,' the constable addressed my master, 'the king's pleasure is that you keep this offender safe, allow him no sport, and he must fast three days a week. As for the female offender – where is she? – I am to keep her at the lodge, where she will serve as dairy-woman.'

I skipped inside to fetch her with the happy news that, whether because of something my master had put into his letter or because, when faced with the fact, the king's own merciful good sense had won out, she was not to lose her tongue after all, but only trade Don Adriano's company for that of His Majesty's milk-cows, an exchange that seemed to please her well. 'Master Moth,' she confided to me, 'I have some reason to believe it was that longface my Lord Longaville who devised that bloody penalty, for the simple frightening of us "frail vessels," and when it came to it, the others could not be so fierce. I am sure I owe Don Adriano nothing in the matter.'

It was clear that he would have had her believe otherwise, by the mooncalf gaze he cast on her as we emerged from the house. 'Maid,' he began, which made me snicker into my hand.

'Man,' she threw back at him, cool as any cucumber.

'I will visit thee at the lodge.'

'It's a short walk.' Her tone implied that she wished otherwise.

'I know where it is situated.'

'Lord, how wise you are!'

'I will tell thee wonders,' he went on, edging close enough to snuffle at her in an undertone, 'I love thee.'

But at this point old Dull noticed things were not going as strictly as they ought, and laid his hand to her arm, demanding, 'Jaquenetta, come!' She looked as happy to make her escape with the constable, as my master looked woeful to see her go.

That grief Don Adriano vented as wrath on Costard, whose sin had been the very one my master would have wished to indulge. 'Villain!' cried he. 'Thou shalt be heavily punished.'

'I am bound and beholding to you, then,' Costard replied, 'more closely than your liegemen, since they are but lightly rewarded.'

This was the first glimpse I had ever had of the wit that underlay the mild giant's supposed foolishness. For the time, however, I simply obeyed my master's command to take the transgressor and lock him up, to fast in prison.

Accepting his sentence with the comment, 'I thank God I have as little patience as another man,' Costard allowed me to lead him away as meekly as if he could not have overpowered me had he so chosen. As I was about to shut the door on his cell, he said to me, 'Lad, how much do you understand of the ladies?'

'I have watched bulls with cows, clown,' I made answer, 'cocks with hens, and stallions with mares.'

'And sweet Jaquenetta? How much do you know of her?'

'That she deserves to be whipped, if tattling tongues speak truth. And yet, for all of that, she surely deserves a better love than my master.'

The prisoner put his hand on the door to prevent my closing it just yet. 'How deep, lad, runs your loyalty to Don Adriano?'

'My father Rousillon and he were cronies in the old king's service, once upon a time, and I think for no other reason than that Don Adriano took me into his service. But for all that' – here I winked – 'the old fool rewards me as befits my size: but lightly.'

Costard appeared to reach a decision, for he nodded gravely. 'Some might say that, good Moth, and yet worth is not measured by size alone. When you grow up to manhood, you will learn that our Jaquenetta is what kindlier tongues prefer to call a generous girl. But such generous creatures run deep risks when they encounter any man with whom they would prefer not to come to it, for if they should cry rape, who would believe them? Moth, she is two months on her way by your master.'

'Then where lies her problem?' I asked. 'Don Adriano wishes nothing better than to marry her.'

'And therein lies her problem! Sweet handful of wit, have not you yourself just now remarked that she deserves a better mate?'

I thought it over, and saw his point. 'Well, what would you have me do about it?'

'Be my eyes and ears in the world outside, good Moth. For the moment, we can only wait and watch what opportunities Fate may unfold for us.'

'That I can do willingly enough! And, to begin, let me spy on Her Grace the Princess of France and watch what happens when she and her ladies come up against our King Ferdinand and his pretty oath!'

Costard chuckled, even as I turned the key upon his prison door, 'Would I were there to watch it with you!'

I was doing nothing for him that I would not have done for myself. Her French Grace's visit on some delicate errand of diplomacy had already been planned before the young king and his closest courtiers had forgotten it in devising their oath, and not for more money than my master had ever gambled away in his worst night would I have missed seeing how they compromised the letter of their vow with the strict necessity of kingly duty.

By good chance, I had barely left the environs of the royal park before I met a stranger striding along: a tallish man of middle years and jaunty attitude, dressed in the height of French fashion and whistling some light French air. 'Garçon!' he cried on spying me.

'Hey, my pretty little lad! Can you tell me where to find His Majesty of Navarre?'

I directed him where he was likeliest to find our high-born scholars at that hour, then took my own course along the path I had seen the Frenchman travel, and soon found the French court encamped in the fields hard by a little copse, where I stole into a comfortable niche among the trees and both saw and heard quite well.

In addition to various assorted noblemen, the French princess had three lovely ladies to wait on her, one pale blonde, one amber-haired, and one dark. As I secreted myself, they were discussing King Ferdinand and his companions in monkish scholarship.

'Lord Longaville?' the pale lady was repeating. 'Madam, I met him at my sister's wedding! A handsome man who does all things well – arms, the arts . . . His only fault is a sharp wit coupled with a blunt will.'

Aside from the bit about his wit and will – I could well believe it was indeed Longaville who had made up the threat that a trespassing woman should lose her tongue – I scarcely recognized our tall, skinny, and dour zealot from the lady's description. But even as I wondered their talk moved on to Lord Dumaine.

'A well-accomplished youth,' the second lady testified, bowing her head as if to hide a blush . . . or perhaps to gather more sunlight into her hair, which I thought borrowed its amber color from some such artifice. 'A round-faced innocent,' she went on, 'so eager to see goodness in everyone, that all who meet him must return the favour. I met him once at my father the Duke Alençon's.'

'Berowne was there at that same time,' cried the dark-haired beauty. 'The merriest and wittiest of them all, if the hour's talk I had with him counts for anything.'

'God bless my ladies!' exclaimed Her Grace the Princess. 'Are they all in love?'

'In love, madame?' the Duke of Alençon's daughter protested, lifting her artfully amber head. I should not have cared to be on the receiving end of the flash in her grey eyes. 'In faith, I am no victim of that shrewd gallow-bait Cupid!'

'No, you'll never be friends with him, will you, Kate?' said she of the dark hair. 'He killed your sister.'

'He made her melancholy, sad, and heavy,' Katharine replied. 'And so she died too young. Had she been light like you, Rosaline, she might have been a grandmother.'

'Light?' Rosaline frowned. 'What do you mean, mousekin, in calling me "light"?'

'Why, that hour you spent lightly chatting with my Lord Berowne was the very same hour in which they found that my poor sister had hanged herself for love!'

'And how were we to blame for that, pray you, when neither you nor anyone else knew of poor Elinor's fate before . . .'

'Enough!' The princess stopped their quarrel with an outstretched hand. 'We were all still too young to understand how young we were, and how little we understood. For now, until we know what present troubles we may run, I will have no more talk of those that lie in the past, but only pleasant banter and play of wits.'

So they bantered, saying nothing more of any great import – except to show me that they had been well informed concerning our king's vow and proclamations as to members of their sex – and leaving me to ponder the fair sweet Elinor, who had been a brave soul – a generous lady? – when she breathed. Then the jaunty old Frenchman whom I had met earlier returned with King Ferdinand and his attendants to grant the princess and her people a diplomatic welcome.

Either to comply with the scholars' vows against their sex or to show contempt for them, the French ladies all raised masks before their faces. I giggled into my sleeve to see how each mask turned towards its bearer's chosen gentleman, and how, vows or none, each gentleman scholar returned the ladies' glances as though attempting to pierce the mystery of which was the she whom he had courted years before.

'You shall be welcome, madam, to my court,' the king began.

'I will be welcome, then,' the princess replied mischievously. 'Conduct me thither.'

'Pardon me, dear lady,' our hapless young monarch stammered. 'I have sworn an oath . . .'

'So I have heard,' she answered. 'An oath as sinful to keep as to break! But now, to cut matters as short as possible, and with as little violence to your vows as we can manage, vouchsafe to read the purpose of my coming and bring it to a speedy resolution.' She passed him a paper, displaying elaborate care not to touch his hand in so doing.

While he read, I noticed that Lord Berowne and the dark-haired Rosaline made opportunity to step a little apart and exchange words, but in voices too soft for me to overhear.

'Madam,' King Ferdinand said at length, a frown creasing his brow, 'to fight his late wars, your royal father of France borrowed of my late father King Charles of Navarre the sum of two hundred thousand crowns, for which as surety he signed one part of Aquitaine to us. Now, he here demands the immediate return of either that land or the sum of one hundred thousand crowns, which he intimates has already been repaid. As for us, we would prefer the money to the land. Yet there would still remain a hundred thousand crowns unpaid even had this first payment ever been made – of which neither my late father nor I have ever seen so much as a penny!'

'You wrong my father, the memory of King Charles, and your own good name,' replied the princess, 'in denying receipt of what was paid in good faith.'

'I protest that I never heard of it!' the king insisted. 'If you can prove to me that this hundred thousand crowns was ever paid, I'll pay it back or yield up Aquitaine!'

'We take you at your word!' the princess exclaimed, shrewd as any merchant (seeing her chance to get the land back for half the original debt). 'Boyet,' she went on, turning to my jaunty Frenchman, 'you can produce the receipt, signed and sealed by special officers of King Charles.'

'So please you, madam,' Boyet replied smoothly, 'the packet which contains that, among other things, has not yet come. It will arrive tomorrow.'

'Until tomorrow, then,' King Ferdinand agreed. 'Fair princess, by the terms of my vow you may not come within my gates; but here in your encampment you shall enjoy such honour, welcome, and good cheer, that you may imagine yourself lodged within my very heart.'

She replied with equal courtesy, and so the king took his leave, as if unwilling to test himself too long in female company. His fellow scholars lingered a little while, pumping Boyet for news of the ladies-in-waiting. I stayed long enough to learn that the blonde, Maria, was an heir of Lord Falconbridge, as Katharine was of Duke Alençon, and the dark Rosaline of her own bold will. When all our men of Navarre had departed, and the French were left to trade wit among themselves, I too skipped away and returned to poor Costard, whom I found languishing in his prison with a mug of milk and half a meat pasty, which Jaquenetta had smuggled him through the same window I used for our conversation.

'One hundred thousand crowns . . .' Costard mused on hearing what I had seen and heard. 'Two hundred thousand! Lord, how lightly the great folk talk about sums of which a mere fraction would keep one of us little ones in comfort for life! Come, Moth, have you any perception how much such a sum may truly be? No more have I!'

'More, at least, than even my master could easily gamble away in a single night, to keep his purse as threadbare as his habit. But think, Costard! This same dead Lady Elinor of Alençon – my master remembers her, too!' And I told him Don Adriano's graveyard meditations of earlier that day.

'He remembers her,' – Costard repeated, 'and that in the same breath with King Ferdinand's late father, and with your own. Well! Supposing that your master was there at Alençon's that same time, what might he tell us of my gentle lords Berowne and Dumaine?'

'That they were tender juveniles, surely,' said I. 'They must have been no larger then, than I am now.'

He shook his head thoughtfully. 'Dumaine, perhaps, but not Berowne. No, my Lord Berowne would have been . . . let me see . . .' He made a great dumbshow of reckoning it up on his fingers, still greasy as they were from the meat pie . . . 'already by then well into his twenties, and his dark Rosaline, for anything I know to the contrary, old enough for some acquaintance with the gentle arts of flirtation, no matter how young Elinor's sister Kate may have been at the time. And now, I wonder, is poor Katharine her father's sole surviving heir?'

'Whether she is or no, she would rather have her sister still alive and be content with the smaller portion, to judge by what I saw.'

'And, surely, folk never put on false faces,' said Costard, grinning as he licked his fingers. 'Yet if our sweet, cherub-faced Dumaine was little more than Kate's own age then, or yours now, my lad . . . Was our grave Lord Longaface there with them at His Grace of Alençon's, I wonder?'

'Lord Longaville? Now that I cannot say. I can only keep my ears open. But how does any of this ancient history help poor Jaquenetta's present case?'

'In no way that I can see.' Costard drank off his milk, wiped his mouth, and shook his head like a dog. 'Yet it interests me curiously. Well, my sweet ounce of man's flesh, your part is to run and spy, mine to sit and ponder.'

Next day in the still-immaculate morning, when I went to seek out my master, I found him at his desk with a heavy folio spread open before him. But, instead of reading, he was penning another epistle. 'Ah, child!' said he, covering it as I came up. 'Sweet child, warble for me. Make passionate my sense of hearing.'

I sang him 'Concoline,' a sweet air and one that seemed suited to his mood. At the song's end, he handed me back the key to Costard's room and bade me 'give enlargement to the swain, and bring him festinately hither,' to be employed as carrier of a letter to Don Adriano's love.

'To Jaquenetta?' Costard inquired, in some surprise at my news.

'Unless his fancy has suddenly lighted on another,' I replied. 'Which would be fast work, especially with all other women forbidden within a mile of the king's grounds.'

'Fate may already be unfolding us opportunities. Pray you, Moth, not a word to make me seem other than the fool folk call me.'

'Thou apple-head!' I assured my new friend with a wink. 'Are not all us mortals great fools?'

Don Adriano had already sealed his letter and was adding the superscript when we arrived. 'Ah, my sweet herald is returned,' he said smiling as we came up, 'bringing my prisoner, as instructed. Sirrah Costard, I will enfranchise thee—'

'Marry me to one named Frances?' Costard asked with a perfect show of round-eyed wonder. 'Oh, that she be both fair and a good cook – or, if not both, at least the latter!'

'Thou rational hind! I mean that I will set thee at liberty, and, in lieu of thy durance, impose on thee no task but this: bear my significant – that is to say, my missive, epistle, or, as the vulgar would call it, letter – to the maid Jaquenetta.'

'Only for this?' Costard asked, making his roundest eyes at the sealed letter as he turned it over and over in his hands.

'Nay, then,' said Don Adriano. 'The best ward of mine honour is rewarding my dependants. Take this remuneration as well.'

' "Remuneration"?' Costard repeated, accepting the trifle my master held out. 'Oh, I see! It's the Latin word for three farthings.'

'Be off on thy errand!' said my master. '*Carpe diem*, buffoon, whilst thou can, or I choose me a better envoy. Nay, Moth, stay thou and sing to me again, lest overmuch study wear out my brain.'

I stayed long enough to lullaby him into a gentle doze, which was not difficult seeing that, among their other fond vows, the king and his fellows had sworn to take no more than three hours' sleep in a night and none in the day, and Don Adriano for all his bulk was striving to ape their example in this, if not in the matters of food and women. As soon as I heard him safely snoring, I seized my chance and tripped out after Costard.

I found him turning my master's farthings in one hand and heavier coins in the other. 'Ah, Moth!' he grinned. 'See here the difference between "guerdon" and "remuneration" – "guerdon" is eleven pence farthing better. My Lord Berowne has given me a guerdon for carrying his letter to the Lady Rosaline.'

'Jaquenetta can break the seal on her own from my master,' I observed, 'and I have had some little practice in unsealing letters and sealing them again so that none but the keenest eye sees the difference.'

Costard chuckled. 'We have but to deliver these letters and be sure to overhear them read. And, to see what it may stir up, I mean to deliver them to the wrong parties, letting it be blamed on my foolishness. But let us take sweet Jaquenetta into the joke, and if she has any interest in hearing what her own tormentor in love has to say to her, we will indeed call upon your skill with wax seals.'

But Jaquenetta could not read – which Don Adriano may have forgotten or never known – and she professed not the slightest interest in hearing his letter for herself. 'It will be long-winded and full of overblown words,' she remarked. 'I would rather milk the cows. You may listen to it for me, and bring me back the gist. When the time comes, however, I would relish hearing what my Lord Berowne has to tell his Lady Rosaline.'

Leaving Berowne's letter with Jaquenetta for safekeeping, Costard and I proceeded to find the French visitors. The princess had brought her court out with one of King Ferdinand's foresters, to shoot by invitation at deer from under cover; the bushes lent me a convenient hiding place to spy on the scene undetected, lest my presence raise too many questions.

'What do you wish, fellow?' the princess inquired on seeing Costard.

'I have a letter here,' said he, turning it over and over as if reciting from mere rote memory, 'from Monsieur Berowne to one Lady Rosaline.'

'From our good friend Berowne?' said the princess. And then, even, as the dark-haired Rosaline stepped forward with outstretched hand, Her Grace turned to Boyet and ordered him to take the letter.

My jaunty Frenchman took it from Costard, glanced at the superscription, and announced, 'But here is some mistake. It is written to one Jaquenetta.'

'We will read it, I swear!' the princess declared eagerly.

Boyet broke the seal and read it aloud to the assembly. It regaled them into waves of laughter, being as long-winded and full of overblown words as Jaquenetta had predicted; and the gist of it was, that Don Adriano compared himself to 'the most illustriate King Cophetua' and

Jaquenetta to 'the pernicious beggar Zenelophon,' and he graciously guaranteed to raise her as high in marriage as Cophetua had raised his beloved beggar-woman.

'What peacock is this Don Adriano de Armado that penned and dared sign his name to this gem?' cried the princess, wiping tears of laughter from her eyes.

'I am much deceived,' said Boyet, 'if I do not remember the style.'

'How could one forget?' asked the princess.

'This Don Adriano is a Spaniard,' Boyet went on, puckering his brow in memory, 'but attached to the king of Navarre . . . this present young King Ferdinand, and also, before his time, to the old King Charles, Ferdinand's father. He was among the Navarrese party that time they visited His Grace of Alençon. And once I encountered him, by chance, in Rome that time I bore your royal father's letter there. I have heard that now he makes sport for Ferdinand and his book-mates.'

'Rare sport he makes for them, then!' Still chuckling, the princess turned back to Costard.

'Well, fellow, thou hast made a rare mistake. Hast thou not another letter about thee, one truly from Lord Berowne to Lady Rosaline?'

Costard shrugged, turned out his pockets, and held out his empty palms. 'Great lady, I told you. I received a letter from my Lord Berowne to a lady of France that he called Rosaline, and I have duly delivered it.'

'Well!' The princess refolded Don Adriano's letter and tossed it to Rosaline. 'Here, sweet chuck, keep it safe to laugh at another day. Come, forester of our royal hermit host, where is the bush that we must stand and play the murderer in?'

'On the edge of yonder coppice,' the forester replied, and led them away, shouldering their bows and balancing their arrows. But, lingering behind, my Lady Rosaline started toward Costard as if to question him further.

Boyet insinuated himself into her path. What words they exchanged were spoken too low for even my small ears to catch, until they ended with quoting a hoary old couplet at each other.

'Thou canst not hit it, my good man'

'If I cannot, another can!'

Thus they drove each other after the rest of the French court, making it safe for me to emerge and confer with Costard even as we hurried back to execute the second act of the farce of the misdelivered love letters.

'Did Her French Highness forget that my master's letter was properly speaking Jaquenetta's property and not the Lady Rosaline's?' I marveled.

'More likely she understood by dint of some feminine mystery that Jaquenetta wants none of it,' said Costard. 'Although I have known great ones to regard as their own right and due any and all property of folk smaller than themselves. But now . . . perhaps it was the way Her Grace likened shooting a deer to murder . . . I suffer certain qualms as to whether poor sister Elinor really did knot that noose with her own delicate hands. Friend Moth, I may accept your kindly offer to examine my Lord Berowne's letter ahead of time.'

This we did, myself reading it aloud to them both – for, though Costard could put his A, B, and C together better than he let show, he was, for all his secret shrewdity, no great scholar. All that we could make of Berowne's fourteen rhyming lines, however, was a love poem, which I recognised as in the form called 'sonnet,' filled with flowery compliments to his lady, and argument why her lover should not be blamed if in homage to her he forswore his vow to king and bookish study. If it held any secrets in cipher, they lay hid far too deep for us to make out.

Since according to our pretext Jaquenetta had received it as if in good faith, we had no need to reaffix the seal; although I, as the only one of us three known to have sufficient education to read the superscript, had great need not to let myself be seen party to the confusion. This time I went ahead, locating and concealing myself near by the bookmen we had chosen for our dupes: the schoolmaster Holofernes and the parson Sir Nathaniel, as pretty a pair of solemn wise innocents as ever sought to outjabber each other in learned prattle. At present they were amusing themselves in talking above the head of poor old Constable Dull, and he in gallantly striving to catch them up with the ancient riddle, 'What was a month old at Cain's birth, that's not five weeks old as yet?' to which they, of course, knew the answer as well as I: the moon, though they called her Dictynna, Phoebe, and Luna. Having attained his venerable years by doing as little as possible of his own volition, as well as being accustomed to my master's freaks and starts, the constable accepted without comment the reappearance of yesterday's prisoner in company with the new dairy-woman.

'God give you good morning, Master Person,' Jaquenetta mischievously addressed the parson. 'I beseech you, be so good as to read me this letter. It was given me by Costard, and sent me from Don Adriano.'

Sir Nathaniel read it out with great cadence and rolling feeling. The schoolmaster Holofernes immediately chid him like a young pupil for misfiring in his delivery, and at the same time compared the verses unfavourably with those of Ovidius Naso.

'But, damosella,' the schoolmaster went on to Jaquenetta, no doubt seeking how such epithets as 'celestial' might apply to her, or wishing to listen again for 'music and sweet fire' in her voice, 'was this indeed directed to you?'

'Aye, sir,' she answered too eagerly. 'From my Lord Berowne –' And then, seeing her slip, tried to cover it with, 'That is, from one of the stranger queen's lords . . .'

Fortunately, both schoolmaster and parson seemed too much bemused by the whole occurrence to pay overmuch attention to Jaquenetta's actual words; and if the constable noticed, he kept his own counsel. Holofernes was already turning the sheet over to examine the superscript. 'To the snow-white hand of the most beauteous Lady Rosaline,' he read. 'Hmm. I will look again for the nomination of the party writing . . . "Your ladyship's" and so forth . . . "Berowne.". Sir Nathaniel, this Berowne is one of those who vowed, along with His Grace the King, to hold neither traffic, congress, nor any communication with them of the delicate gender for full three years, and here he hath framed this letter! Trip and go, my sweet,' the schoolmaster concluded, returning the incriminatory sheet to Jaquenetta, 'deliver this paper into the royal hand of the king. It may prove important.'

'Sir . . .' she began, looking puzzled.

'Concern thyself not with thy womanhood in the royal presence. Should he ask, I have granted thee authority and exemption in this singular instance!' The schoolmaster waved her away as if such authority were his to grant.

Clinging to Costard's arm, Jaquenetta went. I stayed hid long enough to hear the schoolmaster generously invite both parson and constable to go and dine with him at the house of one of his pupil's fathers, where he would further abuse poor Lord Berowne's poetry. Then I slipped away and caught up with my friends.

Myself weaving along in concealment as before, we found King Ferdinand and his three closest vow-fellows together, Berowne berating all the others for having broken their oath by writing love verses to their various French goddesses. When he paused for breath, Jaquenetta seized her chance, not without some quivering, and cried, 'God bless the king!'

'What do you bring me here?' asked His chastened Majesty, turning to her with obvious relief and no word of censure or punishment for bringing her feminine flesh into the royal presence.

'Treason, my lord,' Costard answered for her.

'Grand or petty?' The king heaved a great sigh, having just been caught in a kind of treason, so to speak, against his own law. 'If petty, then take it away again in peace.'

'I beseech Your Grace,' Jaquenetta insisted, 'let this letter be read. Our parson called it treason.'

With another sigh, King Ferdinand accepted it from her and handed it over to Berowne, obviously supposing him the last loyal man present, with instructions to read it aloud. While waiting for Berowne to unfold it, His Grace asked Jaquenetta where she had got it.

'From Costard,' she replied.

'And thou?' the king went on in mild patience to Costard.

'From Don Adriano – Hey!' cried my friend.

Instead of reading his own verses aloud, Berowne had begun tearing his letter into tiny pieces.

'How?' exclaimed the king. 'What's this?'

'A toy, my liege,' Berowne said at once. 'A trifle. Your Grace need fear nothing from it.'

'It moved Berowne to passion, however,' Lord Longaville observed suspiciously.

'It is in his handwriting, too,' cried Lord Dumaine, piecing some of the fragments together. 'See! Here's his signature.'

'Ah, you son-of-a-whore!' Berowne muttered at Costard. Then, turning back to the king and his other companions, he continued in a completely different style, courtly and graceful, 'Guilty, my lord! I confess all.'

'What?' asked the king.

'That you three lacked only me to make our number complete – four fools, forsworn together in love! Dismiss the silly turtledoves, and I'll unveil my full heart to you.'

'Well!' the king said with a grin of relief, dismissing Costard and Jaquenetta at once.

I waited and listened a while longer in my covert before taking my departure, as unseen as I had come, and rejoining my friends. 'They said nothing more that I could hear of any great interest to us,' I reported. 'They quibbled a long while as to whether a beauty as dark as Lady Rosaline could truly be called "fair," and then the other three happily let Berowne prove to them, as well as any lawyer, that black was white and breaking their oath was the one and only true way to keep it safe. Then they all entered into a new pact to woo and win their ladies openly, and so I left them plotting some gallant entertainment for this afternoon.'

'What do you think?' said Costard. 'Did our good Lord Berowne fear nothing else than standing revealed as one more oath-breaker alongside his comrades, or had he some worse discovery to fear?'

Jaquenetta shook her head in puzzlement. 'I could not tell whether he read the letter through before tearing it up, or not.'

'Or whether he even heard you say from where you had it,' I put in.

Costard bit his thumb in thought. 'We know that Berowne and the dewy-cheeked Dumaine were there at His Grace of Alençon's that time the poor young heiress hanged herself for love, as all believe . . . Moth, my comma, thy lamented father was there too, I think, was he not? Did he never tell you any of the tale before his death?'

'None, Signior Costard, but from such few small crumbs as my master has let drop over the years of my pagehood, I gather that was the time when he and my father cemented the bond between them that has left me in Don Adriano's service and keeping.'

'Was it so?' A canyon appeared between Costard's brows, so deep was his frown. 'All the same . . . I wish we knew whether or not Lord Longaville was there at the Duke Alençon's, too.'

'Not "two," sir – "three,"' I quipped, reckoning them up on my fingers. 'Berowne . . . Dumaine . . . and Longaville, like an old tale!'

'At that rate, why not say six?' he quipped back. 'Berowne and Rosaline, Dumaine and Katharine, Lord Longaville the glum and Maria the bright!'

'That's six names,' I rejoindered, 'but only three couples.'

'Four, or eight,' Jaquenetta mused, 'if we count King Ferdinand and her tall, pretty Grace of France.'

'No,' Costard said, half serious again – though no more than half. 'The young king could not have been there at Alençon's, any more than his father old King Charles. As for the French princess . . .' He turned out his hand. 'Who knows?'

'Eight, then,' she persisted, 'with Moth's father and fat Don Adriano—'

'Who will be wanting his dinner!' Costard exclaimed, ruffling my hair, 'and hungry enough to swallow you down as a tidbit if you do not get to him soon!'

I slapped Costard's hand away, which I would never quite have dared do to my master's, for all the flipness of my tongue with him, and hastened back to serve at table. Indeed, Don Adriano had only his cook and myself to perform that service for him, putting what funds he had saved from gaming into filling his belly more richly than graciously; but hearing that the king and his fellow scholars had all forsworn their vows against women, and presumably their vows against sleep and food as well, today my master felt free in conscience to eat as fully as he would have eaten anyway, and this put him in so good a mood that he easily forgave my tardiness in pouring his wine, and asked me no further questions.

He had not quite finished fortifying himself against the afternoon hours when Lord Longaville arrived on an errand from the king. Still maintaining his own discipline so far as to refuse a glass of wine, the solemn nobleman explained that His Majesty required some sprightly play or pageant with which to entertain the French princess in her camp that evening, and knew of none so fit as his trusted Don Adriano to put it together so soon. They also desired the loan of his page – myself – to assist them in a preliminary diversion of their own, for which they required my attendance in an hour's time.

Ever watchful of our opportunities, I suggested to my master, as soon as Lord Longaville was gone, that he might do worse than enroll Costard in his project. Don Adriano found this a delectable plan. Elegant as my master seemed to his own mind, I suspect he thought the clown would set off his own supposed perfections as a pet monkey its lady's beauty, and moreover, he remarked, Costard had become his dependant by bearing his letter and accepting his remuneration.

The three of us next went and enlisted the knowledgeable assistance of Holofernes and Sir Nathaniel, who had swallowed their fill of fine, long words along with the more regular kind of fare at their dinner and showed themselves eager for the pageant. The schoolmaster lost no time in proposing that we present the Nine Worthies. Since we had not nine grown actors, he assigned me to play Hercules strangling the snakes that Hera sent to kill him in his cradle. Poor old Dull, who had neither offered nor, by his own testimony, understood a word of all this, agreed to beat his tabor for the Worthies and do nothing more; but Costard was willing enough to undertake a hero or two.

So I left them, assigning and re-assigning the eight remaining Worthies among the four of them – my master, the parson, the schoolmaster, and Costard – while I obeyed the summons to the other four – Longaville, Berowne, Dumaine, and the king – and found them, if anything, even sillier and more foolish in their newborn antics than the four whom I had left.

They had made up their minds to pay their ladies an afternoon visit disguised as Muscovites, and I was to announce them. In hopes of helping to identify the various ladies, whom this year they had seen only behind masks – indeed, the young king had never seen his princess otherwise, unless in a portrait – each noble swain had sent his fair one some distinctive favor, as a pair of gloves or string of pearls, along with his love verses; and they thought the ladies, supposing them to be outlandish foreigners, would see no reason whatsoever not to wear these costly vanities.

Lord Berowne coached me in my lines. 'Bear thy body thus!' he commanded, pushing my shoulders back with fingers still ink-spotted from hastily repinning his sonnet.

'Thou shalt see an angel,' said the king. 'Yet fear her not, but speak out boldly.'

'An angel is not evil,' I answered. 'I would fear her if she were a devil.'

At that, they all – even Lord Longaville, usually so longfaced – fell to laughing, slapping me and one another, and rolling around in mirth and horseplay, as though they were so many children and I the solemn master standing up in their midst. Watching them, I could not believe that either Longaville or Berowne might deserve my friend's dark suspicions, any more than the cherubic Dumaine or the moonstruck king himself . . . unless guilt were putting on the disguise of innocence, for the benefit of his comrades, far more successfully than the lovers were putting on that of Muscovites for the benefit of their ladies.

But then, glancing toward some bushes, I glimpsed my dapper Frenchman Boyet lying hid, as I myself had hidden several times already that day, spying on us. 'Ha!' thought I. 'The king's disguise will be no mystery at all to the ladies.'

Thus forewarned, I ought to have proved unflappable in my hastily memorized speech. Alas, scarcely had I approached the French camp to announce the supposed Muscovites, and begun to hail the rich beauties, when all four of them, masked though they were, turned their backs to me.

'Out of your favors, heavenly spirits,' I stammered bravely on, 'vouchsafe once to turn your sunbeam eyes—'

The ladies seemed to titter with mirth, and Boyet, standing nearby, remarked, ' "Son-beam eyes" '? No, my boy, they will not answer to that. Better say, ' "daughter-beam eyes"!'

At the same time, Lord Berowne was muttering angrily at my other ear, 'Is this your word-perfection, rogue? Be gone!'

I had heard and seen how fair ladies can discountenance brave men, and now, for the first time in my young life beginning to understand the phenomenon, I was grateful to make my escape.

In the same covert from which I had watched the French camp the day before, I found Costard. 'The schoolmaster has so written it that you and he will appear together, and he will give all the explanation for both,' my friend whispered to me. 'When the time comes, you have only to pick up your snakes, which Jaquenetta is fashioning of cloth stuffed with crushed straw. Wait here and help me spy on them all. Listen closely for any words of poor Lady Elinor, or those unfortunate hundred thousand crowns.'

So we sat and watched the disguised lords pair themselves off with the masked ladies; but much of what they said was uttered far too softly for our ears, and all that we could overhear was mere foolish banter, scraps of attempted lovemaking on the men's part, with the ladies twisting their words away from them into nonsensical fluff. Not a hint could we hear of either questionable matter. Of course, to have brought up the reason why the French had come to Navarre in the first place would have marched ill with my lords' Muscovite disguise . . . but then, from what I could witness, their every step and sentence marched ill, and when they took their leave, it was not in glory.

'Are these the famous wits of Navarre?' the princess asked when they were out of sight, pulling off her mask.

'Hotheads,' chuckled Boyet. 'Rushlights . . . candles . . . tapers – and your sweet breaths have puffed them out!'

As they laughed and joked, we learned that the ladies had all exchanged their suitors' favours beforehand, so that the king unknowingly courted the Lady Rosaline and Berowne the princess, while Lords Longaville and Dumaine similarly sought out each the other's light of love. At this, Costard pursed his lips and pretended to whistle. 'Whose inspiration was that pretence, I wonder now?' he murmured. 'And was it merely for sport, or has someone in the French party hatched suspicions, too?'

'Madam,' Boyet eventually told the princess, 'you may be sure that they will return as themselves, and try to win back what they have lost as Muscovites. Therefore, change favours again.'

Lady Rosaline exclaimed with a peal of laughter, 'Good madam, let us complain to them what fools visited us just now dressed like Muscovites!'

The princess and her ladies retired to their tents, and presently the king and his noble scholars returned, as Boyet had predicted, stripped down to their own proper attire, and requested audience with Her Grace of France.

'I will bear your message, my lord, and I think I can promise you that she will not refuse you a word or two,' Boyet replied with something so greatly resembling courtesy that an uninformed onlooker might not have known the difference.

When the Frenchman had disappeared into the tent, His Highness observed somewhat sourly, 'A blister on that fellow's tongue! He is the one that threw Don Adriano's page out of countenance.'

'He pecks up wit like a pigeon pecking up crumbs of bread,' Berowne replied, 'and buys his ladies' admiration with better men's words. If he had been Adam, he would have tempted Eve, and not the other way around. Why, when he plays, he can charm the very dice to roll as he bids them!'

Beside me, Costard muttered, 'So! Our Lord Berowne suspects the Frenchman of something . . . and the Frenchman, if I read him rightly, may return the favour. This is interesting!'

'Does it tell you something?' I whispered.

'Not so much that, as it strengthens a certain opinion I had already begun to play with.'

'Which is?'

'Hush, sweet Moth,' he answered, as serious as I had ever seen him. 'I'd prefer you not to know.'

'And I would prefer to know!'

He looked at me, plucked a worm from a leaf near our heads, threw it meditatively away, and temporised, 'Not yet, then. Dear friend, promise not to pry into this for a little while yet. I would like your observation fresh and unprejudiced when the moment comes.'

Meanwhile, the princess and her ladies had emerged with unmasked faces to confront the king and his gentlemen.

'We beg to mend our welcome,' His Majesty was saying. 'Pray you, let us lead you beneath our roof.'

'We will rest where we are,' she replied. 'Keep your vow. Neither God nor I delight in perjury.'

Somehow, I felt unsure whether she were talking only about his self-imposed monkish vows of study and fasting, or whether she added some dark hint pertaining to the hundred thousand crowns.

The ensuing scene told us nothing more as to this. The ladies first mocked the Muscovites, as they had plotted, and then revealed their own masquerade, to their suitors' extreme embarrassment. Then they all began to make peace and flirt in apparent earnest; but now Costard and I heard the rest of the Nine Worthies approaching, and went to meet them. Jaquenetta came too, helping bear the bits of hastily improvised costuming, and soon I was tricked out with a strip of bunting wrapped round me on top of my own garments, and a toy snake in either hand.

Costard stepped back openly to the French camp to ask if they were ready for the pageant, now that the 'posteriors of the day,' as Don Adriano called the late afternoon, was upon the world and twilight following apace. On his bringing back word that they were ready, we all approached, though softly as befit actors with every full right and prerogative to lurk concealed awaiting their cues. My master alone, who carried the schoolmaster's elegantly if rapidly penned playbill, seized his chance to go forward and deliver it into the king's own hand, thus seeing the French camp for himself and showing off his boasted chumminess with the crown of Navarre.

'Anointed,' Don Adriano addressed the monarch, using all the precious and pretentious language at his command, 'I implore so much expense of thy royal sweet breath as will utter a brace of words.'

Beside me, Jaquenetta gasped, 'Does he "thou" and "thy" the king's own majesty?' And, in the same moment, I overheard the princess asking Berowne, 'Does this man serve God?'

'Why?' Berowne asked her in return, blinking.

'He does not speak like one of God's creatures!'

Costard raised his brows a little and threw on his costume of toga and helmet, sword and buckler. His sword, like those of the other grown Worthies, was real, though old and imperfectly polished.

Don Adriano rejoined us, puffing out his cheeks in obvious contentment with the impression he had made – if he had overheard Her Grace's comment, he must have interpreted it as a compliment upon his overblown verbiage – and Constable Dull stepped forward humbly but resolutely, and began to drum a solemn rhythm on his tabor.

Costard went first and, if any of us had hoped to carry our pageant off with dignity, my friend dashed that poor hope at once. 'I Pompey am,' he declaimed, puffing his chest and throwing his huge shoulders from side to side, 'surnamed the Big—'

'What schoolboy Latin is this?' Boyet interrupted with a chuckle, showing no more respect for the worthy than he had earlier for me.

' "The Great," clown, "the Great"!' exclaimed Berowne, laughing and clapping the Frenchman on the back. 'But I must be friends with thee, old mocker.'

Had they forgotten their enmity, then? Costard cast them a glance as he acknowledged, grinning, 'It is "Great," sir. I Pompey am, surnamed the Great, that here have come by chance, and lay my arms down at the feet of this fair lass of France.' Laying them down before the princess, he added, as if prompting a fellow player, 'If your ladyship would say, "Thanks, Pompey," I will be done.'

'Great thanks, Great Pompey,' she answered, laughing.

Sir Nathaniel, decked out with a paint-daubed shield and a helmet that looked much like Costard's, sighed and stepped forth next. 'When in the world I lived, I was the world's commander. My shield's device declares that I am Alexander—'

'Your nose says you are not,' Boyet chortled, 'for it is anything but a Greek nose!'

Again Berowne seconded the Frenchman's joke, and between them, with only false and token sympathy from the rest of the noble audience, our hapless conqueror was soon conquered and driven almost in tears from the field. Costard, however, held his ground, as if his own showing had been vastly superior, and all but hobnobbed with the gentlefolk until the princess gently bade him stand aside. I wondered what he was up to.

Now the schoolmaster took me by the shoulder and marched with me into place; and, as if in apology for disgracing me earlier, for once Boyet and the others held their peace, and heard Holofernes through while he explained, half in Latin, that I represented Hercules strangling serpents while still a babe. As soon as he had nudged me off again, however, and commenced presenting himself as Judas Maccabaeus, the lords Dumaine and Longaville joined Berowne and my Frenchman in purposely mistaking Maccabaeus for Iscariot. 'Shame, Judas!' cried gentle Dumaine, and Boyet added, 'To make Judas hang himself.'

By the time they had driven the poor schoolmaster from the scene, even old Dull, who had played his tabor unmolested for every entrance in turn, misfired a little in his rhythm for Don Adriano's appearance.

But my master stepped forth with as much show of confidence as though he actually felt the earth shuddering beneath his footfall. 'The armipotent Mars, of lances the almighty,' he commenced in powerful voice, 'gave Hector a gift—'

'A gilt nutmeg!' guessed Dumaine, fully warmed to it by now.

'No, a lemon,' said Berowne.

'Stuck with cloves,' Longaville added.

'Gave Hector a gift,' Don Adriano struggled on. 'I am that flower—'

'That mint!' cried Dumaine.

'That columbine!' echoed Longaville.

'Sweet royalty!' Don Adriano appealed to the princess. 'Bestow on me the sense of hearing!'

'Speak, brave Hector,' the princess replied. 'We are much delighted.'

Stumbling to his knees before her, he began, 'I do adore thy sweet Grace's slipper—'

'He loves her by the foot,' Boyet observed to Dumaine.

Who answered, 'He may not by the yard.'

'By – Hannibal!' Don Adriano panted, striving to heave himself upon his legs again. 'I – Hector – far surmounted—'

He ended with a scream.

The princess stood some paces in front of her tent. Behind her, between two tents, stood a woman clothed in white draperies, that the twilight already turned to blue. Her head was bowed over a bundle covered with dark stains that she carried in one arm.

Badgered to distraction, my master half shrieked the names of Hector's wife and sacrificed son. 'Andromache! Astyanax!'

Shaking her head, she brought her other arm forward and held it up like the hand of the blind goddess Justice. In place of Justice's scales, a noose dangled from her outstretched hand.

'Elinor!' screamed Don Adriano. 'Ah, sweet, forgive . . .' He sank back down, blubbering.

'Fellow Hector,' Costard said, stepping forward, 'she is gone, is she not? She is quick, and with your child!'

Not until that moment did I myself understand that it was Jaquenetta who stood there, better costumed than any of us male players.

But if Costard had meant to goad Don Adriano into further confession, his move had the wrong effect. 'Thou – villain!' my master shouted, heaving himself up at last and casting about for Hector's rusty sword. 'Dost thou slander me – here, among princes? Thou shalt die!'

'Then Hector will be hanged for murder!' Costard exclaimed, stepping backward and getting Pompey's blade into his hand.

Lady Katharine suddenly cried, 'Elinor! He called her by my sister's name!'

Don Adriano's head whipped back and forth in the gathering twilight, his panic all but palpable. 'I – I challenge thee!' he bawled at Costard, for once ignoring the difference in their ranks.

'A trial by combat?' asked King Ferdinand.

'In our shirts!' said Costard. 'My lords, let him wear no frills and padded sleeves to trip up my point.'

'I will not fight in my shirt!' Don Adriano protested, his vehemence seeming out of all proportion to the counter-challenge.

'You may not refuse,' said Dumaine.

'Sweet bloods, I both may and will!'

Boyet strode forth, laid hold of Don Adriano's doublet, and ripped it open by the buttons. 'Ah!' declared the Frenchman. 'So, you still faithfully wear the wool-shirt they gave you for penance in Rome. And why, my friend, did they give you that penance?' As the Spaniard stood silent, the Frenchman turned to King Ferdinand. 'And here, my good lord of Navarre, is the receipt for your father's hundred thousand crowns, which came in today's packet.'

The king called for light and, when a torch was brought, unfolded and studied the receipt. 'It is signed,' he said soberly, 'by Lord Rousillon and Don Adriano de Armado. Don Adriano, what became of these monies?'

Then, in brief, my master confessed. He and my father – for whose sake Costard had refused earlier to tell me his suspicions – had indeed jointly received the French king's partial repayment, jointly written the acquittance for it, and jointly plotted to keep it for themselves in the trust that should the receipt ever be produced, they could jointly brazen it out with protestations that it had been forged in their names. For the safety of such a sum, all had been done in secrecy between them and Boyet's predecessor in office, under cover of the general gathering. But Don Adriano had already half seduced and half raped the Lady Elinor d'Alençon, and now, through some foolish carelessness on his part, she learned of the embezzlement. She tried using her knowledge to force him into arranging her a match with Lord Berowne.

Had she sought to marry Don Adriano himself, he might have asked nothing better; but, on hearing her preference for the younger and nobler lord, he flew into a rage and strangled her with his bare hands, afterwards hanging her above a volume open to love verses, so as to make it appear that she had killed herself for love.

As for my father, he had died naturally enough; and, for his sake, Don Adriano had kept me in his service. But as for the hundred thousand crowns, my master had gone through first his own share and afterwards through that portion my father had willed him in trust for me, eating, drinking, whoring, and gambling. Perhaps in part he strove mightily to forget fair Elinor and the child he might (for all he know) have put into her, and also the wool-shirt a confessor had enjoined on him in Rome; but surely men do not always need suchlike excuses for suchlike sins, and surely Don Adriano had coveted that money before murdering the poor lady.

Since Don Adriano had committed two crimes, and since that of the embezzlement lay against his own pledged loyalty to the crown of Navarre, Her Grace of France left his punishment to King Ferdinand, who ordered him shut up in a monastery for the rest of his life, and there was an end to it. Having seen the receipt, however, the king held faith with his own word and returned Aquitaine to France, forgiving the rest of the debt.

'How did you know all of it?' I found the chance to ask Costard later.

'I did not know all of it, and what I did know I learned largely by guesswork and suspicion. By your own account, Don Adriano seemed strangely affected by the Lady Elinor's death. He was ever freakish and prone to moods – sometimes, my waggish moppet, I feared for thy own safety when he fell into a temper. But there was his loyalty to your dead father to hold him in check there. Then, too, there was his behaviour with poor, generous Jaquenetta. And then, his clothes were rich once on a time, but that was long ago by the very look of them. Once, he had clearly had wealth. We know where much of it went, but where had it come from? We knew that your father and he had been at Alençon's, as well as their lordships Berowne, Dumaine, and Boyet, when the lady died, and we knew that the receipt for the missing hundred thousand crowns was in Boyet's safekeeping. Now, we did not know that Lord Longaville had been there, and the rosy-cheeked Dumaine would have been little more than your present age at that time; and, when I saw that Berowne and Boyet seemed suspicious of each other, and knew no reason why a guilty man should harbor suspicion of someone else, I signed sweet Jaquenetta to go ahead with our own small plot and see what conscience we might catch. Had we waited, no doubt your new master Boyet would have proved your old one's guilt in the matter of the money by means of the receipt.'

'But without you, friend,' I mused, 'it might never have been known how it was not truly Cupid who killed Lady Katharine's poor sister.'

'Not, at least, Cupid alone and unassisted,' he agreed soberly. 'Well, Cupid may take a year's holiday now, so far as our great ones are concerned.' News had arrived on the heels of our pageant, that the ailing king of France was dead; and Her Grace the Princess, along with her ladies, had enjoined their lovers to retire in earnest from the world for the year of France's mourning, with the gentle agreement that at the twelvemonth's end they might renew their suits if they so chose.

'I do not envy Cupid this "holiday," ' I teased my friend, 'seeing how your small ones are likely to engage his leisure.' For it appeared that the schoolmaster, with more learning of books than of life, had been much smitten with sweet Jaquenetta, and she had not yet decided whether or not to let him win her away from Costard . . . or the other way around . . . in time to give Don Adriano's bastard a better father.

AS STRANGE A MAZE AS E'ER MEN TROD

David Langford

The Tempest *(1611) is undoubtedly Shakespeare's strangest play. Prospero, the Duke of Milan, is driven out by his brother Antonio, and seeks exile, with his daughter Miranda, on a remote island where he enslaves the deformed Caliban and the spirit Ariel. Prospero is a student of the occult, and uses his arcane knowledge to create a tempest which brings to the island an assortment of his friends and enemies, including Antonio, his former counsellor Gonzalo, Alonso the king of Naples, and Alonso's son Ferdinand and brother Sebastian. During the play much is revealed about the individual characters, but all is resolved and Prospero is restored to his dukedom. At the end of the play they all sail for home. That is where the following story picks up the tale.*

> *Yes, faith, and all his lords, the Duke of Milan*
> *And his brave son being twain.*
> (*The Tempest,* 1.2.439)

The sky was clear, the breeze fair, the sea calm as a clock: King Alonso's ship had set its course for Naples and home. It should be possible, now, to forget that island where the party had been so mazed and befuddled by masques, sleights and deceits. Indeed those dreamlike adventures already seemed far distant. Gonzalo sniffed the salt air, peered rheumily at the wheeling seabirds, and wondered why he had all along felt a sense of unfinished matters; of something still taking its course.

And now the king's foolish, cowardly brother was gone. Fallen quietly overboard, perhaps, in a simple lubberly accident. Or perhaps not. In the old days, Gonzalo had helped unravel small intrigues at the court of the old duke (now the restored duke), while missing Antonio's larger treason until too late. If his wits were not too tattered with age, it would be good to pluck out the truth of Sebastian's passing and so make amends of a sort.

Exiled on his wondrous island, Duke Prospero had prepared a revenge twelve years old, twelve years cold. That strangely convenient tempest had delivered his enemies – Antonio the usurper, Alonso the co-conspirator – into the hollow of his hand. The old scholar had gloated over them as they swayed helplessly before him, bereft of sense by what Gonzalo suspected had been potent drugs. And then . . . grudging words of forgiveness. An end to strife. Homeward bound. Was Prospero's heart really so melted by the sight of young Prince Ferdinand burning hot for his daughter?

A shadowed figure moved between him and the sun. 'Mumbling your prayers, old windbag? Or devising another ideal commonwealth?'

Gonzalo blinked. Antonio might no longer be Duke of Milan, but he still wielded a ducal arrogance that gave weight and savage edge to the man's habitual pose of mockery. But there had been a time when Antonio's mockery failed. 'We all become windbags in the last harbour of life,' Gonzalo said comfortably. 'The secret of being a windbag is to tell everything; and so, to have no secrets. This provokes telling in others.'

'Winged words, as ever; winged like a fat capon. And what would you wish to be told?'

'I have studied Prospero's book –' the aged councillor began, and was briefly taken by a sudden convulsion of Antonio's thin features.

'I have studied it too.' The words were edged with ice.

Prospero grandiloquently spoke of having destroyed his books of scholarship and grammarie (if indeed these were different things), but had brought aboard an account of words and doings during those few wracked hours upon his island – written down, he hinted, by those unseen servitors in whom Gonzalo could not quite believe. Alas, Prospero's scribe was sadly accurate, reproducing each and every shaft of mockery directed against Gonzalo by Antonio and his now-vanished crony Sebastian. The strange book also recorded when that mockery had fallen silent.

Even windbags can be blunt, Gonzalo told himself. 'I wondered that, for so long at the last, you kept silence. The tongue of Antonio is a weapon where other weapons fail; yet as Prospero strutted in his hour of triumph, you hurled not a single jest at him. One commonplace barb for the beast-man and his stink of fish, but no more.'

Antonio looked at him indulgently, like a duelling-master who acknowledges a pupil's feeble sally. 'Perhaps I was struck dumb by brother Prospero's generosity. You recall the words with which he prefaced his so gracious forgiveness: "For you, most wicked sir, whom to call brother, Would even infect my mouth . . ." What a gift he has for pretty compliments.'

Gonzalo, with sudden certainty, said: 'That is an easy story, to tell children and old windbags. Behind it I feel there is a hard story.'

'Why, yes.' Antonio granted him a thin smile and a gaze both calculating and almost respectful. 'I thought on the outcome of all our adventures; and I thought as well that, although we are men with small Latin and less Greek, we may say like good scholars, *Cui bono*?' He turned and moved away, sternward along the deck.

Cui bono? For whose good? Who benefits, who gains from the disappearance of Prince Sebastian? Gonzalo, thinking to see a weak place in Antonio's armour of scorn, had hoped for more than this truism tossed like a bone to a toothless hound. He looked about him again. Occasional mariners bustled to and fro, with little to do in this fair weather but make a show of diligence. Trinculo the little jester wore a scowl of glum concentration as he juggled four wooden balls, coming to grief each time he essayed a fifth. There were the young lovers Ferdinand and Miranda holding hands close by the bowsprit, swapping their coy nonsense. Nearer, in the gilded chair placed for him on the foredeck, Alonso gazed placidly out to sea.

Cui bono? Antonio was a man of malice and would first consider motives of malice and vengefulness. Such a reason for disposing of Sebastian had already come into Gonzalo's mind. It all came down to the games of that devious web-spinner Prospero, who blandly kept himself apart in his cabin while leaving his damnable book at large to set the cat among the pigeons.

'Sire,' said Gonzalo with the muted respect due from a courtier of Milan to the King of Naples, 'Might I ask whether you have entertained yourself by study of our duke's chronicle of all that happened since the tempest?'

'I have not,' said Alonso. Which at once swung a barred gate across the path Gonzalo had hoped to take. There seemed no special firmness or concern in the king's voice; only the weariness that follows having come close to death at a wronged enemy's hands, making a great and public repentance, and accepting the burden of being forgiven. But kings must know how to speak deceitfully, and how to snuff out a life with a word. Either of those foppish courtiers Adrian and Francisco might well be Alonso's pet murderer.

If Alonso had read in the book, he would know of Sebastian's plan to slay him while he slept and become King of Naples – or rather, to have Antonio strike the blow while the feebler Sebastian disposed of the possible witness, Gonzalo himself. Apparently Prospero's servitors had interrupted the deed: Gonzalo well remembered waking to find the cronies wild-eyed, swords drawn, prating about beasts that had roared. It occurred to him that, had he been a younger man without the mellowness of a walker knowing himself to be ambling down the last miles before the grave, he too might have meditated a vengeance on Sebastian. Why, he thought, I myself would be the first to attract a thief-taker's attentions. Wiser to accuse an old fool than a king.

If Alonso had read in the book . . . but he chose to deny this. Gonzalo bowed very slightly and decided that it was time to go below.

The gentle swell that heaved the ship's deck was less soothing down here in the stench (it *did* smell like that creature Caliban) and the darkness, where low beams lay in wait to deal lubbers a murderous crack on the head. Here was Sebastian's cabin, aft on the starboard side, where the now sobered and crapulous butler Stephano had carried a plate of ship's biscuit – only to find the cabin empty, the port open wide.

Sometimes, in the old days, it had been a useful rule to suspect anyone who claimed to have stumbled on a body, or lack of body. Gonzalo pondered. Stephano and his henchman Trinculo had behaved badly enough on the island with their inept plans to oust Prospero, take the place and rule it as their own. So they'd been soundly whipped for it at Prospero's command; they might resent ducal chastisement, but what had they to do with Sebastian? When great ones fall, Gonzalo told himself, it is by the hands of other great ones. What folly to conceive that the jester or the butler did it.

The fusty, cramped cabin had little to tell him. Soiled bedding and clothes; a cloudy steel mirror nailed askew to the bulkhead; crumbs mingling with rats' droppings on the deck timbers. Sebastian's writing-box lay shut up on the small table. Gonzalo thought to open this little desk, laid his hand on its polished wood, and felt a stickiness at one corner. A brownish smear which might be blood. The image leapt up before him like one of the mage-duke's seemings: the box hefted by an unknown hand, its sharp corner striking Sebastian's head, the limp prince laboriously pushed through the port into God's own bottomless and watery oubliette.

So much for imaginings. Might the cabin yield further facts? Inside the writing-box he found the expected ink bottles and a vilely cut quill. Within the lid, a few far from new sheets of paper: Sebastian had not been a great letter writer. A seal, and fragments of wax. A tiny pen-knife. One compartment contained a nutmeg. Another held a ball of crumpled paper which Gonzalo idly spread out . . .

> *You were seen to push King A. overboard before you made your brave show of being first rat out of the sinking ship. Let us . . .*

The mind rushed eagerly enough to complete that sentence. 'Let us speak of large sums in gold,' might it be? Next came a great blot which had run to and fro in antic patterns with the crumpling of the sheet. The writing, despite its neat line, had the wavering, slightly florid flourishes of a courtier's hand. A hand that had been trained to begin afresh once a letter had been marred, until the epistle ran smoothly from end to end, never blotting a line.

Gonzalo frowned. This game of *cui bono* was too much like the game of tig: Sebastian's dead hand had touched another, and the mystery of who might wish him ill became the mystery of who else might harbour thoughts of regicide. Which pointed in a most horrible direction indeed.

'Sire,' he said when he had regained the grateful sunshine of the foredeck, 'another question – if I may'

'We await no other audience this day,' said Alonso with mild irony.

'Cast your mind back to the height of the tempest, as the mariners began to cry aloud that our ship was lost. You went overboard. Soon we all did. But you in particular – could you have been pushed?'

'A dozen times, man! The mariners were colliding with us, thrusting us aside in their wild frenzy with the ropes and masts. Our whole craft seemed to spin like a wheel. We were on the heaving deck, we were whelmed in salt water, we were ashore, all as in a dream. And then everything becomes mazier still, as though I were soused in strong wine . . .'

Gonzalo nodded. Prospero and his apothecary's tricks.

'But . . . yes. Now that you stir up the memory, I fancy I recall being pushed in the back. Not a casual bump, but the thrust of two hands. Yet with something half-hearted about it. Could that have been when I tumbled overboard? I cannot say.' The king shivered. 'It is not a recollection that I wish to cherish.'

'Some things are best forgotten,' said Gonzalo, trying not to betray that his words came from the heart. He turned aside, and paced the swaying deck once more.

Cui bono was a harsh taskmaster. He had wondered at Antonio's bitter silence near the end of their island stay, but not until now at another silence before it began. A silence that passed unnoticed in the tempest. The passengers had staggered about a rain-lashed deck, hindering the mariners as the storm raged: Alonso dumbfounded that a mere boatswain should talk back to a king, Antonio and Sebastian swearing futilely at toiling sailors, even Gonzalo himself (he recalled with embarrassment) spinning foolish conceits about how their valiant boatswain was safe from drowning because born to be hanged. One face cried nothing, though. Had that remaining passenger on deck been keeping silence – biding his time – waiting for the moment when, unobserved in the storm-chaos, he might topple the king over the deckrail?

A dark deed, and a futile one: little did that person know that the luck of the tide or the minions of Prospero would bring them all safe to shore, including both the pusher and the pushed. Or that he had not been unobserved after all, and that Stephano would presently suggest an agreeable price for silence. Which would be the death of Stephano.

Gonzalo found himself gnawing at his beard, a bad habit which recurred in times of inner turmoil. Fragments of evidence whirled through his mind as though storm-driven. They came together in a grisly shape; but a shape which, his old sense of caution told him, was not proof to take before the king's justices. Such a story would not serve to hang a dog. But – his eyes narrowed as the proper question formulated itself – what *could* it do?

He sighed. It would be necessary to make a private appointment after dark, an appointment which he did not much relish. Other arrangements too. And, once again, he must consult Prospero's troubling book.

Dark of the moon, but the Mediterranean by night outdid the pale glitter of the stars; the water glowed in great swirls and bands of phosphorescence, and the ship's wake boiled with white fire. Gonzalo had picked a shaded corner of the aft deck, out of sight of the mariner on watch. Presently, noiselessly, the shadows at his side were filled with a dark and somehow sardonic presence.

Gonzalo said without preamble, 'He was first to shore. I remember Francisco babbling of how fast and well he swam: "His bold head 'bove the contentious waves he kept, and oared himself with his good arms with lusty stroke." Just a peppercorn in the balance, but evildoers are well known to flee the scene of the crime. And the spoilt note in Sebastian's writing-box pointed to one who was first out of the ship. Like a rat.'

'You over-top me,' said the voice of Antonio. 'I merely noted that he was the obvious gainer. Of course I had the advantage of hearing from my late ally Sebastian what was done during the storm. Will you name him, or shall I?'

Gonzalo resigned himself to pronouncing the name, whatever devils it might raise. 'Our young lover Prince Ferdinand. For he had everything to gain by removing Alonso: at a stroke he would become King of Naples. Later, having learned more of usurpers and their ways' – Gonzalo sensed an ironic bow from the shadows – 'he would have found it wise to make his assurance of the succession doubly sure by dealing first with the king's brother Sebastian. Who would doubtless have had good advice.' Another mocking bow. 'But Sebastian had also sealed his own death warrant by trying to exact a price for silence about Ferdinand's attempt on the king.'

'Wordy, but well said. There may be reasons after all why God put windbags into the world.'

'Once you think of Ferdinand,' said Gonzalo slowly, 'page after page from Prospero's book of words seems to bear witness. Here he claims to have been weeping for his father, but hears some music and on the instant forgets nine parts in ten of his sorrowing. Were those real tears? Almost at once he is making eyes at the old duke's daughter. Was this real grief? You are a clever man; you marked that.'

'Clever enough to win a duchy, not so clever as to keep it.'

'Even the chess-game in Prospero's cell. "Sweet lord, you play me false," cries the girl Miranda. A man who cheats at chess, the game of kings, may do likewise on this world's greater board.'

'The game of Kings of Naples. Almost, old whiskers, I come to like you.'

'Spare me that,' Gonzalo muttered.

Antonio's voice continued in light tones, as of a courtier embarking on a rare jest. 'Rather let us speak of brother Prospero, and what he likes or likes not. Will it be to his ducal liking that all these clever contrivances have achieved only the betrothal of his daughter to a princeling who has done murder – and has made a fair shot at parricide? What foulness he has so willingly embraced!'

A pause, as the spars creaked with a tiny shift of the wind. 'I think . . . I think it is too much to *your* liking, my lord.'

'Why should I deny it?'

'Because none of it is true,' Gonzalo said stolidly.

The figure in the shadows contracted into new alertness. 'Speak.'

'It seems that one brother of Milan is as adept as the other in mazes and deceptions spun out of air, sleights that vanish into air, into thin air . . . Why should Sebastian *write* that dangerous letter to Ferdinand, when a nod and a wink would suffice? Why, because the blot-ruined draft message was needed to lead old Gonzalo by the nose – together with your gentle hint of *Cui bono*?

'My wits are no longer quick, but after a time I saw that the note did not come from Sebastian's pen – a vilely cut quill that would set down only scratches and spatters. You should have used that pen, my lord, and not your own. Then, who was so well placed to knock him on the head than his special crony Antonio? I could not see Sebastian relaxing his guard for an instant when speaking with an angry Ferdinand. Again, when I bethought myself of the "half-hearted" push Alonso felt at the height of the tempest, my mother-wit said that this was not bold young Ferdinand but cowardly, hesitant Sebastian – observed by *you*, my lord, and assuring you that Sebastian was ready to join you in dark deeds, if only you would take the lead.'

'I fear, old man, that this night contains your death,' said Antonio very quietly.

'That fear I have long left behind. But tell me, why does Antonio, noble pretender to the duchy of Milan, stoop to involve himself in riddles and affairs of death – bloodying his hands for the sake of befouling young Ferdinand's name and discomfiting Duke Prospero? Poor foolish Sebastian was worth little, but deserved better than to be the sacrificed pawn in a new gambit. You had your brother's forgiveness, however poisonously phrased. Was the game of revenge not over?'

'It was not.' The thin voice became more conversational. 'Old man, think on this. My crime was not that great. Did I not rule Milan justly and well? True, it became necessary to exile Prospero when he absurdly clung to all the trappings and titles of power – yet none of the responsibilities. All *those*, he left to me. You see it in his book, even where he rants about my perfidy: "I thus neglecting worldly ends, all dedicated to closeness and the bettering of my mind . . ." Is that the voice of a worthy ruler?'

Gonzalo shrugged. 'I need not debate the greatness of your crime, when there was no great punishment. Befuddlement in a masque of shadows on that island of phantasms, a few hard words, and forgiveness. Was this such cruel retribution?'

'Gonzalo, he took my son.'

'Son?' Confusion filled Gonzalo's head, a medley of winds and fancy lights and forgotten voices. 'Your son?' An elusive name: 'Ju . . . was it Julius?'

'I, even *I*, had almost forgot. I knew at the last that I had lost something dear, and wrestled in silence with my memories. A triple pox on my brother's grammarie and snares of the mind! Then, you see, as we made good sail and the island dropped beneath the horizon, I read it in the book that Prospero made for my torment, the book called *The Tempest*. And I remembered.

'That lucky young fool Ferdinand said it: "Myself am Naples, Who with mine eyes, never since at ebb, beheld the king my father wracked."

"Then he went on" "Yes, faith, and all his lords, the Duke of Milan and his brave son being twain." '

'At that hour, I was the Duke of Milan. My brave son Julio sailed with us. And where is he? Gone, a piece taken from the chessboard, plucked from all our memories by Prospero's whoreson drugs and enchantment, my bloodline ended. I knelt pleading at my brother's feet, and he would only say that perhaps his book was in error. And you, prating loon, you say the game of revenge is over!'

Suddenly, irresistibly, he bore Gonzalo towards the deckrail. There was a terrible wiry strength in that thin body. 'I will have more blood. Blood will have blood—'

There came another disturbance in the aft-deck shadows as something massy leapt from the top of the deckhouse. A great crash of sea-boots striking the deck was followed by a small, dead-sounding thud, and a hiss of expelled air from Antonio's lips. He slumped.

'Stocking full of sand, my lord,' said the boatswain respectfully. 'Hope I done right. You told me to wait until matters went awry.'

'Yes. You have my thanks,' Gonzalo said, breathing hard. 'I owe you more than gold, but gold there shall be.'

The shipmaster emerged from the darkness nearer the stern. He bent and felt the huddled shape on the deck; felt again; opened clothing. There came a long pause. 'Tapped him a mite too hard there, boatswain. But it's for the best, I judge. Lunatics are rank bad luck at sea. The men don't like it. Let's have no more of these dirty games of statecraft on my clean ship. Bestir ye now, Boats – yarely—'

Stepping back, Gonzalo whispered a prayer as the erstwhile Duke of Milan slid into the phosphorescent waters and their waiting sea-change. Perhaps this truly was for the best. When the wits of great ones fail . . . He frowned to himself. Had it been too easy? Surely Antonio would expect a hoary councillor, who had survived so many decades, to take certain precautions before meetings at dead of night. Lofty Antonio, whose overweening pride would never let him plunge to death in an admission of despair; but who, when life held no more, might permit others to soil their hands by giving him surcease.

Gonzalo shuddered. Such imaginings should be dismissed as the stuff that nightmares are made on. But still, but still, he felt curiously reluctant ever again to speak with Prospero. 'O rejoice,' he had found himself saying on the island – that the god from the machine had restored harmony, that Ferdinand had found his wife, Prospero his dukedom, 'and all of us ourselves when no man was his own.' Now that golden joy was darkened, like a once-clear stream that runs turbid and filthy in the aftermath of a tempest.

WE ARE FOR THE DARK

Stan Nicholls

We now turn to the real world of William Shakespeare – or as real as we know it. Despite the fact that he is regarded by many as the world's greatest playwright, we know precious little about his childhood. He was apparently born at Stratford-upon-Avon in April 1564 and educated at the local school. His father, John, was a farmer, but settled in the town around 1551 and became prosperous as a merchant and businessman, rising to become the town mayor in 1568. However, by the late 1570s his fortunes had failed and he lost much of his property. Shakespeare's mother was Mary Arden, the daughter of a local farmer. Otherwise nothing is known of his childhood. This allows Stan Nicholls a free rein in exploring Shakespeare's youth.

Six of the clock ante meridiem, twenty-third day of April, the year of Our Lord 1576.

The dust motes dancing in the beam of watery sunlight made him think of fairies. They set in train the notion of a tale concerning the lives and loves of the fairy-folk, dwelling in their forest domain. He resolved to write down the thought when he was able.

It came to him that fairies and like elfin beings were more in keeping with the balm of a Summer's night than the chill of an early Spring morn. Yet still he populated the shaft flowing through the chapel window with phantasmagorical creatures of ancient lore, moving gracefully to the tune of unseen pipers. Such were the caprices that paraded regularly upon the dais of his mind. Summer it may not be, William Shakespeare reflected, but this day held especial magic for him all the same.

Magister Armitage droned on.

Will fidgeted slightly, his lower back numb against the uncushioned bench. Even after four – no, five years – his body had not ceased rebelling at the hour at which he was required to present himself for schooling. Absently flicking aside a stray lock of ginger hair, he snuck a glance at Guy Spencer sitting beside him. His friend, and the other boys, some five and twenty in number, were blinking, half awake, as the morning sermon rolled on.

Oblivious to his youthful congregation's discomfort, head of masters Geoffrey Armitage continued wading through a passage from the lavishly appointed Bishop's Bible propped before him on the lectern. Will found no fault with the text. His feeling of tedium arose, as ever, from a delivery so long of wind.

Guy caught Will's eye. They fought an urge to giggle.

Armitage's second-in-command, Samuel Gower, standing ramrod straight and rancid-faced beside the row of pews, noticed and sent them a fearsome glare. He brandished his leather strap. The pair sobered at once and returned their attention frontward.

At last, Armitage came to the end of his recitation, urged all to labour hard in the day ahead and reminded them of the virtues of *mens sana in corpore sano*. In clipped tone he dismissed them to break fast.

Outside the chapel, the students fell to whispered boisterousness as they walked towards the refectory or made off to gather books and notes for their lessons. Will and Guy took the cloistered way. To their right, beyond the pillars, lay an enclosed grassy square edged with borders just beginning to flower. On the opposite side of the garden an open latticed gate afforded a glimpse of Stratford, already bustling with marketeers.

In common with the other boys, Will and Guy wore tunics of darkest blue, indicating their status as pupils of the grammar school. The garments were cut from wool, the town's chief provider of trade and prosperity. Will was musing on whether his companion's modest frame would ever grow enough to fill his properly, when Guy spoke, voice pitched low.

''Tis your birth day, Will. Good health. How doth it feel it to reach your twelfth season?'

Will smiled. 'I own I am not quite giddy with the weight of years. Twelve feels much as eleven did. As you will know for yourself soon enough.'

They were joined by Daniel Burrage. His was the only brain that, in truth, Will accepted as nearest to equalling his own. Though he had never uttered this opinion.

'Good morrow,' Will greeted. 'Are you game for Virgil this after noon?'

'A probation of the philosopher's tracts? Aye, I'll match wits with you.'

'And come off second best again, I'll warrant,' Guy opined.

It was meant as gentle raillery, and despite being known for a humourless disposition, Burrage took it as such.

John Dudley fell in beside them, shoulders round, gaze downcast. At ten years he was the youngest of their circle.

'You look troubled, John,' Will said. 'What ails you?'

'I know not the Greek we were set,' the boy replied miserably, 'nor can I grip the summes.'

'You *can*,' Will assured him. 'You lack not the intellect but the mettle.' He laid a comforting hand on his arm. 'Have faith in yourself.'

'I will be beaten.'

'No, you will prevail.'

As he spoke, they were passed by a sobbing child.

'Methinks that was not best timed,' Guy muttered.

'Nor this,' added Will, nodding toward an approaching figure.

Thomas Nashe swaggered up to them. He was a robust lad, short and stocky, heavy browed and with a distinct absence of neck.

'Ah, the swots,' he sneered. 'Save you, Dudley, the runt of the litter.'

'If our company be so distasteful, allow us to bid you a heartfelt good riddance,' Will responded.

'Come, come, ill grace befits you not on such a day.' His words dripped with sarcasm. ''Tis a time for celebration I'm told, and doubtless you will be presenting us with one of your verses. To commemorate yourself.'

'Yes, my fancy is to write of the piling years as like a wide, black well that swalloweth all hope. I would take as my inspiration your mouth, Tom.'

Nashe's face darkened ominously.

'Hold,' Daniel interjected. 'What is this?'

They looked in the direction he indicated. On the edge of the lawn, perhaps ten yards away, Samuel Gower stood in close proximity to Nathan Webb, the Bible studies tutor. It was obvious from their intemperate expressions and gestures that they were engaged in an argument.

It ended abruptly with Webb storming away. Then Gower saw the boys staring and headed for them like a vengeful wraith. He arrived red faced and seething with anger.

'*You!*' he snapped. 'Shakespeare and Spencer. I will broach no disrespect in chapel.' He levelled his strap at them. 'Repeat it and you will feel my sting. And *all* of you will observe the rule of silence when moving about the school. Ignore me at your peril.'

Without further ado, Gower strode off.

None mistook the gravity of his threat. Sharp experience had been their mentor in such matters. As they continued their journey, all, Nashe included, were united in unspoken detestation of the man. Shortly, Nashe departed on an errand of his own. John and Daniel went on ahead, leaving Will and Guy to travel alone to the dining hall.

They were the last to arrive. A master boomed '*privatim et seriatim*.' The crowd of students did as they were told and formed ranks in front of the door. Through it, Will could make out the long, plain wooden tables laid with jugs of water and ale, alongside platters bearing loaves of barley bread, fish, eggs and wedges of pungent cheese.

Having stood in line for several minutes, the duo were at the point of entering when Armitage appeared from behind. He looked into the hall and tutted.

'No sign of Magister Gower,' he complained, as much to himself as them, 'and he is to lead the blessing afore bread is broken.' He addressed the boys directly. 'Masters Shakespeare, Spencer. Go with haste and bid my deputy's presence forthwith.'

Will asked, 'Where may we find him, sir?'

'His study would be most fertile a place to begin. Be gone.'

They chorused assent and set off, finding little joy in the prospect.

To reach their destination meant crossing the garden square. As they trod the spongy grass, Will pointed. 'Look: Tobias.'

The school gardener and jack-of-all-trades, was digging in one of the flower beds. Seeing them coming, his countenance brightened. He doffed his cap.

Falteringly he mouthed, 'Good morrow, young masters.' His pattern of speech, and general aspect, left no doubt that he was a simpleton.

They returned his greeting warmly.

'Still toiling with the fruits of God's bounty, I perceive,' Will commented.

'Aye, master. I am blessed, am I not?'

'That you are, Toby,' Will told him kindly. 'But we beg you forgive our hurry. We carry a message of import.'

Toby grinned. 'Fare thee well then.' He went back to his spade.

''Tis a bitter fate he must bear,' Guy remarked once out of earshot.

'Truly. Though a gentler soul t'would be hard to find. We must remember him when at prayer, friend Guy.'

They arrived at the door of Gower's study. It stood ajar. They knocked. There was no reply. Will called Gower's name, but was rewarded only with silence. He knocked again, with sufficient force that the door swung inward a jot. Deciding the room was empty, they made to leave.

A sound from within halted them. They could not make out what it was. Summoning fortitude, Will entered. Guy followed. The chamber was in darkness, its heavy drapes still undrawn. No candles or lanterns burned, although a thin crack of light did penetrate on the far side of the room, where a second door was likewise part ajar.

Calling Gower's name once more brought the noise afresh. Its identity remained elusive.

'A cat, mayhap?' Guy ventured in a whisper.

Will shrugged, mystified.

Leading the way, he moved further into the study. Then he stumbled against some sprawled obstruction, and nearly fell. There was a groan. Alarmed, he bade Guy draw the curtains. The flood of light revealed a dreadful scene.

Gower lay upon the floor, his head a bloody mess.

Both boys let out involuntary gasps of horror. The first to gather himself, Will knelt for a closer inspection. It took no great knowledge of the human physique to tell that the man had been savagely battered. But as far as Will could tell, no likely weapon was in sight.

Gower made a sound. Will leaned closer. His lips working feebly, the magister was trying to say something. At length, he managed a single, barely perceptible word. Then a crimson trickle snaked from the corner of his mouth and the death rattle sounded.

Will slowly rose, ashen-face, and crossed himself.

Guy did likewise and asked, 'What did he say?'

'It sounded like . . . It could only have been . . . *Fraser*.'

They stared at each other, appalled.

Five and thirty minutes past eight of the clock ante meridiem.

'You are sure that was all he said?' Captain Peregrine Adams asked again.

'Quite sure,' Will repeated. ''Twas but the lone word.'

'And you, master Guy? You are certain that the dying man's utterance did not reach your ears?'

'It did not, sir.'

The Captain of the Watch frowned and cast his gaze around those present in the school's smaller lecture room. Apart from the boys and Armitage, they consisted of Nathan Webb, Latin master Francis Quincey and Henry Savage, who taught Philosophy.

'You have, what, just above two dozen pupils here, Magister Armitage?'

'That is correct.'

'And these gentlemen comprise the teaching body?'

'They and one other. We are fortunate in being well-funded by the Church and private benefactors.'

'And the one other of whom you speak?'

'Ambroise Kean, our general factotum. He is currently supervising the boys.'

'Tell me of him.'

'Unlike my colleagues here, who are Oxford men, he is Stratford born and bred, taken on partly through merit, partly out of Christian charity.'

'How so?'

'He was discharged from the army sore wounded. The affliction left him with a leg all but useless.'

There was a knock at the door.

'Come!' Armitage called.

A member of Adams's Watch entered. He carried a weighty, short-handled hoe. Its iron head was stained with blood.

'I found this, sir,' the man reported, handing over the tool.

Adams inspected it. 'You will observe, gentlemen, not only blood, but on closer examination strands of hair. To my eye, they match the victim's. The murder weapon, no doubt of it.' He nodded at the watchman. 'Good work.'

Will and Guy seemed to have been forgotten. They exchanged surreptitious glances and did nothing to draw attention to themselves.

'Where did you find this?' Adams wanted to know.

'In the lean-to by the gardener's quarters, sir,' the guard replied.

'What more proof is needed?' Francis Quincey exclaimed. 'Gower named his murderer, and now this.'

Adams turned to Armitage. 'Tell me about Tobias Fraser.'

'Another discharged from Her Majesty's service, though of common rank. He was rendered an idiot by a blow to the skull. There was prospect of him becoming a sturdy beggar if not taken in by us.'

'More Christian charity?'

'Indeed, Captain. We are governed by the principles of High Church and saw it as our duty.'

'He has never given cause for concern,' Nathan Webb intervened.

'Yet his mind is not his own,' Henry Savage countered. 'Who can say what let he has over the demons that torture him?'

Will could contain himself no longer. 'Your pardon, sirs,' he piped-up.

They all looked to him, including Guy, though where their expressions held consternation, his was apprehensive.

'You have something to say, Master Shakespeare?' Armitage answered sternly.

'Tobias Fraser has less malice in his smallest finger than most others have in their entire beings,' Will proclaimed. 'It is beyond reason that he should harm another.'

Armitage came back with asperity. 'We are obliged for your

considered opinion, formed as it is by your many years' observation of the human condition.'

Will blushed but persevered. 'It is an impression shared by all who know him.'

'Is that the totality of your measurement of the man, or is there more you would impart?' The head master now barely contained his displeasure.

'His sweetness of nature best speaks for itself, Magister. But I lay before you one verity. Tobias was at work in the garden scant moments before Master Spencer and I came upon the sad scene.'

Adams took up the point, 'And thus could not have committed the atrocity? I think not. There are two doors to Magister Gower's study, both allowing access to different parts of the garden. Fraser could have outpaced you by going the other way. He might have entered the room, done the deed and made his escape before you arrived. Again, he could have undertaken the grisly act *before* you met him.'

'You attribute more guile to him than he is capable of, sir. Moreover, I lay stress on the chance of uncertainty in Magister Gower's dying word. It *sounded* like "Fraser", but he was weak and—'

'Enough!' Armitage snapped. 'All sensible intelligence points Tobias's way. There is no telling what a man of unsound humours might be capable of. And you, Master Shakespeare, are close to impertinence. You will hold your tongue.'

'It doth seem that the man is most likely culpable,' Adams decided, 'and we must act. But I will use the powers vested in me to order that all, students and masters, remain confined to these premises for the rest of the day.'

There was a clamour of protest. 'Surely we should close out of respect?' Armitage objected.

'It is possible that Fraser is *not* the culprit,' Adams conceded. 'In which case I want all where none can flee. More of the Watch will be brought to enforce my wish.'

Armitage bristled at this. 'What if the murderer was someone from outside the school, and has already made off?'

'That eventuality is another reason no one should leave. If word spreads through Stratford that a murderer may be loose, my watch will have panic to deal with.'

'I shall appeal to the vicar of Holy Trinity, Jeremiah Rowley. He has ultimate authority over the school.'

'You must do as fit, sir. As a matter of fact I had already sent a man to bring the vicar here, but he cannot be located at present.'

Armitage sighed. 'You will have your way, Captain,' he reluctantly agreed. 'For the time being. But lessons are suspended. In that way at least we can show our respect for Gower. The boys will spend the hours in quiet contemplation and study.'

Adams gave him a stiff head bow. 'I am obliged, Magister. Watchman, arrest this Fraser and take him to the place of incarceration. Have one other with you, lest he prove violent.'

The guard hurried out, grim faced and purposeful. Will and Guy looked on helplessly.

Eleven of the clock ante meridiem.

The boys had been turned out into the garden square for their mid-morning constitutional, as on any normal day. Ambroise Kean, dragging his withered leg whenever he needed to move about, had been placed in charge of maintaining order.

Guy and Will were standing apart from the others when they observed Toby Fraser being marched off in irons by two members of the Watch carrying pikes. His interrogation had lasted the better portion of two hours. He was crestfallen and looked afraid.

'An outrage!' Guy complained. 'Surely Toby must have turned aside the foul accusation made against him?'

'I fear not. He has little enough wits at the best of times. I wager he could give no good account of himself. We are witnessing a terrible injustice, and are powerless to do anything about it.'

Guy seethed with frustration. 'When my father hears of this—'

'Of course! Father!'

Puzzled, Guy asked, 'What of my father?'

'Not yours, *mine*.'

'Have you, too, lost your wits? What light could your father throw on this matter?'

'None. But he might vest *us* with the power to do so. He has been Chief Alderman these six years past, remember. He owns property in Henley Street, and there is no finer wittawer in all of Stratford. Why, he has even applied for the grant of a coat of arms. John Shakespeare is a man of substance hereabouts.'

'You *have* left your senses. What purpose in telling me what I already know?'

'My notion turns on what it is you do not know. Our attendance here is free, but my father gives money to help maintain the school. He is, I own, the single biggest donator of coin, bar the Church itself.'

'Your gist?'

'A word from his eldest son could end all that. Or at least Magister Armitage might be made to believe so. And with a free hand—'

'We could look into the matter ourselves!'

'Just so. I will go to Armitage this instant.'

'With me at your side.'

Will favoured his friend with a warm smile. 'Then we are of one mind. If Tobias Fraser is not the perpetrator of this heinous crime we shall bend our wills to prove it so.'

They were about to leave when John Dudley and Daniel Burrage arrived to delay them. The rowdy, Thomas Nashe, was not far behind.

'What think you of this tragedy, Will?' John said.

'Your word is well chosen. It is indeed a tragedy.'

All but Nashe nodded in sage agreement.

'And what would you do of it, Shakespeare?' he sneered. 'Write one of your tedious *poems* to put the world to rights? Hypocrites! I for one have no regrets at Gower's fate. The man was a brute.'

'It is said that it takes a swine to know a swine.'

'Save your cleverness. Can any of you in honesty say that you feel sorrow at his passing?' He thrust a chunky finger at John Dudley, making him flinch. 'Can you? After the way he beat and humiliated you? Or you, Burrage, thinking on Gower's belittling of your work?' He glared at Will and Guy. 'In your hearts you know I speak the truth.'

'Gower was severe, I grant you,' Will replied. 'But that does not warrant his death.'

'Does it not? I tell you, Toby Fletcher should be rewarded, not punished, for his deed.'

'You are a sad braggart, Tom, and your empty bravado is far bigger than your honour.'

For a fraction of a second, Guy felt sure Nashe would strike Will.

Instead he barked, 'Have it your way, you snivelling weaklings!' Then he turned and strode away.

'Poor Tom,' Will said. 'All piss and wind, signifying nothing.'

John and Daniel likewise drifted off.

Staring at Nashe's broad, departing back, Will added, 'This makes me think, friend Guy, that if Toby did not put an end to Gower it is not beyond reason that one of our own number did.'

Five and forty minutes past eleven of the clock ante meridiem.

'I can see you are bent on being vexatious, Shakespeare,' Armitage fumed. 'And a meddlesome . . . *child* is more baggage than we can carry at this time.'

Will straightened himself to his full height, a height above the norm for one of his age, and fixed Armitage with an unswerving gaze. Or at least what he hoped resembled one. 'I mean no disrespect, Magister. Can I take it that you will allow me to ask questions of the masters?'

'The threat you imply leaves me little option. For the remainder of this day, yes, you may pry. *If* the masters chose to speak to you. But you are on a hiding to nought. Fraser is guilty.'

'*Dum spiro spero*, Magister.'

'Then mark this, boy. Let not your thirst for story-weaving colour your vision. Nor your silvered tongue lead you into deep waters,' he added portentously.

'I am indebted, Magister.'

Armitage rose from his imposing desk. 'I have matters to attend. I will pass the word that you have permission to ask your questions.' He left the room.

Guy let out a sigh of relief. 'You took a risk.'

'I do it gladly to give Toby his chance of justice.'

'What now?'

'We inquire of Magister Webb the cause of his disputation with Gower.'

'Then make haste. We have but the confines of this single day. Or what remains of it.'

Guy exited. In following, Will's eye fell upon a portrait half hidden by the open door. He had rarely been in Armitage's *sanctum sanctorum*, and the dimly-lit picture was new to him. He lingered, squinting at the likeness and the inscription upon the bottom of its frame.

'Come!' Guy yelled.

Will shrugged and sped after him. They found Nathan Webb in his own study, poring over the Scriptures.

Having made apologies for the intrusion, Will got straight to the heart. 'Has Magister Armitage told you that I have his permission to ask questions of the masters, sir?'

'He did say something about you making inquiries on his behalf,' Webb answered vaguely. 'Is that so?'

Will and Guy realised that Webb, notorious for his vacancy, had misunderstood. He believed the boys were acting *for* Armitage, rather than independently.

'That is so,' Will confirmed.

Guy noticed that his friend had his fingers crossed behind his back.

'Then ask your questions,' invited Webb.

Will took a breath and plunged in. 'Shortly before Magister Gower's death, we saw you and he engaged in an altercation. Pray, what were you arguing about?'

Webb's thin smile froze. He was taken aback. 'There is need for this?'

'Aye, sir,' Will insisted.

'Well, the bad humour that arose between us had to do with discipline. I took issue with him about the way he dealt out physical punishment in such a generous manner. It came to a head at that time because he had just struck a pupil for, I believed, insufficient reason.'

Will remembered the crying boy in the cloistered passageway.

'Of course, I agree that you students should be properly disciplined,' he added. 'Spare the rod, *et cetera*. But Gower was too severe. We are a Christian institution. Love and compassion should govern our actions.'

'I understand,' Will told him.

'You can perhaps imagine how much I now regret remonstrating with Magister Gower so soon before the man's demise. God rest his soul.'

'So say us all,' Guy murmured.

'Is there more?' Webb asked.

'I, uhm, think not, sir,' Will said.

'Then you will excuse me if I return to my studies.'

They thanked him and left.

Outside, Guy brought up the subject of Will's deceit. 'God will forgive you, Will. You dissembled for a righteous cause. What think you of Magister Webb's explanation?'

'It is true we saw a crying boy, and I have no doubt Gower was responsible. And our Bible studies tutor is well known for his generosity of nature. Yet . . .'

'Yes?'

'All men's souls have corners where light does not intrude. We have only his word that the quarrel *was* about discipline.'

'You are wise beyond your years, Will. What shall we do now?'

'Time is short. My idea is that I go to talk with Magister Savage. Meantime, you mingle with the students and sniff out what you can.'

One of the clock post meridiem.

Will was agreeably surprised to find that the Philosophy master had no qualms about speaking with him on the subject of Gower's death. He suspected this was because he was Henry Savage's star pupil, and for the sake of their shared passion for Ovid.

Midway in their hitherto mundane conversation, an intriguing fact emerging.

'In due course,' Savage revealed, 'I fully expected to succeed him as second master here.'

'How so?'

'He let slip that he was preparing to return to his native Cumbria. To take up another teaching post, I presume.'

It crossed Will's mind that Savage's professed sorrow at Gower's demise barely hid his glee at the prospect of taking the dead man's position.

'Now your ambition has no barriers,' Will observed.

It was a step too far. A flash of malice lit Savage's eyes. 'I trust that your finger of suspicion does not point at *me*!'

'I merely—'

'Merely nothing! If you are so certain that the idiot Fraser was not responsible, there are others here with much more reason than I.'

'You would care to name such?'

'Kean, for one. He was mocked by Gower as being an abomination in God's eyes because of that foreshortened leg of his.'

After that, Savage became curiously reticent. Will made an excuse and departed. He met Guy near the kitchens and recounted what had passed with Savage. For his part, Guy reported that enquiries with the other boys yielded little not already known.

'Gower was unpopular, which we knew. More than one student openly confessed little regret at his passing.'

'It seems that there are fewer here *without* a reason to detest the man than there are with.'

'I confess myself confounded, Will. This rivals any plot you have written.'

'As yet, my friend, as yet. I was on my way to Ambroise Kean, in yonder provisions area. Accompany me.'

It took a little longer to draw out Kean than the others they had so far confronted. But in time he came to admit that Gower had indeed mocked his affliction. Will asked gently how he came by it.

'I served in a company with Fraser. We were both struck down in the same engagement, as unhappy Fate would have it. As Stratford men, and good Church-goers, we were offered positions here upon our discharge.'

Will hadn't known about this connection between the men. Another piece was added to the puzzle in his mind.

'Tell me, master,' he ventured, 'do'st thou think Fraser capable of a deed as foul as murder?'

Kean paused before replying. 'I cannot speak of another. Which of us would be so bold as to say they could see into the hearts of their fellow creatures?'

Will was about to pursue the subject when they were interrupted. Francis Quincey and the vicar of Holy Trinity church, Jeremiah Rowley, entered the room in a rush.

'You see?' Quincey exclaimed. 'I said something was afoot!'

The vicar moved forward. 'I am told that you boys have been troubling the masters and other pupils with probings into today's outrage. What game is this?'

'No game, Reverend,' Will returned. 'We believe an injustice is being done, and act with Magister Armitage's blessing.'

'That I did not know. What can you hope to achieve?'

'For a start, whether the victim had enemies.'

A cynical laugh escaped Quincey's lips. 'It would be more pointed to inquire as to whether he had friends.'

'Would you count yourself amongst the latter?'

'If that were my lot I would hurl myself from yonder Copton Bridge.'

Quincey realised he had allowed the heat of the moment to draw him too deep. He tried to dampen the fires. 'Suffice it to say that we ploughed our separate furrows, Master Shakespeare.'

Will turned to vicar Rowley. 'Do you know of any enemies who might have gone to extremes to deal with Magister Gower, Reverend Father?'

'Am *I* to be put to the inquisition by a child now? As I understand it, the dying man uttered the name of his killer before he left this world.'

'It seemed so.'

'Then there is no more to be proven.'

'Perhaps not. Where were you when Captain Adams sought you out earlier?'

'I am not obliged to explain my movements to a minor!'

'As I said, Magister Armitage—'

'May I remind you that I, as a representative of the Church, have dominion over this school and Armitage.'

'You are criticising the head teacher's actions?'

'No! I have known him since he came to Stratford from the north-west. He is a fine man. And I have had enough of your offensive behaviour. You and your compatriot will withdraw at once. Do not doubt that I will consult Alderman Shakespeare about this disgraceful disrespect at first light tomorrow, if not sooner!'

Will and Guy withdrew. They trudged back to the main schoolroom disconsolate and in silence. Once there, Will went to his heavy wooden desk.

'All have their reasons, it seems,' Guy remarked.

'Yet only one reason *enough*. But you are right, Guy. Any of the masters, any of the boys, might have committed this most heinous of sins.'

'Could we be wrong about Toby?'

'I think not. But I am only a child, with a child's understanding of adults, I confess. I would wish I knew more.' He sighed. 'This should be solvable. We are, after all, taught the principles of Logic. And something troubles me. It tickles at the back of my mind . . .'

He reached into his desk and hefted a tome.

Guy recognised it instantly. 'Ah, *The Metamorphoses*. Your beloved Ovid.'

'Aye, and the Good Book given me by my parents.' He produced the Geneva Bible. 'These are my strength, my comfort . . . my inspiration. I would be alone, good friend.'

Four of the clock post meridiem.

The *something* still nagged in the recesses of Will's mind. His hours of communion with the tracts he found so inspirational had not brought it forth. He left the building, head down, and went to the others on the lawn.

'Our day is nearly done,' Guy said.

'Yes, and it closes dark indeed for Toby. We tried, we failed.'

They sat in gloomy contemplation of their defeat.

Tom Nashe arrived. Will felt, for the first time in his short life, that if the bully said anything to upset him he might offer another human being violence.

'Such long faces!' Nashe gibed. 'A poor brotherhood of the intellect we have here!'

'Brotherhood,' Will repeated, eyes glazing.

Guy was baffled. 'Hmmm?'

'Brotherhood . . . brotherhood. *Brotherhood*!' Will leapt to his feet, bounded to Nashe and pumped the startled ruffian's hand. 'Thank you, Tom, *thank you!* Your ignorance has opened a portal in my mind and let in a blaze of light.'

Nashe stared at him, slack-jawed.

'Guy,' Will said, 'I must away to Captain Adams. Be of good heart!'

They watched as Toby, smiling and tearful, was returned.

'*Now* will you tell us how you performed this miracle?' Guy pleaded.

'All pieces were before us,' Will pointed out. He used his fingers to count them off. 'First, the portrait of a man. Second, its inscription.

Third, the chance reference to a north-westerly county. Last, and most shiningly obvious, Gower's dying word.'

'What of it?' Daniel said.

'Gower *was* naming his killer, but in his last moments he reverted to a classical form of expression. The word was not Fraser. It was *frater*.'

'Brother,' Guy translated.

'Precisely. The crime was that most terrible transgression of God's law – fratricide.'

'Look,' John said.

The Watch emerged with their new prisoner, and this time Justice was served.

As the pupils of Stratford Grammar looked on, Geoffrey Armitage was taken away in shame and chains.

'How did you know, Will?' Guy asked. 'Gower and Armitage did not remotely resemble each other.'

'No. Armitage favoured their mother in appearance. But Gower took on the look of their late father, the man in the portrait in Gower's study.'

'And its inscription?'

'That noted an estate in Cumbria. Magister Savage spoke of Gower's intention to return to that region, and of how it was his native soil.'

'What motive could there be for so awful a deed?' Guy wondered.

'Gower was the elder sibling. He stood to inherit the substantial estates on the death of their father. That death took place a week ago. Armitage feared his brother coming into the family fortune. He knew him for what he was: a violent miscreant with a bent for the demon drink. The fortune would have been frittered. They had their last row this morning, and violence triumphed.'

'How came Gower to be here at all?'

'In order that his brother could keep an eye on him. Armitage, by the by, was the family name. Gower was their mother's maiden name. Geoffrey persuaded Samuel to take that name lest he, Geoffrey, be accused of nepotism. All this came out when Armitage was confronted by Captain Adams. He broke and confessed.'

'I do not understand,' Guy admitted, 'why Armitage sent us to find Gower, knowing him to be already dead.'

'Need drove him. It was Gower's turn to say break fast prayers, and *not* to have sent someone for him would have been suspicious in itself.'

'Well done, Will,' Daniel told him. 'You have sent a villain to the executioner's block.'

'I see Armitage as more tragic than black-hearted. Not unlike a character from an entertainment I have been pondering. Of which I have a few lines about my person.'

He reached into his tunic, brought out a parchment and cleared his throat. The boys stirred, a little uneasily.

'Of carnal, bloody, and unnatural acts;' Will read, 'Of accidental judgements, casual slaughters; Of deaths put on by cunning and forc'd cause . . .'

'That's enough!' they cried in unison.

'Go into trade, like your father,' Daniel suggested.

'Or the Watch!' Guy called out.

'Think again, Will,' young John advised. 'Methinks thou wilt never find thy true path as a poet.'

The Tragedy of
Mr Arden of Feversham 

FOOTSTEPS IN THE SNOW

Amy Myers

The play Arden of Feversham *was registered in 1592 and was at one time attributed to Shakespeare, though it has also been ascribed to Thomas Kyd and Christopher Marlowe. It's the earliest domestic tragedy in English and was based on the real-life murder of Thomas Arden, which took place in Faversham in Kent in February 1551. The following story sees Shakespeare and his publisher, Edward White, drawn into trying to solve the forty-year-old crime.*

'I will make thy fortune, Master White.'

I was all attention as young Kit Marlowe burst into the Sun and Moon tavern. I quickly hushed him, however, although business was poor in the book trade, and Marlowe's *Tamburlaine* and *The Jew of Malta* were the rage of London. I grow more cautious with the years.

'Why me?' I asked. 'You didn't come to me to print *Tamburlaine*.'

'Because, Edward' – these upstart young playwrights are over-familiar, but I held my peace while Kit sat on the table, helping himself to my sherris-sack, 'my play will tell the *true* story behind the murder of Thomas Arden of Feversham.'

My fortune *was* made! I am the owner of the copyright in several plays on Arden, which have titillated the public's morbid interest ever since that terrible crime of 1551. It may have been 1590 now, but it was still a certain draw at my bookstall by the Little North Door of St Paul's. If I displayed too much excitement, however, the price of my licence to print from the Company of Stationers might well go up to over fivepence.

The murder of Arden of Feversham has all the ingredients beloved of the theatre groundlings. Alice, wife to the mercenary and jealous Thomas Arden, former mayor of Feversham and customer of the port, was overcome by lust for young Mosby, a tailor turned gentleman's steward. Eager to enjoy more of his favours as well as more of her husband's money, she conspired with Mosby, together with Michael her husband's steward, and other aggrieved citizens to murder her husband. Two dastardly villains, Black Will and Shakebag, were employed for the task, and Arden was murdered in his own parlour while his wife stayed by.

Even as I gloated over my good luck, however, I thought of a snag. 'The truth is known,' I frowned, 'and seven hanged or burned for it.'

Everyone knew the story. Hiding the body in the counting house, while the villains dispersed, this foul woman calmly gave a supper party while her daughter played upon the virginals. The body was later dragged through the garden and back gate, and laid in a nearby field, where it was discovered by the mayor and a London grocer called Pryme. A trail of footprints left in the snow led them quickly enough to Mistress Alice and her confederates.

Kit's ruff advanced perilously close to my nose, as he hissed, 'The verdict was wrong. 'Twas a conspiracy but not as is believed. What I think really happened is—'

'I don't want to know,' I shrieked, as Kit summoned the serving wench for more sherris-sack. The life of a London bookseller and stationer is not thought unduly dangerous, but I dislike taking risks, even if all the participants are long since dead.

'Tush, man. Have you no guts?'

'I have and I would prefer to keep them.'

Kit laughed merrily, slapping his thighs as though I jested. 'It must be printed as by an unknown author, Edward,' and, seeing my disappointment explained, 'Canterbury, my birthplace, lies close to Feversham, and I am known there. My father was born nearby and told me the tale often. Methinks I smell a dead rat or two, and I would fain seek them out. But I will go quietly.'

'I doubt that, Master Marlowe,' I retorted nervously. 'Do you not recall your stay in Newgate last year after a brawl?'

'Twas not my fault.' Kit was indignant. 'Fear not, I am not so much a hothead that I would find it stone cold. But I would seek the truth and justice, and you will have your play.'

I heard no more of *Arden of Feversham* for nearly two years and assumed Kit had forgotten Justice (who is a nimble gentleman), while he lorded it over the group of young playwrights growing up round Philip Henslowe and Lord Strange's Men at the Rose theatre. To make a living in '92, with plague shutting the theatres, I was forced to abandon plays altogether and fall back on my stand-by trade of saucy ballads, and when I heard that Marlowe was at Chislehurst hard at work upon a play, I had little hope that it was *Arden*.

Until, as April opened, I had a visitor to my bookstall.

'Master White?'

I was diverted from my noonday pot of ale brought by my boy from the tavern.

'Master Shakespeare, is it not?'

I knew him slightly by sight but had never talked with him. He was a pleasant-faced young man, not yet thirty, but nondescript had it not been for the keen eyes – which went with his reputation. Ambitious, I had heard, a junior member of Henslowe's playwrights' circle, who pool their efforts to keep the voracious theatre-going public happy.

'I come from Master Marlowe.' Shakespeare waved a script. 'He bade me deliver you this play, and asks that you register it soon so that it may be printed and bought.'

The Tragedy of Arden of Feversham and Blackwill, I read. This was manna from heaven, if it contained no risk to me. I would register it tomorrow, print it and have it on my bookstall at St Paul's within two days. I have an unjust reputation for sloth, but my detractors would gain no evidence of that.

'Master Shakespeare, I am obliged to you,' I replied fervently, as he handed me the script. 'A pot of ale for your pains?' I sent my boy on a speedy mission, as I glanced at it. My attention was immediately caught and I read on as he watched me. I expected something good from Master Marlowe's quill but this had a finesse, a delicacy, a variety, a black humour combined with stark tragedy, and a poetry that delighted the senses. I could scarce speak for excitement. My business may be saucy ballads, but I know true poetry when I read it:

> *Such mercy as the starven lioness*
> *When she is dry sucked of her eager young*
> *Shows to the prey that next encounters her . . .*

I sent for another pot of ale for Shakespeare since he seemed in no hurry to leave. I was in generous mood, for my first reading suggested that I need not fear reprisals from this printing. 'The plot is not so very different from that I am acquainted with,' I remarked happily. 'Master Marlowe had led me to believe some deep mystery lay in this oft-told tale.'

'Kit meant merely that Arden is not the unpleasant man he has hitherto been thought, nor Alice quite so evil,' Shakespeare replied casually. 'Arden's devotion to his wife brings about his death, and his friend Franklin who discovers the body with the mayor mourns over him, as Antony over Caesar. 'Tis a noble theme. The fault lies not in our stars, but in ourselves.'

'How very poetic, Master Shakespeare,' I replied, my mind still on my treasure. I realised I was clutching it to my chest like a babe, for I saw he was observing me with some amusement. 'Forgive me,' I continued, 'Master Marlowe has surpassed even his *Jew of Malta*. This script is to me as golden ducats to a moneylender.'

'O my ducats. O my daughter,' he murmured.

'I crave your pardon?' Will Shakespeare has the reputation of being a trifle absent-minded, and he will never succeed at his trade if he thinks of his family and not his work.

My mind at rest over the content, I registered the play at the Company of Stationers, paying the usual fivepence for it, since thankfully an anonymous reworking of an old theme excited no great fee.

I heard no more from either Kit or Shakespeare. The latter was helping in an interesting piece named *Titus and Vespasian*, and Marlowe was still at Chislehurst. Or so I thought, until he burst in upon me one day like his own starven lioness in search of prey, brandishing one of my copies of his *Arden* (which had been keeping me well in sherris-sack for many a day).

'Good morrow, Kit,' I said brightly. 'Your drama sells well. Has it yet been played upon the stage? I could arrange a special promotion edition at the Rose—'

The book was hurled straight at my face in truly violent fashion, but having some experience in dodging angry authors I dodged it. 'This is *not* my play,' he shrieked.

'Of course not, I have published it anonymously.' There's no pleasing these ambitious young cockerels.

'This is not what I wrote. What have you done with it, you meddling old fool?'

I was highly indignant. 'I may have edited the odd unreadable word but—'

'The odd *word*?' His voice was a falsetto that would stand him well upon the stage, but his hand went to his sword. 'This has Alice Arden still the murderer. The true leader of the conspiracy was—'

'I don't want to know,' I shouted.

'If you don't there are other publishers who will.'

'It's my copyright.'

'*This* version is. Mine is a different play altogether.'

'This is the play delivered as yours. I can call as witness Master Shakespeare.'

I thought he would have an apoplexy. '*Shakespeare* brought it to you? I gave it to Thomas Kyd, with whom I lodge. I will kill them, I will kill them both,' he roared, and off he stomped.

He did indeed go to another publisher, Abell Jeffes, the villain who used to run a stall at the Great North Door. I was forced to go to law, judgment was in my favour and his entire stock was forfeit to me. In revenge, Jeffes burned it first. As for killing, it was Kit who was nearly killed. In September that year he was charged for a brawl with Walter Cronkite, a Canterbury tailor, and although something in the report struck me as odd I thought little of it then.

Poor Kit was always of a quarrelsome nature, and eight months later he was dead, killed in another brawl in Deptford by persons unknown. In his own words, 'Cut is the branch that might have grown full straight', and this terrible news about a young man moved me deeply. Moreover, I felt I might have been instrumental in barring the way to that elusive gentleman Justice. In that year of 1593 I was approaching forty, a time when man is over the summit in the hill of life, and one's maker awaits one's return. I had unwittingly been the source of suppressing what was might have been Kit's greatest play, and my conscience was victorious in the battle with sloth. I went immediately to the Mermaid Tavern where I knew I should find Shakespeare and others of the theatre. Will sat apart from the crowd, weeping into his sherris-sack.

'Alas, poor Kit,' he sighed, as he recognized me.

I sat down and began without preamble. 'Master Marlowe told me that what you brought me was not his play.'

He put on an expression of complete amazement, but I can see why he is a playwright, not a player.

'Did you re-write it, Master Shakespeare?' I spoke mildly, for who knows, I might need his services one day. I had in mind that much could be done with Holinshed's history of King Leire and his Three Daughters.

Will looked at me reproachfully. 'I attach much honour to my family name. Would I make mock of myself by writing a character named Shakebag? I loved dear Kit. You have no quarrel with me, have you?'

'My purse has none. My immortal soul may have, for you have distorted truth, Master Shakespeare.'

He seemed genuinely perplexed. 'What is truth, as Pilate asked? *Arden* is a play, and a play is not history. If I wrote of Richard III that he was unjustly accused of murdering his nephews, does that change history? The task of the writer is to spin images for the dreams of men.'

I was not content. 'I would know the truth, Will.' I slipped easily into the familiar, for one felt comfortable with Master Shakespeare and the tongue became less guarded. 'The copies may be burned by Jeffes, but where is Kit Marlowe's script?'

'Burned also,' Will said apologetically. 'Kit was not pleased with my slight emendations to his script, and he chased me round the room with his sword, so I gave the script to him to take to Jeffes.'

I groaned. 'Why then, you must tell me, Will, what the script revealed. Who *really* killed Arden?'

Will looked very nervous. 'You don't understand how we artists work, Master White. I only read a few pages, with Thomas Arden, Franklin, Alice and Mosby. I saw immediately that Arden could be made much more interesting if he were a nobleman with both good and bad qualities destroyed by enslavement to his wife's charms. Had I read on, poor Kit's style would have influenced me, so

–' he finished shamefacedly – 'I rewrote it all without reading the rest.'

'Very well.' I believed him, though I felt he was keeping something from me. 'Then we both owe it to Kit to find out the truth ourselves. I go to Feversham.' The enormity of what I was saying surprised even me.

''Twas forty years ago. Would you turn constable, my friend?'

'*We* will turn constable, Will,' I said gently. 'You're coming with me, or I'll see no other printer in London touches your work.'

Will had a way of assessing you as if he were sizing you up for new clothes, or for a character in a new play. I might find myself a pot-bellied foolish constable upon the stage, clad in – *New clothes*. I remembered what had struck me as interesting about Kit's brawl in Canterbury last year. 'Will,' I said slowly, 'Walter Cronkite was a tailor, and Feversham lies but a few miles from Canterbury. In the first Arden play I copyrighted, three of the conspirators in the Arden murder, Mosby (Alice's lover), Grene, and Michael Saunderson (Arden's steward) were all tailors by trade.'

Will seemed unimpressed. 'Coincidence. No dramatic reality. Besides, the groundlings would hear of kings and princes. Tailors are for comic characters.'

I kept to the point. 'I do not believe in coincidence.'

We came by water to the Town Quay at Feversham where Arden had been Customer in charge of collecting taxes raised on goods coming in and out of the port, a first step in his rise to power as mayor, before being disenfranchised just before his death. We look lodgings at the Fleur de Lys inn, where we supped in the very room that the murder had been plotted. Indeed, the landlord obviously increased his revenue greatly by this means. 'I'm Fowle,' he greeted us, wiping his filthy hands on his breeches. I saw the gleam in Will's eye and hastened to intervene before his quick wit ruined our chances of co-operation.

'Are you related to Adam Fowle, innkeeper at the time of the famous murder?'

'Grandson.' He swelled with pride.

'Did he believe justice was done, and that Alice Arden was guilty?'

'She was burned for it.'

'But upon what evidence?'

'That she did it. 'Tis written that she were guilty in the Mayor's wardmote book. I send all inquisitive scribblers there.'

So that was our starting point. 'What if the Mayor will not let us see the book, Will?' I asked anxiously, as we dined next morning before setting out on our mission.

'You are a stationer, Edward,' he replied, still sleepy, though it was past eleven. 'Tell him you wish to print his memoirs and he'll be marchpane in your hands.'

I opened my mouth and shut it again. After all, I need not honour my pledge. We walked to the Guildhall at Tanners Green, and after fervently assuring the mayor that he had the most interesting life story, the wardmote book for 1551 was shown to us, with the story of the murder and the trial. There was no doubting it, for it had been written under the eagle eye of the mayor of the day, now long dead. If Alice were indeed innocent, as Kit had hinted, then the truth must lie with the other conspirators. She seemed a most incompetent murderess. There were several failed attempts; then when the body was dragged out of her house to the back gate, the key could not be found for half an hour. Odd, for a planned murder. It was snowing by the time the body was taken to the field where it was found, but it ceased as quickly as it began, leaving their footsteps plain for all to see, leading back to the Arden house. Did none of these conspirators notice that the snow had stopped? It would be the work of a few moments to heap fresh snow upon them.

The following day, intent on pursuing my theory, we took the new stage-wagon service to Canterbury to seek out Master Walter Cronkite. Our journey was much against Will's inclination, for the dark-haired serving wench at the Fleur de Lys was a comely lass and during the last two evenings Will had spent much time convincing her of this. I had heard him whisper to her, 'Shall I compare thee to a summer's day?', and I saw her bosom swell and her dark eyes grow soft. Had I not a wife, and had I Will's years, I would – But, as it was, it was Will slept much of the way to our destination.

I was frustrated to find that Cronkite was too young a man to have taken part in a murder over forty years old, and though his father was a tailor too, he had died years before. Will's pretence of requiring a new doublet failed (he will never make a player) and I had hastily to explain my mission (adding that I was most interested in the memoirs of tailors).

'I was attacked by Master Marlowe, good sir,' Cronkite informed me hotly. 'I objected that he did not pay me my money for a cloak of velvet. He informed me my work was shoddy, and that I, a master tailor *and* weaver, was an ass. And that is the bottom of it.'

He did not look me in the eye, however, as he curtly added, 'Moreover the Canterbury tailors' guild has never had dealings with its Feversham brothers.'

'Are you satisfied now?' Will asked me mildly, as we refreshed ourselves with ale in Canterbury's own Fleur de Lys tavern. 'Methinks you have a bee that buzzes overmuch in your cap where tailors are concerned.'

'I am sorry to have wasted your time,' I replied stiffly.

'Oh, it hasn't been wasted.' He smiled, as at some inward thought of his own. When years later I saw *A Midsummer Night's Dream* upon the stage, I realised why.

Back in Feversham, Will's dark lass proved faithful despite his eight-hour absence, and moreover seemed anxious to help as we supped at mine host's table once more.

'Who told your grandfather Alice Arden was guilty, if he knew nothing of the murder?' I asked casually of Master Fowle.

'Why, Mosby, the witch's paramour,' he growled.

'A tailor, was he not?' asked Will, in teasing mood, his eye on me. 'Master White would have it that 'twas a tailor led the conspiracy.'

'Mosby was a botcher, a journeyman, he would never rise to be received into the guild as a master.'

'I know the present guildmaster of the Feversham tailors, Will,' his wench whispered in his ear, when mine host was sleepy with beer of foreign hops. He should keep to honest English ale.

'He would know nothing of forty years ago, Rosalind.' Will smiled lazily and lovingly into her face.

'He holds the historical records.'

'What a jewel is Mistress Rosalind,' I cried ecstatically, and on the morrow she led us to West Street, where the present guildmaster dwelled, for he would surely help us to the truth. Guilds prize their honour highly, and if a brother falls from grace he is denied the guild for ever. The present master, a venerable gentleman of some sixty years, heard the reason for our visit with some anxiety, but relaxed when I mentioned Mosby, Grene, and Saunderson.

'They were all journeymen,' he replied quietly. 'Not yet master tailors, and our records cannot therefore help you.'

'Nevertheless I would see them, if I may.' There was some mystery here that went beyond those who died for their crime.

I looked down the members' list in search of I knew not what, names, endless names: Edwards, Farthing, Green, Franklin, Cronkite, Duff, Proud – I had seen enough. *Cronkite, Edmund, master tailor, admitted 1550.*

At my cry of triumph, Will peered over my shoulders. 'Ah', he said, 'no doubt Master Walter's father.'

'And perhaps involved in the murder,' I cried, forgetting my usual caution.

'Then why was he not hung?'

'Because, sir,' the master intervened angrily, 'he was innocent. *No* master tailor would dare become involved in crime. He would be expelled from the guild and he would never trade again.'

Will looked worried. 'The groundlings care little for such a theme.'

He was hardly a help. 'Go back to the inn, Will,' I said kindly, 'where you can do no harm.'

I wondered if I followed in Kit's footsteps as I continued my quest. Why should three tailors, perhaps four, want to kill Arden? It must be something they held in common with him. They were all tailors, they lived in a port and Arden had been Customer of that port. Was there substance here? In his counting house at the quay, the present Customer willingly showed me the entry records for the port, of which he was proud, explaining that we stood in the King's Weighing House where traders stored their goods.

'Are any of them tailors?' The heady smell of hops lingered in the air so I had little expectation of progress.

'Wool skins come in for the weavers, and the batches of hollands, but, as you see from the book, few in Arden's time are recorded.'

I had a sudden inspiration. 'Is it possible to import materials and evade taxes with the help of the Customer?'

'Were I a dishonest man, Master White, yes.'

He looked so angry, I asked with resignation, 'I wonder if you've ever thought of writing your memoirs?'

Printing terms for *The True Story of a Kentish Port Official* settled, he explained that there were enterprising individuals who paid dues on wool skins, took the goods to the spinners, and found them a buyer for their cloth among the tailors. An honest calling. 'However,' he continued, 'if the Customer were dishonest by not entering the goods in his records, and sharing the profit with these moonlighters, even more could be made.'

I returned, most excited, to the Fleur de Lys, where it was obvious from the flush on Rosalind's cheeks that Will had employed his time well – on her account at least.

I explained my new theory – nay, certainty – concluding: 'Mosby, Grene and Saunderson were ambitious journeymen who feared Arden would reveal their shared secret, and their leader in conspiracy was Edmund Cronkite, recently accepted as a master tailor.'

Will thought this over. 'No, Alice Arden who was gently born, could not love a tailor. Or even a weaver. A joke perhaps, a masque, a fairy queen . . .'

I ignored him, intent on my theory. 'Why should they kill Arden, you ask? Because he was now a disgraced man and had nothing to lose. The journeymen were about to submit their master's pieces to join the guild and stood no chance of their acceptance if Arden revealed all, and Cronkite would be expelled from the guild.'

Will had doubts. 'Dead men could not make Kit Marlowe fear to put his name to a play.'

'Perhaps Cronkite's son could.'

'Would a son kill to protect his father's good name?' Will mused. 'Hardly. To kill or not to kill. That is the question. His mother's good name? Perhaps. He—'

'Concentrate, Will,' I said sternly. 'If only William Marshall, the mayor who recorded the trial, were still alive.'

'Old Marshall once rented a grange from Arden,' Rosalind put in. 'My grannie was in service there. He used it for business. Smelly, she said.'

'It was Mayor Marshall found the body,' I cried, 'and being in charge of the wardmote book he could falsify the truth.'

'All the perfumes of Arabia will not sweeten his hand,' Will murmured, laying his upon Rosalind's bosom in thanks for her help.

'Stinking wool skins, Grannie said.' Rosalind removed it.

'From the east to western Ind/No jewel is like Rosalind,' Will sighed.

'All is clear.' I was impatient that my brilliance as constable be recognized. 'The mayor was the leader of the conspiracy, for he feared that Arden might take vengeance for his disenfranchisement, and he would lose his post.'

Rosalind snorted unbecomingly. 'From what I've heard Marshall couldn't organize his way through a plate of roast beef.'

Will slapped her behind. 'Why, there's a lass. A cunning brain lay behind this murder.'

'Everyone concerned in the murder is *dead*,' I muttered.

The wondrous bosom heaved. 'No, they're not. Master Franklin is still alive.'

For a moment the name puzzled me, for it had not appeared in my earlier Arden plays, only in Will's (or should it be Marlowe's) version.

'Why didn't you tell us?' Will howled.

'You never asked. And take your hand from under my skirt, if you please. Master Franklin is seventy-five if he's a day now, sans teeth, sans much sight, sans taste, and everything really.'

'A good man,' Will pointed out. 'And Arden's friend.'

'Only in the first scene,' I said meaningfully. 'Thanks to you we've no idea if he turned out to be the villain in Marlowe's play or not. But –' I suddenly recalled – 'there was a Franklin in the tailors' guild book.'

'Methinks you do protest too much,' Will replied tetchily. 'A play with five tailors as criminals and no female interest would have been duller than *Tamburlaine*. Moreover he found the body, and drew the mayor's attention to it.'

'In your version, Will. In everyone else's, it was a grocer called Pryme.'

'So the mayor recorded.'

Perhaps Will is not so absent-minded after all. 'Let us visit Franklin, Will.'

A silence, then a meek: 'I am not a brave man, Edward. I have much to do on Earth before I would visit Heaven.'

'And I also,' I replied swiftly. 'After I've finished printing memoirs, I would find a young author to write me a play entitled *The tragic historie of King Leire and his three daughters*.'

Will looked interested. 'A Kentish theme, eh? I'm in the right place—'

'Once we have visited Franklin.'

Franklin lived with his servants on a modest estate on the London road and our fears for our lives were immediately dispelled.

As we entered the chamber, a white-haired old man with vacant blue eyes rose unsteadily to his feet and pointed straight at Will: 'Howl, howl, howl, howl . . . For God's sake, let us sit upon the ground and talk of kings.'

'Let us talk of Kit Marlowe and Thomas Arden,' I said firmly, seeing my companion once more distracted.

'Are you Kit Marlowe?' he asked Will doubtfully.

'I am not.'

'Pity. You could learn a lot from him.'

'Is there a crime upon your conscience, Master Franklin? I asked gently. 'Was Alice Arden falsely condemned?'

'I always liked the name Alice,' he replied chattily.

'Second childishness, mere oblivion,' I said sadly to Will as we left, whereupon Franklin's piping voice followed us.

'I made the footsteps.'

With one accord Will and I dashed back, but the moment of clarity had gone.

'There's rosemary . . . that's for remembrance.' He stretched his hands pathetically towards us.

'Our murderer,' I said, as we breathed the fresh air once more. 'Cronkite was innocent.' I felt somewhat crestfallen.

'The quality of mercy cannot be strained, Edward. It was not coincidence that the snow fell to make those footsteps. Countrymen know the sky; Franklin, the mayor and the other conspirators had Arden killed in the field or nearby, waited till the snow stopped, made the footprints, and then Franklin fetched the mayor to be with him as they "found" the body and the incriminating footsteps. That accounts for the delay, which the mayor's record attributes to losing the key of the gate. Alice is accused and convicted; the mayor's record would omit any cries of innocence on her part; an innocent bystander is substituted for Franklin as the body's finder, to avoid any suspicion of his involvement.'

'Why did the other conspirators not speak once they were betrayed?'

'Who knows that they did not?'

I was silenced, but took my revenge. 'Only one question remains, Will – why did you change that play? Thomas Arden was a hard and self-seeking man; you made him an honourable man of noble birth, devoted to his wife. You did not know that Alice was guiltless, but nevertheless you show sympathy for her in your play.'

'Surely even a murderess with blood on her hands can suffer remorse. Out, out, damned spot. One day—'

'Will,' I repeated, 'why did you rewrite Kit's play? Why change Thomas Arden's character?'

He blushed. 'I am far from home. My roots are in Warwickshire, and my heart lies there.'

'Why did you do it?'

'Think what you will, Edward, roam as you like it in the forests of your mind.'

'*Why*?'

Tears filled Will's eyes. 'My mother was born an Arden.'

Venus and Adonis 

THE PRICE OF VIRGINITY

Paul Barnett

It was inevitable when compiling this anthology that the figure of Christopher Marlowe would loom large. It is fascinating to conjecture upon his own relationship with Shakespeare, whose talent was only just emerging when Marlowe's was in full flight, even though both were of the same age. In the following story, Paul Barnett uses this potential rivalry alongside the composition of Marlowe's Hero and Leander *and Shakespeare's* Venus and Adonis *as the basis for a very particular whodunnit.*

There was a knock at the door and both Amy and her elder sister, Betts, looked up, expecting a customer to come in. Who would it be? Master Robinson, the young wheelwright from further up Poultry Street, with yet another of his angry missives to the Queen? Master Fenton, the baker, with a new list of the prices of his breads and cakes? Mistress Lancet, who had carried on the fishmongery after the untimely death of her husband, come to complain about the job of work they had done for her last week?

It was none of these. The latch remained unlifted. No one entered.

'The wind,' suggested Betts, 'rattling the oak in its frame.'

'Young Natty Green throwing a clod of earth at the door to show what he thinks about *girls*,' said Amy, giggling uneasily. Young Natty was not the only person in Poultry Street who thought it shocking and against the will of God that old Master Blount should have taught his daughters to read and write – and, worse, to ply a trade exploiting their ability.

'I shall box his ears for him the next time I see him,' said Betts firmly. At the grand old age of eighteen she was very much the matron. Some said it was her severity of aspect that was to blame for her lack of a husband; others blamed her mannish education. Amy knew the truth was that, like herself, Betts was waiting for the man to appear who would be charming, intelligent and, above all, well washed – a rare attribute in these glory days of the Virgin Queen.

Both girls busied themselves afresh with their work, their pens scratching on the rough paper, but both knew that the knock on the door had been neither wind nor a hurled clod of earth, and both had their ears pricked for the slightest sound of someone on the threshold. They heard nothing except the daily noises of Poultry Street – the shouts of the beggars and traders, the clopping of horses's hooves, the footsteps of passers-by and the occasional rattle of wheels on the cobbles.

Betts was the first to let her inquisitiveness get the better of her.

'That gust might have damaged the hinges,' she said, picking herself up from her bench. 'I had best check.'

Smoothing her woollen skirt down over her hips, she crossed to the door and opened it. Amy could see her sister's shape silhouetted against a lopsided rectangle of bustling sunlit colour as Betts looked both ways up and down the street and then half-turned back towards the room. She was just starting to close the door again when she saw something lying on the step at her feet.

'Why, what's this?'

'*I* don't know,' said Amy.

Betts picked up a small object. 'It has your name written on it,' she said, her voice suddenly taking on the note of boredom that always signified she was intensely interested in something. 'I wonder what it might be.'

She tossed the little folded packet onto the desk in front of Amy.

'Watch out! You might have smudged Master Herbert's ode.'

'His ode?'

'Yes, his interminable ode to Calliope, who is clearly not listening to his blandishments.'

The outside of the packet did indeed say: 'To Mistress Amy Blount.' The corners of the paper were held in place by an unintelligible blood-coloured seal, and round the whole was a ribbon of a more crimson red, tied off with a bow.

'I imagine you shall wish to leave that for opening later,' said Betts languidly as she sat down and prepared to resume her work. As always, her eyes betrayed her: she could not stop herself from squinting eagerly towards the package between Amy's fingers.

Amy giggled again. 'I do believe it is another love letter from My Lord Essex himself. His ardour is so tiring, however flattering it might be to be its object.' She pretended to yawn, bringing her long, ink-stained fingers to her daintily pursed lips. 'He must know that Sir Walter Ralegh and I have an . . . understanding, whatever our dear Queen might think of Bessy Throckmorton.'

'Open it!' snapped Betts. 'Open it or, so help me God, I'll strangle you 'til your eyes pop out and your tongue turns blue.'

'*Again*?' said Amy, but she was just as avid as Betts to find out what it might be. She picked at the bow for a moment but then, finding the knot intractable, simply wrenched the paper free of the ribbon. The seal received equally short shrift. She smoothed the paper out in front of her.

'It's a poem,' she said.

'Who from?' hissed Betts.

'No one. I mean, it's not signed. Just a poem . . .'

'Read it out.'

'All right,' said Amy slowly. She read the words quietly:

Come live with me, and be my love,
And we shall all the pleasures prove
That valleys, groves, hills and fields
And all the steepy mountain yields.

She read on a little further, her lips moving silently.

'There is more!' said Betts urgently. 'Tell me what it is!'

'Wait, sister,' said Amy, her forehead furrowing. 'Let me read my own poem – you shall have it later to read for yourself.'

'How exciting, how exciting!' cried Betts. 'Someone has written a poem especially for you, dear Amy. I wonder who it could be! I hope he is fittingly handsome, and perhaps he might even be rich. Do you recognize his hand? Is it perhaps someone whose work we have copied! Shall we ask father?'

Father was the printer Edward Blount. He worked all day long in his cellar beneath them, emerging only at noon to share their bread and cheese and occasionally at other times to greet a customer. He had as fine a memory for handwritings as the sisters' own.

'No, I do not believe I wish to show this to Father,' said Amy. 'It would not seem quite . . . proper to do so.'

To Betts's astonishment Amy was blushing. 'You *do* know the hand, Amy!' she said. 'You *do*! Tell me who it is! Tell me! Do tell!'

'There is nothing to tell,' said Amy, crumpling up the paper and tucking it into her sleeve. 'It is an inconsequence.'

A few weeks later Master Marlowe called by the Blounts' shop with a new manuscript to be copied. The previous year Betts had been commissioned by him to produce the various manuscripts of his play *Edward the Second* as it was revised during the rehearsals for its staging. The sisters had been scandalized not so much by the mode of Edward's despatch as by the notion of men having relations between each other as were more fitting between men and women. Betts had asked Master Marlowe shyly if perhaps he might not be in error about this, but he had just laughed and chucked her under the chin, a chucking she did not mind in the least, for Master Marlowe was fair to look upon – for all that he was nearly thirty – and his eyes glinted in a way that . . . but it was best not to think about it. Amy, for her part, had copied his *Doctor Faustus* for him so many times in that same year that she thought she could recite the whole play word-perfect, were it not for the fact that Master Marlowe kept changing those words, which was why she had had to copy and recopy the play in a fair hand. One day, perhaps, if Master Marlowe could ever cling for more than a few days to the money his fame brought, their father would be given the commission to print and publish both plays.

'Something new for you, my friends!' he cried as he came in the door. The spring sunshine seemed to come in with him. 'This time it is a poem, a poem of such power and passion that all London must soon come flocking to my beck.'

Betts smiled. 'Oh yes?'

'Well,' he said, returning her grin, 'at least perhaps I shall be able to pay my landlord all that I owe him.' A thought obviously crossed his mind and his face clouded. 'I, um, have . . . I have . . .?'

'You have indeed settled all your accounts with us, Master Marlowe,' said Betts, affecting primness. 'We were surprised at the time, and even more surprised when your coin proved good.'

He clicked his fingers. 'I must have made a mistake. In future you may be sure I shall pay you with only the crudest forgeries and, when you try to spend them, we shall all be hanged together – won't that be cosy? Now, which of you two goddesses shall deign to step down from Olympus to bless my awkward scribbling?'

Betts looked ruefully at the sheaf of manuscript on the desk in front of her. Master Shakespeare's plays were proving very popular at the moment, and he was busily churning them out as fast as he possibly could. Betts herself had ploughed through all three parts of *Henry the Sixth*, which she had found turgid and dreary, and had used subterfuge for which she had never been forgiven to persuade her younger sister to take on the task of copying the sequel, *Richard the Third*. 'Never again,' Amy had said with murder in her eyes, and her resolve had not melted even when the next work had proved to be promisingly called *A Comedy of Errors*. Now Betts had not long started making a fair copy of a new play, *Titus Andronicus*; she had told her sister that the only nice thing she could think to say about it was that it was funnier than *A Comedy of Errors*.

'I cannot accept the task, Master Marlowe,' she said with genuine sadness. 'As you can see . . .' She gestured at her desk.

'More of Master Shakespeare's sleeping potions, I see,' said Master Marlowe cheerfully. 'What a bore the man is! Ah, well, I have no doubt that your younger sister can serve in all matters with dexterity equal to your own – is that not so, Mistress Amy?'

Amy darted a look towards Betts. There was something in the way he had spoken which made her wonder if . . . but no, surely not. Betts would have told her. Betts had told her about kissing the baker's boy, Master Fenton's son, hadn't she? And very interesting it had been for both sisters to discover what kissing – *that* sort of kissing, not the pecks they exchanged with their father and each other – was like. ('Not bad,' Betts had adjudged, 'except we seemed to have too many tongues betwixt us.') The sisters had no secrets from each other.

Except one. Amy had still not told Betts who had penned the *billet doux* which had been left on the doorstep. The same person whose hand had scrawled *Doctor Faustus*. Master Marlowe had never made reference to the note, and neither had she; perhaps he had been drunk – for he often was – when some urge had made him send it to her.

'I shall do my best,' Amy said, her eyes lowered, 'as I always do. I must finish a sermon by the end of the day, and then I shall be free to take on new work. What is this fresh poem of yours about, Master Marlowe?'

'Ah,' he said, striking a pose, his hand tucked inside his jerkin, 'it is a grand epic in the classical style – an epic of love and passion. Of the urgencies of youth and' – he pinched the top of his nose between his fingers, removing imaginary tears – 'of their inevitable fulfilment. In short, Mistresses Blount, it is racy enough to attract the sovereigns of My Lord Walsingham, who shall let his toadies titter over it – all the while pretending that they peruse it only in pursuit of classical culture. I have the first two sestiads already done, and the others well forward in their planning.'

'What's a sestiad?' said Betts.

'A grand word to mean a big chunk,' said Marlowe, interrupting his own flow. 'I had it from Master Chapman, who talks about the chunks of the *Iliad* thus, there being six of them. Therefore I shall have six chunks of *Homer and Leander* – for that is my poem's title – and earn favour and respect in consequence. Now – enough of this. When can you have the work finished, little mistress?'

Amy *knew* she was blushing, but didn't know how she could stop herself. For certain her sister must have observed the redness of her cheeks – and so must Master Marlowe.

She took the untidy heap of paper from him and ran her thumb down the rumpled edges. 'Perhaps a week,' she said doubtfully; his hand was not neat, as she knew from *Doctor Faustus*, and so she would have to allow extra time for those instances where the knots of his penmanship proved obdurate in the unravelling.

'A week!' he cried. 'Fair one, you are a goddess indeed – a goddess of industry. I shall return in that time.'

'And do not, Master Marlowe,' said Betts pointedly as he left with a clatter, 'forget to bring your purse.'

'Lumme!' cried Amy. 'Grab an earful of *this*, Betts.'

It was two days after Master Marlowe's visit, and she was making good progress with his manuscript, interrupted from time to time by attempts to scandalize her elder sister.

'Not more about how the Greeks would have loved to have Leander as their catamite?' drawled Betts in the voice she assumed was worldly-wise. She had learnt the word only recently, and used it as often as possible. She now called Master Marlowe's *Edward the Second* 'the catamite play'.

'No, it's your genuine . . . well, *you* know. Having it away. The god Mercury's got hold of some shepherdess.'

Betts quietly closed the door that led to the cellar. 'Read, sister.'

'On her this god
Enamoured was, and with his snaky rod
Did charm her nimble feet, and made her stay,
The while upon a hillock down he lay,
And sweetly on his pipe he 'gan to play,
And with smooth speech her fancy to assay,
Till in his twining arms he held her fast,
And then he wooed with kisses, and at last,
As shepherds do, her on the ground he laid,
And tumbling in the grass he often strayed
Beyond the bounds of shame, in being bold
To eye those parts which no eye should behold'.

When Amy had finished the two sisters stared at each other, both of them slightly shocked – and at the same time slightly intoxicated by their imaginings of the scene.

'He looked at her *bottom*,' said Amy.

'I think not her bottom,' said Betts dryly, 'but near enough.'

'Lumme!' Amy repeated.

Yet she had not read out to Betts an extended earlier passage, during which the uncannily attractive Leander had pleaded lyrically with the beautiful priestess of Venus, Hero, whose charms had elevated him to a sort of oratorical frenzy:

Virginity, albeit some highly prize it,
Compared with marriage, had you tried them both,
Differs as much as wine and water doth.

And:

> *Honour is purchased by the deeds we do.*
> *Believe me, Hero, honour is not won,*
> *Until some honourable deed be done.*
> *Seek you, for chastity, immortal fame,*
> *And know that some have wronged Diana's name?*

All in all, Leander made an argument in favour of Hero's donation of her virginity that was both cogent and passionate. Amy would have thought little of it – she was accustomed to receiving similar suggestions, couched in less flowery language though in their way equally eloquent, when she was on the street or at the market – had it not been for the fact that the description of Leander in the poem was of a sort of idealized version of Master Marlowe, while that of Hero could have been of herself, Amy.

At first she had thought this mere coincidence, but then she had come across a note tucked in among the pages. It had been brief, and in prose rather than verse:

> My most dearly beloved Amy—
> My heart burns for you. My eyes thirst for the sight of you. My fingers are numb for lack of the touch of you. My lips yearn to be wed with yours.
> If my longings are perchance returned, meet me at the sign of the Boar and Hunter, formerly the Bull in Deptford Strand on the evening of June the 1st. I have engaged a room for the night, so that we may converse as late as we list.
> I have a half-sovereign for you.
> Yr humble and obedient servant – nay, your slave!
> *Christopher Marlowe*

He wished to speak with her! No doubt about philosophy, which she did not understand – but she would do her best, for *his* sake. And he had a present to give her! How kind of him.

She had, however, a dim sense that there might be more than conversation involved in his invitation, and that was why she said nothing to her sister – she would make some excuse for her absence on the appointed night. Doubtless Master Marlowe would offer her a physical proof of his love, and then soon the two of them would be wed. She knew that ideally things should be ordered the other way round, but she was not frightened at the prospect of losing what 'Men foolishly do call . . . virtuous'.

Above all, she didn't want to become an old maid like her sister.

'I have come,' said the rustically accented voice, 'to collect the fair copy of my play *Titus Andronicus*.'

Amy looked up, startled. So engrossed had she been in trying to understand a further passage in *Hero and Leander* that she hadn't heard the door open. Also filling her mind had been imaginings of what might occur that very night between herself and Master Marlowe, for the hours had rushed by and it was already the first day of June. His note lay on the desk by her hand.

'Good day to you, Master Shakespeare,' she said.

'And good day to you', he said gruffly. Although he must have been about the same age as Master Marlowe, he seemed far older. Perhaps that's what marriage does to a man, thought Amy. 'Is your sister not here?'

'No, Betts has gone to the fair today.' She got to her feet and stepped across to her sister's desk. 'She finished copying out your play late last night, so she said she would take today as a much-deserved holiday.'

Amy flushed. Her clumsy tongue!

Master Shakespeare laughed, his lips showing pink within his straggly beard. She had never seen him laugh before, and was surprised how much more handsome it made his face.

'She did not find it to her taste?' he said, laughing again.

Amy had expected anger, not mirth. 'Betts f-f-found it very f-f-fine indeed,' she stammered. 'A most n-noble work.'

'But dry as the dust of a dusty day,' Master Shakespeare said, lightly touching her on the shoulder. 'It is not the sort of fare I would expect a young wench to enjoy.'

'That is not what I m-meant.'

'It is not what you intended to say, but it most certainly *is* what you meant.'

She picked up the two wads of paper – Master Shakespeare's original and the copy Betts had made – and carried them back to her own desk. She began to bump the sheets together on the wooden surface in an attempt to make the edges neater.

'Give me just the copy,' he said, his amusement subsiding as he dug in his purse for coins. 'You can throw my scrawl away or use it for lighting the fire, it's no more use to me.'

She was impressed. Paper did not come cheap. Master Shakespeare must be even more successful than she and Betts had thought. 'Very well,' she said demurely.

'And here is an extra shilling,' he said, 'for your sister and yourself. Please buy the finest cake Master Fenton can bake and enjoy it with your excellent father tonight. Your sister has certainly earned as much for her industry in wading through my *Titus*'s dreary pages!'

With a wave of his hand and another burst of laughter he was gone from the shop.

It was only later that, looking for the note which Master Marlowe had written to her, she discovered she had mislaid it.

The Boar and Hunter was crowded and blue with tobacco smoke and foul language, as it always was of an evening. The Cheshire Cheese, a hundred yards or so away, was the tavern where the fashionable and well-to-do went to drink their wines and eat game pies; by preference, the lowlife frequented the Boar and Hunter instead.

Amy stopped in the doorway and looked around her. She had tried to lie to Betts about what she intended, but her older sister had seen through the pretence at once. Promising to tell their father a suitable story to explain Amy's absence, Betts had then lent her the grey-blue combed-wool dress that had been the object of Amy's envy for as long as she could remember. 'You be sure you tell me all about it!' Betts had hissed at her as Amy had slipped out the window of their bedroom. 'Every last grapple!'

Staring into the gloom of the Boar and Hunter, Amy was for the first time frightened by the prospect of her escapade – there hadn't seemed to be the time before. In her mind's eye she had envisaged a richly furnished taproom empty save for a suave Master Marlowe, turning to greet her with a broad smile and a freshly laundered suit. Instead there was this throng, this odour of dissolute maleness.

A few heads turned. There were some whistles and obscene suggestions. Most of the clientele, however, clearly assumed she was either a whore or somebody else's doxy. Her cheeks stung with embarrassment.

At last she spotted Master Marlowe. He was sharing a table

in a dark corner with a number of other men, and hadn't yet noticed her.

It took courage to push her way through the milling crowd to reach him, and hands wandered intimately over her body as she went; to her fury, she found herself enjoying the touch of them.

'Master Marlowe,' she said on arriving at his table, trying to find enough space to curtsy prettily.

He looked up, and for a moment seemed not to recognize her – despite the fact that he had seen her only a few hours before, when he had picked up her copy of *Hero and Leander* and left behind him the manuscripts of three early plays, written in his university days, that he had decided to resuscitate.

'Ah. Amy,' he said at length. 'I have booked a room where the two of us can have privacy to . . . talk. But first' – he gestured around him – 'I must finish my business with these gentlemen.' One of the 'gentlemen' started a crude guffaw, but Master Marlowe silenced him with a look.

Master Marlowe hailed a potboy and gave him instructions. The youth glanced uninterestedly at Amy and then led her through the crush to the rear of the taproom and up a short flight of wooden stairs. At its top he opened a slack-hinged door and stood aside to let her enter.

Inside, she found a room that might have had some splendour in years past but now clung only to its tatters. The curtain, of cheap grey velveteen, had rips in it, and one end hung loose from the rod. The thin carpet was so worn that any pattern it had once borne had long since disappeared. The whitewashed brick walls were covered in stains. By a rickety table with two goblets and a jug on it were two crooked chairs; but the major item of furniture, filling at least a third of the room, was a bed.

Amy stared at it. All the rest of the room disappeared as she gazed at this marvel. She had never seen a bed before outside pictures. Only the rich had beds; ordinary mortals made do with pallets on the floor or shelves cut out of the walls. No wonder Master Marlowe had economized on the other trappings: the rent of the bed alone must have cost him a small fortune.

So much for the pretence of conversation.

She crossed the room and sat down on the bed, patting the topmost cover to either side of her. The surface was quite hard, but it had a springiness she found seductive.

And what use was conversation, after all, except as a prelude to the real reason, she now admitted to herself, for her coming here?

She helped herself from the jug of deep red wine and drained back two gobletsful in a rush, then took a third back to the bedside with her for more leisured consumption. The strong wine went to her head very swiftly – through excitement she hadn't eaten all day. She peered around the candlelit room again and this time, with the edges of her vision softened and fuzzed, it looked a lot better.

She lay back on the mattress, holding the goblet carefully so that she didn't spill any wine. How many bodies had joined here? How many other pairs of lovers had together found here the delicious pleasure she knew that lovers found? How often had the walls and ceiling of this humble room echoed to cries of ecstasy?

The thoughts made her feel hot. Putting the goblet down on the floor, she loosened the laces that ran up the front of her dress, exposing the inner curves of her white breasts. To think! – the loose women of the city often displayed as much in the open street. Well she, Amy Blount, was now as loose a woman as any of them – or shortly would be – and likewise would not fear to show herself.

What was taking Master Marlowe so long? Pleasantly sleepy from the wine and throbbing in some way she found it hard to define, she lay back once more and grinned at the ceiling. Her thighs moved instinctively apart, awaiting him . . .

'And now I must go to join my wench,' said Master Marlowe with a broad smile. 'I've promised her half a sovereign for her maidenhead, and I intend to get full value for my money.'

'Dibble her deeply for me, Kit,' said one of his cronies.

'That I shall do, Ingram, and many a time. When tomorrow dawns there shall be one cock crowing louder than all the rest.'

He got up to leave them and, as he did so, a hooded figure brushed past him. He looked after it, frowning, for a moment, and then shrugged his shoulders.

'Farewell,' he said.

'Good luck,' said someone, laughing.

None of the men noticed when, a couple of moments later, the person in the hooded cloak approached their friend again and engaged him in brief, agitated conversation.

Not long afterwards, the shouting started.

Master Shakespeare clearly hadn't heard the news when he called at the shop the following morning with his new manuscript – a poem, this time, rather than a play. He was looking tired, but he was not so tired that he didn't notice Amy's pinched, pale face.

'Are you ill, lass?' he said solicitously. 'Should you not be resting?'

'It's nothing,' Amy replied before Betts could do so for her.

She summoned a smile from somewhere and did her best to seem bright. 'I am just rather shocked by what I have heard of one of our other clients. Perhaps you knew him? Master Marlowe.'

'Kit Marlowe?' said Master Shakespeare. 'I know him better than I like him, but he is the finest poet in London for all that. Tell me, what has befallen him?'

'He's dead,' said Betts abruptly. She looked not much better than Amy, having been up all night comforting her sister. 'Murdered in a tavern brawl in Deptford.'

'But that's dreadful!' exclaimed Master Shakespeare, going white and almost dropping his manuscript. 'Not unexpected, because of the way he insisted on associating with riffraff and cutthroats, but dreadful nevertheless. How did you hear of this?'

'Master Herbert told us,' lied Betts smoothly. 'My sister and my father are desolated – we were all fond of Master Marlowe, in our different ways.'

'So bright a genius, to be dimmed so untimely,' said Master Shakespeare. 'It is a tragedy.' He shook his head, as if to jolt the knowledge out of it. 'Still, I suppose, life must go on. Have the constables apprehended the culprit?'

'Not that we have heard,' said Amy in a low voice. Staggering home through the darkness had been an experience perhaps even worse than being in the tavern when Master Marlowe, her intended lover, had been slaughtered. Seeing a young woman out on her own in the darkness, men had assumed the worst of her; she had needed to fight off two of them by physical force before a passing constable, taking mercy on her plight, had escorted her the rest of the way. For a wonder, he had not importuned her himself.

Master Shakespeare let out a long sigh. 'I wish I had greater faith in their abilities.' Again he shook his head. 'Nevertheless, as I say, we must continue.' His voice became more positive. 'I have here a new poem which I have written – not a dull play like *Titus*,' he added with a wink at Betts. 'The Muse came to me last night, and I sat up all through the hours of darkness writing, writing, writing. I only hope it seems as good to me tomorrow as it does this morning. Which of you two would like to transcribe it for me?'

'I will do it,' said Amy at once, then wondered why she had. 'I have no other work on hand at the moment.'

'And neither have I,' said Betts. 'I was set to start working on the new selection of plays Master Marlowe left with us yesterday afternoon, but I doubt he shall need them now.' She looked at them worriedly. 'Yet I cannot think it right merely to throw them away – the paper has value.'

'As you say,' said Master Shakespeare, 'yet it has been all scribbled on already. The works are of no use now Kit is dead. Best to use the paper as you treat my own – for lighting the fire.'

He chatted a little further with Amy, giving her directions for the way he wanted his fresh-forged poem to be laid out on the page, and then he disappeared out of the door into the commotion of Poultry Street, still shaking his head from time to time.

'Well,' said Betts after he had gone, 'I shall go to ask Master Fenton and the Goodwife Lancet if they have any tasks for me. If not, I shall help Father in the cellar for the rest of the day. Will you be all right without me, Amy?'

'I'll be all right,' the younger woman said. 'Now that it's daylight, everything seems easier to accept. Besides, it's clear to me now that Master Marlowe's protestations of eternal love were empty and meaningless. He meant to use me as his whore, and then discard me. I am sorry that he is dead, but I cannot find any grief for him.'

'That's good,' said Betts brusquely, as if she herself cared more about Master Marlowe than she could bring herself to say. 'Now, I must be about my business.'

Amy stared dully at Master Shakespeare's manuscript. *Venus and Adonis* it said at the head of the first sheet. She had little appetite for work – and, besides, her hands were shaking too much from shock and exhaustion for her to consider taking up her pen. She would read through the manuscript this afternoon, and then start to copy it tomorrow.

> *Even as the sun with purple-colour'd face*
> *Had ta'en his last leave of the weeping morn,*
> *Rose-cheek'd Adonis hied him to the chase . . .*

She was gripped. Master Marlowe's *Hero and Leander* had impressed her by its skill and wit – and by what she thought of as its romantic passages – but Master Shakespeare's work, doubtless because he had written it all off in a single session, had a rude vigour which conveyed itself to her so directly that she could imagine the man was there in the room, reading it aloud to her. Before she knew it, she was halfway through the thinnish sheaf of paper, eager to discover how things turned out.

And then a rather unsettling thought occurred to her, and she turned back a few pages.

Master Marlowe's Hero had proved to have a curious physical resemblance to herself, but could not the same be said of Master Shakespeare's Venus? The goddess was captivated by the beautiful young Adonis, and yearned to feel his nakedness against her . . . just as she, Amy, had lain in the upper room of the tavern, her body sprawled immodestly as she ached for Master Marlowe's flesh on her, *in* her. And here, indeed, she found a passage where Master Shakespeare told of Venus lying exactly likewise all night long as she throbbed for the caresses of her Adonis.

Amy read even more quickly to the end of the poem.

Adonis insisted that he must lead the boar hunt, leaving Venus distraught with frustration. But the goddess believed that, once the hunt was over, Adonis would come to her and be hers forever; the same delusion Amy had borne concerning Master Marlowe as he sat drinking. Fate in the form of a boar had intervened to leave Venus's lusts forever unrequited: the beast had turned upon its hunter and gouged out his groin with its tusk, killing him. Amy had anticipated the loss of her maidenhead to Master Marlowe at a tavern called the Boar and Hunter, and the poet's murderer had not only stabbed his eye and slashed his throat but also cut him privily.

And had not Master Marlowe habitually referred to Master Shakespeare as 'that bore'? Surely Master Shakespeare must have known of this.

Was she holding in her hands what was, in effect, a *confession*?

By his own account, Master Shakespeare had written the poem swiftly, inspired to stay up all night writing it. Could his inspiration have been not the Muse but his own crime? And why would he have committed that crime? What had driven him to it?

The note! That note from Master Marlowe which had gone astray. Had it become tucked in among the pages of *Titus Andronicus* and so been borne away by an unsuspecting Master Shakespeare? He might have discovered it later, realized what was afoot, and moved swiftly and ruthlessly to protect her honour . . .

Or to confound a rival lover?

Master Shakespeare had always been friendly towards her; she flushed as she remembered she had often been curt with him, because he seemed so rough-made with his country ways. Might it be that he had, despite her rudeness, fallen in love with her? Or did he, rather, regard her with the fondness a father might have for his daughter? – for she was almost young enough.

She could not fall *in* love with Master Shakespeare, but just in the past few days she had learnt to like him very much. She could come to love him as a daughter did. And she *would*, for had he not risked his life to save her from a vile fate? Now that the scales had been stricken from her eyes, she knew what the consummation of her tryst with Master Marlowe would have led to: an existence of progressively greater degradation until, homeless and diseased, she crawled the gutters in search of the basest of men in hope of a stale crust.

Master Marlowe had known of the course that destiny would likely afford her, yet he had not cared at all. Her fate was irrelevant beside the immediate gratification of his desires.

Master Shakespeare, seeing the same, had made sure it would never come to pass.

Amy neatened the pages of *Venus and Adonis*, and drew her pen and inkwell towards her, as well as some fresh paper. She would say nothing of Master Shakespeare's unwitting confession – she would not even mention it to Master Shakespeare himself. It would remain to eternity a secret, and no one would ever know the mystery of who had killed Kit Marlowe.

Her hands were no longer shaking as she began to write.

* * *

Edward Blount was glad enough when, towards the end of the afternoon, Betts came down to the cellar with the heap of unwanted manuscript. Even during the summer it could grow cold down here, and he was running low on fuel.

Once she had gone he opened the grate and, just before consigning the papers to the flame, glanced at the topmost sheet. 'Christopher Marlowe,' he read in a hushed voice, and then he grinned.

It was a fine irony. That bastard Marlowe had deflowered beloved Betts, and Blount had discovered only too late. But then he had found the rumpled note on the floor upstairs yesterday afternoon, and had known that he could at least save Amy – and at the same time avenge Betts. His sharp-bladed printers' knife had been all he had needed as accomplice in the performance of the lethal deed.

Still smiling, he thrust the papers in on top of the ashes that were all that was left of his hooded cloak.

THAT SAME PIT

Margaret Frazer

When Margaret Frazer opted to write a whodunnit based on Titus Andronicus *I wondered just what she was going to do. Everyone avoided this play when I was compiling the first volume because it is so full of murder, mayhem and carnage that it does not lend itself to a subtle mystery. The play was one of Shakespeare's earliest, written perhaps in 1589, and its violence is attributed to Shakespeare's youthful exuberance. Indeed some scholars have suggested the play may not even be by Shakespeare. I hope you are as intrigued as I was to find how cleverly Margaret Frazer used the play as the basis for her Shakespearean whodunnit.*

The hour was grown past merely late into the last long watch before dawn. Cold had crept in from the room's far corners and white-plastered walls as the fire died, and the candle was burned near to guttering, but the two men at the table talked on regardless. It had been a while since they'd last met, not since the end of their shared boyhoods in Stratford, when their manhoods were still too young to give certainty of what they might become. They'd gone their different ways, swearing they'd not lose touch with one another, and then of course they had, but now were met again as men in London.

There had been stories to tell, wine to drink, laughter shared, until now they were down to the end of the wine and, it seemed, the end of things to say, Will drawing wine-drop to wine-drop on the tabletop with a long forefinger while Robin held and stared into his wine glass as if he badly needed to hold and stare at something and the glass was all there was.

Will, therefore, in his way of guessing more from the things he saw than others, was half-ready when Robin said, 'I sought you out for more reason than old friendship, you know.'

'I know,' Will said, though he'd not admitted it to himself until then. In their boyhood years, there had always been a part of Robin that kept apart from ready fellowship, no matter how much the rest of him joined in. Tonight that part of him had not shown by so much as a mocking glance or the faintest twisted word, it was so completely gone that either Robin had gravely changed or else was keeping it deliberately hidden; and if he was hiding it, Will feared in the back ward of his mind, he was in some manner of deep trouble.

But seemingly he was ready to talk of it, and Will set himself to listen, but was not ready for Robin to say, '*Titus Andronicus*. The play you wrote when you were still schoolmastering in Stratford. I've heard it's been performed here in London.'

Will groaned. *Titus* was a wordy flourish from his callow youth, its crass plot and characters taken from a popular pamphlet and given every classical embellishment he could manage. He'd carried it with him through the years since leaving Stratford, the way a once-besotted lover carries a picture of a long-outgrown love, because it had once been precious to him. An acting company desperate for a play had actually performed it, and he'd found there was nothing like seeing youthful effusions set out on stage, in bare daylight and bold action, to sober a man out of any conceits he harboured. With unfeigned embarrassment, he asked, 'How did you hear of that? Yes, it's been done, but all it deserves is utter oblivion.'

Ignoring his embarrassment, Robin asked, 'Is it possible it could be done again?'

'Not this side of hell if I can help it.' Not now that he knew how much better he could write than that. 'Besides, I doubt there's any company that desperate for a play at present.'

Robin slipped a leather pouch out of the purse hung from his belt and tipped out on the tabletop a handful of coins whose size and lustre could not be mistaken, even in the sinking candlelight, for anything but gold. 'Would this be enough to change anyone's mind?'

Will looked up sharply into his friend's face and asked, awed and suspicious both, 'What have you been doing?'

Robin laughed, openly pleased. 'Using my time wisely.' He sobered and said as if it were an unjoyous thing, 'I'm rich, Will.'

Will looked around the inn chamber, comfortably furnished and cleanly kept, but not near to what could be had by someone with that kind of money in his purse.

Robin answered his look and unasked question. 'I wanted us to be just you and I tonight, not you and I and my money.' He smiled wryly. 'It's always my money first with most people. I wanted it to be just us for a while.'

Will leaned back in his chair, the initial surprise of the gold over and Robin rekindling his interest. 'But now?'

'Now I want to ask if you'll re-write me *Titus* in certain ways I'll tell you and help me find a company to perform it.'

'Why *Titus*? It's a farrago of treacheries, murders, mutilations. Then more treacheries, more murders, more mutilations, and finally cannibalism and more murders after that. I wrote it . . .' *When he was young and wild to do something with words, he didn't know what.* 'To see what I could do. I can do better now. It was only performed because the company was desperate.'

Robin gestured at the coins. 'And everyone's always desperate for these. Will, this isn't in idle sport. I'm serious. For this – and there's more if need be – will you re-write that play in ways I desire and see to it being put on?'

'When?'

'Next month.' Robin leaned toward him, clearly hoping he was coming around, which, faced with that much gold, Will was. 'There are some gentlemen from where I now live coming to London then, for Hilary-term court. They'll surely come at my invitation to see an entertainment. I want it to be this.' He hesitated, then said, 'Will, it's to make a murderer known.'

'You're jesting.'

'Never the least.'

No, he wasn't, Will thought, and they were both most achingly sober – or else more strangely drunk than Will had ever been.

Almost whispering, Robin said, 'Will, there's been murder done and no one suspects the murderer except me. He'll be here, one of these gentlemen. If I can put enough of his crime into the play, they'll see, they'll know. He may even give himself away.'

'If you know so much about him, why do you need the play to trap him?'

'I can't tell you that. Not yet. The thing is a desperate tangle and this is the only hope I have of bringing his crimes home to him.'

'Crimes? More than murder?'

'Murders. That's why your *Titus* came to mind.'

There were murders enough in *Titus*, that was sure, but despite liking Robin, Will had never noted in him strong inclinations toward dispassionate justice and asked, 'Why does this matter so much to you?'

'There's a child.' To Will's raised eyebrows, Robin laughed ruefully. 'You remember my way out of Stratford? As secretary in a wealthy widow's household. She was a good lady to me. So was her husband when she remarried. I served them well, earned their trust . . .' He paused, visibly moved by memory. 'The point is, they're both dead now and I have the wardship of their only child.'

Will made a long, low whistle of appreciation. Robin had made no idle boast about being rich. Wardship of the heir of a wealthy inheritance was a very profitable thing to have.

'It's the child I'm afraid for, Will. This man brought on my lord and lady's deaths. He could well want the child's next. What I hope is that once he knows he's known, knows that these men understand that the things that they thought were only happenstance and chance were actually his doing, he'll be warned off doing more.'

'There is no other way? One that might bring him to justice?'

'There isn't that kind of proof. I have to hope certainty will be enough.'

Will took a deep breath, and let it slowly out. 'Well, then. What are these changes you think will serve?'

The weather was bright-skied and, for January, warm, but Henslowe wandered the yard below the stage, grumbling about potential trouble. Henslowe was devoted to potential – 'The potential for profit in this . . .' 'The potential for disaster here . . .' – but happily was adroit at grasping the former and avoiding the latter, and had agreed to his theatre and company being hired for *Titus* when he once understood there was no chance he'd take a loss on it. He'd muttered over his reputation, but between his cash box and his reputation, his cash box always had the upper hand. Robin, therefore, was going to have his *Titus Andronicus*.

The cast was even going to have a completed script, though it would be a near thing, Will thought, grimly penning at the paper tacked to the board on his knee against the small, ruffling wind finding its way into the open circle of the theatre. The wooden 'O' was three tiers high, eleven bays given to the audience, three to the tiring-house, with the stage thrust out from it into the encircled space. Will was sitting two tiers up in the last bay to stage-right, where he could watch what was being done to his play in rehearsal while writing its ending.

'I *know* it's "Tamara",' Ned groused from the stage at someone's correction. 'Tamara, Queen of the Goths. What I want to know is why the hell it was changed?' He raised his voice, though it had been carrying well enough as it was. 'Hey, Will, how come she's changed to "Tamara" from "Attava"?'

'Whim!' Will called back.

It was actually one of Robin's changes but at least it hadn't messed the scansion. Other changes had been more troublesome. Tamara was given a third son, for Titus to sacrifice, thereby setting her hatred and the tragedy under way. The Emperor's son was changed into his brother, one Bassianus, who with another change rivalled the Emperor for Titus's daughter Lavinia and won her, earning his brother's resentment. As before, the Queen, now Tamara, and her lover, a Moor, set her sons on to murder Bassianus ensuring that two of Titus's sons were executed for the crime; but now the rape and mutilation of Lavinia, instead of taking place after her brothers' deaths, happened with her husband's death. And then . . .

Behind Will the door in the bay's end opened, and John, appearing up the ladder from the tiring-house, said with hand thrust out, 'Page.' Without looking around, Will handed back a completed sheet for him to take to the two scribes presently at work in the bay above Will's, copying out each actor's cues and speeches separately so that each actor had only his own lines and no more. They did not even have the plot in detail until the first time they all rehearsed the play through. It was a complicated way to work, but it kept the play from being pirated by other acting companies, since the whole script was never in anyone's hands but Will's and John's.

Now John grumbled at Will's back, 'Does this last scene have to be so rewritten? Doesn't everyone end up dead, same as before?'

'This way they're more dead,' Will said, still writing.

'It's a hellish lot of trouble.'

Will grinned over his shoulder at the best of all his London friends. 'A trouble that's bringing us enough money to put together our own company of players. Is the Lord Chamberlain still interested?'

John grinned too, grumble forgotten. 'If we put a company together, he'll give his name to it, he says. Write on.' And left, still grinning, as from the yard below Henslowe called up, 'This tree, Will,' pointing at a large, leafless limb lying beside him, waiting to become a tree in the murder-of-Bassianus – rape-of-Lavinia scene. 'Can't we have a rock instead? Trees are so damnably awkward to stage!'

Will sympathised. A plaster-and-painted 'rock' was to be preferred to a sprawling branch, but he called down, 'It has to be a tree. An elder tree.'

'Damned if I'm putting leaves and berries on the thing!'

'No need!' He'd already written '. . . the elder tree Which overshades the mouth of that same pit . . .'

The pit, wherein Tamara's sons threw Bassianus' body, was no problem – open the stage's trapdoor and they had it – but Robin had been insistent about the elder tree, and four lines later there was, 'This is the pit, and this the elder-tree,' to make no mistake.

The last problem was the re-arrangment of the final scene. Will agreed with John that the old way had worked. After serving Tamara a pie made of her dead sons, Titus had killed the Emperor and her, condemned her equal-in-evil the Moor to death, killed Lavinia, and then himself. The end. But Robin had insisted, 'Titus kills Lavinia first, then Tamara. Then the Emperor kills Titus and someone kills the Emperor. *That's* the end.'

'And the Moor's condemned to death,' Will had said; and added, hopefully, 'Unless he's left out altogether?'

Robin's refusal had been absolute. 'The Moor has to be there.'

Will hadn't argued. As far back as Stratford and the pamphlet *The Tragical History of Titus Andronicus* that they had read together and inspired Will to the play, Robin's greatest delight had been in the Moor. 'He makes things happen and no one knows he's done it! They're all fools to him!'

He'd even had Will add two new murders for the Moor – a

Nurse and a Midwife to hide that Tamara had borne him a blackamoor child.

But . . .

But what?

Will didn't know. He only suspected that if he took time to think more about the whole business, he'd like it even less than he did. But there wasn't time to think, only time to write . . .

'Page,' John said behind him.

They'd done it. He didn't know where Robin was tonight, nor did he care, but tomorrow the re-made *Titus* would go before its first audience and so Will was wrapped in his usual throes of uncertainty, sitting at John's table with head in hands, saying, 'I don't know if the thing's any good at all.'

'You never know at this point,' John said cheerfully, used to him.

'Should we have let James and Hal switch their parts?'

'Too late to worry on it now.'

'Why did James want to?' At least it was something simple to worry on, that three days ago, after the first full run-through of the play, James had asked to trade his plum part of Chiron, one of Tamara's murderous sons, for young Hal's Bassianus who died a great many scenes before Chiron's throat was cut, leaving his actor to play anonymous servants and soldiers the rest of the show.

'He said he wanted to be early-dead so he could leave to work a minstrel-job across town,' John said. 'Hal does Chiron fine. It's Dick I'm going to throttle if he says "I don't think I can play her old enough" one more time.'

Will sank his head farther between his hands. 'Oh, God. Does any of it work at all? Who's going to believe anyone would behave the way these people do?'

'Who pays to see believable? "Believable" is what you see for free in the streets and at home.' John reached out and shook Will's arm. 'You've done better than believable with this. This shows the ugliness that comes of passions given their full play. It's not fate or chance that destroys anyone in the play, but choices deliberately made by themselves or others.'

'But will anyone else see that? Oh, God. There has to be a better way than this to make a living!'

'Surely,' John agreed cheerfully. 'But this is what you're best at.'
Will groaned.

He watched the final morning rehearsal of the last scene's complicated plethora of killings and speeches, with Robin, from the middle tier of seats directly fronting the stage. This afternoon Robin's country gentlemen would sit there – 'Not the most fashionable place in the theatre,' Robin had said, 'but they don't know fashion from a bodice-lace, so it doesn't matter' – and Robin would watch both the play and them from where Will had sat while writing during rehearsals. Will didn't know yet where he would be or do, except he wouldn't be with Robin.

Working together had worked them apart. They'd hardly spoken together once the script was set, though Robin had been there every day, watching as he was watching now, with Will trying, as he was trying now, not to see his eagerness at the horrors done on the stage below them and most particularly not see his glee at everything the Moor did.

But despite himself, Will's vague suspicions kept shifting toward certainties, and even more despite himself, he now asked, 'Robin, how much of what you had me change and put in the play is real?'

Robin looked around at him, into his eyes for a long moment, before saying evenly, 'Enough.'

'What . . .'

'Will.' Robin said it most quietly, still looking at him. 'Don't know too much.'

With the thought of snakes staring down birds, Will pulled free from Robin's look and left him.

Will watched from the stage-left spyhole of the tiring house as the theatre filled that afternoon, and saw Robin bring his guests to their front seats in the centre bay. There was much flourishing of hats and bowing among them before Robin removed himself, to reappear alone in his boxed bay to stage-right to more bowing and acknowledgments over the heads of the groundlings. These preliminaries were brought to an end by the drums and trumpets that served to settle everyone onto their seats for the play's beginning.

It ran well from the first, carried along on the actors' usual first-performance desperation after too few rehearsals. By mid-way through there was no doubting the audience's delight in it, but Will, still at his spyhole, was watching a different play from the rest, seeing unease grow gradually on Robin's gentlemen – at first no more than occasional glances among them as the play progressed, with sometimes one or another shifting uneasily on their bench and casting a look toward Robin. But mention of the elder tree roused them all at once, first to look sharply at one another, then toward Robin who smiled and bowed his head to them in acknowledgement of something.

No one returned his smile and after that their disquiet grew, their glances at each other and at Robin more frequent, sometimes one leaning to speak in another's ear, until the words 'Cornelia the midwife' brought several of them to rigid attention, first staring at the actors, then at Robin who this time feigned not to notice, intent on the stage as, a moment later, the Moor, having claimed Queen Tamara's bastard child for his own, killed the Nurse who had brought it to him, shortly promised the same death for the midwife, and ordered both women's bodies buried in the fields so his secret could be kept.

At that, one of the gentlemen began a violent rise to his feet. Another pulled him down but the others were almost as disquieted. Talk spasmed among them all and their looks at Robin were now prolonged, the end of the scene ignored.

Their neighbours were beginning to be restless with them when Will abandoned his spyhole, to thread his way among the actors crowded backstage and up the ladder to the door to Robin's box. Keeping low to be out of sight, he edged to behind Robin's high-backed chair, and Robin, not looking, said, 'Yes, Will?'

'You didn't do all this to trap one of those men into showing his guilt,' Will whispered fiercely. 'You did it to show them what you'd done.'

'Did I?'

'You're "the Moor", destroying people or else bringing them to destroy each other.'

'Am I?'

'Yes. Why?' Will demanded.

With satisfaction thick as cream on milk, Robin said, 'For the sport of it.'

Below, Titus, driven half-mad by griefs, was sending arrows skyward with messages to the gods.

'But why want people to know what you've done? What you are?' Will asked.

'Because it's boring being so clever that no one knows I am. And now that they know, what can they do? What can I be accused of? It's only a play. They'll be certain, but all they can do is live with their certainty while I live with the pleasure of watching them able to do nothing.' He turned his head slightly, saying without looking away from the stage, 'Will, I didn't start the hatred between my "Tamara" and her "Titus". I happened to be there and I made use of it for my own amusements. That's all.'

'The child. Your lady's child. The child you have in ward. Is he yours? Like in the play?'

Robin smiled. 'Oh yes.'

'And you did these things? All these things?'

Robin's smile deepened. 'Enough of them.'

Will slipped backward to the ladder and down, and through the backstage seething of Titus and his men coming off while the Emperor and his court went on, and made his way out into the rearyard, to walk and think. He was still there, pacing, when the play ended to such applause and cheers there was no doubt it had succeeded with the audience at large. He was still there when John found him a while later, to tell him that Robin was dead.

'Still in his chair when his gentlemen friends went along to see him at the play's end, because he didn't come to them,' John said. 'Stabbed from the back and through the heart.'

Before the Sheriff came the audience was long gone, none the wiser there had been a true killing among all the staged ones. His questioning of the actors and Robin's gentlemen was brief. None of the actors knew anything; they had all been too busy to notice. The gentlemen, with time, Will guessed, to have talked it quickly over among themselves, knew nothing either, beyond Robin had invited them to the play and at its end, when they had gone to thank him, he was dead.

For his part, Will admitted he'd talked with Robin during the play, but he'd been seen leaving Robin by more than a few men backstage at a time that could be pinpointed by where they were in the play, while the gentlemen swore Robin had smiled and nodded to them after that. In fact, they were certain he'd been alive right to the final scene.

'But during that scene none of you saw anything?' the sheriff asked.

'It was the end of the play,' one of them said. 'We were watching what happened on stage.'

'And none of you left the others at any time?'

None of them had.

The sheriff's conclusion was that it was likely to have been a cut-purse, come up the gallery stairs to take advantage of a rich man sitting alone. There seemed general willingness to agree with that. Even Will nodded vague acceptance because 'cut-purse unknown' was a straight-forward and simple answer, never mind there were safer ways to take purses than risking being seen in the gallery behind the box, and that it would have had to be an inefficient as well as an unusually murderous cut-purse: Robin's purse still hung untouched from his belt.

Being unseen in the box itself was no problem, Will knew. Reaching there unseen was the trick, but the answer to that lay, he thought, in the certainty that Robin had been killed in the last scene, when during the play's horrendous final moments, there would have been small risk of anyone looking anywhere but at the stage, and moreover, backstage was nearly empty for the only time during the play, with just John left there, tucked with the prompt book into a corner where he could not see the ladder, and 'Chiron' and 'Demetrius', too lately dead to go back onstage in new guise. Everyone else in the cast was onstage as principals, servants, or soldiers.

Except for James who had given up 'Chiron' to Hal so he could leave before the play ended.

It was Hal who Will found in the far corner of a tavern the actors rarely visited, sitting alone on a bench's end behind a table, an ale mug in front of him but no signs on him that he'd drunk much. Sliding in beside him, having had time to think things through even further, Will said without other greeting, 'So, Hal, it wasn't James but you who wanted to trade your parts, wasn't it?'

Hal stared at him. 'What? No. James wanted it, not me.'

'Wanted to trade a larger part for a lesser? James? Haven't you been on at him these past weeks about money he owes you? Until these last few days?'

Hal muttered something about 'too busy'.

'That's never slowed you before. You cancelled the debt in return for him giving up Chiron to you, didn't you?'

Hal could act but apparently couldn't lie. He looked away.

'Why?' Will asked, and answered when Hal didn't, 'Because as Chiron you'd not be on stage in the last scene. You'd be backstage with only Geffrey who is "Demetrius", and can always be counted on to nip off for a quick pint somewhere when there's a chance like that, leaving no one to see you go up the ladder to the box.'

Hal flashed him a hunted look.

'It was something in the play, wasn't it?' Will persisted. 'James asked for the trade right after we'd run through the whole play for the first time. What did you see then that gave you reason to want Robin dead?'

Hal roused. 'I didn't kill him!'

'But if you *had* –' Will chose the words carefully '– what in the play might have made you?'

Hal held back, then said, wary and bitter together, 'Maybe that my mother was named Cornelia and was a midwife.'

Will made a sick lurch toward understanding both what Hal had done and, worse, what Robin had. 'She's dead?'

'These three years now. A while after I came to London.'

'How?'

Hal wanted to tell him. 'She and another woman went to deliver a lady at a remote manor, where few of her household were attending on her, with not even her husband there. The story given out afterwards was that my mother and the other woman fell ill at the birthing, and the lady's secretary, in charge and fearing plague, ordered out what few household folk there were. When he allowed them to return, he said that the lady and her baby were well but the midwife and nurse had died and he had buried their bodies for fear of infection. Your Robin . . .'

'Not mine,' Will said quickly.

'. . . was the secretary. I knew him before I left home and recognised him here.'

'But he didn't know you?'

'I was an unbearded boy of no account when I left home, but I remember him well enough, and most of the gentlemen he had here today. They're all from where I lived.'

'But why kill the women? The baby's colour can't have been the trouble.' The reason in the play for killing the women.

'Women cry out things when their birth-pains are on them. Maybe in her's it wasn't her husband Lady Thomasine cried out for,' Hal said into his ale mug. 'It's my only guess.'

Will silently agreed.

'There's other things, too,' Hal said after a while. 'I still have news from friends at home sometimes. As about the long quarrelling between Lady Thomasine and a lord there, over one of their properties. Even before I'd left, the eldest of her three sons by her first husband was killed in it, and she'd married a man who had wanted to marry her enemy's daughter but the girl had chosen his brother instead. After that, things were done on both sides. For one, the brother's murdered body was found hidden near an elder tree, a boundary mark for the disputed properties. At the same time, the girl was raped and so brutalised – though not like in the play – she could tell nothing about what had happened.'

So there was the reason for some of what Robin had wanted in the play. 'And then?' Will asked.

Hal sighed. 'For one reason and another and despite his father almost beggaring himself to save him, her brother was executed for her husband's murder. And then the local gentry made one last attempt, about a year ago, to make peace, not knowing how far gone in rage and grief the lord was. It seems, from what was told afterwards, that his daughter's wits were gradually returned and she had accused the two grown sons of the lady, her father's great enemy, of her husband's death and her rape. On the way to the reconciliation, he ambushed and killed them both, though no one knew that when both sides met. Then . . .'

His spate of words ran out. Will prompted with, 'He didn't . . .'

'No. No sons cooked in pies for their mother to eat. But the lord threw in everyone's face that he'd killed them and why, and then in front of everyone he killed his daughter and, before he could be stopped, killed Lady Thomasine, whereon her husband killed him and was in turn cut down by some of the lord's servants.'

So much for thinking all the play's murdering and counter-murdering were past belief.

So much for wondering why Robin had wanted the order of deaths re-arranged at the play's end.

So much for . . . 'What Robin didn't count on was his own part as "the Moor" being fulfilled, too,' Will said slowly. 'He didn't count on some cut-purse making casual end of him just as . . .'

'I . . .' Hal began.

'*Some cut-purse*,' Will said, 'who'll surely never be caught.' Because among so much guilt, how could justice be sorted out?

It was only later that Will, drifting homeward alone and the better for drink, had the thought that, still and all, using a play to make a murderer known was maybe something he could use in a play himself sometime.

MURDER MOST FOUL

Richard Butler

The following story is not based on any one play but considers the lives and rivalries of the actors in Shakespeare's company.

Nicholas Kyte was looking forward to murdering Cowley.

It was not that he had any quarrel with him – just the reverse. He and Richard Cowley were on excellent terms, even though Cowley had an eye for Deborah Godwit at the Gilded Magpie and she, as all the world knew, was the property of Nick Kyte. And had not Richard saved him from vile imprisonment by lending him money from some mysterious source that would not bear questioning? Aye, a goodly friend, Dick. But Kyte was to sup with Deborah that evening and the hour was later than he had thought. So the sooner he was done with his murdering, the sooner he could be off to the Gilded Magpie and a night of bliss with sweet Deborah, whose knowledge of the arts of Venus was as astonishing as it was delightful.

He scowled at his image in the cracked, full-length mirror in the tiring room of the Curtain Theatre. Aye, he looked villainous enough. Black beard. Scar on his cheek. Ferocious frown. And, of course, the horrid hump on his back that always drew yells of disgust, scorn and hatred when he limped on stage. Most excellent sport, that! 'Twas ever his favourite role, that of Richard, Duke of Gloster.

He listened to the end of the fifth scene of the last Act. The Earl's Men were performing *The Third Part of Henry VI*, written, for the most part, by Will Shakespeare but in which poor Kit Marlowe had had a hand. Aye, poor Kit indeed! Murdered but a week ago in a tavern brawl.

Kyte could hear the lad Williams who played Queen Margaret railing about 'that devil's butcher, hard-favour'd Richard'. Nearly done now.

And here they come! Applause as the burly King Edward strode off with the Duke of Clarence, pushing Margaret. King Henry's queen along, while two soldiers hauled Prince Edward's corpse. 'The Devil take ye both for a pair of whoreson rogues!' complained the bereaved Queen, staggering into the tiring room after a vigorous shove. 'Must ye heave and buffet me about as if I were a god-damned donkey?'

'Enough, boy! Did not Producer Killigrew say the script called for ye to be led off forcibly?' King Edward took off his crown to scratch his head and spoke to Richard Cowley, crowned as Henry VI and waiting to go on. 'A pox on this hot weather, eh, Dick?'

Cowley grunted. He had, as all agreed, been singularly morose of late. He turned to Kyte: 'I looked for ye ere the play began, Nick.'

'I was late.'

'I have seen little of ye these last few days.'

Kyte grinned. 'I have been much occupied.'

'Ha!' Cowley snorted. 'With Deborah Godwit. Can ye sup with me later?'

'Dick, I thank ye but I am engaged to her for the evening.'

'Can ye not put her off? I must talk to ye concerning Kit Marlowe's death—'

'Master Cowley!' Thomas Killigrew rushed in. 'Have ye no ears?' From beyond the curtain came the impatient yells of an audience kept waiting in the hot May sun. 'Our patron, Lord Durbridge, awaits. Make haste, make haste!'

Cowley went to sit with a book in the curtained-off space at the rear of the vast stage, the Lieutenant of the Tower in attendance. The audience well-nigh drowned the voice of the stage-hand who held up a placard and bawled, for those who could not read. 'A Room in the Tower!' The curtain was twitched back. Kyte lurched onto the stage, glaring about him.

As soon as he appeared there was a howl of execration from the penny stinkards, those who stood in front of the stage. 'Vile Crook-back!' 'Foul murderer!' One threw a half-eaten orange. 'Poxy son of a bitch!' Kyte dodged it and gibbered at them, menacing them with his painted wooden sword. They loved it and shrieked the harder.

Then they quietened as he turned to the King to say with a sneer:

Gloster: *Good day, my lord. What, at your book so hard?* King Henry: *Ay, my good lord: – my lord, I should say rather; Good Gloster and good devil were alike.*

Gloster dismissed the Lieutenant and taunted the King, boasting that he had killed his son. The King responded with a dignified scorn that goaded Gloster into a fury.

King Henry: *The owl shrieked at thy birth – an evil sign . . .*

'Aye,' shouted a man leaning on the apron. 'And well it might, at such a monster!'

Gloster limped up and down, growling and rolling his eyes. The audience booed and hissed delightedly.

King Henry: *Thy mother felt more than a mother's pain,*
And yet brought forth less than a mother's hope,
An indigest deformèd lump . . .

Gloster snarled, threatening the King with his sword. From the upper gallery a woman shrieked. 'Leave the poor King be, ye wretch!'

. . . Teeth hadst thou in thy head when thou wast born,
And if the rest be true which I have heard,
Thou cam'st—.

Gloster: *I'll hear no more!* He ran at the seated King and pressed the blunt point to his chest. *Die, prophet, in thy speech!* The audience screamed, almost drowning Henry's meek speech of forgiveness before he slumped, dead.

They shrieked even harder when Gloster stabbed him again.

I'll throw thy body in another room,
And triumph, Henry, in thy day of doom.

He cackled horribly as he dragged Cowley off, the audience roaring like Bedlamites.

The tiring room was empty. Kyte said, 'What of Kit's death, Dick?'

'He was about to reveal – But later. See, they await ye on stage!'

'Deborah may wait, then. After the next scene ye shall tell me all!' He hurried to take his place near King Edward's throne.

Edward gloated at his success. Gloster delivered a threatening aside followed by a hypocritical speech of love to the infant prince.

Then King Edward brought the play to a close:

Sound drums and trumpets! farewell, sour annoy!

For here, I hope, begins our lasting joy.

A hope not destined to be fulfilled. For, as he and his Queen, with Gloster. Clarence and the rest trooped into the tiring room, they found Richard Cowley sprawled on the floor in a pool of blood, with two stab wounds in his chest.

Then followed complete confusion, with cries of 'Perchance he lives still!' and 'A surgeon, ho!' But, since confusion was common enough in the tiring room, Thomas Killigrew did not seem unduly alarmed when he bustled in to give his customary end-of-performance tongue-lashing. Nor was he surprised when told that Cowley had been stabbed, pointing out irritably that he had been stabbed every afternoon for a month, except on Sundays. Still talking, he was led to the corpse. He looked at it, shocked.

'Jesu, Nick,' was his first reaction. 'Ye have ruined my play, ye wretch! Cowley was no Burbage, to be sure, but—'

'Ye accuse me?'

'Why, to be sure! Who else? A theatre full of witnesses saw ye stab him twice.'

Stout Tom Burslowe, who played King Edward, said, 'I doubt not it was some dreadful mishap, Nick, and ye took a real sword on stage—'

'Not so!' Kyte showed his wooden toy. 'I used this and none other. God's blood, he was alive when I brought him in here! He spoke to me—'

'Who saw ye?' Burslowe asked.

'Well, no one, but—'

'It looks black for ye, Nick.' Killigrew sighed. 'Ye owed him money ye could not repay, did ye not? And all the world knows ye were rivals for the favours of that wench at the Magpie—'

'For the love of God, Killigrew, ye cannot think me guilty of this!'

Burslowe said, 'Let us search for the weapon with which the murder was done. It may tell us something.'

The search did not take long. When young Williams opened the door of Kyte's cupboard they all stared, horrified.

'Aye,' Killigrew said grimly. 'It tells us something, right enough.' He pointed to the sword, its steel blade caked with blood that was already turning brown as it dried. 'It tells us to send for the officers.'

'But that sword is not mine! Master Killigrew, ye cannot let them arrest me on such flimsy—'

'Nick! Nick!' Killigrew shook his head sanctimoniously. 'Ye know our standing with the City fathers. They think our theatre profligate, a haunt of whores and thieves. For our patron's sake, I may not conceal this crime.' He turned to the stage hands who had come to cluster, awestruck, in the doorway. 'One of ye, run for the Sheriff's men!'

Kyte's mind raced as he stared at their grave faces. He had been in the hands of the Sheriff before on small matters and knew he would have no chance of proving his innocence from a prison cell. He sprang to his cupboard and seized the bloody sword. 'Stand back!' He menaced them with it and rushed to the door, the stage hands hurriedly edging aside.

'Nick, I prithee do not be foolish!' Burslowe cried. 'To flee is testimony of your guilt!'

'Who follows after me will surely die!' He turned and ran. Angered, confused and fearful though he was, he could not but feel pleased with his exit line. Perfect pentameter, i'faith, and worthy of Will Shakescene himself!

A gaggle of women screamed and fled as he ran down the lane. And with good reason, he thought. He was still dressed for the stage, his padded hump on his back and a bloodied sword in his hand. He stopped, wiped the blade clean and stuck it into his belt. Now what? As Killigrew had said, the theatres were anathema to the Lord Mayor of London and his Council so the Curtain was built in the fields north of the City walls. Beyond them lay the warrens that Kyte knew well. But he could not hide in them for ever. His only course was to clear his name by finding Cowley's murderer.

First, then, to his lodging at the Gilded Magpie and change his attire.

He went in quietly, hoping to reach his chamber unperceived. But a voice with a round Warwickshire accent called from the dining room where a smallish man, his dark hair thin on top but grown long over his ears, sat alone, writing. 'Nick! Nick Kyte!' He put down his quill.

'Why in the Fiend's name are ye costumed thus? Have ye lost your shirt at dice?'

'Nay, Will. Do but come to my chamber. 'Tis a grim tale I have to tell.' He turned back to add, 'And for the love of God bring me a sup!' Will Shakespeare called for ale. When it came he pocketed his manuscript and followed upstairs.

Kyte unstrapped his hump and rummaged for a doublet. 'There is little time. The officers will soon be here. In brief, Richard Cowley is slain and I am charged therewith.' He donned grey patterned trunk hose, black knee-length canions and grey stockings, while he recounted what had happened in the tiring-room. 'First Kit Marlowe. now this.'

'Aye.' Shakespeare handed him a mug. 'And Dick Cowley was sore distressed by Kit's death, more than most of us, and melancholy as a gib-cat.'

'Indeed he was.' Kyte drank some ale and felt better. 'Now he has met the same strange end – except that Kit's murderer is known.'

'Is he?' Shakespeare looked at him over the rim of his mug.

'Why, to be sure. He was stabbed by one Ingram Frisar—'

'Who has disappeared.'

'—After supping with him before witnesses—'

'Who have also vanished.'

'—In a quarrel concerning the score.'

'So 'tis buzzed about. But although Kit was dissolute, hot-tempered and heretical, he was never mean-minded. He would never shrink from paying his share. And, bethink ye, Nick – for ye knew the man – if attacked, would he have drawn a knife?'

'Nay,' Kyte said slowly. 'No more would you or I. The poniard be more a French or Spanish cut-throat's weapon than an English one. In a tap-room scuffle, there being no room for swordplay, we would upset the table, wield a bottle, use our fists but not draw a knife.' He paused. 'Would that Dick had told me more.'

'Aye.' Shakespeare was silent for a moment. 'Did ye know that Kit was in the employ of my Lord Burghley?'

'The queen's spymaster?' Kyte stared. 'Nay, I did not. How can ye be sure?'

'He told me when in his cups. And now ye say he shared some secret with Dick Cowley. Perchance it cost them their lives.'

Kyte said, 'Who is this Frisar? Another spy?'

'I know not. But it is a curious name and full of anagrams.' Will finished his mug. 'Perchance ye had better find him, starting at the Fouled Anchor tavern at Deptford. Have ye money?' He smiled. 'Ah, I forgot. Ye're an actor.' He pulled out his purse and threw it onto the bed. 'My Lord Southampton has been generous.'

'Nay, nay, Will. I thankee but I can make do. I shall use my pack of marked cards—'

'Jesu, Nick, ye know full well ye be so inept at cards ye cannot win even though they be marked! This be a loan, no more.' He stood up. 'Have a care ye be not taken. Alter your appearance, your gait. For, if this be a political matter, as I believe, ye will have no hope of justice.'

When Will had gone, Kyte cut off his beard, arranged his hair differently, then left, avoiding Deborah on the way out – there was nought to be gained by making her an accomplice. He entered the City at Bishop's Gate, then crossed the river, pushing his way past the crowded shops and booths that lined London Bridge. He turned his back on the Southwark stews, his birthplace, and tramped downriver, reaching Deptford in the golden glow of the summer evening. The Fouled Anchor was hard by the river. He requested a chamber, giving his name as James Edwards, a ship's chandler.

He ordered supper and spoke of the recent murder with the inn-keeper. It was, mine host agreed, a wicked crime but he knew nought of it, having been abed with the colic on the evening in question. Nay, he knew no one called Frisar. His wife? Visiting her sick aunt. The potboy had been in charge with a serving wench but they had seen nought.

Kyte ate his supper and sat with a mug of ale. And it was not long before a fair-haired, full-bosomed maid begged leave to share his bench, even though the room was half empty. He bought her a cup of sack. She was Molly, came to the Anchor often, had not seen him afore. Was he a stranger to Deptford? In need of company, perchance? Prices were mentioned, for an hour or the whole night. He chose an hour then whisked her up to his chamber.

She was practised, but lacked Deborah's fire. Afterwards, he said, 'Were ye here on the night when the playwright was murdered?'

'Aye!' She came up on one bare elbow, her blue eyes wide. ''Twas terrible! I had entertained a gentleman and gone downstairs for refreshment when—'

'Was the landlord there?'

'To be sure – he and his wife. I kept out of their way – the wife likes me not. Master Marlowe was at supper—'

'Ye knew him, then?'

'To be sure.' She smiled reminiscently. 'A hot-blooded, generous man. He sat alone—'

'Alone?' he said sharply. 'Ye're sure?'

'Aye. I was thinking to join him when two men came in. Ugh!' She made the sign of the cross on her naked bosom. 'Evil, hard-eyed bastards as ever were! Cloaked, their hats pulled down. They went to speak with Master Marlowe. He stood up. They crowded him close. I heard him say. "It strikes, it strikes! Now, body, turn to air!" – I know not what he meant—'

'It was from a play he wrote last year. A speech at the end, when the devils came to drag Faustus down to Hell.'

She shivered. 'Then he fell forward across the table. One of the men laughed and said he was vilely drunk. They left. At first I thought it was red wine that was spreading over the table. But, when the screaming began, I slipped out.'

'And that is all ye saw of them?'

'Aye. But stay! One had a fine ruby ring on the left hand that held his cloak.'

'Know ye a man named Ingram Frisar?'

'Ingram Frisar?' She shook her blonde curls.

'Well, I thankee. Molly. Now, here is a sovereign for ye and a piece of advice. If ye value your life, never mention to a living soul what ye have told me.'

She looked fearful. 'I have told no one but yourself – and that only because ye did not treat me with disdain when ye had done with me, as do most men.'

He slept ill that night, slipping in and out of dreams of violence. *Ingram Frisar . . . a name full of anagrams . . . if this be a political matter, as I believe, ye will have no hope of justice . . . a political matter . . . would that Dick had told me more . . .*

He awoke with the dream still upon him to find the sky flushed pink and gold beyond Greenwich Reach. *Would that he had told me more . . .*

Had Dick told anyone else? Nay, Kyte thought. With a secret he was close-mouthed as an oyster. He must have had good reason, some foreknowledge of peril, to make me his confidant. Had he perchance written it down? Unlikely, but . . . Kyte sprang out of bed. There was only one way to find out.

Dick had lodged with an ancient widow in a cottage near Islington. She knew Kyte so, in spite of his disguise, he took no risks but waited until she had trotted off towards the village with her basket before sneaking in at the back door.

The chamber showed no sign of occupancy. Dick's clothes, his personal possessions – all had gone. There remained only the simple bed, a small table near the window and an empty chest.

Someone had been there before him.

If there had been a secret paper, Dick would surely have hidden it. But where, in an empty room with blank walls? He searched but without hope. Not in the chest. Not behind it or beneath it. Not on the table or beneath it. Not in the bed, or under it. He pulled it away from the wall.

A small piece of paper that had been jammed behind the headboard fluttered to the floor.

He pounced. Then cursed. A bill for washing two shirts. He turned it over. Durbridge House, written in Dick's hand. The Blackfriars residence of the dissolute Earl of Durbridge.

By nightfall he was down at Blackfriars and at the rear of the house, in the garden that went down to the Thames. All seemed quiet without and within. No dogs. Dim lights, indicating the presence of servants, with my lord not at home. Good. He went silently to a small, unlighted window. Bolted, of course, but fortunately his wide circle of drinking companions included more than one informative burglar. From his kerchief he took out the slice of bread and honey he had bought for the purpose and slapped it onto one of the small panes of glass. He struck the glass sharply. It cracked. When he withdrew the bread, most of the glass stuck to it. He picked out the rest, put a hand inside and slid back the bolt.

Inside, he felt his way among barrels and sacks. Then a door to a kitchen, where a fire glowed in the hearth beneath a cauldron of stew. Another door, ajar, a light beyond it. He peered cautiously through the crack. A panelled hall, a staircase and—

Jesu! A servant coming straight towards him.

He flung himself against the wall, behind the door. The man came through. Behind his back he slipped silently through the doorway and into the hall. At the far end was a heavy door which doubtless opened onto the street.

Even as he looked at it, there was a loud knock. Sweating, Kyte scurried up the staircase an instant before a large major domo appeared. He opened the door and said. 'I pray ye walk in. Captain. His lordship is expected at any moment.' Kyte lay flat on the floor and squinted down. The man's back was turned but Kyte saw a hand unfastening his cloak.

A hand that bore a fine ruby ring.

The servant ushered the guest into what seemed a lamplit dining room. Kyte flitted down the stairs, the better to listen. He had barely positioned himself behind a carved screen in a corner of the hall when the door opened again and Lord Durbridge strode in, followed by three men, their hats over their faces. The bowing major domo led them into the dining room. Kyte heard the Earl say, 'Ah, Captain, ye arrived before us. My friends, may I present to ye Captain James O'Malley, the instrument of our design. Master William Knox. Sir James MacNorton. Master Thomas Killigrew.' There was a murmur of salutations and a command from the earl that supper be served forthwith.

Killigrew! At supper with the man whose ring betrayed him as the murderer of Kit Marlowe! Kyte was so astounded that he forgot that he was trapped, his way of escape through the kitchen blocked. He listened to the clink of glasses. The earl said, 'Gentlemen, ye may speak freely – my servants are loyal. Let us drink to the success of our enterprise and to Queen Arabella!'

'Queen Arabella!' they chorused. *Arabella*? Kyte asked himself. Who the devil is she? Some Spanish princess?

A Scottish voice – Knox or MacNorton, doubtless: 'So wull the martyred Scottish Queen be revenged and the Stuarts come to their ain at last!'

Stuarts! To be sure – Arabella Stuart! The eighteen-year-old niece of Mary, Queen of Scots, and therefore in line for the thrones of both England and Scotland!

Durbridge said drily, 'And by the same happy stroke will our sickly fortunes be healed.' Footsteps passed Kyte's hiding place as servants took in trays and steaming tureens.

Spoons and knives began to clink. An Irish voice. The soldier O'Malley: 'What of that actor, Killigrew? Have ye tracked the wretch down, now?'

'Er – not yet, Captain. But I have his lodging watched. I'll have him ere long.'

Durbridge said, 'Methinks, Master Killigrew, ye were over hasty in getting rid of Cowley.'

Getting rid of Dick? *Killigrew*?

'Aye.' A different Scottish voice. 'He did good work as an informer.'

'And was well paid therefor,' said the Irishman.

So that is where Dick's mysterious wealth came from! Kyte wondered if he was in a dream.

'My lord,' Killigrew said, 'he was squeamish, which no man may be when engaged in such a design as this. After he told us that the spy Marlowe was on our heels, he expected us to abandon the design. When, instead, we silenced Marlowe, then did he mope, saying the death was on his conscience and he must make amends. The hazard was too great.'

'Did he make Kyte his confidant, think ye?'

'My lord, I heard him say, "I must talk to ye concerning Kit Marlowe's death". Kyte must be given his quietus.'

'And soon!' snapped O'Malley. 'On Monday, but four days hence, that Devil's spawn Elizabeth goes to visit Burghley at Theobalds. I want no whoreson soldiers seizing me as I leap from the crowd and shoot her in her carriage.'

'There will be no soldiers,' Durbridge said. 'For, when the Queen dies, all government dies with her. Parliament dissolves, all justices lose their commissions and no man is empowered to arrest ye until the new ruler takes the throne.'

'Is't true?' the Irishman demanded.

''Tis our law. So do your work, remembering that, when Arabella Stuart makes me chief of her council, an Irish earldom shall be yours.'

Kyte had heard enough. Time to make his escape. He walked softly to the front door. And at that same moment a girl came out of the kitchen behind him.

She stared. Kyte smiled at her. One shriek and he was lost. He said quietly, 'Good night to ye, my dear.' She smiled uncertainly. Then, taking him for one of the guests, she bobbed a curtsey as he unbolted the door and hurried out into the street.

He blended with the darkness, wondering what to do next. He, a wanted man, could hardly go to the justices and accuse Lord Durbridge of attempted regicide. He must consult with Shakespeare. Clever Will would have a plan.

'And so they come again, like the plague in summer.' William Cecil, 1st Baron Burghley, nodded his white head. 'Parry, Babington, Throckmorton and many others conspired the Queen's death. Now Durbridge. But, Master Shakespeare, whence comes your intelligence?'

'From one who has penetrated the very heart of the plot. I know him to be dependable.'

'So? But it is one thing to accuse, another to prove. I may not arrest my Lord Durbridge without evidence of his guilt.'

'I have the means of providing it, my lord, by a device I have often thought to include in a drama. Do but have men ready in the Curtain theatre on the morrow. Durbridge will be there to find women, as is his wont, and will proclaim his own guilt.'

'Well, let it be so, Master Shakespeare. At the Curtain tomorrow.'

Kyte stood among the stinkards as *The Third Part of Henry VI* drew towards its close. His Gloster, he thought, was far better than this ranting fellow's. The audience watched unmoved as he murdered the new King Henry.

I'll throw thy body in another room.

And triumph, Henry, in thy day of – er. *day of doom.*

He dragged the corpse off. Up in the gallery, Kyte saw Lord Durbridge yawn. The man next to Kyte said, 'A poor wretch. Would that we had that other fellow back, he who slew the King to perfection!'

'Indeed,' Kyte said, highly gratified. 'Well, well, perchance he may return.'

'But what is this?' the man said. The audience were watching as the widowed Queen returned, alone. But now she was wearing a red wig beneath her crown.

And now, as Gloriana I return
To make a summer progress through my realm,
My loving people's homage to receive—

The bemused audience stirred. From the curtained-off inner stage a sinister cloaked figure tiptoed out, carrying a pistol.

Assassin: *But I, O'Malley, will the tyrant slay*
And with my Lord of Durbridge and his crew,
Sir James MacNorton, Killigrew and Knox,
The kingdom seize for Arabella Stuart!

He raised the gun. 'Beware, Majesty!' shrieked a woman in the audience. But, even as the assassin stood menacing the oblivious Queen, the Earl of Durbridge stood and shouted. 'What means this mummery? Killigrew, ye bastard, have ye betrayed us?' He drew his sword. Even as he did so, soldiers entered the gallery. A brief struggle and they had him fast.

The audience milled about in a state of bewilderment. A stage hand tugged at Kyte's sleeve. 'By yer leave, sir, Master Shakespeare would speak wi'ye in the tiring room.'

The Sheriff and a captain of soldiers were with Will. Kyte hung back but Shakespeare beckoned him forward. 'Killigrew confessed all at the mere mention of the rack. The other villains will be taken in London or as they flee to the ports. All will be tried and no doubt meet a traitor's end.'

Kyte repressed a shudder at the thought of the hanging, castration and disembowelling. 'Am I now free, then?'

'Aye,' the Sheriff said. 'That ye are. Ye have done right well, Master Kyte.' He clapped him on the shoulder and went out with the captain.

Kyte said, 'Thank God. But, alas, the Earl's Men, without patronage, are at an end.'

'They are indeed. But I have it in mind to form my own company, with a new play to be called *The Comedy of Errors*. If ye wish, I can find a part for ye.'

'Will, I thank ye most heartily. But have I your leave to ask a favour?'

'Aye?'

'I prithee, do not give me such doggerel to recite as ye gave the Queen and her assassin just now.'

'What! That was not of my doing! The whoreson villains chopped and changed it to suit themselves. Jesu!' Shakespeare said indignantly, 'they cut out a most pretty philosophical passage in which the Queen ponders whether 'tis nobler in the mind to suffer the slings and arrows of outrageous fortune or to take arms against—'

'Peace, Will. Put it aside and it may earn ye a few pence one of these days. Come. let us to the Magpie and I will buy ye a pot.'

LOVE'S LABOUR'S, LOST?

Peter T. Garratt

Two obscure references are all that remain to suggest that Shakespeare wrote a play called Love's Labour's Won *probably between 1594 and 1597. A play with that title was published during Shakespeare's lifetime but whether that was the same play we do not know. Amazingly, all copies have disappeared. What happened to the play? That's the mystery that Peter Garratt sets out to solve.*

I was trying to decide about the sign.

I'd got used to living in lodgings in my time in Wittenberg. Of course, I'd had the best rooms in the town then, and in London the strings of my purse were pulled tighter; but I hardly remembered the palace of my childhood, and I never wanted to be reminded of the great, corrupted fortress my father had built to command the entrance to the Baltic. My new bedchamber was cramped, but I had a large room by the top of the stairs for an office. There was no kitchen or dining room, but as I could afford no cook or servant, I ate in a tavern, as I often had in Wittenberg.

The Player King was my first visitor. I froze at the first creaking of the stair-treads, but the goldsmith from whom I rented the rooms kept three strong servants and a pair of mastiffs. That was why I had chosen those particular rooms.

He wore a new doublet, much finer than any I had seen him in before, and his beard and receding hair were neatly trimmed. I, in contrast, was getting shabbier, something which could not have happened in my student days.

The short sword was new as well, the scabbard carrying his crest of falcon and spear. He wore it as an ornament, not a weapon. It seemed odd to me that a player could become a gentleman just by applying: even one who also wrote plays.

I offered sack, which he declined, and small beer, which he accepted, to my surprise, as there is probably no beer in England, or anywhere in Europe, to match our Danish brews, and I only kept the wretched stuff to save expense. He didn't sit, but looked at the few books I had been able to buy, the tracts and handbills I had had printed. He read from one: ' "Privileged Investigation is offered, into your private suspicions, by a Mr Christian, recently come to London, who previously revealed the hitherto unsuspected death of one of Europe's most illustrious monarchs as most bloody and unnatural murder!" ' He looked around the admittedly bare chamber, noticing no doubt the spider I had named 'Claudius' and which I'd allowed lodgings in a corner, and said: 'Have these gained you many commissions?'

'Not yet. Perhaps gentlefolk seeking my services are uncertain as to where to seek me out.' I indicated the sketches the sign-writer had prepared. 'I had felt a sign would show them where to look, but then I thought . . .'

His eyes held some sympathy, but also reserve, as one might look at a former friend out of favour at court. He finished for me: 'You feared a sign might slight your new profession as a form of trade: that commissioners might doubt you are a gentleman. And if, as you see, a mere play-writer can become a gentleman, then you, Prince Hamlet Christian, cannot cease to be one!'

I nodded glumly. He turned to my book, or rather tract, *Against the Monstrous Murderer of the late King Hamlet Frederick of Denmark*. He said: 'A Prince's Pennyworth of Privileged Investigation! So, you showed this to Her Majesty. Did she indicate an opinion?'

'She was very gracious. She asked her man Walsingham, who said it could be printed, but that one part should be in very small type, so one can hardly . . .'

'Let me see . . . the part where you explain how your enemy, King Claudius Christian, was *elected* king because you were too young to succeed your father?'

'That's true, and it's an important passage! It was necessary to explain that we do things differently . . .'

'No you don't. Kings are *not* elected. Not in England. Not in books printed in England.' He put down a groat for the tract, and said: 'Talking of books and printing, I need your help. There's a mystery I need you to investigate, though it might seem a small matter, compared to the death of kings.'

At that moment the main bell of the Cathedral of St Paul rang loudly for One, and within seconds those of the many lesser churches in London joined it. He said: 'I have to go to the Rose. It will be easiest if you come to the play too.'

'Is it one of your own?'

'No, but it's a kind of play I might consider writing. You might also.'

It was strange, walking those narrow, crowded streets with a wealthy commoner, only recently granted a coat of arms. It had happened a few times in Wittenberg, usually at night, when mixed groups of students had toured the taverns. Here, I had to keep reminding myself that safety required I should not be recognized, but should hope to be mistaken for a player's apprentice, or a young writer down from an English university, looking for someone with a real theatre to give his work a try. And had that been what I was, the Player King would certainly have been an appropriate mentor. Many people knew him. Older gentlemen walking with servants nodded. Young men in fashionable clothes and long swords greeted him warmly, asking after his latest production. I noticed they seemed to value his writing more highly than his playing. Workmen in leather aprons, street women in low dresses, even urchins in rags, all shouted 'Hello, Will', as if his brusque nod of reply indicated he knew them well and valued their greetings. From time to time I considered offering a handbill concerning my skills as a Privileged Investigator, but the time never seemed to be right . . . either the nod would be too formal, or the greeting too brief, or too exclusively focused on my companion.

We crossed the river by a bridge lined with shops. I could smell the water but hardly see it. At least it smelled better than the ill-swept streets. On the south bank we came to an area which offended the eyes more than the nose. Every other building seemed to be a brothel. Disgusting, ill-favoured women paraded their off-putting flesh in dresses so low they unintentionally warned their customers of the corruption which was all they had to offer. Two plough horses, huge but nervous, pulled a wheeled cage in which a ferocious black bear snarled and attacked the bars. My companion noticed my reaction. He said: 'The Puritans who control the City proper rate all forms of entertainment as the same. I take it you have not been on this licentious side of the river before?' Before I could reply, he went on: 'In that case, you won't have seen my recent work: *Love's Labour's Won*?'

'Not if it was only performed in this district!'

'You'd be surprised who comes here . . . but you're right. We put the play on twice at the Rose, almost as rehearsals, and once privately for one of my leading patrons, the Earl of Southampton.'

We arrived at the Rose. It was purpose-built, like the other public theatres I had seen. We went in through a doorway separate from those for commoners, or even well-born persons who could afford seats in the gallery. We entered the backstage area, which was lit by windows of cheap, dark glass, and a couple of heavily scented candles. These were needed, for there was a rank smell of sweat and theatrical paint. Actors were rushing about wearing tin armour or other parts of stage costumes. Some were attaching pointed beards and mustaches, the play being *The Spanish Tragedy*. The Player King was evidently not part of the cast, and in contrast to the street, the people here gave him no more attention than they would a prop not needed for that particular play. He led me past the changing area to a heavy oak door. He produced a key: 'This writing office is always kept locked.'

Inside the sealed room it was lighter, its windows being small, but with clear glass. All were bolted. There was a writing table with three chairs, and a number of locked chests and cabinets. He used another key on a cabinet marked with the arms of the Lord Chamberlain, the main patron of his company. He said: 'We keep some of our plays here. Only the partners in the Lord Chamberlain's men have keys . . . and our patrons, as a courtesy, though they never use them.'

The cabinet was full of sets of handwritten sheets tied together. 'A year ago we had a success with a play of mine called *Love's Labour's*

Lost. It played here, in the homes of patrons, even in front of Her Grace. It was well received, and is to be printed. As sometimes happens, we were asked soon after for another work in similar style.' He shrugged: 'Some of your University men think it unbefitting the gentle profession of writing to produce a work to order. We who live by our quills think otherwise. I shut myself away and wrote *Love's Labour's Won*. It wasn't my best work, but did contain scenes which delighted my patron, and a few for *them*.' He pointed dismissively to the public part of the theatre, from which the voices of commoners could be heard agitating for the show to start.

'I only wrote one copy. The clerk took down the parts for the main actors, and we bundled them all together and locked them in the cabinet we keep here. I did not have time to arrange fair copies for our own theatre, nor for my records.

'Recently our clerk had enough time to catch up with such jobs, and I brought him here to see the play, and *take it out*. But though we found all the other works we keep at this theatre, there was no sign of *Love's Labour's Won*. My only copy!'

'I see. Did the clerk have a key?'

'No, he isn't a partner in the Company.' A flourish of trumpets sounded from the stage area. 'Let's find some seats. I'll explain what I need you to do later.'

He locked the cabinet and the office, and led me to a small door which opened into the best part of the gallery, a boxed-off area very close to the stage. Seated there were a richly-dressed couple, a man in his mid-twenties and a woman a few years younger. My companion gave a little bow and said: 'My most illustrious and discerning personal patron, Henry Wriothesly, Earl of Southampton.' As the Earl was looking at me curiously, he grasped me on the shoulder with a comradely but very firm grip which indicated that I too should bow, and added: 'This is Mr Christian, recently arrived from Elsinore.'

I did make a bow, or at least an inclination forward. It pained me to think that I must be the first Prince of Denmark ever to bow to an English Jarl, but I could hardly proclaim my true rank. Besides, he wore more jewels on his doublet than my father had on his crown. The Player King went on: 'Mr Christian is a gloomy Dane, sent to our more cheerful climate to be cured of his Melancholy. And he has recovered, and adopted a new profession, that of Privileged Investigator!' He gave one of my handbills to the earl, who looked at me curiously.

I wondered if he guessed who I was. His companion looked at it over his shoulder, then raised a mask in the shape of a cat's face and peered at me through the eyeholes.

Southampton said: 'It would be a privilege to be investigated by a Christian, unless he were a Puritan, in which case t'would be gloomily Dane!'

They all laughed, especially the woman. She wore a satin dress which imitated the style of the court, but betrayed her profession by exceeding the permitted lowness at the front. By some artifice it forced her breasts upward, as if they were the shaved heads of damned souls struggling to escape the Pit. She had covered her face, but I could see her hair was tightly curled and dyed, almost painted, bright shameless red, evidently imitating the style of the Virgin Queen. I wondered that such a woman could venture to imitate either of those conditions.

The flourishing of trumpets and marching round the stage now stopped, and an actor in a white ghost mask and a shroud began speaking the prologue. Southampton said: 'We should attend to this tragedy, though we would prefer one of yours. Or better still, a comedy. How about *Love's Labour's Won*?'

The woman echoed him, in a surprisingly well-bred voice: 'Yes, let it be *Love's Labour's Won*!'

The Player King looked embarrassed, and hurried me through to the more public part of the Gallery. Plenty of seats were empty, but instead of sitting he led me slowly round the back, looking up and down as though seeking someone, until we were almost opposite Southampton's position. There, although it was more crowded, and mostly with those whose tasteless gaudiness marked them as prosperous traders rather than gentlefolk, he beckoned to an usher to get us to the front row, where an unbroken line of people were looking at the action on the stage. He ploughed through the protests of the people in the next row until we were directly behind a man in his twenties who had balanced an inkwell on the parapet and was scribbling frantically on a book of blank leaves. He had a thin beard and wore a fine yellow doublet. As I was wondering what we were doing in this uncomfortably crowded position, my companion said 'Excuse me!' very sharply and pushed between the scribbler and his neighbour as if intending to sit in that narrow space, making a sweeping gesture with his arm which sent the inkwell flying, some of its contents spilling over whatever the young man had been writing, the rest landing on his bright doublet like a crowd of black flies obscuring the sun. He jumped up with an oath, gripping his quill as if it was the steel-tipped pen with which Caesar fought his attackers, but when he saw who was looming over him, supported by the usher, and in his eyes by myself, (though the nature of this quarrel was a mystery to me) he started to back away. As he was backing through the most crowded part of the gallery, he fell over someone's foot, hitting someone else's knee on the way down. They all cursed louder than he had, and he struggled to his feet and ran off, leaving his papers and inkwell behind him.

My companion gave one of his enigmatic smiles to the crowd, and led me to empty seats further back. By this point in the play, clowns were entertaining the commoners, and people in the gallery were talking. He said: 'A curse that has recently fallen on London is a scurvy breed of men called publishers, scoundrels who come between author and printer with no aim but the filling of their own purses. Their agents are a pox-ridden crew, as you just saw, men who steal the words of others, or what poor shadows of better men's words they can bother to write down, then have these bastard lines printed for their own profit. As you saw, we have to keep watch, but I fear that worse subversions are being used.'

'You mean . . . you think these men and their agents have stolen your play?'

'Yes, and the worst part is, they must have suborned one of my partners to do it. No one else would have the key.'

The clowns finished, and the serious actors returned. My English had improved so much I could follow almost all of it. The lines did not trip so fast on the tongue as my companion's, but were well enough received: indeed, the gallery broke into applause when the act finished and the clowns returned. As the clapping died down, I said: 'This missing play, *Love's Labour's Won.* Was it a success?'

'Yes and no. The lines were well-liked, considering it was fast written. The main players did their work well. However, the theme that had been suggested was one where the nobles of the Court adopt a monastic life in order to study. The ladies, aiming not to be outdone, adopt a similar vow, until they hear the men are secretly planning to break their's and visit a bawdy-house.' He looked at me as though I must inevitably know what happened next, but I had no idea, and he went on: So, the ladies contrive to take over the bawdy house . . . I see you have too lofty a mind to enjoy such entertainments, but they fill the Company purse.

'The play had more women's parts than usual, and these have to be played by boys. Sadly, the Player Queen you met, and our other experienced boys, all reached the end of that stage of their apprenticeship at the wrong time. Their voices had lasted well, but we had taken insufficient care to replace them.' He smiled grimly: 'So the curse of the play was small boys playing large female parts!'

At Wittenberg I had been taught the ancient philosophy of Logic. 'Surely there is inconstancy in the reasoning of your Puritan city fathers. You are not allowed women on the stage, and have to rely on boys, who may outgrow their parts at any time. Yet women flaunt themselves in the audience!'

He shrugged. 'There's more gold in the purse of a beggar than Logic in the mind of a Puritan. I've heard that ladies sometime act behind closed doors, but . . .'

'Ladies act always! Or are acted! Why, from the cloth of her dress and the cut of her accent, one might have thought Southampton's doxy a lady!'

He looked shocked, and clamped his hand hard on my arm. 'Doxy! Mistress Vernon *is* a lady . . . in fact a lady-in-waiting to Her Grace! Please don't speak so of my patron's companions, here in a public gallery!'

I shrugged. No one knew better than I that companionship to a queen did not imply proximity to virtue, but I had escaped from one treacherous Court, and had no desire to create more dangers for myself in another. The serious part of the tragedy was resuming, and this time it ran right through to the final act with no pauses for inappropriate laughter. I found myself warming to the piece. Its hero, starved of justice, made his diet revenge, and that is a food of which I could never have excess.

Afterwards, as we walked through the dispersing crowds, I asked my companion about the author of *The Spanish Tragedy*.

'Tom Kyd? I think you met him. A fine man, a little older than myself, though his looks were bent by more years than there actually were between us. He came on tour the year we went to Elsinore, though he wasn't an actor or a full member of the Company. We gave him what work we could, for he had lost his patron.'

He stopped and gave a wave and a little bow. I saw that Southampton and his lady, now in ermine-lined capes, and accompanied by others dressed as richly but with less taste, were strolling towards one of the jetties from which boats ply up and down the river. My companion did not attempt to join them, and when they were definitely out of earshot, went on: 'Poor Tom was too friendly with Kit Marlowe, a man of even greater talent but no discretion. Ideas scholars scarcely whisper among circumspect friends they spoke loudly, and even worked into plays.'

I started to ask what ideas these were, but he ignored me completely, and went on: 'So poor Tom lost favour. We were able to help him only in the years when we toured abroad. Later he died, prematurely white and withered . . .'

'I remember him now! A young man when you came to Wittenberg, he'd aged a lifetime a couple of years later. He was the man who kept asking about revenge, about the first Hamlet, on whom I modelled myself, and the revenge he took!' I paused, confused and ashamed. There were scholars in Wittenberg who claimed that that first Hamlet was a yarn spun by a chronicler who was more poet than pedant. I, of course, was certain my ancestor *had* existed. Had his spirit not haunted me, along with my father's? But though that Hamlet had bided his time admirably, he had taken a decisive revenge when the time turned for action.

'Of course!' The Player King stopped and snapped his fingers at the air, as though an idea of unparalleled brilliance had struck him. 'Did you know Kyd worked the things you told him into a play?'

'No!'

'He did . . . it wasn't one of his indiscretions . . . it was a success in fact, though alas most of the performances were after his death. It's a work that could do with improvement . . .' He grasped my arm and hurried me along, saying: 'That's it! I had thought to have you tour the printers posing as a collector of plays, but if you say you're working on one, and want it printed yourself . . .'

'That'll interest the rogues! Perhaps I can find one cheaper than the bloodsucker who did my tracts and handbills!'

'Meanwhile, dine with me tonight. There's a tavern where most of my partners will repair. You can meet them, and scrutinize their characters with an eye undimmed by too much close reading of them!'

I woke the next morning with eye and head alike made dim by too much sack, from a dream (or was it a vision in the corner of the room?) of my father's spirit standing silently. How much nobler his sad dignity was than the gaudy ghost from the Rose! How clear a reminder that the last act of my own revenge tragedy must be played in Elsinore, not on a London stage next door to a bear-pit!

The sun was already shining through the shutters, and by its light I could see there was nothing in the corner but an arras of unlaundered clothes hanging over a chain. It had been a dream: the spirit was not seen in its insubstantial person after dawn. By the light I could see also my purse on the table, empty save for groats and farthings. I needed funds, both to live and to pay the asylum keeper to whose care I had entrusted my uncle's courtiers, Rosencrantz and Guildenstern. My own revenge might never be should they be released to make contact with his other agents. I rose, realised I was still dressed, washed and broke my fast with stale water, then made my way upstairs to office. The Player King had given me a list of printers, and I wanted to record my impressions of his partners from the night before.

I sat making notes, as I had for my theses at Wittenburg, but it wasn't easy. Who can tell the character of a player? My clearest impression was that these were all experienced drinkers, men who could keep their counsel as they emptied their cups. Only the Player King had drunk moderately.

I did not hear the footsteps on the stairs at first, being absorbed by the character of Richard Burbage. He was regarded as the best of the players, and had the largest stake in the Company. However, over supper, I had begun to wonder if acting in plays was really the same as the courtierly falsehood I knew too well. On stage that afternoon, he had hurled his bogus emotion at the faces of the audience like a catapult: a true deceiver would have slipped it into their backs like a knife.

I was considering that Burbage had a brother who did not himself act, when I became aware of feet moving quietly up the stairs. I had opened the office door to get light from the landing window, and I think it was a shadow rather than a sound which disturbed me. I jerked upright and my hand flew toward the drawer where I kept my bodkin: then I saw my visitor posed only dangers from which no weapon could protect me. She stood in the doorway both bold and nervous: bold in the low cut of her dress, nervous as any woman who even pretended respectability would be to venture up strange stairs alone. She wore a black eye-mask with little cat's ears at the corners. It did not cover her whole face, but had a double curve over her painted cheeks, an odd reflection of the tops of her breasts. Her outfit exposed what should be concealed, but hid what should be open to inspection. Despite the half-mask, I recognised Elizabeth Vernon, lady-in-waiting to the Queen, mistress to the earl. She moved into the office, still nervous, said: 'Thank Goodness I found the right place! It isn't every day one has to seek out a Privileged Investigator!'

I didn't know how to answer. I felt like telling her to get to a nunnery, but she was a client for my new profession, and any one of the rings she wore would rid me of Rosencrantz and Guildenstern for a year. As for her emerald necklace, its cost would enable their madness to become lifelong. I reasoned that there were no nunneries in England, and offered her a chair and a cup of sack.

'Thank you, a small one,' she said, but she did not sit. Instead, she examined my small library on its single shelf, picked up *The Murder of Gonzago*, and remarked: 'I haven't seen this play,' then commented: 'You have the books of an educated gentleman, if not the outward show. I feel you are a man I can trust.'

I tried to tidy myself. She turned to face me. 'As you are a gentleman, I know you will help a lady in distress. I . . .' Her cheeks flushed beneath their white makeup, and I realised she wore the mask to conceal tears. 'Recently you saw me with a very fine and noble man, a veritable modern Lancelot, or so he would have me think. Often he has pleaded his love for me, seeking as he did so, certain . . . favours.' She did not need to identify the favours concerned, nor whether she had granted them. 'Despite his protestations he will make no formal proposal, nor even swear to forsake all others, as any man would swear for such favours, whether falsely or not!' She paused, wracked with sobs, and I could see the tears creeping from under her mask and down her make-up, like balls of slush rolling through snow.

'So, your paramour is not a liar. Shouldn't you be grateful for that?'

'No!' she snapped, stamping her foot so hard I feared for the goldsmith's ceiling. 'Most men lie every day in such circumstances. For a woman, the only promise that matters is made in a church, whether it's a lie or not!'

Female tears are always dangerous, especially to me, however often I try to steel myself. 'I will help, if I can. But how?'

'You can investigate who is stealing the earl's affections from me!'

'Another woman?' I found myself saying: 'But who could be more beautiful or well connected than you?'

'Woman?' She turned to my bookshelf: 'I see you have read your Tacitus. Men of fashion adore the Romans, and their great old ways.' She opened the book, and declaimed, without actually reading: ' "He was an invert, he lusted after boys past their prime!" Why do you think he applauds the Player Queen so loud? Why do you think they make their boys play women's roles at all?'

She calmed down a little, said: 'Boy, woman, something else entirely, something steals his affection from me. Find out what it is!'

She left a small purse . . . in Wittenberg days it would have seemed very small, but now it was a relief. I put on my best clothes, carried the rest to the washer-woman, gave her a farthing to clean my rooms. I knew she was afraid of spiders, so I said she could leave Claudius. Then I set out on my tour of the printers. On the way, I began to realise that I was planning to put our family tragedy, my father's spirit, my mother's shame, onto the stage. What prince had ever done such a thing?

On the other hand, Mr Christian had put it into a tract, and I started at the place where that had been printed. The printer was a prosperous man who wore spectacles and clean clothes. There was very little ink on his fingers, and I gathered his apprentices did most of the work. He also ran a book shop, and said few of my tracts had been sold, but he was willing to try the play. As my version hadn't even been started, I decided to put on the disposition of a book collector. Such men are always proposing to write something themselves, but are usually too busy reading, collecting, and cataloguing their collections to finish anything.

He assured me that a play would sell well, far better than a tract on what he seemed to think an obscure subject. He said *Love's Labour's Lost* had sold well, and several other plays had completely sold out. I shrugged as though I obviously had all of those, and asked if he could supply anything less common: '*Love's Labour's Won*, for instance. I missed that one, but I heard it might be printed.'

He looked blank, but said he would look out for it. And that was the reaction I got for most of the morning. Some of the printers I visited had been asked for the play before, but none made any real promise to get it.

By noon I was tired and hungry. But I now knew the streets, and had been making my way towards Southampton's London house, or rather mansion. It was a big place, on the corner of a busy street. I had it in mind to put on the disposition of one seeking patronage, perhaps for the proposed play about my ancestor, and worm my way into his confidence enough to learn about the rival feared by my new client. As I approached, I started to wonder if that was the best plan. I saw a shabbily dressed man knock at the front door, and be refused admission. How could a prince, even in exile, risk such humiliation for a painted woman? Hovering uncertainly, I, or rather my nose and stomach, noticed a smell of fried salt bacon from a tavern called the Black Dog very near Southampton's home: from its window one would see who else came to his door. I would break my fast like a Dane from a great family, not a beggar's whippet, and consider my next move carefully.

To my delight, I found the tavern keeper offered Danish ale in bottles as well as a magnificent meal of bacon with green beans and eggs. I was unable to sit in the window, as the table there was occupied by two men in black doublets, a tall balding fellow, and a short, intense character with a spade beard, who looked familiar from somewhere. I was unable to check Southampton's visitors, as although they seemed to have finished their meal these two remained at the window table throughout the time it took me to savour mine.

Southampton had met me as an investigator. I decided it would be best to approach in that capacity. He had expressed an interest in *Love's Labour's Won*, and there was even a possibility he might know something. I bought him a bottle of the best Danish ale as a present, and boldly crossed the street.

The earl's doorman made me wait in a small, gloomy lobby. I reflected as I waited that I was already living on Mistress Vernon's purse. I also wondered how I could find out who an earl slept with if I could not even secure an interview.

In fact I was shown in quite soon. Two or three ladies were just leaving: I tried to memorize their faces, while doubting a secret mistress would come in with a group. Southampton welcomed me in a large, airy study. I noticed that his hair, while keeping a natural fair colour, was almost as long and elaborately curled as his lady's. I wondered if that had aroused her suspicions.

He seemed a manly enough fellow, pouring a cup of the ale for himself. He asked how I had met the Player King, then questions about the theatre in Denmark, and how the players dealt with the language problem. I replied that they mostly did masques or classics in Latin. This didn't surprise him: he was superbly educated, and even knew plays in Greek, from the lost dawn of the theatre.

I got him to compare ancient and modern plays, then worked him round to *Love's Labour's Won*. His eyes brightened at once. 'That's a very fine play, one of his best. It was lost on the groundlings at the Rose, of course, but I loved it and commissioned a performance for my special friends.'

'Did they appreciate it as much as you had hoped?'

'Alas, no! It seems the Player Queen and the rest of his class are now "past their prime"!'

This comment luckily drew both of my investigations together. I said excitedly: 'How strange it is that the main roles are taken by men in the prime of life, but the female parts by boys whose experience doesn't extend to shaving!'

He shrugged. 'Of course, ladies act in private, but the players are too scared by the Puritans to think of engaging actresses. In this case, their relatively experienced lads had been replaced by a crew of street urchins no one had bothered to lick into shape. Anyway, no doubt before long they will be ready to revive it.'

'There's a concern, I gather, that a copy has gone missing.' I didn't say it was the only one. 'You're well informed, and I was wondering if anyone might have offered you a copy. Or asked for a contribution to the cost of printing?'

He shook his head. 'I know the players suffer, if their written ships are taken by privateers. Mind you . . .' He rose and left the room, leaving me alone to wonder how I could turn the conversation to the possible rivals of Mistress Vernon. Shortly he returned with a small bunch of keys: he did not use them, however, but instead used a separate key to open a drawer of his desk and then lock them away. He said: 'I have much enjoyed discussing plays with you. If anyone offers me a copy of *Love's Labour's Won*, I will try to find out how he got it, and ensure it is returned to its owner. Anyway, it is good to meet a man like yourself with a good knowledge of the theatre.

If you are interested, I am invited tonight to bring selected friends to a very special event . . . a surprise. Please join us.'

I had been dismissed, but not without reward. I had been invited to join a select company for a very special event. What it was I had no idea, perhaps a performance of a Greek play, or some other work too elevated for the common theatre. If someone had privateered the affection owed to Elizabeth Vernon, that person might be present: it might even be obvious who it was.

I took a different route back to my rooms, slipping cheerfully back into the disposition of a book collector, but a somewhat antic one, for at every printers I chided them over their prices. I had no luck, perhaps because my mood was wrong . . . or perhaps no one was planning to print the stolen play.

That thought sobered me up. I was no nearer solving my first case. Unless Southampton was very promiscuous, Lady Vernon would not employ me often, while it was obvious plays were privateered all the time. Suddenly, the narrow streets of London seemed dark and threatening, full of inpenetrable mystery. I even fancied I could see someone following me, as if I were still in Elsinore.

The last place I tried was a shop near my rooms which only sold books. I didn't expect much . . . after all, who would buy a handwritten manuscript these days? Yet the bookseller said he *had* had enquiries after *Love's Labour's Won*.

'There was a woman . . . well, a lady. Didn't ask about much else.'

'You mean . . . a real lady, or . . .'

'Spoke like a real lady. Mind you, a lot of them do, these days. She didn't leave an address, so who's to know?'

I left in a state of high excitement. Some printing privateer must have hired a doxy to seduce one of the partners into giving her the play, but not until she'd made sure she couldn't just buy a copy. But how could I decide which partner?

'Good afternoon . . . Mr Christian, is it?' I froze: two men had come up, one on each side. They wore black, and I recognized them from the tavern near Southampton's mansion. The one who had spoken had a beard. I said to him:

'Yes, but I'm afraid I've forgotten where we met.'

'Perhaps at Secretary Walsingham's.' This wasn't good: officially

Walsingham was the Queen's secretary, but I knew he was also her master of spies. This one said: 'You visit many shops, but buy no books.'

'I'm looking for a particular one.'

'Let me guess. Something in Latin? Something *Roman*, perhaps?'

'No!' I knew it wasn't illegal to be a Catholic in England, but that a man could be hanged for showing any sign of being one. I didn't understand the law, but knew people were terrified of falling foul of it. 'I'm a good Danish Lutheran!'

He nodded: 'Then you have strange connections.'

'I've just been visiting your great Earl of Southampton!'

The other man, the big one, spoke for the first time. 'Even an earl can have . . . connections. No one cares if a beggar breaks his bread with a papist, whether they think there's blood in their wine or not. But an earl . . .'

I snapped: 'I am no one's bad connection! Search my rooms if you like!'

I started to regret that offer as they followed me heavily up the stairs. I had no Catholic books, but I remembered Tacitus was a heathen who had spoken ill of the church. Was that allowed in England?

Luckily, it seemed it was. The smaller man admitted there was nothing suspect in my room. He reminded me that all Lutherans were allies of the Queen, and as her guest, it was my duty to report any sign of popery.

I was soaked with sweat, and my doublet was starting to stink. I undressed, sluiced myself with the last water in my pitcher, looked for my best clothes, then stopped. It seemed anyone could belong to the Church of England whatever they believed, as long as they said and did nothing. If Southampton was a covert Catholic, perhaps he assumed I was of the same persuasion. Perhaps his special surprise event was a secret papist Mass: if so, to celebrate it would be as dangerous as attending the licentious rites of a coven of witches.

I paused, irresolutely. I could not call on the example of the first Hamlet: he had been a heathen. Then I thought of my father, who had never allowed anything Catholic in Denmark. Southampton at least knew I was a Dane!

Meanwhile, Claudius sat in his web and waited to strike, just as the other Claudius would strike if I ran out of money and his agents were released.

I put on my best suit of clothes, gold thread on a black doublet, a set I had yet to wear in England. It was getting dark as I walked through the streets. Passers-by hurried nervously, and strange figures skulked in the mouths of alleys. There would be robbers as well as spies and agents; but I was Hamlet the Dane, from whose ancestors' fury the English had begged the Lord God to deliver them, and whatever dangers there were, I would face them down.

I found Southampton preparing to set out by carriage. He was with some other well-dressed men, whom he did not introduce. It seemed at first he assumed I knew them, but as we rattled through the increasingly empty streets, I started to wonder if this special thing was so secret it was best to not know who else attended. They were all men, and it occurred to me that popish priests do not marry.

We reached a big complex of buildings by the Thames and stopped. I could see little by that time, and as we got out, I asked what place it was.

'This was once the London home of the Black Friars,' he replied solemnly. 'When they were dissolved, their living quarters were sold to private persons of substance. There is also a small theatre, though the common players are not allowed to use it.'

He led the way to a hall, brilliantly lit by candles and oil lamps, with a stage at one end. Servants were circulating with jugs of wine and plates of food, and several more of Southampton's friends were already there. Several had ladies with them. He greeted all of these with kisses to the hand or cheek: but though Elizabeth Vernon was not present, none engaged his special interest. After a few minutes of thus circulating, he raised his hand for silence: 'Dear friends, I cannot tell you what entertainment we have tonight: but I do think we should thank the Lord for our good fortune, that we can lead such a wonderful life, riding into the night with the excitement of the unknown, but with no fear of danger. Whatever we are about to receive, enjoy!' He led them in a sort of theatrical grace: I remembered that among papists, only priests can lead prayers: and these prayers were in English.

All the lights were moved to the stage, and we settled down for the show. It began with a group of young men impersonating students . . . if it was impersonation, for they sounded younger than Southampton's friends. They were well spoken, and did not bombard the audience with words like professional players. The theme appeared to be that as scholars they should lead a monastic life: this left me uneasy, for I well remembered that monks had once prayed and studied in this building, but were now banned forever from its halls and cloisters.

Then an extraordinary thing happened. The men exited, and a group of ladies entered. At first I thought they were tall boys skillfully padded, but soon I realised from their necklines, low as depravity, that they *were* ladies. They wore half-masks, but I soon realised that the lead female, one Emilia, was played by Elizabeth Vernon. This group too was intending to withdraw from the world and study. As soon as there was a pause for refreshments, I whispered to Southampton: 'You realise this is the missing play, "*Love's Labour's Won?*"'

'Of course. But why missing?'

'There's only one copy, and it's clear now who has it!'

He frowned a little, and felt something in his purse, but the action resumed before he could reply. It was clear the Vernon woman had contrived to steal the play: but not being its author, I forgave her that. Indeed, by the end of the evening, I would have forgiven her anything. In the study scenes she pleaded that colleges should be opened for women with such passion that the role of Emilia might have been written for her, not some immature comedian; but in the scenes at the bawdy house she was a total revelation. She sang and danced and wore a gown so flimsy that some tricks of the candle-light made it appear she wore nothing but her mask: thus attired she so seduced the most reluctant and monkish of the scholars that at the end he made a proposal which sounded more real than acted, and she of course accepted, though I saw her eyes stare at Southampton through the mask holes as she spoke.

As the crowd applauded, I turned to him and said: 'With such a mistress, what man could ask for anything more?'

'No man. Though my mistress would like more, of course. She would be scholar, wife, and whore, all rolled into one.' I was starting to remember that that would be impossible, when he said wistfully: 'If I were minded to marry so soon, of course I would marry her. But I value freedom and danger, the drive into the dark. Besides, she needs to learn that not all keys were meant to be fitted into their holes by her fingers!'

He rose and led the way to a room behind the stage. I guessed it was the ladies' tiring room, but a few of the youths from the cast were there also. The audience held back till Southampton entered, then started to follow him in. In the middle of the room was a long table, lit by an open oil lamp in the form of a maiden holding a glass bowl full of oil, which cast the light through the glass onto a row of hand written sheets, the parts for the play which I had been commissioned to recover. Elizabeth stood beside it, pointing something out to a friend. Southampton walked over to her, saying: 'My dear, a performance to prove that women should never act before Puritans, lest they be driven even madder than they already are.'

She turned and smiled, and said: 'Perhaps, but there is an act for every audience.' In the lamp light, her beautiful, painted face and hair looked quite natural. Southampton nodded, and said:

'I will commission a part just for you. Perhaps the story of the girl lawyer and the Jew you liked so much.' He paused, and put his hand into the purse at his belt. 'Also, I have a present for you. A ring.'

'A ring!' her face lit up brighter than all the candles in the hall: she did a little twirl and pulled at a little cord at the neck of her dress, so that it flew off and left her standing only in the flimsy brothel gown; then she pulled off her mask and thus almost naked threw herself at him and smothered his face with kisses. He enjoyed this for as long as a man could hold breath, then pushed her away, and pulled from his purse the keyring I had seen earlier.

'With this ring, I hold the keys entrusted to me by my friends the players and writers, which you must have filched while I slept.'

He handed it to her: her face flushed red as her painted hair, and she shouted, almost screamed: 'What! In front of all my friends!' and hurled the keyring back at his head. He ducked, and overbalanced into the glass maiden with her bowl of oil. It crashed over, spilling burning oil all over the precious playscript. It flared up, every sheet instantly ablaze. They all cried out in horror and flinched back: I alone realised the extent of the danger. Seeing the girl's outer stage dress lying discarded on the floor, I grabbed it and hurled it over the fire to blanket it out.

The next day I dined with the Player King, handing him the few charred fragments I had managed to save. Though he had gained nothing by hiring me, he gave me a purse for them. I realised he had come to see the actions of his patrons as whims no more to be controlled or railed against than those of the weather.

Mistress Vernon rewarded me too, in her own way. Perhaps it was suggested to her. Lots of people were talking about her performance, and the fire. She sent me a sign, superior to that of any tradesman, in the form of a very fine silver key. And with that sign, I decided to proceed with my new career.

BENEATH WHICH HOUR?

Peter Valentine Timlett

Here is a mystery which is not based on any of the plays but centres on the building of the Globe Theatre which was opened in Southwark in 1599.

He came down the Shoreditch road, the post-horse moving easily and steadily beneath him, and stopped to stare across Finsbury Fields. They were still there, the ruins, he could still make them out. The old Theatre, built by Richard's father. Aye, The Theatre, the very first theatre in the whole of England, built by James Burbage over twenty years before in the year of Our Lord 1576, in the reign of her most gracious majesty Queen Elizabeth, and there he had trod the boards with the best of them. Ah, they had been good days, but the Theatre had grown old, and with a lease soon to expire and a landlord grown greedy it had been time to move. But where?

The horse dropped its head and began to placidly crop the grass, and he let the reins hang loose. It was Richard and Cuthbert who had found a suitable site in Maiden Lane in Bankside, across the Thames on the southern side, and had taken a 25 year lease, but money had been short. The Burbages could only afford half the cost, and the other half had been borne by the senior players, himself having a twelfth share.

Well, it would either bankrupt them all or make their fortunes. Or send them all to Clink prison if the truth were ever known as to how they had built the new theatre.

Shakespeare sighed and turned his horse south. They had been right to move, they had been given no real alternatives. But it had been touch and go, and still was. He remembered the night that Richard and Cuthbert had mentioned their scheme. It was the age-old problem of money. 'Even with the owner-shares, yours and the others,' Cuthbert had said, 'we still cannot afford all the building costs.' He eyed the playwright cautiously. 'If we didn't have to pay for the main support timbers, the great oak supports that hold the whole thing up, we could just about manage.'

Then he had told them his idea – it was mad and crazy – and over and over they had argued, but again and again Cuthbert had come back to the same point – no main timbers, no Globe Theatre – and so they had agreed. About twenty of them had gone, Richard, Cuthbert, himself, Will Kempe playing a part far removed from his usual clown's role, and some dozen or so workmen led by Peter Street, the carpenter. The 28th December had been the chosen date, a dark and gloomy day, though London was still festive and paying little heed to them. All day it had taken them, and every moment he had cursed himself for having agreed to such a mad venture. The workmen had torn off the thatch that had roofed the galleries and stage, had stripped out the lathe and plaster infilling, knocked out the wooden dowel pins that held the frame together, and had dismantled the twelve-inch square oak beams, some of them more than thirty feet high – and they had been heavy, by all the gods of theatre were they heavy!

From Finsbury Fields the City of London stood between them and the Thames, and they couldn't take the great carrier-carts through Bishop's Gate and across London, not without attracting too much attention. So they had skirted the city to the west and barged them down the Fleet to the Thames at Bridewell and so across by barges and wherries to Bankside – and by heavens had he been thankful to see Maiden Lane again.

Then building began apace, with him more fretful than most at every passing day, until Richard had said: 'Go home to Stratford, William, go see your great new house. Put flowers on your son's grave. There is nothing for you here until we open. Come back in August for the rehearsals – *Julius Caesar*, as agreed.'

So he had gone north, and stood by Hamnet's gravestone, grieving anew for his eleven-year-old son, played with his surviving children, renewed his love for Anne, and celebrated his father's grant of a coat arms – '*Not Without Rights*' his father had said with a twinkle, 'no bad motto for a family to have' – and so now he had returned, August in the year 1599, August as he had promised Richard.

He passed under the portcullis at the Bishop's Gate set in the old city wall, and into London itself, the largest and most exciting city in Europe, bustling and vibrant, drawing people from all over the realm, aye and from across the seas: courtiers seeking royal favour, merchants searching for business ventures, tradesmen seeking a living, actors and playwrights like himself, and of course the scoundrels, the vagabonds, always after easy pickings. He made his way south down Bishopsgate Street and then down Gracechurch Street though the throng of people, his very soul drinking in the shouts and cries, past the sumptuous town-houses of the wealthy, at the back of which was a maze of twisted streets, the rickety over-hanging houses leaving them constantly darkened, in perpetual gloom. And the smells! After several days on the road in the fresh air, the smells of London hit him anew, the reek of garbage and human excrement, sewage simply dumped in the streets, foul-smelling butcher's waste, blood and entrails piled in alleyways or thrown in the river – and dead dogs thrown over the city wall at one particular point into the ditch the other side, the hound's ditch.

But he was a playwright, an observer of human character, and though London excited and thrilled him, as always, he was not blind to its darker side – the gangs of vagabonds that roamed the streets at night, hordes of cut-purses and pickpockets, the dark crimes of foul murder and rape, the sad sight of unwanted children tossed onto rubbish heaps and left to die – and the stench, an accepted fact of life, and the frequent outbreaks of disease, of smallpox and cholera and the plague, the Black Death that struck at high and low alike.

As he crossed over Lombard Street and down to London Bridge he saw the great spire of St Paul's to his right, glimpsed briefly along an alley; St Paul's whose central nave, Paul's Walk, he knew would be crowded with 'gulls', fashionable young fools parading up and down, showing off their fine clothes, catching up on the latest gossip, buying titbits from shopkeepers who had their stalls set up inside, even using the tombs as shop counters to lay out their wares. Aye,

London was the greatest city on Earth but it was not for the weak or the faint-hearted.

He passed under the gate and onto London Bridge itself, the only bridge across the Thames, jammed with high narrow dwellings, built so close that carts could scarcely pass one another beneath, the bridge crowded with people and animals and carts, the cries and calls filling the air, and then he came to the gatehouse at the southern end and could not prevent himself from glancing upwards to see the dozen or so heads of traitors stuck on spikes for all to see.

Then he came off the bridge into the borough of Southwark, passed St Saviour's on his left, and turned right and came at length to Maiden Lane – and there, beyond the narrow dirty little streets, beyond the brothels and the drinking dens, there it towered, exactly as they had visualised it – the huge Globe Theatre, thirty yards across, room for two thousand people and maybe more, with its motto over the entry door *Totus mundus agit histrionem*, 'all the world's a stage', and over the motto the figure of Hercules holding the globe of the world upon his mighty shoulders – The Globe!

He took a deep breath, and the fear that had sat athwart his shoulders all these weeks dissolved and vanished. He grinned ecstatically and moved forward, and as he came to his lodgings Richard saw him coming and raced to meet him. 'Will. Will, by all the gods of stage and craft, it's good to see you.'

Shakespeare looked at his friend, at the long narrow face and receding hairline, at the countenance that even in his pleasure seemed dark and full of woe, as befitting, mayhap, the visage of the greatest tragedian in all the realm. 'Well, Richard, your hair cut short, and what's this I see, a new embroidered shirt, slashed and slitted, with a fancy yellow silk lining pulled through the slits – and a new bonnet too, in green velvet. My, my, Richard, quite the gull you have become.'

'It's French, the latest, but never mind all that.' He flung his arm aloft, as he had so often on the apron. 'Well, what d'you think?'

The Globe towered above them as they walked towards it. 'It's the old Theatre reborn, a twenty-four sided polygon, looks like a giant wooden "O".'

'Yes, yes – yes, yes – but what do you *think*?'

William grinned. 'It's beautiful, Richard – it is quite beautiful.'

Richard grinned happily and pointed north across the fields towards where another theatre could be seen. 'Philip had apoplexy when he heard.'

Philip Henslow ran the Rose Theatre and his company the Lord Admiral's Men employing his son-in-law, Edward Alleyn as the leading tragedian. 'They are a good company,' said Shakespeare, 'but Edward does not have the same sharpness of role as you do, Richard.'

'That's true,' said the actor. 'I am the best.'

'Though not the most modest.'

Richard at least had the grace to laugh. 'Come,' he said, 'let's see inside.' They walked towards the only door, and as they went in William gasped. 'As you can see, it's virtually complete.' There was the apron stage jutting far out into the pit, and there were the three tiers of galleries, and the lords rooms, and there aloft was the mechanism to lower actors to the stage beneath, and everywhere was the rush and bustle of a myriad workers and props men and wardrobe mistresses. 'The canopy is yet to go up,' said Richard, 'it's being embroidered with the sun and stars even now, and the thatched roof has to go on the galleries, but we will be ready in about a week, and certainly we can open on the 21st September as we planned.'

'With *Julius Caesar* – as you agreed?'

'Oh yes, I anticipate it will be every bit as popular as your comedies. By the way, did you finish *Hamlet*?'

'Yes, yes I did, and I have to borrow your modesty and say that it's the best thing I've done so far.'

Richard Burbage looked at him. 'We had a tragedy here a few days after you left. There was a young boy who worked at the bear-baiting court just across from The Rose, a youth, can't think of his name just now.'

'Stephen,' said Shakespeare, 'Stephen Palmer – nice lad – looked after the two bears, fed them, cleaned out their quarters, that sort of thing.'

'Well, not any more he doesn't, he went missing. Then the owner found great pools of blood and some bones in the inner part of the bears' cage, and after a lot of rushing hither and thither it was decided that someone had deliberately thrown the boy to the bears who promptly tore him apart. It was reported that Robert Small had been seen near the bear-pens on that day.'

'Robert Small, the butcher's son?'

'Yes, a fit of jealous rage over Agnes Tuffin. He's in Clink prison now charged with murder waiting for the next Judges Assize in October.'

Agnes Tuffin was the only child of old Henry Tuffin, one of their carpenters. 'Good God – and what about Agnes?'

'Distraught, as you can imagine.'

Shakespeare shook his head. Henry Tuffin was a widower, dour and silent, a massive fellow, more bear himself than man, but a good carpenter, one who had served the Burbages for many years. His daughter, Agnes, who kept house for him, was a comely wench who stirred the loins of many a youth in Bankside – and who stirred yet darker passions too, it would seem.

The following morning he called at Tuffin's lodgings and found Agnes hard at work sewing a costume. 'A sad business, Agnes,' he said. He leaned forward, his hands on his knees. 'Have you been to the prison to see Robert?'

'Yes, once. His father asked me to take some pies in for him.' She looked up at him. 'People do say I egged him on to do it, but that be not true, Master Shakespeare.' She shook her head vehemently. 'That be not true.' She flung the costume down. 'They are vile to say such of me!'

He looked at her closely. Oh yes, at sixteen years of age Agnes Tuffin was a wench to stir a loin or two, a lithe-limbed and full-breasted young woman. It was not difficult to understand how passions could rise. But for whom did her tears fall, for Stephen or Robert?

'Do you like Robert?' he said softly.

She tossed her head, reddening slightly. 'Oh he's just one of them that keeps a-calling. They're like flies.' She looked up at him. 'Every girl has flies a-buzzing.'

He thought of his own daughter and knew that he did not like flies. 'Did Stephen come a-buzzing?'

She snatched up the costume and busied herself, her head lowered. 'He might have done,' she said in a small voice.

He leant forward and gently took her chin and tilted her face up. 'Was it Stephen you cared for?' he said quietly.

For some long moments she said nothing, and then the dark waters of her grief welled up anew and spilled once more upon her cheek. 'Oh Master Shakespeare, he was so strong, so handsome. He was only a bear-baiting boy, I know, but he sang and laughed and when

I was with him I felt as I had never felt before – and now he is dead and I wish I was dead too!' and she burst into fresh tears.

He waited patiently for the storm to subside, and when her shoulders stopped heaving he said: 'And Robert?'

'He wanted to speak to my father,' and her voice was so quiet that he could scarce hear her, 'but I would not let him. I hate him, I hate him, him with his dead fish eyes – but father would have welcomed him, I know.'

'Oh, why is that?'

She flung a disdainful look at him. 'Because Robert's father owns a butcher's shop and because Stephen didn't even know who his father was.'

'Was that why Robert killed him?'

Her eyes were bleak. 'I don't know, I don't know. One minute I think he wouldn't be man enough, and the next I can see him bolstered up with drink and rage and capable of anything.'

As can most men, he thought. He rose and went to the window. The glass was crude and thick but he could still see the youth lounging across the alley. 'That lad there,' he said, 'the one with the truculent manner and the sneer on his face. He was there when I came in. Who is he?'

She rose and peered through the discoloured glass. 'Oh him. That's Alfred Fletcher. He's wherryman, well a sort of apprentice wherryman – works his father's boat sometimes.'

'He's a big fellow.'

'Oh yes, Alfred Fletcher believes himself a very big man indeed.'

He turned to her. 'Is he one of the flies?'

She nodded grimly. 'The loudest and the most persistent.'

Emerging into the sunshine, his face settled into a grim expression. Noble or peasant, young or old, men were more oft driven by their loins than ought else. He crossed the alley to where the youth was lounging against a wall. 'You are Alfred Fletcher? he enquired politely.

'What of it?' said the youth sourly.

He was a big fellow with great shoulders and a powerful frame. 'William Shakespeare. Perhaps you should be aware that when Henry Tuffin is at his work in the theatre – *in absentia*, you might say – I am happy to stand *in loco parentis* to young Agnes.'

'Er?' said the youth.

Shakespeare looked up at him. 'It means,' he said softly, 'that if anyone harms or even upsets Agnes they will have me to deal with,' and he fingered his sword-hilt thoughtfully. 'And on behalf of Agnes you should also be aware that I am investigating the death of Stephen Palmer.'

The boy looked down at him, weighing the situation. 'What's that to do with me?' he said truculently.

'Nothing, I hope – for your sake.' He looked up at him. 'The Sheriff has a noose waiting for the one who murdered Stephen Palmer, and a hangman's rope is strong enough to hang anyone, even one as big as you,' and he turned and walked away. He perhaps ought not to have spoken as he did, but he did not like the fellow. It would, however, serve to spread the word throughout Bankside that Master Shakespeare himself had taken an interest in the matter.

The following morning he rose early and went to Clink prison, a grim, dour building near St Saviours. He banged on the great oak door for a good many minutes before it was finally opened and a thin weasel of a man peered out. 'Waddaya want?' he growled.

'A civil tongue from you for a start,' said Shakespeare firmly, pushing open the door. 'Take me to the jailer.'

The man grumbled but led the way down a dark and dingy corridor to a small cluttered office. The jailer was a fat, ugly man smelling of ale and much else, and Shakespeare's nose wrinkled with distaste. But he was the authority here, and after some haggling he agreed on sixpence to see the prisoner. Grumbling and wheezing the obese jailer led him down into the basement and unlocked a cell. 'You can have five minutes,' he said sourly and handed over the candlestick.

The stygian darkness of the cell gave way reluctantly before the yellow light. It was a dank stone cell, the normally perpetual darkness relieved only by a tiny window high up on one wall. The stench of urine and excrement was obnoxious but Shakespeare grimly took a pace forward and held up the candlestick.

In the far corner a figure lay on the ground, knees drawn up, arms and hands held protectively over his upper body and head. 'Robert Small?' said Shakespeare. There was no reply, but he could see the pallid skin shiver as would the skin of a horse shiver under the torment of flies. 'Robert, I need to talk to you.'

'Go away,' came a muffled voice. 'I didn't do it. I told 'em, over and over I told 'em – I didn't do it!' and the voice rose to a shriek that set Shakespeare's skin crawling.

'Perhaps you didn't. That's what I'm here to find out.'

'Go away! Go away!'

Shakespeare felt oddly disappointed. It takes a strong emotion to commit murder – greed, jealousy, a lust for power – and some courage or at least desperation in view of the ever-looming noose – but certainly there was no strength in that weak cry, no courage in that fearful posture. 'Get up!' he said sharply and prodded the body with his foot. 'Don't lie there snivelling.' The man lowered his hands and peered up at him, and then gradually and fearfully unwound his body. Then, using the wall as support, he hauled himself to his feet.

'That's better. Now, I am here on behalf of Agnes Tuffin.'

The man gave a small, weak cry. 'She wanted that bear-boy.'

'Really? Is that why you killed him?'

'I didn't kill him, I told 'em I didn't kill him!'

'You were seen near the bear-pit that evening, a scant hour before the crime was discovered.'

'I weren't the only one, Master Shakespeare, including the one who said he saw me.'

'Since you recognize me you know that if I can demonstrate that you did not commit the crime then I have may have enough influence to get you out of here. Quite possibly there are some people who don't like plays, but the Sheriff does.'

The following day Shakespeare went to see the owner of the bear-baiting court, a surly churlish fellow. 'The Palmer boy's gone, and the butcher's boy's in Clink for it,' he growled. 'Let it be, Master Shakespeare, let it be.'

'Robert Small didn't murder Stephen Palmer, I'm sure of that. He's too much of a snivelling coward, and he's a weak puny little fellow whereas Stephen was a big lad.'

'Aye,' he said, the burr in his voice betraying his west country origins, 'you can't be a weakling and tend bears.'

'And the weakling, Small,' said Shakespeare witheringly, 'is supposed to have picked up this robust, strong lad, far heavier and taller than himself and tossed him to the bears! I tell you, master bear-man, someone's brains around here are as addled as old eggs, but mine aren't. And another thing – where are the bones!'

'Bones? What bones?'

'The bones of the dead boy – you were supposed to have found them in the bears' inner quarters.'

'The surgeon took 'em – Branson's his name – down by St Saviours.'

Shakespeare stamped away in a foul mood. Great god in heaven, doesn't anyone round here use his brains! As he passed the Globe and into Maiden Lane he saw Alfred Fletcher leaning up against a fence-post, and when the boy saw him a mocking smile rose to the surface of his features, and Shakespeare stormed over to him. 'Well, I can tell you one thing, Fletcher – Robert Small did not murder Stephen Palmer and I'll have him out of prison by the week's end.'

The boy shrugged insolently. 'So what's that got to do with me?'

Shakespeare thrust his face close to the boy's, though he had to reach up on the balls of his feet to do it. 'Because, Alfred Fletcher, it needed someone big and strong to toss the Palmer boy to the bears – and that fits you, my friend – and the only other person known to have been near the bear-pit that evening was you. You have the strength to have committed the crime, you were at the scene, and you had just as good a motive as Robert Small – young Agnes. That's what it's got to do with you – and with Robert Small released the Sheriff is going to want the real murderer – and if that's you then I'll take great pleasure in preparing the hangman's noose myself for your detestable fat neck!' and he turned and strode away red with fury.

All the way along Maiden Lane he kept trying to regain his composure. 'Calm down, calm down – what ails you, man, to rant and rave – there is no real evidence against Alfred Fletcher. What do the vagabonds say, what's that slang word? Ah yes, a queer cuffin, a hoggish and churlish man. Well that's Alfred Fletcher all right, a queer cuffin, and I'd lief as not like to see that oaf swing, evidence or no evidence.'

He found Branson's surgery room in a back street, a dirty, untidy chamber, cobwebbed and grimy. The bare wooden table had been splashed with water to get rid of most of the blood from recent operations, but the edges of the table and the legs were encrusted with the dried blood of earlier tortures. On a crude bench set against the far wall were some surgical instruments – a barbaric looking tooth-puller, an amputating saw, some forceps, and a hand-drill whose probable purpose made him shudder.

The surgeon came bustling in, a small, sour-faced man with a tiny pointed beard and ferret's eyes. 'Yes?' he said curtly.

'I understand you took away the remains of Stephen Palmer

from the bear-pit on the night of the murder some months ago.'

The man nodded. 'I took some bones,' he agreed.

There was a silence for some moments. 'Well, may I see them?'

The man shook his head. 'Can't – I threw 'em to the dogs.'

The playwright could scarce believe what he was hearing. 'Human remains – you threw human remains to the dogs?! They were evidence, man – the mortal remains of Stephen Palmer!'

'Really? Then he was a very peculiar young man.' The surgeon smiled a cruel cold smile. 'The poor lad was afflicted with the shin-bone of a horse, the rib-bones of a cow, and sundry bits and pieces of bone from sheep, dogs – oh and probably badger and fox. They were the sort of bones you'd find in any butcher's rear yard.'

Shakespeare could not take it in at first. His mouth kept opening and closing until finally all he could say was: 'You're sure?'

'Of course. When you've sawn and drilled and amputated as many human bones as I have you get to know the difference. I prepared a deposition to that effect soon after the incident and lodged it with the Alderman's Court to await the Assize.'

So, the Alderman's Court has known about it all these months, and they would not have dared do other than inform the Sheriff – and all this while poor Robert Small, snivelling little creature though he is, has been languishing in Clink prison and the authorities do not even have a body!

It took Shakespeare four days before he was finally granted an interview with the Sheriff, and a half-a-dozen subsequent meetings before he could persuade him to reluctantly release the prisoner. 'I am perhaps allowing myself to be persuaded against my better judgement, Master Shakespeare,' he said, 'and if Robert Small did not murder Stephen Palmer then who did?'

Robert Small was released the following day and came to see him, pathetically grateful. 'If there's anything I can do for you, Master Shakespeare, you let me know.'

'Well, stay away from Agnes Tuffin for a start, she's not for you.'

The boy looked up at him craftily. 'I hear tell you think Alfred Fletcher done it.'

'Got to be – if it wasn't you, who else – who else was buzzing around Agnes who would want Stephen Palmer dead?'

Robert Small remembered the many times Alfred had boxed his ears, or knocked him down, or snatched the jug of ale from his hand. 'It was 'im, I know'd it.'

Three days later Shakespeare was sitting on the green in front of the Globe when Richard Burbage saw him and came over. 'Well, it's playwright turned constable I hear.'

Shakespeare shrugged. 'Someone had to take an interest otherwise Robert Small would have been hanged for a murder that he did not commit.'

'And now the whole of Bankside is buzzing that you're after Alfred Fletcher.'

'He seems the most likely.'

'Forget it Will, it wasn't Alfred Fletcher. The lad had a commission that evening to row some quality down river almost to Chelsea, saw them pulling down river myself.'

Shakespeare threw up his hands. 'So why didn't you tell me?'

'Because you didn't ask, and how was I to know that you'd go rushing round Bankside like some avenging angel?' Richard Burbage looked at his friend and saw the anguish. 'You did a fine thing, Will, getting that boy released, but there is nothing more you can do. Good God, you don't even have a body now. For all you know Stephen Palmer fled Bankside to escape from Agnes Tuffin!'

'But . . .'

'No, Will – forget it. We start rehearsals tomorrow. Your responsibility is to the Globe,' and he strode away.

Shakespeare sighed. Richard was right, but he hated an unsolved mystery. It was evening now and down by the Globe he saw the workmen streaming away to their lodgings, among them Henry Tuffin, and as the carpenter came past Shakespeare nodded. 'Evening, Henry. You've a good lass in young Agnes.'

The burly man did not break his stride. 'Aye, that she is, and she'll be with me a few years yet.' He glanced at the playwright and a very curious smile flitted across his face. 'It's all I ever wanted,' and he passed on down towards Maiden Lane.

Shakespeare stared after him, a horrid possibility surfacing in the dark waters of his mind. Henry had been in charge of driving the pilings and filling the foundations. Oh dear god, not Henry – big enough, burly enough, wanting to keep Agnes at home – but where is Stephen Palmer – where is the body? And the playwright's head swivelled and he stared at the Globe – a twenty-four sided polygon: twenty four like the hours in a day!

Dear God in heaven, beneath which hour does Stephen Palmer lie?!

All's Well That Ends Well 

METHOUGHT YOU SAW A SERPENT

Peter Tremayne

It is not exactly certain when All's Well That Ends Well *was written, and it has been suggested that this was the final title for the presumed lost play,* Love's Labour's Won. *This would mean it was written before 1598, but internal evidence suggests that it was written, or extensively revised, between 1601 and 1604. Peter Tremayne has opted for 1601 and has linked the play to the execution of Queen Elizabeth's one-time favourite, the Earl of Essex. You do not need to know the plot of the play to follow the story, as everything you need to know is revealed in due order.*

> 'Methought you saw a serpent,'
> *All's Well That Ends Well*, Act I. Scene iii.

Master Hardy Drew, the newly appointed deputy to the Constable of the Bankside Watch, gazed from the first floor latticed window onto the street, watching in unconcealed distaste as a group of drunken carousers lurched across the cobbles below. The sounds of their song came plainly to his ears.

Sweet England's pride is gone!
Welladay! Welladay!
Brave honour graced him still
Gallantly! Gallantly!

The young man turned abruptly from the window back into the room with an expression of annoyance.

On the far side, seated at a table, the elderly Constable of the Bankside Watch, Master Edwin Topcliff, had glanced up from his papers and was regarding the young man with a cynical smile.

'You have no liking for the popular sympathy then, Master Drew?' the old man observed dryly.

Hardy Drew flushed and thrust out his chin.

'Sir, I am a loyal servant of Her Majesty, may she live a long life.'

'Bravely said,' replied the Constable gravely. 'But, God's will be done, it may be that your wish will be a futile one. 'Tis said that the Queen's Majesty is ailing and that she has not stirred from her room since my lord Essex met his nemesis at the executioner's hands.'

It had been scarcely two weeks since the flamboyant young Robert Devereux, Earl of Essex, had met his fate in the courtyard of the Tower of London, having been charged and found guilty of high treason. Rumour and disturbances still pervaded the capital and many of the citizens of London persisted in singing ditties in his praise, for Essex had been a hero to most Londoners and they might even have followed him in overturning the sour, ageing Queen, who now sat in solitary paranoia on the throne in Greenwich Palace.

It was rumoured that the auspices were evident for Elizabeth's overthrow and even the usually conservative Master William Shakespeare and his theatrical company had been persuaded to stage a play on the deposing and killing of King Richard II but a couple of week's before Essex's treason was uncovered. It was claimed that many of Essex's supporters had, after dining together, crossed the Thames to the Globe to witness this portentous performance.

In the middle of such alarums and excursions, young Master Hardy Drew had arrived to take up his apprenticeship in maintaining the Queen's Peace with the ageing Constable. Drew was an ambitious young man, who wanted to create a good impression with his superior. The son of a clerk, he had entered the Inns of Court under the patronage of a kindly barrister, but the man had died and Hardy Drew had been dismissed because of his lowly birth and lack of social and financial support. So it was, he found himself turning from one aspect of law to another.

Old Master Topcliff rubbed his nose speculatively as he examined his new assistant. The young man's features were flushed with passionate indignation.

'I would not take offence at the songs you hear nor the people's sympathies, young man. Times are in a flux. It is a time of ebb and flow in affairs. I know this from reading the Almanacs. What is regarded as seditious today may not be so tomorrow.'

Master Drew sniffed disparagingly. He was about to make a rejoinder when there came a banging at the door, and before he or Master Topcliff could respond it burst open and a young man, with flushed features, his chest heaving from the exertion of running, burst into the room.

'How now? What rude disturbance is this?' demanded Master Topcliff, sitting back in his chair and examining the newcomer with annoyance.

The youth was an angular young man of foppish appearance, the clothes bright but without taste. Topcliff had the impression of one of modest origins trying to imitate the dignity of a gentleman without success.

'I am from the Globe Theatre, masters,' gasped the young man, straining to recover his breath. 'I am sent to fetch you thither.'

'By whose authority and for what purpose?'

The young man paused a moment or two for further breaths before continuing. He was genuinely agitated.

'I am sent by Richard Burbage, the master of our group of players. The count has been found murdered, sirs. Master Burbage implores you, through me, to come thither to the crime.'

Topcliff rose to his feet at once.

'A count, you say?'

'The Count of Rousillon, master.'

Topcliff exchanged an anxious glance with his deputy.

'A foreign nobleman murdered at a London theatre,' he sighed, 'this does not augur well in the present travails. There is anxiety enough in this city without involving the enmity of the embassy of France.'

He reached for his hat and cloak and signalled Master Drew to follow, saying to the youth: 'Lead on, boy. Show us where this Count of Rousillon's body lies.'

The Globe Theatre was a half a mile from the rooms of the Constable of the Bankside Watch and they made the journey in quick time. There were several people in small groups around the door of the theatre. People attracted by the news of disaster like flies to a honey pot.

A middle-aged man stood at the door awaiting them. His face bore a distracted, anxious gaze and he was wringing his hands in a helpless, almost theatrical gesture. Hardy Drew tried to hide a smile for the action was so preposterous that the humour caught him. It was as if the man were playing at the expression of agitated despair.

'Give you good day, sir,' Master Topcliff greeted breezily.

'Lackaday, sir,' replied the other. 'For I do fear that any good in the day has long vanished. My name is Burbage and I am the director of this company of players.'

'I hear from your boy that a foreign nobleman lies dead in your theatre. This is serious.'

Burbage's eyes widened in surprise.

'A foreign nobleman?' He sounded bewildered.

'Indeed, sir, what name was it? The Count of Rousillon. Have I been informed incorrectly?'

A grimace crossed Master Burbage's woebegone face.

'He was no foreign nobleman, sir.'

'How now?' demanded Master Topcliff in annoyance. 'Is the constable to be made the butt of some mischievous prank? Is there no murder then?'

'Oh, yes. Murder, there is, good Constable. But the body is that of our finest player, Bertrando Emillio. He plays the role of the Count of Rousillon in our current production.'

Master Topcliff snorted with indignation while Master Drew did his best to hide a smile.

'An actor?' Master Topcliff made it sound as though it was beneath his dignity to be called out to the murder of an actor. He gave a sniff. 'Well, since we are here, let us view the body.'

Burbage led them to the back of the stage, where several people stood or sat in groups quietly talking amongst themselves. One woman was sitting sobbing comforted by another. Their whispers ceased as they saw the constable and his deputy. From their appearance, so

Drew thought, they were all members of the company of actors. He glanced across their expressions, for they ranged from curiosity to distress to bewilderment, while others seemed to have a tinge of anxiety on their faces.

Burbage led them to what was apparently a small dressing room, in a darkened corridor behind the stage, which was full of hanging clothes and baskets and all manner of clutter. On one basket was a pile of neat clothes, well folded, with leather belt and purse on top.

In the middle of this room lay the body of a young man who, in life, had been of saturnine appearance. He was stretched on his back, one arm flung out above his head. The eyes were open and the face was masked in a curious expression as if of surprise. He wore nothing more than a long linen shirt that probably had once been white. Now it was stained crimson with his blood. It needed no physician to tell them that the young man had died from several stab wounds to his chest and stomach. Indeed, by the body, a long, bone handled knife, of the sort used for carving meat, lay discarded and bloody.

Master Topcliff glanced down dispassionately. Death was no stranger to the environs of London, either north or south of the river. In particular, violent death was a constant companion among the lanes and streets around the river.

'His name is Bertrando Emillio, you say? That sounds foreign to me. Was he Italian?'

Master Burbage shook his head.

'He was as English as you or I, sir. No, Bertrando Emillio was but the name he used for our company of players.'

Master Topcliffe was clearly irritated.

'God's wounds! I like not confusion. First I am told that he is the Count of Rousillon. Then I am told he is an actor, one Bertrando Emillio. Who now do you claim him to be?'

'Faith, sir, he is Herbert Eldred of Cheapside,' replied Burbage, unhappily. 'But while he treads the boards, he is known to the public by his stage name – Bertrando Emillio. It is a common practice among we players to assume such names.'

Master Topcliff grunted unappeased by the explanation.

'Who found him thus?' he asked curtly.

As he was asking the question, Master Drew had fallen to his knees to inspect the body more closely. There were five stab wounds to the chest and stomach. They had been inflicted as if in a frenzy for he saw the ripping of the flesh caused by the hurried tearing of the knife, and he realised that any one of the wounds could have been mortal. He was about to rise when he saw some paper protruding under the body. Master Drew rolled the body forward towards its side to extract the papers. In doing so he noticed that there was a single stab wound in Bertrando's back between the shoulder blades. He picked up the papers, let the body roll into its former position on its back and stood up.

'Who found him thus?' Master Topcliff repeated.

'I did,' confessed Master Burbage. 'We were rehearsing for our new play in which he plays the Count de Rousillon. It was to be our first performance this very Saturday afternoon and this was to be our last rehearsal in the costumes we shall wear. Truly, the stars were in bad aspect when Master Shakespeare chose this day to put forward his new work.'

'You are presenting a new play by Master Shakespeare?' queried Hardy Drew speaking for the first time. He had ascertained that the papers under the body were a script of sorts and presumably the part was meant for Bertrando.

'Indeed, a most joyous comedy called *All's Well that Ends Well*,' affirmed Burbage albeit a mite unhappily.

'Let us hope that it pleases the loyal subjects of the Queen's Majesty better than your previous production,' muttered Master Drew.

Master Topcliff shot his deputy a glance of annoyance before turning back to Burbage.

'This is a comedy that has turned to tragedy for your player, master director. All has not ended well here.'

Burbage groaned theatrically.

'You do not have to tell me, sir. We must cancel our performance.' His eyes widened suddenly in realisation.

'Z'life! Master Shakespeare is already on his way from Stratford to attend. How can I tell him the play is cancelled?'

'Isn't it the custom to have an understudy for the part?' asked Hardy Drew.

'Usually,' agreed Burbage, 'but in this case, Bertrando was so jealous of his role that he refused to allow his understudy to attend rehearsals for him to perfect the part. Now the understudy has no time to learn his part before our first performance is due.'

'What is known about this killing?' interrupted Master Topcliff, bored with the problems of the play-master.

Burbage frowned.

'I do not follow.'

'Is it known who did this deed or who might have done it?'

'Why, no. I came on the body a half an hour since. Most of us were on stage reading our parts. When Bertrando did not come to join us, I came here in search of him and found him as you see.'

'So you suspect no one?'

'No one would wish to harm Bertrando, for he is one of . . . *was* one of our most popular players with our audiences.'

Hardy Drew raised an eyebrow.

'Surely that would not endear him to his fellow actors? What of this understudy that he has excluded from rehearsals? Where is he?'

Burbage looked shocked.

'You suspect one of our players of such a deed?' he asked incredulously.

'Who should we suspect, then?' demanded Master Topcliff.

'Why, some cut-throat from the street who must have entered the playhouse in pursuit of a theft. Bertrando surprised the man and was stabbed for his pains. It seems very clear to me, sir.'

Hardy Drew smiled thinly.

'But not to Master Topcliff nor myself,' he replied quietly.

Master Topcliff looked at his young deputy in surprise and then swiftly gathered his wits.

'My deputy is correct,' he added, addressing Burbage.

'Why so, sir?'

Master Topcliff gave a shrug.

'You tell him, Master Drew.'

'Easy enough. Your Bertrando, master-player, did not enter this room to surprise a thief. Bertrando was already in this room. Someone then entered while he was presumably dressing to join you on stage. The purpose of that person was to kill him.'

Burbage looked at him incredulously.

'Do you have the second sight? By what sorcery would you know this?'

'No sorcery at all, sir, but by using my common sense and the evidence of my eyes.'

Master Topcliff was regarding his deputy anxiously. He did not like the word 'sorcery' being levelled at his office. Such a charge could lead to unpleasant consequences.

'Explain yourself further to the good Master Burbage,' he suggested uneasily.

'I will and gladly. There was a single stab mark in Bertrando's back. I would say that the culprit entered the dressing room while Bertrando was donning his clothes with his back to the door. He had only his shirt on. The murderer raised the knife and stabbed Bertrando between the shoulder blades. It was a serious wound but Bertrando was able to turn, with shock and surprise he recognised his assailant. The assailant in a surge of emotion, raised the knife and struck not once not twice, but in a frenzy of blows, born out of that emotion, delivering five more stabs to Bertrando's chest, each a mortal wound. That is an indication of the rage that the murderer felt towards him. Bertrando sank to the floor. Either he was already dead or dying within seconds.'

Master Topcliff looked on approvingly.

'So you think this was done by someone who knew Bertrando or whatever his name is?'

'Sir, I am sure of it. No cut-throat would commit a murder in such a fashion. Nor is there sign of any theft.'

'How can you be so sure?' demanded Burbage.

Master Drew turned to the neat pile of clothes on top of the basket.

'I presume that these are Bertrando's clothes of which he divested himself, stacking them neatly there as he changed for the stage?'

Burbage glanced at the pile as if seeing the clothes for the first time.

'Yes,' he admitted. 'Yes, I recognise his jacket. He was a vain man and given to gaudy colours in jacket and hose.'

Master Drew pointed.

'Then I suppose that the leather belt and purse is Bertrando's also?'

Burbage's eyes widened.

'That they are,' he agreed, seeing where the logic was leading.

Master Drew leant forward, picked up the purse and emptied the contents into his hand. There fell into his palm a collection of coins.

'Would a thief, one who had been prepared to murder so violently to secure his theft, retreat leaving this rich prize behind? No, sir, I think we must seek other reasons as to this slaughter.'

Burbage bowed his head. His nose wrinkled at the smell of blood and sought permission to cover the body with a sheet.

'Now,' Drew said, turning to Burbage, 'you say that most of you were on stage when you noticed that Bertrando was missing from your company?'

'That is so.'

'Can you recall anyone who was not on stage?'

Burbage thought carefully.

'There were only a few that were latecomers, for I needed everyone on stage to rehearse the final scene, that is the scene set in the Count of Rousillon's palace where the King and all the lords, attendants and main characters gather.'

Master Hardy Drew hid his impatience.

'Who was not with you then?'

'Why, Parolles, Helena, Violenta . . . oh and young Will Painter.'

'You will explain who these people are.'

'Well, they are all characters in our play. Well, all except Will Painter. He was the understudy for Bertrando who was excluded from the task. The only thing I could give him to do was to be a voiceless attendant upon our King.'

Master Drew scratched his chin.

'And he was one with a motive, for, with Bertrando dead, he could step into this main role and win his reputation among the luminaries of your theatre. Fetch this Will Painter to us.'

Will Painter was scarcely as old as Hardy Drew. A fresh faced youth, well dressed and with manners and mode of speech that displayed an education that many theatrical players did not possess.

'Will Painter? That is a familiar name to me.' Master Drew greeted, having once more sought the permission of his superior to conduct the inquiry.

'It is my father's name also and he was admired as a writer of plays,' replied the youth nonchalant in manner.

'Ah, indeed. And one who provided well for his family. It is strange that his son would seek such lowly footings in the theatre.'

'Not so,' flushed the youth. 'To rise to be a master-player one must know and experience all manner of theatrical work.'

'Yet, methinks, that you would have preferred to play the role of the Count de Rousillon in this new comedy?'

'Who would not cast an envious eye at the leading role?'

'Just so. Did you cast such an envious gaze in Bertrando's direction?'

The youth flushed in annoyance.

'I do not deny it.'

'And were you irritated beyond endurance by the fact that Bertrando was so jealous of his part that he refused that you understudy him in rehearsal?'

'Irritated by his popinjay manners, yes. Irritated, yes, but not beyond endurance. One must bear the ills with the joys of our profession. I admit that I liked him not. But dislike was not enough to slit his throat.'

'Slit his throat? Why do you use that expression?'

Will Painter frowned.

'I do not understand.'

'What makes you think that his throat was slit?'

'Why, Master Burbage waxing lyrical about a cut-throat having entered the theatre in search of plunder and killing Bertrando. What other method would such an assassin use?'

Master Drew uncovered Bertrando's body.

Will Painter saw the stab wounds and turned his face away in disgust.

'I liked him not but 'tis oppressive to see a man so reduced as this.'

'And you can not hazard a guess to the identity of anyone who would wish him so reduced?'

The young actor shrugged.

'In truth, if I were to name one, I would name many.'

'How so? Master Burbage says he was well disposed to the entire company?'

The youth was cynical.

'Well disposed, but more to the feminine gender of our company than ought else.'

'Women?' asked Master Topcliff aghast. 'Do you mean that you have women as players?'

'Aye. Master Burbage experiments in using women to play the female roles as is common in Europe. Bertrando cast his net like a fisherman and trawled in as he could. However, he lives . . . *lived* with Hester at the Mermaid Tavern in Mermaid Court.'

'Hester? And who is she?'

'The maid that plays Helena in our comedy. I saw Bertrando and Hester arrive at the theatre together. She was already dressed for her part and so Bertrando went towards the dressing room, presumably to change. I saw Bertrando no more.'

'Did you go near the dressing room?'

'Not I. I went off to seek a flagon of ale in the Globe Tavern opposite and there I remained until I heard the sound of disturbance. Master Fulke will tell you that I departed as he arrived, for he brushed past me as I quit the theatre, although he didn't greet me.'

'Master Fulke?' And who is Master Fulke?'

'You have not heard of Raif Fulke who plays the part of Parolles in our play?'

'Parolles?' mused Master Drew. 'Let me stick with Master Fulke and not be confused by such a choice of names. You say that Master Fulke brushed past you?'

'I did.'

'Did he go to speak with Bertrando or Hester?'

'I did not stay to see but I think not. He is at enmity with them for Hester once lived with Master Fulke and he bears no fondness for Bertrando. It is well known that Fulke is jealous of Bertrando and his success both on stage and with women.'

'Well, Master Painter, do you go to call this Hester here but do not go beyond the confines of the theatre until we tell you.'

The girl Hester came almost immediately.

Old Master Topcliff and his assistant, aware of the niceties and refinements, had stopped her from entering the dressing room with the dead body and proceeded to question her outside. She was an attractive woman whose silk gown may have seen better days but which still enhanced the contours of her figure, leaving little to the imagination. That she had taken the news of the death of her lover badly was written on her tear-stained features. Her skin was pale and her eyes red with sobbing.

'I hear you were Bertrando's lover?' began Master Drew without preamble.

The girl sobbed and raised a square of muslin to the corner of her eye and dabbed it.

'Lover? I am Mistress Herbert Eldred,' she announced, raising her chin slightly. 'So have I been these past two years. I have a paper to prove it.'

Master Drew blinked, but it was the only expression that he gave of surprise.

Master Topcliff sighed as if totally puzzled.

'Faith! Who is Herbert Eldred?' he demanded in bewilderment.

Master Drew glanced swiftly at him.

'The actor, sir, Bertrando Emillio. Herbert Eldred is his real name.'

'Ah, I had forgotten. Why these people cannot stick to one name, I have no understanding.' He looked hard at the girl. 'I am of the impression that no one in this company of players knows that you were married?'

'Herbert – Bertrando as was – felt it better that we keep our marriage a secret lest it impede his career. If you want proof of our marriage, then I have . . .'

Master Topcliff made a dismissive gesture with his hand.

'No need for proof at this stage. So, if you are the dead man's wife you, therefore, had no cause to kill him?'

The girl stared at him in indignation.

'Of course I had no cause to kill him! But there be others . . .' She hesitated as if regretting what she had said.

Hardy Drew was swift to follow her words.

'Others?'

Her eyes were now narrowed in suspicion.

'But why speak of that when I understood that a thief had attacked him and killed him?'

'Who told you that?'

'It is common talk among the players.'

'Were you in this part of the theatre while the others were gathering on stage for the rehearsal?' pressed Drew without answering her previous question.

'For a moment, no more.'

'When did you last see Bertrando?'

'I came with him from our lodgings to the theatre. I left him to change for the rehearsal while I did the same and then I went to the stage but Bertrando was not there. When he did not come, Master Burbage went to fetch him.'

'You left him well?'

The girl pursed her lips in a grimace.

'Bertrando was always well. I left him entering that room behind you. Is that . . . ?'

Master Drew nodded in answer to the unfinished question.

'Please wait for us in the theatre and send us who plays the part of Violenta.'

A tall, fair haired young girl appeared shortly after Hester Eldred had left them. From a distance, she looked the picture of maidenly virtue and innocence. Only when she grew near did Hardy Drew see the hard lines around the mouth, the coldness of the blue eyes and the smouldering resentment in her features. Her body was too fleshy and would grow to fat in middle age, and the pouting mouth would turn to an ugly form.

'I am Nelly Porter,' she announced, her voice betraying signs of the West Country. 'What is your need of me?'

'I understand that you play the part of Violenta in this new drama?'

'A joyous "comedy",' she sneered. 'And what of it? I have played many parts in the French theatre.'

'How well did you know Bertrando?'

She gave a raucous laugh.

'As well as any maid who trod the boards of this theatre, aye, and who came within the grasp of the pig!'

'There is hatred in your voice, mistress,' intervened Master Topcliff mildly.

'Hatred enough,' affirmed the girl, indifferent to his censure.

'Hatred enough to kill him?' demanded Hardy Drew.

'Aye, I'll not deny it. I could have killed the pig who ravished girls and left them to bear his children and fend for themselves.'

'He did that to you?'

'So he did. Two years ago. But my child died.'

'And did you kill him for vengeance's sake?'

'No, That's God's truth. But I do not grieve nor do I condemn his killer. If that is a crime, I am ready to be punished.'

'You are honest enough with your dislikes. Where were you just before the rehearsal?'

'I was late getting to the theatre from my lodgings, that's all.'

'Did anyone see you arrive at the theatre?'

'None that I know of. I went straight to the stage on my arrival so only the people there saw me.'

'I see. Wait for us now on stage and send us the actor who plays Parolles. I believe his name is Master Fulke.'

She walked away without another word and they watched her go before exchanging glances.

'She is not exactly grieving over her former lover's death,' Master Topcliff observed, stating the obvious.

Master Fulke was poised, could pass as a gentleman, but was not exactly handsome. He was too round of the face, and too smooth of skin and too ready with an ingratiating smile.

'Well, Master Fulke . . .'

'You want to know where I was before I joined the gathering on the stage?' Fulke greeted a little breathlessly.

'You seem to know my mind,' replied Drew gravely.

The genial actor shrugged.

'It is hard to keep a secret among so small a company. I was delayed, if you wish to know. I arrived late at the theatre . . .'

'Late from where?'

'From my lodgings in Potters Fields. I have a room in the Bell Tavern overlooking the river.'

'That is but ten minutes walk from here.'

'Indeed so.'

'Why were you delayed?'

The man rolled his eyes expressively.

'A rendezvous,' he smiled complacently.

'And this, this *rendezvous*, it made you late arriving? Did anyone see you arrive?'

'I brushed by that young upstart, Will Painter.'

'But you did not see Bertrando?'

Master Fulke sneered.

'Bertrando! Yes, I saw *Master Herbert Eldred*. He, too, had a rendezvous . . . I saw him go to his dressing room. Then I saw someone enter after him. It was not my concern. So I went on my way to join those on stage for the rehearsal.' He sniffed. 'We were fifteen minutes into the rehearsal when Master Burbage began to worry that Eldred had not appeared. I told Burbage where he might be found.'

Master Topcliff tried to suppress his excitement.

'God's wounds, man! Do you tell me that you actually saw his murderer?'

'No, I do not, sir. I said I saw someone enter his dressing room after Eldred had gone in. I have no way of saying this was the murderer. I did not stay longer, as I said, but passed on to the rehearsal.'

'Describe the person,' Topcliff ordered sharply. 'Who else would it be but the murderer?'

'A man, short of stature, of wiry appearance I would say. He wore his hair long and dark, underneath a feathered hat. There was a short cloak. He wore boots. The colours were dark and tailored in the latest fashion. I could see no more in the gloom of the passage. In truth, though, there was something familiar about him, though I cannot quite place it. It may come to me later.'

Master Topcliff was pleased. He dismissed Master Fulke and turned to Hardy Drew with grim satisfaction on his face.

'Well, at least we know our killer was a man, and that he was no common cut-throat but someone who could afford to dress well.'

Drew looked at his mentor blankly.

'Yet this does not lead us any closer to apprehending the man.'

'There are too many of this description on the streets of this city for us to single one out and charge him,' agreed the old Constable.

'Do you plan to leave it so?'

'For the time being. Come, Master Drew. I will have a word with this Burbage and his players before they are dismissed.'

The company was standing or sitting on stage in gloomy groups. A tall, balding man, well dressed, was engaged in earnest conversation with Burbage.

'Ah,' Burbage turned, 'this is the Constable, Will. Master Topcliff, this is Master Shakespeare.'

The balding man inclined his head to the Constable.

'What news? Can you say who engineered the death of our player, sir?'

'Master Fulke saw the murderer enter your actor's dressing room and has given a full description . . .'

There was a gasp from several members of the group and all eyes turned to Master Fulke, who momentarily stood with flushed surprise. He had not expected the Constable to reveal his attestation.

'So you mean to arrest the culprit?' queried the playwright.

'Not immediately, Master Shakespeare. We will consider our move for a while. Master Fulke here has given a good description, but he has not, so far, recalled where he has seen the person before, though he is sure he recognised him. We will wait to see if his memory improves.'

Fulke made a move forward as if to deny the Constable's interpretation, but Master Topcliff turned and glared at the man, so that Fulke lowered his head and hurried off.

The old Constable turned to the assembly and bowed low, flourishing his hat. As he left the theatre, Master Drew came trotting in his wake.

'I do not understand,' he ventured, as he hurried to keep up with long strides of the Constable.

Master Topcliff paused in the street and turned to him.

'Are you city bred or country bred, young man?'

'City bred, Master Constable.'

'I thought so. I am country bred and raised in the fields of Kent. When the quarry goes to ground, what does the huntsman do? You know not? Of course, you know not. What is done is that you prepare a lure.'

Hardy Drew frowned.

'Then you have prepared Fulke as a bait in a trap?'

'If our murderer is one of the gentlemen of Master Burbage's company, he will come this night to make sure that Master Fulke's memory does not return.'

'A harsh judgement on Fulke if we are not there when the murderer visits him.'

'Indeed, but be there we will. We will go to the lodgings of Master Fulke and prepare our snare with Fulke as the unknowing decoy.'

Master Drew looked at the old Constable with a new respect.

'And I thought . . .'

Master Topcliff smiled.

'You must learn the ways of the gamekeeper, young man, and learn that it is always best to tell the poacher where you have set your traps for him.'

They took themselves to the Bell Tavern in Potters Field. A few coins pressed in willing hands were able to secure a booth with curtains from which they could view the front entrance of the tavern. This station fell to Master Topcliff while Hardy Drew, being the younger and hardier, took up his position at the rear entrance of the tavern, so that either entrance to Fulke's rooms might be observed.

A little the worse for drink Raif Fulke entered the tavern towards ten o'clock and made his way immediately up to his room.

It was well after midnight that there was a scream and the innkeeper's wife came running to Master Topcliff, her eyes wide and frightened.

'E's dead. Master Fulke is killed!'

Master Topcliff called to a young man hefting barrels to run around the back of the inn and inform Master Drew. Master Topcliff tried to make for the stairs but found the innkeeper's wife clinging to his sleeve and expanding in detail on her fright.

No one had entered from the back door, of that Hardy Drew was certain. He hurried into the inn and up the back stairs to the bed chambers. He saw one of the doors open at the end of a corridor and ran in.

Master Raif Fulke lay on the floor. A candle burned nearby but it scarcely needed the light to see that there was, dark blood oozing from several wounds on the man's chest. Miraculously, Fulke's chest still rose and fell. He was not yet dead. Drew knelt by him and raised his head.

'Who did it Fulke, who did it?'

The actor opened his eyes. Even in his condition, he smiled, though grimly.

'I would not have known him . . .' he wheezed painfully. 'Like Rousillon, I knew him not . . . Why? Why, young sir? Jealousy is a fierce foe. That was the reason.'

He coughed suddenly and blood spurted from his mouth.

'Take it easy, Fulke. Name the man.'

'Name? Ah . . . for, indeed, he was mad for her, and talked of Satan, and of Limbo, and of Furies, and I know not what . . .'

He coughed again and then smiled, as if apologetically.

'The web of our life is of a mingled yarn, good and ill together; our virtues would be proud if our faults whispered this not; and our crimes would despair, if they were not cherished by our virtues.'

'The name man, quick, give me the name.'

Fulke's breathing was hard and fast.

'I am a'feared the life of Helena . . . was foully snatched . . .'

'Helena?' demanded Drew. 'Do you say that Helena, Hester Eldred, that is, is now in danger from this man?'

Fulke forced a smile.

'Helena? Methought you saw a serpent . . .' he began.

Drew compressed his lips in irritation.

'Concentrate, Fulke, name your assailant.'

Fulke coughed again. He was growing weaker and had not long.

'The play . . . the play's the thing . . .'

Then his eyes dilated and for the first time he realised that he was going to die. The moment of truth came for Master Fulke in one horrible mute second before he fell back and was dead. Master Topcliff hurried in having shaken off the terrified innkeeper's wife.

'Did he say aught?' he asked breathlessly.

Drew shook his head.

'He was rambling. His last words were something about the play being the thing . . . what thing?'

Master Topcliff smiled grimly.

'I fear it was only a line from Master Shakespeare's tragedy of the Prince of Denmark. I recognise it well for it is a play of murder and intrigue that held much meaning for me. "The play's the thing wherein I'll capture the conscience of the king." No use to us. This is my fault. I was too confident. I let this murderer out of my grasp.'

'How did he get in? I can swear that he did not pass me at the back door.'

'Nor from the front,' vowed Master Topcliff.

He peered round. The window was still open, the curtain flapping. There was a small balcony outside built out above the waters of the Thames. The river, smelly and dirty, was lapping just below. The window and balcony was in the side of the building, for it was built sideways on to the river and was blind to the scrutiny of anyone watching the front and back.

They stared out onto the darkened waters. The assailant must have come by rowing boat and pulled up against the wall of the inn, under the balcony. It was high water, and easy to pull oneself up towards this balcony and then climb through Fulke's window.

'Our man will be long gone by now. Now, truly, all we can do is return to our lodgings and secure a good night's repose. Tomorrow morning, I think we will have another word with Master Will Painter. Logic shows him as our likely suspect.'

Hardy Drew sighed with exasperation as he stared down at the actor's body.

'Faith, he rambled on so much. Had he known he was dying I doubt whether he would have quoted so much from his part in this play.'

He suddenly spied a sheaf of papers on the bed. Bending, he picked them up and perused them.

'*All's Well That End's Well*,' he quoted the title. 'A bad ending for some.'

He was about to replace it on the bed when he spotted a line on the pages to which the playscript had fallen open. 'Methought you saw a serpent,' he whispered. He turned to the old Constable. 'Are you sure those words "the play's the thing" comes from this other tragedy you mentioned? Are they not used in this new play?'

'I have seen the tragedy of the Prince of Denmark but I have not seen this new comedy, nor has anyone else, remember? They were just rehearsing it for its first performance.'

'True enough,' Drew replied thoughtfully. After a moment or so, with a frown gathered on his forehead, he tucked the playscript under his arm and followed the old Constable down the stairs, where Master Topcliff gave instructions about the body. There was nothing further to do but to return to their lodgings.

It was morning when Master Topcliff, sitting over his breakfast, observed a pale, and bleary eyed, young Hardy Drew coming into the room.

'You have not slept well,' he observed dryly. 'Does death affect you so?'

'Not death. I have been up all night reading Master Shakespeare's new play.'

Master Topcliff chuckled.

'I hope that you have found good education there?'

Drew sat down and reached for a mug of ale, taking a mouthful. He gave an almost urchin-like grin.

'That I did. I found the answer to many mysteries there.'

Master Topcliff gave him a hard look.

'Indeed?'

'Indeed. I learnt the identity of our murderer. As poor Raif Fulke was trying to tell me – the play's the thing, the thing which reveals the secret. He was quoting from the play so that I might find the identity of his assailant there. But you are right, that line does not occur in this play but the other lines he quoted do.'

An hour later they stood on the stage of the Globe with the players gathered, in sombre attitude, about them. Burbage had recovered his shock of the previous day and was now more annoyed at the loss of revenue to his theatre by the delays.

'How now, Master Constable, what now? Two of our good actors are done to death and you have named no culprit.'

Master Topcliff smiled and gestured to his deputy.

'My deputy will name the assailant.'

Drew stepped forward.

'Your comedy says it all,' Drew began with a smile, holding up the playscript. 'Herein, the Count of Rousillon rejects a woman. She is passionate to have him. She pursues him, first disguised as a man.'

There was a muttering.

'The story of the play is no secret,' pointed out Burbage.

'None at all. However, we have Bertrando, who actually plays Rousillon, in the same situation. He is a man of several affairs, our Bertrando. Worse, he has rejected a most passionate woman, like Helena in the story. Bertrando is married and likes to keep his marriage a secret, is that not so Mistress Eldred?'

Hester Eldred conceded it among the expressions of surprise from the company.

'So one of his lovers,' continued Hardy Drew, 'that passionate woman, likes him not for his philandering life. Having been rejected, like Helena in the play, she pursues him. However, unlike the play, she does not seek merely to win him back but her intention is to punish him. She stabs him and ends his life.'

'Are you telling us that a woman killed Bertrando?' gasped Burbage. 'But Fulke saw a man enter the dressing room.'

'Fulke described a man of short stature. He was positive it was a man. Unfortunately, we,' he glanced at his superior, 'decided to allow Fulke to act as bait by pretending he knew more than he did. Thus lured out, the assailant who murdered Fulke before we had time to protect him. Luckily Fulke was not dead. He survived long enough to identify his assailant . . .'

He turned to Hester Eldred. She read her fate in his eyes, leapt up with a curse and ran from the stage.

Master Topcliff raised a hand in signal and a burly member of the guard appeared at the door and seized her.

A babble broke out from the company.

Burbage raised his voice crying for quiet.

Nelly Porter moved forward.

'I thought you were going to accuse me. I was Bertrando's lover and thanks to him my child died. I had more reason to hate and kill him than she did.'

Hardy Drew smiled softly.

'I did give you a passing thought,' he admitted.

'Then why . . . ?'

'Did I discount you? When we arrived, Hester was on stage in a dress. Now her part, as I read the play calls for her, as Helena, to appear in man's clothes. Yet she clearly told us that she had arrived at the theatre with her lover, left him to change while she went to change herself. Presumably from her own clothes she would change into that of her part as a man. But Will Painter said that he saw her arrive with Bertrand in man's clothes ready for her scene. She told me that she had left Bertrando and went to change into the clothes for her scene. When we came to the theatre she was in a dress and had been so from the time of the rehearsal. She had, therefore, killed her husband while in the male clothing, changed into a dress, and joined you all on stage.'

'But her motive? If she was passionately in love with Bertrando, why would she kill him?'

'The motive is as old as the Earth. Love to hatred turned. For Bertrando was just as much a ladies' man during his marriage as ever he had been. Hester as his wife could not abide his philandering. Few women could. She did not want to share him with others. I could feel sympathy for her had she killed in hot blood. But she planned the scene and brought her victim to the theatre to stage it. She also killed Fulke when she thought that he had recognised her . . .'

'Who knows,' intervened Master Topcliff, 'maybe he had recognised her. Didn't Will Painter say they had lived together before she took up with Bertrando? Painter implied that Fulke still loved her. Even when dying, perhaps for love, he could not name her outright but, for conscience sake, gave you the coded clue instead?'

'One thing this deed has also killed,' interrupted Master Burbage.

'We shall no more experiment with women as players. They bring too many dangers with them.'

Master Hardy Drew turned and smiled wanly at Master Topcliff.

'By your leave, good master, I'll get me to my bed. It has been a tiring exercise in drama.' He paused, smiled and added with mocking tone. 'The king's a beggar now, the play is done.'

DESDEMONA'S DAUGHTER

Edward D. Hoch

As we have seen, in Shakespeare's day all the acting parts were usually played by men, which was one of the reasons why Shakespeare's plays have so many women disguised as men. It was not until after the restoration of the monarchy in 1660 that actresses were allowed to perform in public. In this story Edward Hoch uses that as the basis for his whodunnit.

By 1660 the death of Oliver Cromwell two years earlier had left a void in English life that only a king could fill. Thirty-year-old Charles II returned from exile and the monarchy was restored. Cromwell's body was disinterred from Westminster Abbey and hanged as a traitor. Life in London changed almost overnight from Puritan strictness to the joyfulness of Charles's reception.

The theatres, closed from 1642 by the Civil War and Puritan condemnation, had been allowed to reopen on a limited basis in 1656, but it was not until 1660 that they became free of Puritan regulation. And on 8 December Ann Marshall was about to become the first woman ever to act on an English stage, appearing in Shakespeare's *Othello*.

'Desdemona!' her stage manager said, coming into the area that had been converted into a dressing room for Ann and the other actresses in the company. 'Who would have thought a woman would be playing Desdemona on an English stage?'

'Women perform on the stage in France and Italy. Why not here?' She was tall and dark-haired, with her mother's almond eyes. The women in their company owned shares just as the men did and one of them, Margaret Hughes, would soon take over the Desdemona role. But for tonight it was all Ann's. Her father had died five years earlier, and she regretted he hadn't lived to see this moment of her triumph.

It was then that a messenger entered. He held a thick letter with a red wax seal firmly attached to its back. 'This is for Ann Marshall.'

'Who is it from?' she asked, accepting the missive.

'A solicitor here in London. His instructions were to deliver it to you.'

He was gone in an instant, and as she broke the seal on the letter the stage manager departed too. 'The play begins in thirty minutes.'

'I don't come on until the third scene,' she reminded him. 'I'll be ready.' She was curious about the lengthy letter in her hands, and started to read it.

'My darling daughter' (it began), 'if you are reading this it will mean that my fondest dream has come true, that you are among the first actresses to perform on a stage in England. As I write this, in the spring of 1655, I know that my days are numbered. I have reached the grand old age of 65, when even Will Shakespeare lived only to be 52. Civil War and the tyranny of Cromwell have kept the theatres closed for most of your short lifetime, but I feel that will change soon. Until then, this letter will reside in the drawer of my solicitor, waiting the time when it can be delivered to you.

I want to tell you the truth of what happened during the theatre season of 1604, half a century ago, when a ghostly terror strode along the banks of the Thames one day. I was but a lad of fourteen playing the part of Desdemona in the master's newest play, *Othello*. I had been with the company for three years at that point, performing at the Globe in Bankside and travelling with my father on tours of the provinces. When we travelled, my mother remained in London with the rest of the family, which was the customary arrangement. At that age I longed for the companionship of young ladies, but life in the theatre was strictly a masculine pursuit. This had its advantages for a travelling company. The actors could all share one large room in the country inns where we stayed. And males were more likely to cope with the strenuous life on the road.

The winter theatre season in London usually began on St Stephen's day, 26 December, often with an indoor performance at the court of Queen Elizabeth. With her death in 1603 and the coronation of James I, many things changed. Shakespeare's acting company, known as the Lord Chamberlain's Men, became the King's Men. Since theatres had kept the traditional shape of the inn courtyard, even such a handsome one as the Globe had no roof over the pit to protect the groundlings from the elements. They stood during the performance, while the better classes sat on cushioned chairs in the galleries above, much as it remains today. With *Othello* as the opening production, a decision was made to begin the season of 1604 in November when the weather was a bit better. Because I was taller than the other boys in the company, I was chosen to play Desdemona.

Shakespeare himself often acted in his own plays. He rarely took the lead, though, and one of his favorite parts was the ghost of Hamlet's father. Perhaps it was this fondness for the supernatural that attracted a man like Horace Spade and brought about the terrible event of that day. Certainly there were many characters in his works with ties to the supernatural. *A Midsummer Night's Dream* had been performed often by 1604, and a year later he would create the weird sisters of *Macbeth* because of King James's scholarly interest in black magic. James had actually written a tract on demonology, which came to the attention of this man Spade.

Horace Spade was a necromancer given to the black arts who had alleged communication with demons and the dead. He had a few followers who like himself strode the banks of the Thames dressed all in black, hoping to communicate with devils. I have never forgotten my encounter with the man. It was just after the opening of *Othello* in November 1604. The company had first performed Will Shakespeare's newest tragedy in the old banqueting hall at Whitehall on All Saints' Day, and it opened soon after at the Globe. All performances took place by afternoon daylight, of course, with the theatres flag being raised to signal the start of the play. On this day after the performance I'd wandered up from the Globe to the nearby Thames to watch the sunset on the water. I noticed a man dressed all in black walking in the same direction but didn't realize he was coming to me until he spoke.

"You are the boy Sam Marshall who played the part of Desdemona in this afternoon's entertainment," he said, making it a statement rather than a question. I saw that he was a somber man with long hair and a mustache, wearing a wide-brimmed hat that cast a shadow over his face. He had a slender build but was taller than me by several inches, and as he towered over me I felt a passing fright.

"I am that, sir," I responded, holding my ground.

"Horace Spade is my name, and I am a dealer in demons."

"Yes, sir." I acted as if it was the most natural occupation in the world, akin to being a miller or fishmonger, though in truth his words filled me with a nameless terror.

"The woman you play, Desdemona, has *demon* in her very name. Little wonder that she comes to such a sorry end!"

"I never thought of that, sir."

"Well, I have. It is but another example of Will Shakespeare's fascination with the dark side."

He laid his hand upon my shoulder and I gave an involuntary shudder. "I must return to the theatre," I told him. "They are waiting for me."

"Are they, now?" His lips curled back into a sort of grin, showing a row of blackened teeth.

I broke away then, running as fast as I could back to the Globe. It was not until I had safely reached it that I dared to look back. Horace Spade was nowhere to be seen.

The following day Sarah Caudell, the woman who sewed our costumes, came by the theatre to see if any minor repair work was necessary. The men in the more vigorous roles would often split their seams when tussling, and since the costumes were very expensive they had to be kept in good condition.

As she worked I mentioned my encounter with Horace Spade. She was properly horrified. Her little eyes closed for an instant and she shook her head. "No, no! You must stay away from that bad man. He is a devil!"

"Why do you say that, Sarah?" I thought of her as a woman old enough to be my mother, though in truth she was still in her twenties.

She put down the sewing needle and reached out to take my hand. "There are more things in this world than a fourteen-year-old boy can imagine. Sometimes people like Horace Spade can see evil everywhere except within themselves."

Her words remained with me all through that day. When I had once more been smothered by Othello to the audible gasps of our audience, I waited backstage until the end of the play. After our bows I caught up with Ben Bull, the actor playing Iago, and asked him about Horace Spade.

"Has that man been coming around again?" he asked. The actor was anything but bull-like, his slender features giving the Iago character more the appearance of a rodent.

"Sarah doesn't like him."

"And with reason. He was rough on her."

"What do you mean, rough?"

"That's not for you to know, lad. Be gone, now."

The following afternoon's performance went well, though an autumn chill in the air caused both audience and actors to dress a bit warmer. Beneath Desdemona's nightgown I wore my shirt and breeches. Being killed by Othello every afternoon was both strenuous and tiring. I didn't wish to be cold as well. As our audience filed out I found Sarah Caudell patching a rip in one of the younger boys' breeches. His name was Todd and he played the part of Emilia, wife to Iago.

"Do you have something for sewing too?" Sarah asked me in her most severe manner.

"No, I am all of one piece today." I pulled the nightgown off over my head. "I want to go down by the river again to see the sun set. Do you wish to join me?"

"Oh, all right." She put away her sewing things and we went out the back door together.

Walking across the field, still muddy from a morning shower, I tried to tell myself that I hadn't asked her to join me simply because I feared another encounter with Horace Spade. Yet I knew that was part of the reason. I had been scared out of my wits by the earlier encounter, and now I was asking protection from Sarah Caudell, the mother-figure. She knew it, of course, and when we reached the river, dank and ugly at low tide, she asked casually, "Is this the place where Horace Spade appeared?"

"It is," I admitted, glancing about nervously.

"Do you think he might come after you again?"

"He believes I am some sort of demon because I take the part of Desdemona."

We began strolling as we talked, and soon she told me of her own experiences with the man in black. "I do not travel with the company outside London, of course. They manage their own sewing in the provinces. But here at the Globe, and the Rose, and the Swan, and the Fortune he has sought me out. He calls me an evil woman, Sam, but he is the evil one himself. He professes to dabble in the black arts, though this is only his excuse for molesting women and boys like yourself. He caught me one night outside the Swan and forced me to come with him to a nearby tavern. It was horrible!"

Suddenly I noticed a man ahead of us on the river path. Even at a distance I recognized Ben Bull. He seemed excited and waved when he saw us. "What is it?" I asked when we reached him. He was no longer the devious Iago but only a badly frightened actor.

"Don't go any further," he warned. "There's a body in the river!"

"A body?" Sarah repeated.

"I think it's Horace Spade."

We watched from a distance as Spade's bloated, black-clad body was pulled from the water. The cause of his death became immediately obvious when the man was rolled over to reveal a dagger plunged to its hilt into his back. As the body was taken away the news spread rapidly through the tightly-knit society of actors and theatre people. The murder weapon had been a dagger from the theatre itself, and all of us were under suspicion. By evening Horace Spade's murder was the talk of every tavern in London, but there was no sorrow in the news. It was as if the threat of a plague had been lifted from our lives.

I searched around for Master Shakespeare himself at the tavern, viewing this as an excuse to speak with the great man. He was standing near the fire with Burbage, our Othello, both wearing white ruffs around their necks like proper English gentlemen. They were close friends, and had built the Globe along with other investors. Seeing they could not be interrupted, I settled for James Rodgers who played Cassio. He was a handsome actor in his twenties, always striving to please women and attract their admiration. Shakespeare himself was said to have chosen him as Cassio.

"Well, good Marshall, I see you are breathing again after your latest smothering!" he greeted me.

"I was present along the river when Ben Bull found Spade's body," I told him with a touch of pride. It made me feel like a man, to have viewed death even at a distance.

"There was someone who deserved to die," he said in all seriousness. "He consorted with devils and dabbled in nameless vices." He seemed to remember something then. "The constable was here looking for you. Did you see him?"

"Constable?" I had a natural fear of all things legal, imagining somehow I might be separated from my father. His name was Robert, as you know, and he always supported my career on the stage. We were living at home with my mother during the winter season in London. As soon as my father finished playing the part of Roderigo, he usually departed for home, leaving me to come along when I wanted. Sometimes there would be a caution not to stay out much after dark, and I knew the dangers of the streets where ruffian gangs might set upon me. But I was only a mile from home once I'd walked across London Bridge.

I decided then that I should start for home since it was already dark. Leaving Rodgers at the tavern I set off in the direction of the bridge. But before I had covered a hundred yards I was accosted by a looming black shape who shone a lantern in my direction. "Is that you, Master Sam Marshall?"

"Who–?" I uttered in surprise.

"Constable Cleary here. I don't mean to frighten you."

"I'm on my way home."

The constable was a large man who wore a beaver hat with a badge of office on its front. "We are investigating the murder of Horace Spade this afternoon. I have questions to ask you."

"I didn't find him," I said quickly. "That was Ben Bull. Miss Caudell and I came along later."

"When the coroner examined the body he found something clutched in the dead man's hand. This!" He held up a damp and muddy piece of cloth, shining his lantern on it. At first I didn't realize what it was, but then I saw by its design that it was one of the pieces from our drama.

"It is the Egyptian handkerchief, spotted with strawberries, given to Othello's mother and thence to him! In our play Othello has presented it to me – to Desdemona – as a token of his love. When she accidentally loses it, the handkerchief falls into the hands of Iago. He puts it in Cassio's room, and for Othello it becomes proof of his wife's unfaithfulness."

"I am somewhat familiar with the plot of Shakespeare's latest effort," the constable replied, "but thank you for the summary." We walked toward the torchlit bridge as he spoke, and now I saw that the handkerchief had been torn, as if ripped from the killer's hand by the dying necromancer. "Are you the last one to have this in your possession during the play?"

"Far from it, sir! The handkerchief drops to the floor where it is retrieved by Iago's wife. She gives it to him and he in turn drops it in Cassio's chamber. Cassio gives it to his mistress Bianca who shows it in front of Othello, bringing about the final tragedy."

"It was never returned to Desdemona?"

"Never. But anyone might have taken it after the final curtain."

Constable Cleary nodded, deep in thought. "The evidence of the handkerchief points to some member of the King's Men as the murderer."

"I cannot believe that."

"You grant there is no other handkerchief like this one?"

"That is true. It was specially made, so the strawberry embroidery would be visible from the front of the audience. We must find something else for tomorrow's performance."

"Then the murder took place just after the play's end, shortly before Ben Bull sighted the body. It is a wonder none of the departing audience saw the fatal blow being struck."

"The sun sets early these days," I pointed out, "and it was already cloudy." But something was bothering me. Someone should have witnessed the crime, unless it happened before the performance ended. Unless—

I left Cleary and continued toward London Bridge. The tide was rising now and the river was running swiftly. Watching the glimmer of dark water I thought I saw a shape in the darkness, lit only by the distant torchlight from the bridge itself. There was sudden movement and he was upon me!

"It's time to settle scores!" he snarled, gripping me by the throat.

It was Horace Spade, the necromancer, returned from the dead to end my days on earth!

We struggled there in the darkness, on the edge of the great river. With that powerful hand locked around my throat I was unable to cry for help. I pictured myself doomed for all time, dragged down to the lowest pits of Hades by this creature of the undead.

Then, just as my strength was leaving me, there came a slender fury to the rescue. It was our seamstress, Sarah Caudell, who leaped upon Horace Spade's back and pried his fingers from my throat. He broke free and whirled to face his attacker, his face twisted into a Satanic grin. "The she-devil herself! We would make a pair, sweet Sarah!"

She picked up a loose stone from the bridge abutment and hurled it straight at Spade's head. Her aim was true. He gasped and staggered backward, then toppled over the bank and into the river. We watched his body twisting in the water until it was swept away by the night.

"You saved my life!" I told her. "He was going to kill me."

"He is a hard man to kill," she said, catching her breath. "We thought him dead this afternoon."

"We were mistaken, but let us get away from this place before other demons rise from the river."

Sarah hurried after me. "But how do you explain what happened? How could he return from the dead?"

"All in good time. I will feel safer if we talk in a tavern with others around us."

"You suspect that someone from the King's Men is involved in this?"

"Perhaps."

We crossed the bridge by torchlight and found shelter at the White Hart. Sarah ordered a pint of ale and gave me a taste. "Is he dead now?" she asked finally.

"As dead as he will ever be."

"But why not earlier?"

I licked the ale from my lips. "You and I were never really close to the body. We relied much on Ben Bull, who told us only that he thought it was Spade. The corpse was dressed in the necromancer's familiar black garb, but I remember thinking he appeared bloated from his time in the water. This was clearly impossible. He clutched the strawberry handkerchief which is a key costume piece in our drama. It had been used during this afternoon's performance. The man in black had been dead only minutes when Ben Bull found him. The body was not bloated but merely overweight, and that meant it wasn't Horace Spade at all."

"Then who was it?"

"We know some of Spade's followers wore black as he did. I believe this was one of them, perhaps sent by Spade to cast a spell on us. Spade had threatened me the day before yesterday, so it was natural for someone seeing the man in black on the river path to suppose that the necromancer had returned."

Sarah sipped her ale. "You're a smart lad."

"Somehow Spade blamed me for his friend's death, which is why he tried to choke me just now.'

"Who do you think did it? One of the company? Ben Bull or Rodgers? Certainly not Burbage or Shakespeare."

"No."

Her eyes widened. "Of course! It was Horace Spade himself who stabbed his friend! Why didn't I think of it before?"

"If Spade had done it, he'd have taken advantage of the mistaken identification and laid low for a time, perhaps even left London. Besides, how could he have gotten hold of that handkerchief without entering the theatre and coming backstage for it?"

"Then it was one of the company?"

I shook my head, suddenly wiser than my years. "They all had to remain backstage. The entire cast appears at the end to take their bows. The killer was someone with access to the backstage area, yet who was free to leave before the performance concluded. Someone with a motive for killing Spade and the opportunity to take the dagger from the theater's properties. Most important, someone who might logically be in possession of a torn handkerchief used in the play."

"You have described me!" she said with astonishment.

"Exactly, Sarah. On this day you murdered Horace Spade twice."

She was silent for some moments before she spoke again. "You are only a lad of fourteen, thrust into an adult world. What do you know of such things?"

"Ben Bull told me Spade had been rough on you."

"He once attacked me, and at your age you cannot know the

shame and fear such an act brings to a woman. I took a dagger from the weapons box backstage and started carrying it 'neath my skirts. I swore that it would never happen to me again. You told me he'd accosted you yesterday and I feared the devil might try to have his way with you. Just before the performance ended I went outside and thought I saw him walking along the bank. The black suit and the failing light fooled me, along with my own hunger for revenge. I went up behind him and stabbed him in the back, watching as he toppled into the shallow water. Then I quickly returned to the theatre, mending Todd's torn breeches to divert suspicion from myself."

"And the handkerchief?"

"It ripped during the performance. I noticed the tear and took it to sew. It was protruding from my pocket when I stabbed him, and he grabbed for me, dying with it clutched in his hand."

We sat together sombrely for some time before she finally asked, "Will you tell this to the constable?"

"No," I decided. "Horace Spade was a man who deserved to die. Perhaps your first victim, his follower, deserved it too. Certainly you saved my life tonight, and I am eternally grateful for that."

When the company left London to tour the provinces in the spring, Sarah Caudell stayed behind. I never saw her again.'

Ann Marshall finished the letter's final endearments and put it down. It was a story her father had wanted to tell, all these years, and had finally done so after his death. Why he'd waited so long was something she'd never know. At least there was this bond between them, between herself and the fourteen-year-old boy who'd played the part of Desdemona in the first production of *Othello*.

She was, in a very real sense, Desdemona's daughter.

Then they were calling her on stage, and she walked out from the wings with a firm stride and spoke her opening lines. 'My noble father, I do perceive here a divided duty . . .'

CONSPIRACY THEORY

Tina and Tony Rath

Like Arden of Feversham, A Yorkshire Tragedy *was based on a genuine murder committed in April 1605 when Walter Calverley was alleged to have killed two of his three sons and seriously wounded his wife. Calverley refused to plead and was executed that August. The murder caused a sensation and it is likely that the play was composed during that summer of 1605. The play is generally ascribed to Thomas Middleton, though it is possible that George Wilkins also had a hand in it, whilst some scholars have connected it to Shakespeare. In the following story, Shakespeare along with Ben Jonson and other fellows, undertakes a stirring reconstruction of the murder in an attempt to find out whodunnit.*

Scene: The Mermaid Tavern. Don't be misled by that word tavern. It's not the kind of establishment you might have expected, full of singing roisterers and improbably upholstered serving wenches. Indeed, to address Moll, Meg, Marion or Margery, the girls who wait on customers here, as a 'wench' would be asking for a black eye and a suggestion that you should take your custom to The Boar's Head in East Cheap where they're not so fussy about that kind of thing. It's afternoon, anyway, and fairly quiet.

Three men are sitting in a private booth. They are not really here to drink, though they have cups of wine in front of them. Two of them use this place more as an office than a drinking haunt. Their table is covered with papers, and they have been discussing business, but now that discussion has turned, somehow, into a murder investigation.

The papers on the table are plays, plays printed, plays in manuscript, and prompt copies with scrawls all over them, showing that they have been used in production; plays being the business of two of this trio. And there is also a pamphlet which advertises itself as being the story of 'Two most unnaturall and bloodie Murthers: the one' (which is the subject under discussion) 'by Maister Cauerley, A Yorkeshire Gentleman, practised upon his wife, and committed uppon his two Children, the three and twentieth of April 1605.' That year may mean something to you. It may not. At present, to our three tavern-detectives, it means nothing at all.

'You see,' says the youngest of the three, a Yorkshireman, with, as it happens no theatrical connections, apart from his acquaintanceship with the other two. He has local knowledge of the events in the pamphlet, though, and he has been co-opted into a discussion about producing an improved version of a play based on those events, a play at present called *A Yorkshire Tragedy, Not so New as Lamentable and true*. It is that truth that the young man is not at all sure of, and even if true in general it is certainly not accurate: 'they didn't even get the name right. It's Calverley. Walter Calverley. Of course, they don't use the name at all in the play.'

'No. They just call the protagonists Wife and Husband. And then there's a Maid and a "lusty servant",' says one. 'But it's very plain who they're talking about.'

'The Calverleys are an old family,' says the other.

'An old recusant family,' says the young man.

'Ah.' And they all understand that perfectly, for they are all Grammar school boys in a time when the only grammar worthy of the name is Latin, they can all conjugate the Latin verb *recuso*, I refuse. Refuse, in this case, to attend the services of the new reformed church. The Calverleys can hardly be called an old Catholic family in a country where every family was, until recently, Catholic, but they have continued to be Catholic even under the penal laws designed to discourage that religion.

All three men know this well. One is a militant young Catholic, another was, for a while, a Catholic convert, (he will have carved on his gravestone a Catholic petition for prayers for the dead: *Orate Ben Jonson*, though so ambiguously that later generations will mistake it for a most graceful epitaph – 'O rare Ben Jonson,'), while the third has remained a Catholic almost absent-mindedly. You would say that he has hardly noticed the Protestant Reformation. Besides, he is protected. He belongs to a company of players with a noble patron, and no one would wish to see him hang at Tyburn for his religion. But ah, what a last dying speech Will Shakespeare would make to the crowd!

'What exactly happened?' he asks the young man.

'Oh, it's all there!' he flips over the pages of the pamphlet contemptuously. 'Walter Calverley was a gamester and a womaniser – supposedly. He wasted his estate, then demanded that his wife sell her dowry to get him more money for his pleasures. She went to London to see her relatives to arrange it, but instead they offered to find him a place at Court, with an income attached. When she told him this he went mad – literally. He stabbed his eldest son to death, attacked and mortally wounded the second boy, threw the maid down the stairs when she tried to defend him, and then, when his wife caught up the child, stabbed him in her arms, and struck at her three or four times. He thought she was dead, but her whalebone bodice saved her from the worst injuries. One of his servants tried to stop him, but Calverley fought him off – injured him quite badly by kicking him with his spurred boots, according to the story – and then he rode away like fury, with the alleged intention of killing his youngest son as well. The child wasn't in the house at the time because it was quite a young baby, still with its wet-nurse. Calverley never got there, because Providence arranged for him to fall off his horse and he was arrested.'

They have been listening carefully, picking the meaning out of his strongly accented speech and they have to think for a moment before Will says: 'But the pamphlet stops there. And so does Middleton's poor scrap of a play.'

'Scrap indeed!' says Jonson. He quotes: '"Murder his wife, his servants, and who not? For that man's dark where heaven is quite forgot?" Middleton should be writing mottoes for ale house tapestries! A Yorkshire Tragedy indeed!'

'A most vile phrase,' Shakespeare agrees, absent-mindedly. 'But what did happen after the murders. Did anything new come out at the trial?'

'There was no trial. He refused to plead.'

'Stood mute,' murmurs Will who collects words and phrases like a magpie. He particularly likes technical terms from other people's trades and professions.

'So,' says Ben, robustly. 'They pressed him, did they?'

He means the death called *peine forte et dure* (a strong and hard punishment which it most certainly is). If you refuse to plead, the law says you must be stretched out upon the floor, and loaded with increasingly heavy weights, until you either die, or change your mind about pleading.

'Yes. There's a story that he asked the bystanders to jump on his chest as they were laying on the weights, to finish him off quickly. He's supposed to have shouted: "Them that love Sir Walter, loup on, loup on!"'

Shakespeare winces, and signals to Marjorie for more wine. 'And a mutton pasty or two if you've got any ready,' he adds.

'Oh, yes, Master Will, we've got some lovely and hot,' she says. The girls like Shakespeare. He talks to them, and listens to them too, which is unusual even amongst the more polite clientele of the Mermaid. He sometimes writes the things they say down in his commonplace book too so some people take him for a government spy. But none of the girls believe this. Nor do they believe that he puts their words into his plays, although that happens to be true.

'Why d'you think he did that?' Ben Jonson is asking.

'To keep his estate in his family,' says the young man. 'If he'd been tried and convicted of murder it would have been forfeited to the Crown. It should have been forfeited years ago, of course, because of their religion, but the Calverleys were wheeler-dealers in a small way, and they'd managed to hang on to most of it.'

'So he volunteered for a long and painful death to make sure his wife and surviving child kept an estate that he'd wanted to sell only weeks before,' Shakespeare says, reflectively.

The young man nods. 'And what's more his wife, who's supposed to have seen him kill her little boy in her arms, and then try to kill her, petitioned for his pardon.'

The pasties arrive. Shakespeare gathers the papers up and stacks them neatly at the edge of the table to make some room.

'They've got some apple and a bit of cinnamon in them, Master Will, to give a relish to the mutton,' says Moll. 'Don't let them get cold now.'

She knows men. They'll talk and talk, and let good food go to waste unless someone reminds them not to. And sure enough, they're sitting now, staring at each other, ignoring the lovely pasties. She leans over and cuts one in half and the smell of cinammon and savoury mutton does what her words could not, and the men do begin to eat. But they hardly seem to know what they're eating.

'Did he say anything at all – when he was arrested?' Ben Jonson asks through a mouthful of mutton. He's been arrested himself and he knows the drill.

'They say he admitted the murders and said he'd done it because he knew the boys weren't his, and he was afraid of his wife.'

'What?' says Shakespeare.

'His actual words were,' the young man takes out his commonplace book, and consults it, '"he hath had an intention to kill them for the whole space of two years past . . . the said children were not by him begotten and that he found himself to be in danger of life sundry times by his wife".'

'Was there any gossip about her – any suggestion that his accusations might have been true? Could she have been a wanton who desired her husband out of the way?' Shakespeare asks. 'She might have tried to get him pardoned because she felt she'd driven him to murder.'

The young man shakes his head impatiently. 'She had travelled down to London to persuade her relatives to sell her dowry, simply because he'd asked her to. That sounds like a concerned and loving wife to me. And there was no gossip.'

'They had a young unweaned baby, you say, so this talk of a two year estrangement is nonsense, too. Jealousy is a kind of madness,' Shakespeare, who has created a whole gallery of jealous husbands, says thoughtfully. 'And there was talk of madness in that family.' He knows something about the Calverleys, although he comes from a different part of the country. There is a network of recusants all over England. Priests, outlawed, and hunted as they are, travel between them to bring them the Mass and the Sacraments. They also bring news and, human nature being what it is, gossip.

'His grandfather, old Sir Walter, tried to get his son William – that's our Sir Walter's father – they're all either Walter or William, it can get a bit confusing – out of the Marshalsea gaol by claiming that he was mad, but that means nothing,' the young man lowers his voice, and glances over his shoulder, a gesture so habitual in this kind of conversation that no one else notices, 'your own father said he couldn't go to church on Sunday because he was afraid of being arrested for debt.'

Shakespeare smiles. His father is comfortably off and anyway you can't be arrested for debt on a Sunday, but none of his fellow town councillors is ungentlemanly enough to query this explanation for not attending the new reformed service. Perhaps old Sir Walter wanted his son at home and thought that a madman was more likely to be released into the community than a professed Catholic. Perhaps he was right.

'So what do you say did happen?' Ben Jonson demands. 'The children actually are dead, and the wife half killed – no one's contesting that, are they?'

'The children were murdered and the wife wounded all right, but I don't believe Calverley did it,' says the young man stubbornly. 'It's not as if it's the first time. Look at all those lies they told about Clitherow's wife. She was arrested for harbouring priests, and they spread all kinds of filthy stories about her. They even claimed she'd killed herself in prison, when she'd refused to plead, like Calverley. Probably she wanted to stop her children being brought into court to swear her life away. Anyway, she was pressed to death too. Like Calverley.'

'I remember,' Shakespeare puts down his pasty. 'Unlike Calverley, she was pregnant.'

There is a brief silence while they think about this. The youngest man, the only one with no children, that he knows of, is the first to recover.

'So you see –' he says, 'they don't care what lies they tell about us.'

Jonson shifts uneasily at that word 'us'. Shakespeare sips some wine. 'But how, but how? The tale seems plain enough. Now how would I do it, if I were to write a whole new play – a better piece than this one of Middleton's perhaps. Cunning images of wax devised to make witnesses think they saw the dead children's bodies and the children themselves spirited away? Sir Walter's mad twin, kept hidden in the attics, who escapes – or is let out – to wreak havoc – the murders done by the Devil in Calverley's shape – no, baby tales all,' he says dismissing these solutions as soon as he voices them. Jonson, who has written a play about the Devil taking on human form, bristles a little, and Shakespeare smiles. 'Well – let's see how he did it,' he says abruptly. 'Where does Middleton set this scene? In the upper gallery isn't it, so the Husband can throw the maid down the stairs?'

'The upper gallery?' says the young man. 'What's that?'

'Theatrical jargon,' says Jonson, loftily getting his own back for that slight to his plot, 'theatres are built like inn yards where the first plays were performed: you have your platform which is the stage, and above that a gallery where the musicians sit, and sometimes scenes are played. It can be hidden by a curtain, which can be drawn back, so players are seen sitting, or lying in bed or whatever. Discovered, we call it.'

'In theatrical jargon,' says Shakespeare. The two men smile, silently agreeing to take the contest as a draw, although technically Jonson is one down to Shakespeare.

Will raises his voice, and calls for the Host.

That gentleman, who has been gossiping with some of his regulars, discreetly paying no attention to the three in the booth, comes over instantly. 'Yes sir. What's your pleasure, sir? What d'you lack?'

'A staircase, and a couple of your people,' says Will. 'Moll and Marian would be excellent – and one of your pot-boys – Ned if you can spare him. He makes a rare player and I want to act out a scene.'

This is precisely what the Host is afraid of. He lives in daily expectation of discovering that neat-fingered Ned, one of the few lads who can weave between the evening crowd with a trayful of brimming tankards without any fear of accident, has run off to join the players. Rather than encourage Ned he offers clumsy Francis instead, a substitution which is good-naturedly accepted.

The three men, and a straggle of onlookers move to the main staircase. Jonson brings the play-book and the pamphlet. The Host follows, nervously moving anything breakable out of the way. Master Will has tried directing troublesome scenes from work in progress here before.

Jonson reads from the play-book:

'Enter a maid with a child in her arms, the mother by her asleep.'

'Sleepwalking?' asks the young man, puzzled.

'No, no, it means someone pulls back a curtain, and the audience see the mother asleep, with the maid attending to the child,' says Jonson.

'They are discovered,' says the young man.

'Right, right,' says Shakespeare, pleased to see someone else taking an interest in technical terms. 'But we have no curtain, so that we must leave to the imagination of our spectators.'

'Think, when we talk of curtains, that you see them,' says Jonson, but Shakespeare is absorbed in directing his small scene to notice.

Marian, rather inclined to giggle, is arranged over two chairs, as if asleep, and Moll stands beside her, gripping a cushion wrapped in a shawl as if she suspects it of harbouring plans to escape ('It's a baby. Dandle it,' Mr Shakespeare tells her absent mindedly, and she obediently gives it a few sharp shakes every so often.)

'It was a toddler, rather than a baby,' says the young man. Shakespeare scans the audience swiftly, sees no child small enough to take the part, and decides to stay with the cushion.

'What time is this?' says Jonson. 'Late at night?'

'No, it was daytime,' the young man tells him.

'The lady might well have been asleep by day. Melancholy makes for deep and most unrefreshing sleeps, as I have observed. And early wakenings, too. And she was a lady with a great cause for melancholy, if all is true,' says Shakespeare thoughtfully.

'What must I do, sir?' Francis asks, unhappily.

'Ah – give him a dagger, someone,' says Shakespeare.

The Host, wisely, supplies a length of broom handle.

'Now, you run up the stairs, and try to snatch the child from the maid,' he sees Francis is looking bewildered, and explains, kindly, 'try to take the cushion away from Moll and throw her down the stairs when she resists—'

'Carefully,' the Host interjects.

'Look,' says Shakespeare, who has been an actor for as long as he has been a playwright, 'it's quite easy to fall without hurting yourself.'

He demonstrates, rolling down the stairs to the horrified delight of all the bystanders.

'Don't you try it, Moll,' says the Host, somewhere between advice and an order. He doesn't want one of his girls off with a broken ankle.

'It'd take more than he to throw me over the stairs,' says stout Moll.

'Try anyway, Francis,' Shakespeare says, absently, getting up, and putting his doublet to rights.

'Whore, give me that boy!' Jonson quotes helpfully.

Francis shambles gamely up the stairs, waving his broom handle. 'Whore – begging your pardon, Moll, I'm sure – give me that boy!'

'O help, help! Out alas, murder, murder!' prompts Jonson, but Moll does not waste her breath on words. She lets out a volley of screeches which brings Marian leaping from her couch to take the child from her arms, allowing Moll to wrench the broomstick from Francis's hands to hit him about the head and shoulders with it. This drives him back until he loses his footing and rolls down the stairs, sustaining rather more damage than Shakespeare.

'Call me whore, will you?' says Moll, dusting her hands.

Two or three of the audience lift Francis to his feet and brush him down. Someone gives him a draught of ale. They all urge him to have another go.

'They do say that madmen have exceptional strength,' says Shakespeare. 'So perhaps he would have had better success than our Francis. But I do wonder that no one heard the screams. What now, Ben?'

He consults the pamphlet and announces: 'Her fellow servants find the maid at the bottom of the steps, and think she's fallen down by accident, because she's been knocked out by the fall, so she can't tell them anything about it.'

'But she told her story later?' Shakespeare asks sharply.

The young man and Ben Jonson exchange glances. They understand his point without having to say anything. They've both served as soldiers in the Low Countries, where getting knocked on the head is a way of life (and quite frequently, of course, of death too). And they know the effect that a knock-out blow has on the memory.

'Apparently. But at first they didn't know what was wrong –' says the young man.

'And hadn't heard any screams,' Shakespeare repeats.

'Perhaps the girl was too surprised and scared to scream –' Jonson suggests.

'But the child must surely have cried out when his father attacked him? In pain, if not in fear?'

'Unless he was killed at once,' suggests a voice from the audience.

'But he wasn't. It was the child staggering down the stairs, bleeding from a mortal wound, that made the servants realise that something worse than a clumsy girl falling down the stairs was going on,' says Jonson, consulting the pamphlet again.

'And what about the wife, who was, according to the story, trying to fight off her mad husband, who was bent on murdering her and her baby – why was she doing it in perfect silence?' Shakespeare asks.

'I'm sure I shruck loud enough,' says Marion.

'And so did I,' says Moll.

'So you did,' says Shakespeare, 'and quite right too. Well, the child has staggered down the stairs –' Moll hurls the cushion to the foot of the stairs, and gets a round of applause – 'what happens now, Ben?'

'A lusty servant goes up to see what's happening.'

Shakespeare darts up the stair, taking on the part of the lusty servant. Finding himself face to face with Moll, he shakes his head impatiently.

'Moll, down the stairs with you. Francis, you come back here.'

Francis and Moll hurriedly change places. Moll flops down at the foot of the stairs.

'Good. Marian, you've been stabbed, so you're down too –' she drops obediently. 'And I come face to face with you, Francis, with your bloody dagger –' he starts back with a look of horror and surprise: 'O, sir, what deeds are these?'

'Base slave, my vassal! Comest thou between my fury to question me?' reads Jonson.

'Base slave –' Francis intones nervously.

'No! No!' says Shakespeare. 'Like this: "Base slave, my vassal!"' he thunders – and then stops. 'Give me the dagger!' Francis hands it over willingly enough. 'So. Handy dandy. Which the butcher, which the butchered?'

Jonson and his young companion stare up at Shakespeare. 'Base slave, what dost thou with my children dear?' Will shouts, hurling himself at Francis, who, hopelessly taken aback, falls backwards down the stairs again, into the helping hands of the audience. There is some laughter, but it dies away when Shakespeare, with a stricken face, drops to his knees beside the fallen Marian.

'Oh speak my love – oh grant me but one word,' he murmurs.

Marian, caught up in the spirit of the scene, raises herself on one elbow, essays a slight dying moan and flops back.

> *'What, all my pretty chickens and their dam*
> *At one fell swoop? I have no time to rave*
> *There's yet one left and him I'll die to save'*

says Will, and, waving his dagger over his head, he leaps to his feet and rushes off down the stairs. There is a patter of applause, and several people remark how surprising it is that that quiet Mr Shakespeare can act a bloody murderer to the life, so natural as you'd ever wish to see, while Ben Jonson, who is a murderer (killed his man in a duel, besides his service as a soldier), can't do it at all.

'Will that be all, Master Shakespeare?' the Host asks hopefully.

'Yes, I think so. No, stay, there is one thing. Has your wife a whalebone bodice?'

'No, Master Shakespeare, that she has not,' he exclaims, slightly shocked that Master Shakespeare should think his wife might forget herself so far as to wear or even own a garment so far above her station. Buckram and wood are the proper stiffening for a decent woman's stays. He adds, so that Master Shakespeare won't think she is short of clothes: 'She has a very good bodice, in flame coloured velvet, stiffened with buckram, for holidays, but I don't think she'd want to lend it –' he glances at Moll, who has been joined by Marion now at the foot of the stairs. And besides, he thinks rather proudly, it wouldn't fit either of them.

'No, no, of course not. Just a thought of mine. Let Francis bring us some more wine if you will – and –' he slips a coin to Moll, and another to Marian. 'Very prettily done, my dears. I could wish some of our players were as able.'

They blush, more pleased with the compliment than with the coin. Shakespeare wonders what it would be like if his Rosalind, for instance, were played by a young woman, instead of a boy actor. A girl pretending to be a boy, played by a real girl? Interesting, surely . . . too interesting perhaps. They'd never get away with a girl in breeches, and more's the pity . . . he thinks, pleasurably, about girls in breeches, and loose lawn shirts for a moment . . . but he is brought back to the matter in hand by his companions as they return to their booth.

'The serving man killed them,' says the young man. 'I saw it as soon as you changed places with Francis.'

'But how – a household conspiracy?' says Jonson.

'No need,' says Shakespeare. He takes a long swallow of wine. 'Say the servant was a government agent.'

The young man nods vigorously. He can believe that. He wants to believe it.

'They either put him into Calverley's household, or turned one of Calverley's own servants using bribery or blackmail, or even patriotic arguments—'

'Oh, yes. I expect they told him that we're plotting to bring the Spanish Inquisition over here and burn all the good Englishmen—'

'And rape good Englishwomen,' says Jonson.

'That goes without saying,' the young man agrees.

'Well, however they did it, they got an agent in the Calverley household. And he, probably, got himself an accomplice by an old and well-tried method.'

The others look blank and Shakespeare explains: 'The maid. She had to be in it. He probably seduced her, or promised to marry her. Or again, used bribery or blackmail. He must have been powerfully persuasive, whatever methods he used, because I think it was she that killed the two little boys.'

'Would a woman do that? Whatever the persuasion?' says Jonson.

'Do you know, I think she might. A servant, always at someone else's beck and call, waiting on another woman and her children – who knows what resentments might build up? If the children were spoiled, and the wife sullen, as all must be sometimes, especially after childbirth. Perhaps all he did was put a match to a powder-train.'

'Why did she have to kill them?' says the young man. He hasn't bargained for a woman.

'Because,' Shakespeare says, 'there were no screams.'

There is a small pause, and then Jonson says: 'Ah! I see.'

'I don't,' says the young man, rather sullenly.

'This whole scenario, of the child torn first from the maid, then from the wife, and stabbed just doesn't work,' said Shakespeare, 'we've just seen that it doesn't. The screams would have brought the whole household up those stairs. The children were attacked silently, perhaps while they were asleep. Indeed, I hope they were asleep. But she bungled it. Calverley walked in and found her about it. Perhaps he really did throw her down the stairs. Who can blame him? The dying child staggers after her, the wife wakes, and doesn't know what's happening for a moment or so, but the servant, below stairs does. He runs up to finish the job. I think both Calverley and his wife were supposed to die. Probably the maid was going to pretend to find the children dead, and make an outcry that Calverley had killed them and his wife. The servant was to dash upstairs and finish the job. They would probably have put it about that Calverley killed himself.'

'So the servant tries to retrieve the situation. He stabs the wife –' says the young man.

'But he doesn't know – as her husband would have known – that she's wearing whalebone stays, so he does less damage than he thinks. And he doesn't have time to finish her off because Sir Walter goes for him and gives him a good kicking. Now, his wife is covered with blood, and, as far as he can see, dead or dying. The two boys are dead. He knows or guesses that this attack has been planned to wipe out his whole family, so he rides off in desperation to try to save the youngest. Save. Not kill. And he did, in some sort, save him, because no one could claim that his father murdered him when he was arrested before he ever got to him.'

'So why doesn't the wife tell the authorities the truth?'

'Perhaps she does. But someone tells her to keep quiet if she wants to see her remaining son grow up to inherit his father's estate. And if she wants to live herself. Perhaps she consulted with her husband in prison, and he told her to keep quiet. After all, he was willing to endure a ghastly death to keep the estate in the family. All she can do is petition for pardon. Which isn't forthcoming.'

'But why, that's what I want to know,' says Jonson. 'Why should the government take against Walter Calverley?'

'Religion,' says the young man. 'The Calverleys were just too good at wheeling and dealing, and keeping their property without compromising their faith. I expect they annoyed someone. You know what this government's like. Rotten to the core.'

This time it is Ben Jonson who glances over his shoulder. He is not personally anxious for another spell in the Fleet prison.

But the young man continues relentlessly: 'They wanted to wipe out the Calverley family because they were Catholic and because they were clever. When Walter fought back they turned the whole thing round and used it as a splendid piece of propaganda against Catholics in general and the Calverleys in particular. Now they've got that, they probably don't care if the estate stays with the youngest child.'

'A dirty business,' says Shakespeare.

He may mean politics in general, or religious persecution, or something else entirely. Ben Jonson brings everyone back to the matter in hand.

'So will you be turning this Yorkshire Tragedy into a kind of domestic Macbeth?'

'Oh – I think not,' Shakespeare fills his cup again. 'It's not really my style.'

'Pity to waste the work you've already done.'

'Why not do it, Will, but give them the truth?' the young man demands. 'Tell them what this government did. What it does every day.'

The two older men – wiser in the ways of the world or simply more cowardly – exchange glances. 'Because I don't think anyone would produce it –' Will begins, but Ben Jonson, waving the remnants of Will's pasty which he has thriftily decided to finish, and scattering gravy over the pamphlet, protests:

'But after all, is it the truth? I mean, I know Will's made out a good story, but we still don't know for certain. I mean, would the government go to those lengths—'

'Oh, I think there's no doubt that they would,' Shakespeare picks up his wine cup and peers into the depths, as if into a dark crystal. He sighs. 'Who knows what sort of conspiracies they're hatching even now, eh Guido?'

THE NAME-CATCHER'S TALE

John T. Aquino

To say anything about the following story would be to say too much. You will find that it follows on very neatly from the previous one, though we see Shakespeare in an entirely different light . . .

In spite of what the song says, old soldiers do indeed die – it just takes so long.

If you are an old soldier, like me, you have three choices: to deliberately die by drink or blade; to wage old battles in the mind until canker death takes the field and the prize; or to serve new masters. I, who fought the Spanish papists in Flanders, thought that I was fortunate to find the third choice in the person of Salisbury.

My name is Henry Bagnet. After my arm was shattered by a Spanish charge, Robert Cecil, baron of Estendon, lately first Earl of Salisbury, and King James's favourite, took pity on a fellow cripple and gave me employment as – well, his man. Twisted at birth and close to dwarfness, Salisbury said that he needed an investigator at his beck and call. 'You can be my strength, my sword, my eyes,' he said, looking up at me.

The duties were rudimentary at first – watching the Earls of Northumberland and Oxford to see if they did anything to tip the king's tolerance of their Catholic recusancy; submitting reports on

Lord So-and-So, who had dined with a woman who had a sister who married a man who had lived in Catholic Spain; and attending the theatre a great deal, since Salisbury insisted that playhouses were where people met to become inspired in intrigue and treason. I actually became an eager theatre-goer, revelling in the language that sharpened my mind, and experiencing the reality of unreality. I saw men cry real tears at made-up words.

But my duties and the atmosphere about them changed in October in the year of Our Lord sixteen hundred and five. It was then that drink or death seemed the better choice. Both are what they seem to be.

I was asleep at around midnight when three of Salisbury's servants roused me and took me, still dressing, to him. He was always seated when I saw him and never smiled, although he often said something like, 'Good to see you' or 'I hope you are well.' This time, he was writing, brusquely bade me sit, and, eyes on his work, shoved a written sheet toward me with his shrivelled hand. The paper was not signed, and I could barely make sense of it, but it was a warning to someone not to come to Parliament. One sentence stood out, 'They shall receive a powerful blow, this parliament, and yet they shall not see who hurts them.'

'What do you make of it?' Salisbury barked at me, obviously not willing to have me ask where it came from and how he received it.

'A powerful blow to Parliament that no one sees. A man usually sees his opponent. But in the service, one says of a dead man who has been struck by cannon fire, "He never knew what hit him." You do not know what hits you if someone blows you up with explosives. "Blow" must mean "blow up." Now, unless an enemy floats some form of cannon boats on the Thames, there will be some other kind of explosion that hurts Parliament.'

He listened silently with his narrow, blue, almond eyes staring inward. Finally, he muttered, 'You know how to play with words, Bagnet.'

'Not I my lord. But I can catch the meaning of those who do.'

'No matter.' He turned away and gestured with the slightest nod of his head to the men who had brought me. They gave me gold and brought me back to bed. I knew enough not to talk about it and simply thought from his dismissal that the letter was one of many such threats that came his way.

A week passed, and again I was awakened, just before dawn on the fourth of November by the same two men. This time they smiled, almost apologetically, and held my cloak as I put it on. The reason for their embarrassment became clear as we walked from my house in St Andrews to the long cold stones of Westminster Palace, and then continued trudging past closed shops, empty taverns, and shuttered lodgings, to Parliament Place. We finally stopped at a tiny dwelling that was at a right angle to the House of Lords. In centuries past, it may once have been a place where nobles disrobed and robed for palace ceremonies, but now it was obviously being used as a store room. When I started to upbraid my two warders for bringing me to look at barrels, I noticed that standing nearby in the shop shadows were Thomas Howard, Lord Chamberlain and Earl of Suffolk, Baron William Parker Monteagle, and a third man whom I did not know (but who later turned out to own the house).

'I am Bagnet—' I started to say to the earl.

'So you are the "name catcher," the man who figured out what "blow" meant, although I must tell you the king has decided that he had the sudden illumination himself. As a result, he will not shower you with gratitude for saving his life because – well, he feels he saved himself. But, others will reward you, have no fear.' His talk of my personal reward seemed to make him aware that we were not alone. He waved his hand toward Monteagle and said, by way of introduction, 'It was Monteagle here who received the warning, although he does not know why. What do you make of this?' he gestured to the room, which was filled with billets and barrels.

'What have you found? Something to cause a blow?'

'We have no warrant. But the king has asked us to search the area, for fear that there is a papist plot. The king convenes Parliament tomorrow, and he fears the papists—'

Suffolk started to lecture me about the history of recusancy, those who practise the old faith, the Catholic faith, in secret to avoid the arm of the law, and the real fear that they were plotting to install the old religion and its pope in place of England's church. There were rumours of secret trips between the Midlands, where they were very strong, and Flanders, where Hugh Owens and William Stanley, who headed the papist contingent in England, hid. Papist schoolteachers from Warwick to Penton were said to poison the minds of young boys and send them across the channel to Douai where they trained to be priests.

But my mind had moved away to a dark and cloaked figure standing in the shadows a few houses down, who came into my sight almost on cue. I also had a glimpse of a second man. By the time I reached them, there was only one – a tall bloke with reddish beard and moustache. 'Whom do you serve?' Suffolk asked, coming behind me.

'Thomas Percy.'

Suffolk nodded in recognition. 'Papist,' he whispered as if by reflex. 'And the room—'

'His.'

I started to take red beard by the arm to escort him away when Suffolk said, 'Let him go. We must first to the king.'

I pushed my face to Suffolk's and said what anyone would know. 'If you let him go, he will be gone.'

Suffolk matched my glare. 'We'll to the king.'

I spent the day dozing outside of Salisbury's chambers while he met with King James at Whitehall. At times, I was roused by the cheers and shouts of a performance of *Henry V* at the Globe across the river and thought how I would much rather have been there, although I had seen the play twice. It was not until midnight that we were authorized to return to the dwelling at Parliament Place. And – red beard was still there! In the same place. He was arrested at once, the dwelling searched by warrant, and the barrels were found to contain gunpowder, enough to blow up the king and Parliament.

The Lord Chamberlain had questioned him and let him go. And yet red beard had stayed – almost as if waiting to be caught.

In the upcoming days, we agents of Salisbury scurried around like rats with a purpose. Parliament had been convened and briefed by the king on the plot. Red beard was identified as a Guido Fawkes, who had served in the Spanish army in Flanders – we actually might have faced one another in battle. He had gone by the name of Johnson, Percy's servant, in order to rent the house so close to the site of their planned blow. It was rumoured that he had a mining background, and that he had been brought from Flanders by Owens and Stanley to dig a mine under Parliament and blow it up.

The king and queen and all who make the law would have been dead if the plot had succeeded. The king's surviving family were to have been kidnapped and made puppet rulers. Those, like myself, who had mostly tolerated papists as misguided now saw them as makers of treason and terror. Their hope of having their religion recognized, to have a new king fulfill his reported promise to do so, was now as dead as the king would have been.

I cannot describe the mindless horror of that time, when all that was treasured was deemed at risk and, as a result, values were sent out of sight for a while.

By king's order, the ban on torture was lifted for this Fawkes, and within a few days, names began to drift out in addition to Percy's – Robert Catesby, Percy's cousin; Christopher and John Wright; the brothers Wintour; Ambrose Rookwood. All had Catholic roots or connections. All had fled when Suffolk and I first discovered Fawkes. All were being pursued. There was also a watch on Henry Percy, the Earl of Northumberland, a known Catholic sympathizer, and, not coincidentally, Salisbury's chief rival.

I sensed that, having been so close to the situation at the beginning, I was being given menial assignments, so that I would not appear favoured. I was asked to pore through Salisbury's intelligence files, which were voluminous, dating back to the time of his father Thomas Cecil Burghley, councillor and favourite of Queen Elizabeth. I was to search for mention of those already named. So much for my reward! My theatre connections were also tapped. Among the rumours were that Catesby had dined with playmakers Ben Jonson, William Shakespeare, and Thomas Dekker, the month before at a tavern called the Irish Boy. Also, I was told that the performance at the Globe of which I had heard the cheers was reportedly paid for by Catesby. What was tricky about this assignment was that the company that played at the Globe was sponsored by the king himself and called 'The King's Men.'

The obvious place to begin was at the Globe. I knew that Shakespeare was the author of the play in question, a co-owner of the Globe, and a reported guest of Catesby – all good reasons to question him. I found him seated alone on stage – on a theatre throne. The playhouse, which had been closed during the investigation by the king's order, was deserted.

He was a smallish man, slightly plump, and jovial in face, even when he worried, which he was when I told him why I was there. He told me to sit, and, with my good hand, I pulled up a neighbouring throne, slightly smaller, perhaps for Henry the Fifth's queen. I asked him what he knew about Catesby and the other plotters.

Shakespeare told me that Catesby was a friend of Jonson and Dekker and that they had simply brought him along to dinner, that he barely knew Catesby and actually knew more about his ancestor, whom he had portrayed as a supporter of the villainous king Richard III in a play of the same name. When he spoke, defending himself, his voice could be heard at the theatre's rear. The playhouse was designed so, which is why I could hear the cheers across London.

'From your speech, you are from the Midlands, are you not?'

'Stratford.'

'Ah, I am from the Midlands myself. Coventry, although I have not been there for years. Have you bade farewell to Stratford forever or do you intend to return?'

'I have bought a new place there, and will go there when I retire.'

'Ah, that is wonderful. But as for Catesby, he was from Lapworth, just a few miles north of Stratford. So were the Wrights. Rookwood from Clopton, a stone's throw. Robert Wintour was from Huddington—'

'And what of that, sir –' and suddenly I noticed that he had controlled his voice to a whisper. 'My father was a merchant, and I moved in different circles from the men you mention. It is not as if I went to school with them.'

'And your friends Jonson and Dekker?'

'Each man knows his own mind. You must ask them to share theirs with you'

'Does Jonson frequent the Irish Boy?'

'Or the Mermaid's.'

'And Dekker? You wrote a play with him about Sir Thomas More whose performance was prohibited because of its papal leanings.'

'Anthony Munday wrote the play. Dekker and I merely added some scenes. We could not save it. It happens that way sometimes. One works with what one has. As for Dekker, I have not seen him for days.'

'Nor has anyone,' I said as I rose to leave. 'I must add, Master Shakespeare, that I am a great admirer of yours. When we were boys, those of us who revel in the made-believe had to wait months for mummers to wander by. Now there are – how many – a half a dozen theatres in London? I attend them frequently. You are at least partly responsible for this great flood of beautiful language and action. In listening to your words, I have attuned my ear to language.'

'Yes,' he smiled. 'You are the "name catcher." '

I grinned, but then asked him, pointedly, 'Tell me, who chose *Henry V* for performance on the fourth of November?'

'We have a schedule,' Shakespeare said, implacably.

'And you are an owner and control the schedule. What a coincidence that a play about a legendary – or shall we say, ideal – king was performed on the day papists were planning to blow up King James. Do stay in the city, Master Shakespeare. And, by the way, you look – at home – on your throne.'

Jonson was indeed at the Mermaid's Tavern. He too was stout and short – making me think it was an occupational hazard of playwrights. We went to the back room, I sat and he said, without waiting for my seat to settle—

'Shakespeare and Dekker brought me to Catesby's dinner.'

'And you barely knew Catesby.'

'Hardly at all.'

'And Percy? Rookwood? Robert Wintour? Is it not true that you frequent recusant circles?' The poet cheerfully shook his head, no. 'Do they not come here?' I persisted.

At that, the poet smiled. 'So I have been told.'

'How well do you know Shakespeare?'

'I know him well, but I do not know him. I call him "Invisible Will." He is there, but he is not there. He shows you only what he wants you to know.'

'Unlike yourself?' Jonson shrugged. 'And Dekker?'

'A colleague. Someone I dine with. Nothing more.'

'Is he not Dutch?'

'I believe—'

'And is not Flanders where Owens and Stanley reside—'

'So I am told—'

'And where is Dekker?'

'I have not seen him—'

'For several days, I know. We will search for him.'

Jonson pulled his chair closer and whispered. 'Look, my gallant friend, do not waste time with me. Join the heroic brigade that descends to catch the traitors at Holbeach House.'

'How – how would you know about that—'

'Because,' Jonson whispered, 'I too am Salisbury's man. If I frequent Catholic circles, it is to spy for him.'

Jonson was right. Catesby, Percy, and many of the others had been surrounded at Holbeach House. They were outnumbered and also weakened from having blown themselves up – having laid their gunpowder out to dry and carelessly ignited it. Catesby and Percy were shot and killed – by the same bullet. A John Streete of Worcester claimed the thousand pound reward for this remarkable feat. Francis Tresham, one of the conspirators, had just died in prison, and the cause of death was unknown.

Salisbury had me read the conspirators' confessions in his presence. I noticed how shaky was the signature of 'Guido Fawkes' after his long torture, as opposed to those of 'Thomas Winter' and 'Ambrose Rookwood' who were captured later. He also had me read the lieutenant's report from Holbeach House. 'Well,' he asked as he often did. 'What do you think?'

I dropped the papers down with disgust. 'A magic bullet that kills two men. A mysterious explosion that blows up the men who attempted to blow up the king. A man dies in prison before he can talk. It is stage managed, my lord.'

'Sometimes things are what they are, Master Bagnet.'

'And sometimes we are made to believe what is not. It is called theatre, my lord. And speaking of the theatre, is Benjamin Jonson, the playwright and poet, in your employ?'

This time my lord Salisbury smiled. 'Ah, Jonson. He writes me poetry – "What needs hath thou of me or my muse/whose actions so themselves do celebrate" – and then he dines with Catesby. He supports both sides so that he thinks he will not lose. And by so playing, he will not win. He is harmless'

'How are those who mislead and deceive harmless? I believe that men should be what they seem.'

'I know you do. Your virtue and your failing. All right, we will have Jonson watched.' Again, he waved at his men who gave me more gold.

But I would not leave without asking, 'And Thomas Dekker?'

'Has he been found?'

'Not yet. But do you know him?'

The little man looked up and in complete blankness said, 'He is of no use to me, and so I do not know him.' And as he turned away, I sensed that it was the last time I would see him, that he would no longer know me. Others would become his strength, his sword, his eyes. Or already had.

* * *

I had some occasion to go to Worcester and, while there, tried to find this John Streete in order to question him about his magnificent shot, felling two men with one bullet. Interestingly, no one in the entire city had ever heard of him. It was possible that, like me, he had left his home town years before and never returned. Or – something else.

In January, I attended the trial of the surviving eight conspirators in Westminster Hall and watched as they were led away – Rookwood, Pater, Fawkes, Digby, Keyes, Grant, Robert and Thomas Wintour. I remember that Robert towered over his brother and that Thomas gave a coin to his jailer, doubtless for some favour.

Three days later, Robert Wintour, Digby, Grant, and Pater were hanged, cut down while still alive, and then cut into quarters at St Paul's Churchyard. The next day Rookwood, Fawkes, Thomas Wintour, and Keyes were also drawn and quartered. I made a point of standing next to a man I saw in the crowd. Afterward, I invited William Shakespeare to dine with me at the Duck and Drake.

'Sorry business,' I said. 'Those of us who served in combat have made a deal with death to die at once. To see men butchered so, that is not death, that is damnation itself on Earth.'

Shakespeare nodded curtly and sipped his ale.

'Master Shakespeare,' I said, pulling my chair closer and whispering in the manner that Jonson had taught me, 'I need your help. This is such an amazing list of mysteries: the anonymous letter; Suffolk making me wait an entire day before arresting Fawkes; Fawkes, the conspirator who, although alerted that the government was investigating, does not flee; a bullet that kills two men; the disappearance of Dekker. You know the basics of this case. And you are trained in analyzing human character. Is it possible, as many say, that the Earl of Salisbury – do you know him, by the way?—'

'Slightly,' he said, as if caught off guard.

'—is it possible that the Earl of Salisbury himself arranged it all – the letter, the magic bullet, the death of Tresham – all to trap the papists, disgrace Northumberland, and give himself even more power than before? That this was not a huge papist plot but the mad, doomed-to-fail scheme of a group of a dozen rebels that Salisbury blew out of proportion?'

'This is dangerous talk, Master Bagnet,' said Shakespeare, not really nervous.

'This is strictly between us.'

Shakespeare seemed suddenly interested. 'I have read of such things. I am actually working on a play about a Scottish lord, Macbeth, who killed the king while seeming to be his friend and who then took the crown.'

'Very topical. But is it altogether – wise?'

'I think so,' he laughed. 'Banquo and his son in the play are ancestors of King James. The play extols his reign.'

'I see. So you have multiple purposes.'

'Oh yes.'

'I believe you usually do. Do you know – I told you I admired your work – I was able to deduce that "blow" meant "blow up" because of something you had written in your play *Hamlet*. "I will blow their mines and blow them at the moon." Is it not interesting that you anticipated the idea of blowing up mines under Parliament and used the same wording as that in the letter – "blow" – meaning "to explode" – rather than "blow up." Some would say that this would mean that *you* had written the letter. But for that to be true, then you would have to be one of the traitors.'

'Master Bagnet, what are you saying?—'

'When I asked you if you knew Catesby and the others – who were born near you in Stratford – you said, "I did not go to school with them, after all." It is true you were not schoolmates. But it is interesting that you chose that concept of school because your schoolteachers at Stratford – Simon Hunt, John Cotton – were papists. Cotton was hanged, as was your schoolmate Robert Debdale. There is a file on you in the Earl of Salisbury's collection that is as thick as my arm. Your father welcomed Father Edmund Campion to your home when you were just seventeen. When Campion was arrested, you fled to serve in a papist household in Houghton. Not only did you know Catesby, you dined with him, bringing Jonson along. Dekker, whose parents were from Holland, was a papist as well. When Catesby and the others began their scheme, who else would they turn to but boyhood papist friends – you from Stratford, Dekker from St Paul's.'

'This is rot, Bagnet. Fawkes did not name me—'

'Because he did not know you. He was the outsider, the munitions expert, fresh from Flanders. Catesby and Percy knew you, but they are both dead and cannot implicate you. Interesting that they were both killed by one bullet. Only an unknown from Worcester claimed to have killed them. Why? Was it because no one would take credit for shooting such brave men in the back as they attempted to surrender, for blowing them up and shooting them down like dogs on Salisbury's orders so that they would not talk, so that they would not implicate people like you, traitors to traitors. Or is Streete a shared name for this band of reluctant killers? To quote Iago in your *Othello*, "Men should be what they seem—" '

'Look,' Shakespeare said, getting up from his chair. 'This is madness.'

'Sit down!' I ordered him. 'I know enough to have you arrested this second. Your freedom depends on me. So sit.'

He sat and said, 'Why?'

'Why what? Why would you join them or why did you betray them? As to the latter, how did you put it – you have a "new place" in Stratford. You are rich and successful. And you are, after all, "a king's man." Whatever sparks of the old faith Catesby and Percy kindled in you were drowned by your comfort in your success. Ironically, it was you and not Jonson who was Salisbury's man. Salisbury knew a great deal about the plot before the anonymous letter to Monteagle – in which you wrote "blow" rather than "blow up." The letter just gave him the avenue to inform the king of the conspiracy. Fawkes left the gunpowder after the Lord Chamberlain and I discovered him, but was persuaded to come back – and the others were convinced that the letter had not been believed – by a master persuader, a playmaker, who convinces audiences that wooden chairs are thrones and that boys are queens. A man who can control all manner of theatrical effects such as his whispered voice in an empty theatre and a solitary figure positioned in the shadows so as to be seen only at a certain point in time. That was you I caught a glimpse of in the shadows with Fawkes, was it not? A long way from your house in Cripplegate.'

'It was not me!'

'Of course it was you, although I did not see you clearly. Jonson calls you the "Invisible Shakespeare," so accustomed did you become in your papist upbringing to hiding your true self and so used are you in your playmaking to working behind the scenes. I told Salisbury that the whole business had been stage managed and stage managed by London's master playwright at that. Everything was written out and rehearsed. Why wouldn't Suffolk let me arrest Fawkes? It was because you and Salisbury wanted the others to flee, to be spread out across the country where they could be picked off.'

I had unloaded the bulk of my artillery on him. When I was done, he sat and blew his breath to whistle but made no tone. 'I am indeed a play-maker, Master Bagnet,' he said finally. 'I take events as I see them, and I mould them. One does what one can with what one has. I make no excuses. In another time and another place, I might write it differently. I follow my destiny. In my own way, I may live forever. Now that would be something. But I offer no excuse and neither do I confess. This can all be said easily enough, but not proved.'

'Salisbury tried to protect you and still may. But in this atmosphere of accusations and name calling, you would not endure. A pity too, since you have attempted so hard to survive.'

Shakespeare breathed hard. 'Yes, that is what the priests taught us. To survive was everything. What will you do?'

'I have thought a lot about that,' I told him, honestly. 'I believe it was what happened to Thomas Wintour that directed me.'

'What do you mean?' he said, as if he knew.

'The two Wintours always spelled their names "W–i–n–t–o–u–r." It comes from the Welsh "Gwyntour" for "white tower." But in his confession in the Tower, Thomas signed his name as it is pronounced – "W–i–n–t–e–r." He was short when I saw him, and his brother was tall. Not impossible but unusual. Thomas bribed the guard – why? Perhaps so that they would be hanged on different days and the difference in their heights not accentuated. You and I know that Thomas Wintour is free, and the man on the scaffold was Thomas Dekker.'

I got up and looked down at the quiet Stratford man. 'I abhor your religion, sir. I detest what you and your friends tried to do to the king and Parliament. And yet, Dekker died for what he believed. He gave his life so that another might live. That I admire. And he evidently had the same choice as you. Salisbury said he did not know Dekker because he could not use him: again, an interesting choice of words. But he used you. You betrayed your friends to save yourself. I cannot take your confession, Master Shakespeare. And for what you did, there is no excuse. As for your punishment, I will simply let you live. That will be enough for a coward.'

As I walked away from him in a tavern full of noise, I heard his voice, perfectly projected so that it would reach me and only me, say, 'At last, "name catcher," you have named me.'

I left him alone, which is mostly how he spent the rest of his life. His best work was past, although he did write *Macbeth* for King James about the man who seems to be everyone's friend while he plots his own advancement – 'False face must hide what false heart doth know.' What he mostly wrote was not under his name. I was amused to see published various works under the name of 'Thomas Dekker.' Many of them denounced papists – such as a marvellous play called *The Whore of Babylon* which recounts another assassination attempt of an English monarch, only this time it was of Queen Elizabeth but, again, it was by papists. When I saw it, I felt like I was watching the conspirators' discarded plans for killing King James as recounted by Master Shakespeare. In the years following, because of works such as these, Dekker became known as a patriot – much to the comfort of his wife and children and to their financial benefit. Shakespeare may have been seeking repentance, and after he died, Jonson must have taken over writing for Dekker, as a final favour. It was this sort of thing that led to wrangling about who wrote what play, which continues to this day. Dekker was even supposed to be in debtors' prison for ten years – a clever ruse to hide his absence. As Dekker himself had shown, a bribe to a local constable goes a long way. None of the higher-ups care once the attention has moved on – to continue our theatre images.

Northumberland, who had supported the gunpowder plot, as it was soon called, had his life spared but died in disgrace. The conspirators were indeed papists and had plotted to kill the king and parliament. But the action of these few caused all papists to suffer extreme persecution. Salisbury became more powerful than ever.

And, of course, Shakespeare lived and died a patriot too and, as I write this, his work, his wonderful work, lives on as well.

As I said at the beginning, the choice I made was not the right one. With suicide and drunken revelry, while they may be cheats, at least they are not lies. I prefer combat that is head-on.

I, old soldier, continued living. And, amazingly, that was not the end of my involvement with Master William Shakespeare and attempts on the king's life. There was the cannon shot aimed at the king during the premiere of Shakespeare and Fletcher's *Henry VIII* while the king was in the audience that led to the burning of the Globe Theatre. But that is another tale.

MASTER ELD, HIS WAYZGOOSE

Chaz Brenchley

Shakespeare's sonnets have always sparked a lively debate. Who was the dedicatee Mr. W.H.? Who is the youth of the early sonnets and the Dark Lady of the later ones? And why, when the sonnets were probably all written before 1600, were they not published until 1609? Those are the mysteries. Here's the story.

'Brat?'

'Yes, sir?'

'Know you what we do here, Brat?'

'Yes, sir.'

'Well?'

'We print books . . . Ow!'

'You know nothing. We are printers; we despoil death. We cheat time, Brat. We confer immortality on our friends.'

'Sir?'

'*Vitam mortuo reddo*, I restore life from the grave . . . Do I make any sense to you at all?'

'No, sir.'

'No. You are a brat, with no thoughts higher than your own low belly, and I should throw you back into the gutter I plucked you from. Though what use you would be to anyone there, I cannot imagine. Well. Scrub the ink from this for me – carefully, mind! – and then break it up. The type is Bastarda, which is fitting, Brat, is it not?'

'I don't know, sir.'

'No. As I said, you know nothing. Be away, boy, be about it . . .'

The printing-house of Master George Eld was his own house also, where he lived and slept. There was a door to one side of the workshop, with stairs beyond that led up to his private rooms.

Two massive gates gave onto the yard outside, and stood wide all day to let the light in. One had a postern set within it, for any night-time traffic: through that the journeymen and apprentices left at the day's close, to sleep in their own house opposite. All but Brat. Named and claimed by Master Eld – seized, indeed, with his hand in Master Eld's purse, seized and kept and never freed since – Brat had his own pallet in a curtained enclosure at the back of the workshop. 'If I must keep a devil,' Master Eld had said, 'then the devil may keep the house.' Even the postern had strong bolts, but there were clever thieves in London, 'more clever than you, Brat,' and fire was a risk always; best to have a boy there, to cry the alarm at need. No longer the youngest, nor the smallest, nor the newest apprentice in the shop, still it was Brat who closed and barred the shutters each night, who watched his master lock the postern and throw the bolts across, who stood in the guttering shadows of his master's lamp and watched him walk to his private door; who often stood and listened to the stair's creaks as it bore his master's weight before sidling through the dead dark – no lamp allowed for him, no flame left unsupervised where there was so much that could burn – till his groping fingers found the curtain, and the stiff straw of his bed beyond.

The curtain was for the clients' comfort, not for his. He shared his space with a barrel full of piss.

* * *

This day as every day bar Sunday, he fetched a bucket of that piss – his own and every man's else, even Master Eld used the barrel at need – and carried it and the locked chase, heavy with type; carried them over to his stool in the corner where the stones were stained black from years of splashing.

He dipped a coarse brush into the bucket, set the chase on his knee and began to scrub. The sticky ink gleamed darkly; if any were left to dry, that type would be unusable until it had been soaked, perhaps boiled, and then picked clean with care, not to scratch the lead. That was another task that fell to him, as the blame did, always; he preferred to scrub.

Even so, even with his head bent to his work and through the sounds of his own hard scrubbing he knew when a client stepped in through the gates. No one stilled, they were all better-trained than that, certainly neither man nor boy would be staring; but suddenly the whole shop was quieter at its work, the apprentices moved faster and the men more slowly as the great presses were raised and lowered and raised again, the damp sheets of paper set on the tympan's pins or whisked away, hung on the frames to dry while the formes were inked to print the next.

From his vantage-point, low and half-hidden, shadowed by the bulk of the machines, Brat could stare, and did. Master Eld had never trained him better; indeed, had never tried.

A new client, this, a stranger: a man bigger in his belly than his boots, brushing back the hood of his cloak to show a face framed with neat-cut hair and a trimmed and pointed beard. Both hair and beard were touched with grey; the skin between was stained wine-red. Brat saw so much, and more. He saw how the man carried himself, how his head rode above his shoulders as he walked forward, as Master Eld went to meet him.

Brat saw and turned the brush in his hand, worked one stiff fibre loose and strained his ears to hear.

'Master George Eld?'

'Indeed, sir. And you are—?'

'Thomas Thorpe is my name, though I would prefer that you not publish that abroad. I am a man who values his privity. I wish you to undertake a commission for me, a small book of sonnets . . .'

'It would be a pleasure, Master Thorpe. Come through to the back here, where we can speak more comfortably.'

That was unprecedented; ordinarily Master Eld would take a new client directly into his private office to discuss a job of work. Brat watched the two men draw closer, seeing how his master's bald head overtopped the other's by the span of a big man's hand; then he ducked his own head down and made busy with his hog's-hair bristle, picking as though there were encrusted ink on the type, not to feel one big man's hand across his ear now or later.

'Sonnets, Master Thorpe?'

'I have them here.' Brat risked a glance, through the tousle of his flopping hair; he saw a roll of papers bound with string, fetched from inside the man's cloak and passed over almost furtively.

Master Eld cut the string with his knife, and flattened the papers on an imposing stone. For a moment there was silence; then the rustle of turning pages, and, 'The sonnets of William Shakespeare. Well . . .'

'Do you know Master Shakespeare?'

'I have seen him, among his company. Many times.'

'Then you know that there will be a demand for these.'

'Indeed. No other printing-house has seen them?'

'You were recommended; I came to you first.'

'Well, then. You will take a glass of wine with me, sir . . .?'

And now he did lead Master Thorpe to his private office, taking the papers with him; Brat saw how he bore them loosely, carefully in his hands, like a man who carried unexpected treasure.

Brat had unlocked the chase and was distributing type from the forme into its case when the office door opened and his master appeared, ushering the visitor out with uncommon subservience, bowing him through the gates and across the yard to the street beyond. Master Eld was always polite, never effusive; Brat watched, and wondered.

When he returned to the shop, Master Eld came directly to where Brat was working.

'Well, young devil?'

'Sir?'

'What make you of our new client?'

'He is over-fond of sack, sir.'

'Aye, but that is hardly my concern, nor yours. What more? Do you think his name is truly Thomas Thorpe?'

'Oh yes, sir.'

'Why so certain? I am in some doubt myself.'

'He asked you not to speak it about, sir.'

'Not to publish it. He did. But he might as easily have offered me a false name and asked the same, not to spread the lie too far.'

'Yes, sir – only he knows that you might catch him in the lie, and so he spoke the truth.'

'Oh? And how might I do that? He gave me no direction to his house.'

'Ask for him at Whitehall, sir, or at Greenwich Palace. His name will be known there, though you should probably call him Sir Thomas.'

'Explain yourself, Brat. He was not dressed for the Court.'

'If he wants to pass unrecognized, a man may borrow his servant's cloak – but not his boots. He wore good kid on his feet, though the heels were worn down. And he carries his chin as if he were used to a ruff beneath it.'

'Brat, you are exemplary.'

'Sir?'

'You are a warning to us all, not to confuse ignorance with stupidity. Nor so ignorant now; sharp-eyed and quick-fingered still, but you will make a better printer than you ever were a thief. We deal with a dishonest world; a printer must know his man. His heels were worn, you say?'

'Yes, sir. I think he wants money.'

'Aye. Hence this book. That will make money for us all. But I wonder how he came by Master Shakespeare's sonnets, indeed I do . . .'

It was not for his own security that Brat was locked in at night, or not any longer; by day the other apprentices named him lucky devil, for the errands he was sent to run took him all through the city. Not an hour after Thomas Thorpe's departure, Master Eld called him into the office. The sheaf of sonnets was spread all across the desk, all but for a small space where his master was folding and sealing a single sheet of paper.

'Here, lad,' as he pressed his thumb into the warm wax: there was a ragged scar across the ball that made a print known everywhere as Master Eld's. 'Take this to the Company of Stationers, fast as you can.'

'Yes, sir,' with a quick smile that won him a frowning scowl along with the paper. Brat rarely asked questions; he rarely needed to. Master Eld might be suspicious of their provenance, but he wouldn't let these sonnets slip. The Company of Stationers was as rigid in its rules as any guild; intention to print a title had to be registered, but once that was done no other man in the craft could bring out a rival edition. None that was sanctioned, at least. There were always pirates, but the Stationers were strict in their enforcement; the lifetime of a pirate's shop was usually brief.

The clerk who received Brat was an old acquaintance. He grunted a greeting, took the paper, checked the seal and unpicked it. The volume of registered titles stood open and ready; he reached for a pen and dipped it, murmuring aloud as he wrote.

'Master George Eld, "Shakespeare's Sonnets", an edition of one thousand copies. Very well. Have you heard the news, lad?'

'What news is that?'

'An actor in Master Shakespeare's company was found dead last night. Stabbed, he was, and his room ransacked . . .'

Brat bore that news swiftly home. Master Eld blinked, frowned, gazed at the panting boy; at last said, 'Did you learn his name?'

'No, sir.' If the clerk had heard the name, he would have spoken it.

'No matter. Have you ever seen the players, Brat?'

'No, sir,' or not as his master meant it. In the streets, in the taverns, yes, and picked their purses too when they were fat; but not in the Globe or any other playhouse, not at work.

'Mmm. Well, tonight you shall.'

Guttering torchlight, vivid colours, voices that boomed above the rowdy pit – this was his reward, Brat knew, for guessing his master's interest in that actor's death. Another night, he would have been enthralled. The life of an apprentice was often dull, after the life he'd lived before: by his wits, by his nerve, by his fast fingers and faster feet. Bolted in and abandoned to his lonely pallet, he could yearn sometimes for the open city in the night outside, for the crush and noise of a crowd, even for the rush and terror of a hot pursuit.

Tonight, though, he was distracted. His master had not come

here to see the play; therefore, neither had he. Soon separated in the squeeze, he kept one eye on the stage and the other on Master Eld's bare bald head, to be sure of finding him again; both ears had other work to do.

And did it: so that when at last the play ended and the pit emptied into the street, when he felt his master's hand grip his elbow and steer him into a quiet alley, he was more than ready.

'The player's name was Richard Spence,' said Master Eld.

'Yes, sir. And his room was in Mistress Taylor's house, on Timiny Lane.'

'Indeed. Anything more?'

'Yes, sir.' Everyone in the pit had been talking, inevitably, and all on the same fascinating subject. 'He was a young man, barely out of playing skirts, they said; and Master Shakespeare's particular friend, they said that too.' They'd said that often, particularly when a melancholy-looking man in his middle years had been on stage, his voice barely carrying above the hiss of voices. Throat-full with sorrow, Shakespeare had been that night.

'Yes. I heard that. Tomorrow, I think, I may find an errand for you, Brat. To Timiny Lane . . .'

'Mistress Taylor?'

'Aye, that I am. What do you want, boy?'

'Please, mistress, I'm to be apprenticed at the Globe, and they said you might have a bed for me here . . .'

'Well, I might at that, for a small 'un. I've a roomful of apprentices at the back that I could squeeze another cot into. Wishful to be a player, are you, boy?'

'Perhaps, mistress. Errand-boy for now, but Master Shakespeare said he'd train me himself . . .'

'Did he so? Well, you're pretty enough, I'll say that. If you don't mind wearing skirts.'

Pretty enough for a player, or pretty enough for the man? She didn't say, Brat didn't ask. He followed her into the house and up the stairs, his fingers groping the wall in the half-dark; on the first landing, a door stood open and a girl appeared suddenly, with a sloshing bucket in her hand.

'Mistress, I've scrubbed and scrubbed, but that stain – Oh! Your pardon, mistress . . .'

'That's all right, Betsy. It's only a boy wanting a bed. And don't mind the stain, either; my gentlemen won't. You wouldn't, would you, boy? Not that you're getting a sight of my best room, but . . .'

'Stain, mistress?'

'They do say a murdered man's blood won't wash.'

Brat widened his eyes, dropped his jaw, thought that he could indeed find a place with the players, if his current place hadn't suited him so well. If Master Eld hadn't kept him so closely . . .

'Murder, mistress?'

'Aye, and in my own house, when I was down in my own kitchen, it must have been . . .'

And now she was well away, and Brat need ask no questions further: only grunt and nod and listen, listen hard.

Such a sweet young gentleman Master Spence had been, he heard, far too good for that rabble of players he'd made his life with. Born to a good family too, a noble family, though he never would name his father; Spence was a name he'd taken, not his own. There'd been a dispute, seemingly, foul words and fury; he'd left his home and his weeping mother, as wild boys will, and had sworn never to go back.

And he'd taken up with the players then, handsome young thing that he was; and a fine turn he'd given, in skirts or breeches. She was never one for the play ordinarily, but she went to see him, time and again.

He'd been a special friend of Master Shakespeare, that wrote all those plays; and the company had been to Court, summoned by the queen herself, to play for her. Though he'd been reluctant to go there, her sweet Richard: for fear of seeing family, she'd thought. A great success he'd scored there, by all reports, a triumph; and had had more callers after, women in fine dresses and the finest gentlemen, though she'd hesitate to call them lords and ladies by the way that they behaved . . .

Yesterday, though – oh, it was terrible. He'd kept his room all morning, as his custom was, so late he'd come in the night before; but then at noon he'd had a caller, a woman, a stranger got up in the Moorish style, veil and all. Master Richard had sent the boy out for a jug of wine, and he'd been laughing, so pleased he was with his visitor. After she left there'd been another, a man who'd called a time or two before; Mistress

Taylor had seen him on the stairs, on his way up to Master Spence's room.

There'd been no sign of the lad, then or later; she'd thought he must have drunk himself stupid and gone back to bed. At last the Globe had sent a runner to fetch him, for that night's play. And they'd found him dead on his bed, stabbed through the heart and his room in chaos. She'd been that overset by the sight of him, it had fair torn her heart . . .

'A woman, and then a man?'

'Yes, sir.'

'And she knew the man, but not the woman. Mmm. Describe him.'

'Claret-coloured, she said he was, sir, the size of an ox and the shape of a pig well fatted.'

'Does that sound like our Master Thorpe to you, Brat?'

'Yes, sir.'

'To me also. Well. Let me alone now, boy, I must overlook these sonnets.'

Master Eld stayed up late that night, turning leaves in his office, turning and turning. Brat lay on the pallet behind the curtains and tried to stay wakeful, anticipating a call. The dark was oppressive, though, he couldn't keep his eyes from closing nor his mind from dreams. When he woke it was rising day, the glimmer of his master's lamp was long gone and the blanket he'd left deliberately on the floor was warm across his shoulders.

Master Eld had another visitor that week, another man who came in his servant's clothes, though this one wore them better. It was his voice that betrayed him, or rather the tone of his voice as it slipped cool and commanding from the printer's office, as Brat strained to listen at the door.

A journeyman's hard hand interrupted that endeavour; Brat scuttled necessarily back to his work, silent and aggrieved.

A minute later, his curiosity was somewhat assuaged. He and every boy, every man else stood quite still, as their master's response thundered out into the workshop.

'You presume, sir, to stand there cloaked and nameless, and to tell me what books I may or may not print in my own shop? . . . No, sir, keep your purse, keep it, I say! I have no interest in its contents. No, and none in your name either, nor your family's. You will leave this place, sir, and leave it swiftly, before I call my men to throw you out . . .'

He had no need to do that; his own physical presence was enough, and more than enough. The office door was wrenched open, Master Eld's body loomed beyond it; his visitor – shorter by a good head, and slim as a wand beneath the disguising cloak – all but ran out, though he paused in the gateway to cast one vituperative glare back. His voice rose, shrill with anger now: 'You will regret this, printsman. Oh, you will . . .'

Master Eld took one, two paces forward, big hands rising; the man ran indeed, across the yard and out into the street.

In the silence afterwards, Brat could hear his master's breathing, clear across the shop; no one else, he thought, was breathing at all.

Then, 'Peter, Henry, leave what you are doing – you will begin to set the pages for Master Shakespeare's book of sonnets. Immediately. I will work alongside you.'

'Yes, sir . . .'

It was the law, that printers were forbidden to manufacture their inks within the city walls; the base varnish was made by boiling oil and gum together over a slow fire, and the mix was apt to overflow the kettle and catch fire, to the great danger of surrounding buildings.

It was Master Eld's happy habit to convert necessity to pleasure and make a wayzgoose, a celebration of the day. When the weather was apt, he would lead all his house, men and boys together, out to the spot where his many fires had blackened the high stone wall that girded the city. The boys hauled a wagon that held all that was required, including a butt of sack and dough collected from the baker as they passed.

The journeymen would make rolls and fry them in the heating oil; if the apprentices got short commons – what was burned or left over, cold and unappetising, dense with the pungent taste of linseed – that was only what they were accustomed to, and welcome none the less. It was the natural condition of an apprentice, to be eternally hungry.

It was Brat's natural condition to be eternally curious also, and so eternally bruised. Even he did not quite dare question his master, as he might a journeyman; but this sunny day, while he watched the fires beneath the kettles, he still kept one eye on Master Eld.

Who was pacing, not drinking as his men were; who was paying no heed to the work nor to the conversation, but rather continually gazing back toward the distant gate into the city. Not the traffic on the road that held his attention, Brat thought; he guessed that his master's eye looked further.

And was proved right when a beckoning finger summoned him.

'Brat, I dislike leaving the house abandoned, without a watch. We want ink, and I would not waste a sunny day with the weather so uncertain; even so, I am not easy in my mind. I think you and I will go back to the workshop now. If all is well, I will leave you there – with some small comforts, as restitution for your missing the wayzgoose – and then, if trouble comes, you can run for the constable or summon help from our neighbours. Do you understand me?'

'Yes, sir.' Mostly, Brat understood that he would eat better than his fellows that day, for all that they picnicked in the sun; he had tasted Master Eld's comforts before, a time or two, and they were better than linseed rolls. Better by a distance . . .

His mind made up, Master Eld was suddenly in a tremendous hurry, his long legs and broad shoulders driving him through the crowded streets. Brat trotted at his heels, and was all but blown before they reached the printing-house.

The yard gate had been locked as they left. Master Eld paused, with the key in his hand. He listened, pressing his ear to the planking; then he touched Brat's lips for silence, and beckoned him to follow.

They went down the stinking alley behind the journeymen's quarters, to the rear wall of the yard. There they found a handcart upended, leaning against the wall; Master Eld set one boot on the axle and leaped up, took a grip on the coping-stones and heaved himself over. Brat swarmed up after him and sat atop the wall for a moment, breathless and intrigued.

He saw a darkness in the great doors to the workshop, where the postern had been forced open; he saw a man standing before it in cloak and hood, gazing in; he heard the sounds of breaking.

He saw his master stoop to snatch a stave from the woodpile; he saw him cross the yard in three massive strides; he saw the cloaked man start to turn, too late. He heard the thud as stave met hooded head, and winced.

The man slumped to the ground; Brat slithered down the wall, as Master Eld stepped through the postern.

Cries of alarm from within. Brat sprinted across, more to watch than to help his master, who he thought would need no help from him.

Just as he reached the postern he was knocked aside, almost knocked down by a hectic, charging body. Others followed, three men altogether; one was bleeding from the scalp, one clutched his arm as he ran. They scrambled up the woodpile and over the wall, and Brat heard the sounds of their footsteps fade.

Master Eld appeared in the postern, breathing hard.

'Well, Brat,' he said, 'here's a pretty mess to come home to.'

Then he stooped, heaved the unconscious man up and carried him inside. As he did so, the hood fell away; Brat recognised the slim, clean-shaven visitor who had made his master so angry, who had cried threats as he left.

Master Eld bore the man all through the workshop; Brat followed slowly, gazing about him. Even in the dimness of the shuttered room, he could see a pretty mess indeed: all the cases of type overturned, the set formes wrenched apart and their chases smashed, damage too to the heavy presses themselves.

No time to gawp. His master pushed through the curtains into Brat's own little space, and he hurried after.

He'd thought to see the man laid out on the pallet there, till he should recover his wits; but he'd mistaken his master's impatience, or his wrath.

Master Eld let the man fall, then lifted him again one-handed, by the neck. He thrust the man's head deep into the barrel of piss, held it there for a slow count of five – Brat counted his master's breaths – and let it rise.

The man spluttered, choked, struggled weakly; Master Eld grunted, and pushed his head under again.

The third time, he held it for a count of ten. Then he did shove the man down onto the pallet; stood over him, and said grimly, 'Now, sir. You will tell me who you are, and what you are about.'

'Yes, yes! I – my name is Antony de Vere . . .'

He was a young man, a frightened man: frightened of more, Brat thought, than Master Eld's presence looming above him.

'And why have you wrecked my workshop, Master de Vere?'

'You must not print those cursed sonnets, you must *not!*

You would disgrace my family, shame my name, I cannot permit . . .'

'Brat.'

'Master?'

'Go to my office. You know where I keep those things I most value; check there, to see if master Shakespeare's sonnets be safe. Run.'

Brat ran.

There was a loose board in the office floor, and a strongbox beneath. The key was hidden behind the skirting. Brat fetched it, worked the stiff lock, rummaged till he found the roll of papers. Spelled out some few lines to be certain, then put all back as it had been.

As he approached the curtains he heard his master's voice, the other man's.

'It was you slew the young player, Master Spence. You went there dressed as a woman, and you killed him. Why?'

'He was my brother,' frankly sobbing now: sobbing with disgust, Brat thought, as much as fear. 'I despised him, but I went to plead. We knew he had those verses, he had said he meant to make them public; the man Shakespeare had written them from love of him, he said, and he would publish that.

'He thought it a great jest, when I appeared in woman's dress. He said, he said he'd make a player of me too; I could have killed him then. But I begged him one last time, for his family's sake, to destroy that filth that shamed us all; he scorned me. And so I, I . . .'

'And so you slew him.'

'Yes. And fled; and never thought to search his room, how could I, when he lay dead on the bed there, and his eyes still watching me . . .?'

'Brat.'

His master could see through curtains; that surprised him not at all. He stepped between them, and said, 'Yes, sir?'

'Run to fetch the watch. Here is the yard key; they need not climb the wall. Then when you have brought them here, go back to my men, and call them home. Bid them put out the fires, and return. Our need for ink is not so urgent now; the wayzgoose is delayed.'

Brat spent much of that day on his hands and knees, picking type and leading from the workshop floor. His fingertips were sore with scrabbling before Master Eld called an end by lamplight.

'Enough now; bed, all. We've more to do tomorrow.'

Brat sat back on his heels and watched him usher them all out, men and boys together; watched him wedge shut the postern; watched him turn.

'Master?'

'Yes, Brat?'

'How did Master Thorpe come to have the sonnets?'

'Master Thorpe went to buy them from the boy, I think; perhaps to steal, if he would not sell. He knew their value, and had tried before. This time he found the boy dead, searched the room and came away with what he sought, at no cost to himself. Or so he thinks. Master Thorpe stands in fear, I fancy, of the de Vere family; rightly, if that young killer is an example of the breed. That's why he seeks to keep his name unconnected with the book.'

'What will you do?'

'Do? I will repair my shop, and then I will print the sonnets. And no, I will not put his name upon them; that I swore, and I keep my oaths.' Lamp in hand, he stood by the doorway to his private rooms; and smiled, and held his hand out. 'Brat, come.'

Brat went.

SHAKE-SPEARES
SONNETS.
Neuer before Imprinted.

AT LONDON
By *G. Eld* for *T. T.* and are
To be solde by *William Aspley*
1609.

FORTUNE'S OTHER STEWARD

Mary Reed and Eric Mayer

As if there were not enough mysteries surrounding Shakespeare's life, there is just as much mystery about his death and burial. He had apparently retired to Stratford and his burial was registered on 25 April 1616. Some years later the story circulated that he had died following a drinking bout with Ben Jonson and Michael Drayton. So what happened? It is to this final mystery that our last story turns.

> *Shakespeare is dead but his Wit lives on,*
> *His Wit shouted murder, though Shakespeare was gone.*
> —Edward Bunne, poet and publican

My verse is humble but I polish it every day. And hang me for a cat if it isn't true. It was I who unmasked Will's murderer.

What murderer?

Pull up a stool. Have some more sack. I'll have a drop myself. 'Tis a pity the anchovies are all gone.

Don't you recognize me? Listen. 'Banish plump Jack and banish all the world!'

Now do you see me? Sir Jack Falstaff and none other! Whenever London fogged his mind, Will left for Stratford and sought me out at the Goat and Gibbet. I was his Wit.

No, sir, as you see, I'm not Jack to the very life. He was merely corpulent, while I'm an imposing figure, and forthwith a man known for discretion, rather than cowardice. And I'd be a whoreson knave if I shared my theatrical counterpart's monstrous appetites.

Why yes, I will have another half cup of sack, to warm my tongue to the tale. But as to wit . . . ah, as to wit, there we are as like as two snowflakes, Sir Jack and I.

And a lucky circumstance it is, too. You'll remember, being an educated man yourself, that after Prince Hal became king, Will promised at the end of the play to bring the jolly knight back. 'If you be not too much cloyed with fat meat,' he wrote, 'our humble author will continue the story, with Sir John in it.' But as it turned out, he left it to me to write that very tale!

I solved the murder of the man I had inspired on St George's Day, exactly one year after Will's death and 53 years after his birth, for he was born and died on 23 April. There are stranger things in life than art, my friend, and more than mere coincidences.

Was it coincidence that brought Will's old friends to the Goat and Gibbet on that raw, rainy anniversary, or were they were drawn there by Will's spirit? Even after he grew wealthy and well-known beyond the dreams of men, as I have mentioned, he often stopped in for ale and a few hour's merriment. Sometimes, now, when the candles burn low I fancy I see him in the shadows, and he almost speaks . . . but I digress. Let me take you back to that fateful morning.

Tom Jenks was first to arrive. I hadn't finished sweeping the floor when he barged through the door, furiously shaking rain off his patched coat.

'I'm off to be a soldier for Her Majesty,' he roared.

It wasn't an unexpected statement, since it was made as regularly as the times his debtors or my Lord of Oxford's men came to find him, which is to say fairly often.

I asked him if he had been making free of my lord's pheasants again.

'Nothing like that, Master Bunne.' He grabbed my arm with a powerful hand, glancing around as if the deserted inn was full of large-eared knaves and cutpurses, before leaning down to whisper in my ear. 'When I'm away, I'd deem it a favour if you'd keep a kindly eye on Rose.'

'You won't find a more wakeful watchman than I, Tom,' I assured him. 'But you know Mistress Rose has had nothing to do with any part of another man, except for the heads she turns. And that's nature's fault, not hers.'

Tom grunted, giving me a dark look. I wondered if I was about to lose her excellent housekeeping services. She had probably worked, at one time or another, for every household in Stratford, since Tom's unfounded suspicions invariably cut her employment short. Will confided in me once that he had drawn some inspiration for Othello, the jealous Moor, from poor Tom Jenks. I poured Tom ale and left him to contemplate his military career, laying snares for Spaniards rather than pheasants perhaps, while I finished sweeping and then clearing out the fireplace.

As I carted out a bucket of ashes, a woefully thin figure in a mud-spattered doublet and cloak turned towards the door. He seemed to have been contemplating those few ragged brown leaves still shivering in the branches of the oaks along the street. Yet the leaves were not so forlorn as the sodden, drooping feather in his hat.

'Simon Deacon!' I cried, for I must admit that I was surprised, for I thought he was in London, and said so.

Another voice echoed my words, in an even more petulant tone. 'Yes, it's Simon. For pity's sake, let us in, out of the rain!'

Only then did I notice the fair man closing the distance between the rutted road and my doorway. For a second I failed to recognize him, for he was in breeches.

'And Matthew Reynolds! I still recall your Juliet, even though it's been –' I am, sir, a cultivated man, as you have doubtless surmised.

So, indeed, is Matthew Reynolds. He was not, however, on this occasion too gracious in his speech, for he cut me short with a surly, 'Nearly as long as I've been standing in the wet. I've lately played Desdemona and Ophelia, and I expect I'll die as untimely as they, if I don't get out of this weather.'

I think we can forgive him his churlishness, don't you?

Deacon, his fellow thespian, however, seemed little impressed. 'A moment please,' he rumbled, 'as I alighted from the carriage I espied a single crow. One for sorrow, it is said. I would that I should see a second, because two is for joy.'

'You have your joy, here's your second crow,' I pointed out, for striding down the street was the foreboding figure of the midwife, Mistress Scuttle, dressed in her habitual mourning black.

She overheard my comment. 'Crow! And what's this that greets me? A man's hide stretched over a great pudding!'

'There's Will's Lady Macbeth,' I whispered to Deacon. 'She's delivered more tragedies than Marlowe.' And then to Mistress Scuttle, as we entered the inn: 'This is the actor Simon Deacon, renowned for his Hamlet's pensiveness, his Lear's madness, and his Falstaff's fatness.'

'My tones have grown rounder in recompense,' Deacon reproached in mellifluous manner, sweeping off his hat and bowing low to Mistress Scuttle.

She, however, was unimpressed, frowning as she pointed out that he might say they had both brought Will Shakespeare's children to life. 'And I pray, good sir, you've had more thanks than I,' she concluded darkly, with more than a hint of the sound and fury for which she was renowned.

'You can't expect thanks for delivering only two or three of the human sort,' I pointed out.

Noticing her glare, Reynolds hastily enquired that as far as Will's literary children went, which would be her favourite, if pressed to name one.

'My favorite's Falstaff,' Mistress Scuttle admitted, warming to the rogue – Reynolds, that is. 'Such a witty, clever nimble-tongue. He always makes me laugh. We don't see his like here in Stratford.'

'You don't have the eye of a poet,' I told her, boldly indeed, but then am I not a man of courage?

Ignoring my wit, she responded 'Landlord, an ale, if you please.' Her expression was sufficient to make strong men faint.

'And the same for us,' Reynolds added, 'and will you not join us?'

Tom Jenks looked up suspiciously when we joined him at the plank table by the fireplace.

'Aye, I'm still here,' he muttered in answer to my eloquent glance, 'and I may have to delay serving Her Majesty so long as Stratford is filled with strange men wearing feathers in their hats.'

'We're actors, sir, theatrical players,' intoned Deacon at his mellowest. 'We have braved the long road from London to pay tribute to our great friend William, on this memorable day, and to convey our respects to his widow, Mistress Anne.' I did observe that the great tragedian looked even more care-worn than he had at Will's funeral. In his youth, he had indeed been fat and happy, but as time passed he had taken on the physical characteristics of those mostly tragic figures he so brilliantly played.

'We also wished to inquire about rumours lately circulating in London, concerning unperformed manuscripts,' Reynolds confided. 'If I am at all fortunate, he finally wrote one drama where the heroine does not die horribly. It is said that you were close to Will, landlord. Do you know anything of such matters?'

Well, sir, a man has his dignity after all, and I am not ashamed to say that I was outraged at the very suggestion. 'Unperformed manuscripts? And doubtless a few sonnets, a galliard, and a portrait or two painted in midnight oils, betimes, all executed in the dead of night and unbeknownst to us, who were as brothers to him?'

He did, at least, have the grace to look as crestfallen as the wet feather on his hat.

'Mistress Anne said nought to me about new plays,' confirmed Mistress Scuttle, 'and I consider us the closest of friends. I always keep in touch with my families and,' she glared at me as she said it, 'most show their gratitude with small remembrances.' I began to wonder if I should have added a little extra recompense to her fee when she last attended my wife. Women have long memories, sir, long memories.

But let me continue. Even after that, Deacon persisted in adding to Reynolds's folly, for he in turn revealed that, as he put it, it was 'his hope, most fervent, that William indeed penned one final play.' He rapped the tabletop with his knuckles, no doubt hoping for good fortune granting his wishes. I found it very odd that a man of the world would be so superstitious, but then again theatrical players are notorious for it, so 'tis oft said.

He would be fortunate indeed to find an unpublished play with another tragic hero to match the stature of those with which he had already attained his great reputation, I thought.

Mistress Scuttle remarked that she would rather see Sir John Falstaff again. A murmur of agreement went up, for as Reynolds commented: 'Everybody loves Sir John.'

Tom, alone, had no opinion on the matter. He sat hunched over his ale, wary as a black bear in the pit, his brooding gaze darting from one actor to the other.

What a scene it was, sir. In this very room, the King's Men and more, what with the very people whose shadows, reborn, peopled the stage. A brooding Othello, Macbeth's harpy of a wife, Juliet, Desdemona, Ophelia, Hamlet, Lear, Caesar. And no less than two Falstaffs – yours truly, who inspired Will to his greatest creation, and the paler version, the theatrical mimic.

And there we were, on that rainy day, characters with no play, all of us thinking in various ways about dear dead and departed Will. In the spirit of the day, we almost expected ill tidings from abroad, ominous portents, a strange and sinister messenger. As it happened, what we got was Parson Prentice, blown in with a few sere leaves, pale and gaunt as the ghost of Hamlet's father.

Now the parson, sir, is one of those tiresome villains who likes to hear himself overmuch. A plague on them, I say! To him, every day the sun rises is Sunday, and any pair of ears a congregation. Faced with two of England's greatest thespians, the parson seemingly decided that what the scene needed was his own voice. Evidently he too had been thinking of Will that morning, for, warming himself at the fire, he spoke at some length.

I'll save your gentle ears from his sermon on mortality. More sack, sir? When I hear about mortality, I always reach for the sack. At any rate, our actors' feathers were dry by the time the parson arrived at Will's deathbed, which he described in a suitably dramatic fashion. Even a parson, I vow, glories in reflected glory. Now here is the crux of the matter, for what he said surprised even our worldly visitors from the stews of London.

He was telling us about the last time he saw Will, who was then in his final hours. 'Will sent the doctor out of the room. "A word in private," he whispered to me, "for 'tis of vital import"' Now I'd be a credulous man indeed if I believed every word I've ever heard.' This brought a low growl from Tom, but the parson paid him no more heed than a parishioner who snored during one of his sermons, continuing unruffled: '– but Will's words were passing strange. "Tell them," he said to me, "that my wife will be ill-pleased, but that it is Will's way." '

'But what would she not be pleased about?' wondered Simon

Deacon for all of us, 'excepting of course that she was about to be widowed?'

'Fevers prattle more than bad poets, and that's all I took it for, until the will was read,' the parson nodded, reminding us of the ensuing scandal.

'You mean all the gossip about how Will left his wife his "second best bed"?' Mistress Scuttle remarked, with, I may say, somewhat unseemly relish, continuing, 'Although it was a bequest I would not have been displeased to have.'

Tom, who is sensitive to such topics, grimaced. 'If Will saw his wife as being in his second best bed, who did he suppose was in his best? That's what I ask myself!'

It must be admitted that we were all probably asking ourselves the same question.

'Remember that the bequest was written in, after the will was completed, as an interlineation.' Parson Prentice pointed out, somewhat smugly. 'As I remarked, I believed it was feverish ramblings, but this morning, thinking on it again . . .'

'Could it have been some kind of secret message?' wondered Reynolds. 'And if so, from whom? From Will, or another? By which I mean, was it in someone else's handwriting? If it wasn't, and from Will, for that matter, for whom was it intended? A man of so many, and finely-chosen, words. Could he have not been a little clearer?'

We sat and looked into the embers of the fire. By this time the sack had warmed my liver and set my brain ablaze. What is sack but the distilled essence of imagination? A single, sober Shakespeare can set a Falstaff upon the stage, a hundred drunken monkeys might populate the boards with an Ancient Pistol, but a sack-fired Edward Bunne can hear a chime at midday, as Mistress Bunne oft remarks.

Well, sir, inspiration flew in and perched on my shoulder, whispering in my ear.

'Murder,' I cried out. 'It was murder! And the whoreson villain responsible sits among us!'

My announcement was greeted with the kind of gasps that usually greet the display of Titus Andronicus's body parts.

'Did none of you think it odd that Will was carried off so suddenly by this fever?' I asked. 'Deacon and Reynolds, you both saw him only a week or so before his death. Was he not in rude health then? Mistress Scuttle, you often popped in to his house to visit Mistress Anne. Was he out of humour? Mistress Rose was working for the Shakespeares just before Will died, was she not, Tom? Did she mention he seemed ill?'

Tom lumbered to his feet. 'What is this about my Rose?' he demanded, somewhat unreasonably, of the assembly.

'Moonbeams,' Reynolds put in, with a dismissive toss of his blonde hair. 'Nothing but moonbeams.' Seeing Tom's look, he hastily added that of course he was not referring to Mistress Rose.

'Skewer me for a liar if I'm not telling the truth! Can you not see? Will had his suspicions. He gave us a clue, in his will, just in case.'

Mistress Scuttle cawed with laughter. 'What clue, you bloated bladder of bile?'

'What clue, Mistress? If you'd midwifed your own birth you'd have added to the world by your usual subtraction,' I said, refusing to be insulted, for my goodness of heart is as legendary as my intuitive brilliance. 'The clue is "the second best bed." Something is concealed in the bed. We must betake ourselves to New Place at once!'

At this point there broke out at the Goat and Gibbet the sort of frenzy that would have reduced even the eloquent playwright himself to a terse 'alarums and excursions.'

I will not bore you, sir, with a recital of how I masterfully took hold of that yapping pack and shook them into some semblance of a mob, or how I grabbed the tall candleholder off the floor by the hearth before we galloped to New Place, where Mistress Anne Shakespeare still lived, along with Will's second best bed and – unbeknownst to her – his secret. When Parson Prentice's timid knock went unanswered, I was forced to leap courageously to the fore and, having done so, delivered a volley of blows to the door that would have sent Hotspur into a maiden's faint.

Will's widow answered the door, brandishing a heavy ladle, but before she could set about us with it, I pushed past her into the hallway. Sometimes, when circumstances demand it, sir, a gentleman must forget his manners.

I am sorry to say that Mistress Anne almost forgot hers, crying, in an uncivil manner, to say the least: 'Master Bunne, what is this havoc?'

'The pursuit of justice! Point us to your bed!'

But Mistress Scuttle, having scuttled in – for what is in a name, sir, what is in a name? – as I say, having scuttled around us while we wasted time hobnobbing in the hall, was already mounting the stairs, the actors not far behind. Panting up after them, I thought I heard Simon Deacon mutter something about hidden manuscripts to his fellow actor.

'Here's the bed,' crowed Mistress Scuttle, leading our charge into a small room at the back of the second storey, 'and a fine piece it is, too!'

The company fell upon it. We had already tossed its furnishings to the floor by the time Mistress Anne arrived.

'What outrage is this? Out of my house, villains!' she cried.

'The villain has long since come and gone and the outrage cannot be stayed good lady, but only avenged,' I assured her, thrusting my brave makeshift pike into the mattress. The air was choked with feathers, thicker than the French saw on Crécy's arrows.

Will's misguided widow grabbed my arm but I pulled away. Deacon and Reynolds set to with a will – ah, sir, I see you appreciate my humour – and in a tick we had the whoreson mattress drawn and quartered. Mistress Scuttle wailed her disappointment, while the parson cowered at the doorway, sputtering protests feebly. Mistress Anne looked at the wilderness of feathers and wept.

'There's nothing here,' whined Reynolds, tossing handfuls of feathers over his shoulder, looking as if he would weep himself.

Deacon scrabbled blindly around the floor, Lear in an indoor tempest. 'Nothing! Nothing!' he boomed, his tones nicely rounded, despite his distress. As you can see, sir, I am an observant man. And a determined one.

'Treacherous bed! Give up your secrets!' I persisted, prodding what remained of the mattress.

At that moment Tom Jenks finally lumbered into the room. He was already half maddened with his own lurid imaginings. The awful words 'treacherous,' 'bed' and 'secrets' were flames to his tinder. With a horribly incoherent roar of rage, he leapt at the bedframe, the very foundation for his worst fears. Oak snapped like bone under his assault. We stood and gaped. Even I had never seen him in such a blinding rage.

In short time, Will Shakespeare's second best bed lay in splintered ruins. But unfortunately there was nothing hidden within, no mysterious note or accusing last message secreted in the mattress or concealed in a hollow leg.

Mistress Scuttle's face was as pale as her gown was black. Reynolds had sustained a wound in the fray; a drop of blood blemished his cheek. Deacon looked more haggard than ever. Tom Jenks still looked suspicious, although calmer. As for me, my brave makeshift candleholder-pike had been broken. The two pieces clung together, disconsolate, by the merest fibre of carved wood.

I felt a fool, and said so to Mistress Anne, begging her pardon.

She nodded. 'Only a fool could have concocted such a tale. My poor husband murdered and secrets concealed in his second best bed, indeed!'

'Moonbeams!' was Reynolds's scornful observation.

'Yes, I've been a fool,' I agreed, for I am not a proud man, sir, and admit to my faults, though they be small, 'because in the heat of the moment I forgot that my good friend Will was, above all else, a poet, a master wordsmith, a veritable paragon of literary artifice, and thus I had stranded myself high and dry on the reef of the base and common meaning of the words he employed so artfully. But now I think on it further, do you tell me, what bed is it that is one's "best bed"?'

'Surely the bed one sleeps in?' Deacon sounded bored, brushing feathers from his sleeves.

'Just so. But if a man has such a bed, his first and best bed, in which he sleeps during his lifetime, does he not then have a second best bed, in which he sleeps through all eternity? Are you blinded by the brilliance of it? The second best bed Will referred to is his grave!'

More sack? I'll have just one more cup. You are a visitor, of course, and so perhaps do not know that Holy Trinity Church lies very close to the River Avon. On cold April days the wind off the water can cut to the bone. There are those who say that such winds contributed to the fever that carried off Will. But we know better, do we not?

It was such a day then, as I have mentioned, and indeed so cold was it that in relating my story, I can still feel its icy rain lashing at me. Colder than Lady Macbeth's heart, as you might say.

Well, then, our Will is buried inside the church, in the sanctuary. When we went in, even out of the wind and rain of that melancholy day, the whole place was cold, a still, congealed sort of bitterness of place and time, as if the world was holding its breath, waiting for me to unmask Will's murderer. I remember our breath glimmered in front of our faces in the watery coloured light that filtered through the stained glass.

We trod hastily across stones concealing the bones of strangers, until we came to the slab beneath which Will lay at rest. Reynolds and Deacon were at my heels. Deacon's wonderful voice quavered as he quietly read out the verse carved on the stone floor before us, for of course he had not been back since Will's funeral and had not seen it before.

Good friend for Jesus sake forbear
To dig the dust enclosed here,
Blessed be the man that spares these stones,
And cursed be he that moves my bones.

Reynolds mused aloud as to the hand which had penned such a verse. Well, sir, I was and am proud to say that I composed it, at Mistress Anne's request.

'My finest work, if I may say so,' I said modestly, raising my voice so the parson could hear. 'For, you see, Mistress Anne knew Will was afraid his bones would be moved to the charnel house, to make room for others. It often happens.'

Deacon hastily stepped away from the slab, distancing himself from the stone and its threat.

'So far as I'm concerned, a curse and a groat will get you a cup of ale, and nothing else,' sniffed Reynolds.

You must remember, of course, that these were men of the world, not simple country folk such as you or I. But even so they both looked startled when I reminded the assembled company that we were there to look for Will's last message.

'You can't be thinking to desecrate a tomb?' quavered the parson.

I pounded the stone protecting Will with what remained of my candleholder. 'Open your ears,' I commanded my companions, 'for did he not direct us to this very place?'

'Open our ears so you can pour in the poison?' Mistress Scuttle enquired with venomous sweetness.

'The poison was poured long ago,' I said, refusing to take offence.

'Will was afraid he might be taken untimely from us, but perhaps he did not entirely trust his instincts, and could not bring himself to accuse a friend, even though' – here my imagination was again inspired – 'even though he might have actually received threats.'

'Do you accuse someone in particular?' demanded the parson, who obviously didn't like anyone else orating in his church. 'None of us are capable of such a black deed.'

'No? And yet Will saw the hardness of a Lady Macbeth in one of us, didn't he? One who may have felt slighted to receive so few – what did you call them – remembrances, even after delivering his children.'

'You blasted bombard of bilious lies! Will died of fever, not poison!' The lady cursed. And in a church, too.

'Perhaps whatever lies beneath our feet will secure your innocence, Mistress Scuttle. But, then too, do not think you are alone in being under suspicion. Was not Othello's murderous jealousy inspired by poor Tom Jenks, whose wife worked for the Shakespeares?'

Tom Jenks, who had been remarkably quiet after the debacle at Will's house, spoke up with a typical response, to wit, that a quick poison would not have been agony enough for anyone who trifled with his Rose.

'Enough of this!' Deacon's voice cut through the icy air. 'What could you hope to find beneath this accursed slab, anyway? Do you imagine Will carried an accusation on his person into his very grave?'

'Perhaps he did. Perhaps . . . perhaps he scribbled down that Matthew Reynolds had pressed him, under threat of death, to write a play where the heroine didn't die, because said thespian had been driven mad, dying so untimely and so often on stage, and all in a single life!' Even I was amazed, sir, at the flights my brain was taking.

'Moonbeams!' screamed Reynolds, looking moonstruck enough to prove the theory on the spot. He flung himself at the slab, tearing at its edges with his fingers. 'Help me move this stone! The truth will out with Shakespeare's bones!'

My small army surged forward, ignoring the parson's protests.

All, sir, save Simon Deacon.

'Stop, fools,' he thundered, that golden voice echoing around the freezing church. 'That stone is cursed! Don't touch it! We'll all lose our mortal souls!'

It was then I fixed the great actor with my gaze. 'It is your soul which is lost, Simon Deacon. For it is you who murdered our friend Will.'

'Fat rascal, you disgrace yourself with your calumny!'

'You must have slipped a subtle poison into Will's ale on your last visit. It would have done its work slowly.'

Deacon's fellow actor Reynolds had ceased clawing the slab. He looked aghast. 'Will wrote the characters that made Simon the greatest tragedian. Why would he want Will dead?'

'Tragedy is fine, so far as it goes,' I said. 'But the first part Simon played was Sir John Falstaff and everyone loves that merry knight. Didn't the Queen herself command the play that became *The Merry Wives of Windsor*? Alas, Simon, you were not the queen, to command Will's muse. And after the *Merry Wives* Will wrote no more parts for the character for which you were so loved.'

'Lies!' shouted Deacon, raising echoes in the icy church. But it was his storming's last clap of thunder.

Everyone seemed at a loss for words, except the parson, who observed: 'Well, since we are all pointing fingers, I suggest that before these vile rumours go further abroad, we all take an oath on the altar that we are innocent of Will's death. I include myself –' here he looked straight at me, '– for, after all, I was one of the last to see him alive, was I not?'

'Yes, let us all swear to the truth of it – but on Will's grave!' Inspiration flew in again, and I continued, 'Better yet, on Will's bones!'

Parson Prentice naturally protested at this, but not so strongly as Deacon. 'Cannot you read? There's a curse on that grave,' he shouted, 'and if it's opened, we'll all be damned, innocent and guilty alike.'

An interesting choice of words, do you not think? However, I poked at the slab with what remained of the candleholder. 'I'm not superstitious,' I said, 'even if you are. I think we are all agreed that there's a message of some kind in there, so let us see what Will has to tell us.'

Deacon turned pale as a loon, and when he spoke his voice was suddenly as weak as a death rattle. All his golden mellowness had gone. 'For pity's sake, don't disturb those accursed bones!' He began to weep. 'He was a liar. He promised to continue, to write another story in which my Sir John would return. He said so, right at the end of the second part of *Henry IV*. But when *Henry V* finally appeared

– why, in the play, Falstaff was already dead! And so too, died all the joy of my career. I waited, but Will never kept his promise, despite that I reminded him of it year in and year out'

Well, sir, we stood agape, as witless as geese at a fair. But had we all recited chapter and verse of every play that Will wrote, not to mention the unknown masterpieces he supposedly penned, still Deacon would not have heard us, for having once begun confession, he was driven to complete it.

'Yes, the poison did its work slowly, but not so slowly as he killed me. Once I was a round, rollicking knight, and everyone loved the man who played Sir John Falstaff. Look at me, now. Who am I? A gaunt Lear, a grim Macbeth, a tortured Hamlet. Yes, they all applaud me. The great tragedian. But who is there who loves a Lear, or a Hamlet, or a Macbeth?'

So, sir, my brave tale is coming to an end, along with the sack. You may ask what became of that cold-hearted murderer? As you have perhaps surmised, Deacon never saw a second crow outside the Goat and Gibbet that morning. Indeed, he never saw the inn itself again. That solitary bird, or at least Deacon's superstition, indeed foretold his sorrow, for if he'd not been so superstitious, so in terror of the lifting of that cursed slab . . . well, perhaps Will had carried to his grave some clue as to his murder. He had written stranger tales. Or maybe his lost manuscripts are mouldering there with his bones. We all carry our secrets and unfinished business to the grave with us, after all.

You ask for the end of this tale?

Well, then, this is it. Deacon demanded sanctuary, since he was already in the church. A strange sanctuary it must have been, imprisoned so close to Will. Perhaps that was why, in the end, he left before the allotted time was up. Perhaps he had heard that – let us say – certain interested parties were watching and waiting for him, and he determined to escape. Perhaps his guilty heart drove him out. Many things have been rumoured. But be that as it may, he left sanctuary, as Parson Prentice himself has stated, one monstrous night, and, so we did hear, blundered into the river and drowned. There are those who say he threw himself into it, playing Ophelia. They found him a few days later, but we never saw more of his feathered hat. I like to think it was swept downriver and now adorns a more deserving pate.

And now, irony of ironies, he lies in Trinity Church graveyard, not far away from Will. I suppose that eventually he will be moved to the charnel house. Will, of course, is still in the sanctuary and I am certain always will be. All these 'wills': I am sure that he would appreciate the wordplay, for that was, if you like, Will's way.

And isn't it a vexing puzzle, that, for all Will Shakespeare's wondrous writing, it was Edward Bunne's clever little curse that exposed a murderer? But then, wasn't Falstaff said to be Fortune's steward? And thus, as I once wrote:

Although great verse, our humours sway,
Sometimes, it's doggerel saves the day!

THE CONTRIBUTORS

Gail-Nina Anderson, *A Man of Middle-Earth* and *The Duke of Dark Corners*. Gail-Nina Anderson is an art historian and journalist who has side-line interests in vampires, ghost stories and Fortean phenomena. She has organised two major exhibitions of Victorian painting and recently published an article about the Angel of the North sculpture.

John T. Aquino, *The Name-Catcher's Tale*. John Aquino (b. 1949) is an American author with a special interest in the Elizabethan period, especially its relationship with the demise of the world of faery. He contributed *When the Dead Rise Up* based on *King John* to *Shakespearean Whodunnits*. His wife Deborah Curren-Aquino is a Shakespeare scholar of note. She has compiled both a detailed annotated bibliography and a volume of essays about the play *King John*.

Cherith Baldry, *The Chimes at Midnight*. Cherith Baldry (b. 1947), a former teacher and librarian, is best known for her children's books, particularly the *Saga of the Six Worlds*. She is also an Arthurian scholar and has written several stories seeking to redeem the character of Sir Kay. She contributed *The House of Rimmon* based on *The Merchant of Venice* to *Shakespearean Whodunnits*.

Paul Barnett, *The Price of Virginity*. Paul Barnett (b. 1949) is a Scottish writer and editor who has written most of his fifty or so books under the name John Grant. His fantasy novels include *Albion, The World* and, under his own name, the more recent space opera series starting with *Strider's Galaxy*. Among his non-fiction books are *The Encyclopedia of Walt Disney's Animated Characters* and *The Encyclopedia of Fantasy* (edited with John Clute). He contributed *Imogen* based on *Cymbeline* to *Shakespearean Whodunnits*.

Stephen Baxter, *All is True*. Stephen Baxter (b. 1957) is one of Britain's leading writers of science fiction. His related novels include *Timelike Infinity, Flux, Ring* and the collection *Vacuum Diagrams*. One of his most popular books was *The Time Ships*, a sequel to H.G. Wells's *The Time Machine*. He contributed *A Midsummer Eclipse* based on *A Midsummer Night's Dream* to *Shakespearean Whodunnits*.

Chaz Brenchley, *Master Eld, His Wayzgoose*. Chaz Brenchley (b. 1959) has made a living as a writer since he was eighteen. He is the author of eight published novels, mostly in the mystery and horror fields, including *Dispossession*, about love, death, amnesia and a fallen angel. He is also completing a major fantasy series, *The Books of Outremer*, based on the world of the Crusades. He held the post of Crimewriter-in-Residence at the St Peter's Riverside Sculpture Project in Sutherland, which he recalls as a bizarre experience and which led, indirectly, to his collection *Blood Waters*.

Richard Butler, *Murder Most Foul*. Born and educated in England, Richard Butler emigrated to Australia in 1963. His first book, the adventure novel *Fingernail Beach*, appeared soon after. He taught in Tasmania and Victoria until the publication of his fourth novel, *The Buffalo Hook*, when he turned to the dual career of writer and professional actor, producing novels, scripts and feature articles and working in films, television and live theatre. To date he has published nineteen books including the historical novels, *The Men That God Forgot, And Wretches Hang, A Blood-Red Sun at Noon* and *The Devil's Coachman*.

Margaret Frazer, *That Same Pit*. The Margaret Frazer alias originally hid the identity of two writers, Gail Frazer and Mary Monica Pulver, who between them produced the popular series of Dame Frevisse novels, which began with *The Novice's Tale* in 1992. Although Mary Pulver has gone her own way (after an amicable parting), Gail is continuing the Dame Frevisse series, but keeping the pseudonym. Gail contributed *The Death of Kings*, based on *Richard II*, to *Shakespearean Whodunnits*.

Peter T. Garratt, *Love's Labour's, Lost?*. Peter Garratt (b. 1949) is a lecturer and a writer of science-fiction and fantasy. Much of his work has appeared in the British magazine *Interzone*. He contributed *Buried Fortune*, based on *Timon of Athens*, to the first volume.

Anne Gay, *The Fire that Burneth Here*. Anne Gay (b. 1952), sold her first story in 1982, but only began writing regularly after the success of *Wishbone* in the Gollancz/Sunday Times best SF story competition in

1987. Her novels include *Mindsail* (1990), *The Brooch of Azure Midnight* (1991) and the much acclaimed *Dancing on the Volcano* (1993).

Susanna Gregory, *A Gift for Killing*. Susanna Gregory (b. 1958) is the author of the historical mystery novels about Matthew Bartholomew, a teacher of medicine at Michaelhouse, part of the fledgling University of Cambridge, in the mid-fourteenth century. The series began with *A Plague on Both Your Houses* in 1996. She previously worked in a coroner's office, which gave her a special insight into criminal behaviour. She contributed *A Villainous Company* based on *Henry IV* to *Shakespearean Whodunnits*.

Lois Gresh, *Three Meetings and a Funeral*, with Robert Weinberg. Lois Gresh (b. 1956) works in the computer industry as a programmer and systems analyst, and has written hundreds of technical manuals and related texts. She is the proprietor of Technohell, Inc., which designs and codes corporate websites, software and systems. She has sold many short science fiction and horror stories and her first novel, *The Termination Node*, written with Weinberg, is in the works, along with *Computers in Star Trek*.

Claire Griffen, *The Wine-Dark Cup*. Claire Griffen has previously appeared in *Classical Whodunnits, The Mammoth Book of New Sherlock Holmes Adventures* and the magazine *Boggle*. She is Australian, and spent several years as an actress and dramatist before turning to writing fantasy and mystery stories.

Edward D. Hoch, *Desdemona's Daughter*. Edward Hoch (b. 1930) is a phenomenally prolific American short-story writer with over seven hundred to his credit. He has created many fascinating detectives, including Captain Leopold, Dr Sam Hawthorne, Nick Velvet, Ben Snow and Simon Ark. His stories appear regularly in *Ellery Queen's Mystery Magazine* and *Alfred Hitchcock's Mystery Magazine* but only a small percentage has made it into individual story collections. Well worth tracking down are his Simon Ark series, *The Judges of Hades, City of Brass* and *The Quests of Simon Ark*, the Nick Velvet books *The Spy and the Thief* and *The Thefts of Nick Velvet*, and the Sam Hawthorne stories, a few of which have been collected as *Diagnosis: Impossible*. He contributed *Toil and Trouble* based on *Macbeth* to the first volume.

Tom Holt, *A Good Report of the Worm*. Tom Holt (b. 1961) is best known for his immensely popular comic fantasy novels, which began with *Expecting Someone Taller* in 1987 and include *Who's Afraid of*

Beowulf?, Ye Gods!, and *Faust Among Equals*. A lesser-known fact is that Holt is an expert on ancient Greece and Rome and has written two novels set in classical Greece, *Goatsong* and *The Walled Orchard*. He contributed *Cinna the Poet*, based on *Julius Caesar*, to *Shakespearean Whodunnits*.

Phyllis Ann Karr, *Love's Labour's Discover'd*. Phyllis Ann Karr (b. 1944) is a noted authority on King Arthur having compiled *The King Arthur Companion*, recently revised as *The Arthurian Companion*. She also wrote the Arthurian historical mystery *The Idylls of the Queen*.

Andy Lane, *As Near to Lust as Flame to Smoke*. Andy Lane is 35 and a full-time civil servant. In his spare time he has written four original *Doctor Who* novels, one *Bugs* novelisation, two *Babylon 5* episode guides and several short stories, as well as co-writing a book on James Bond. He is married and lives in London.

David Langford, *As Strange a Maze as E'er Men Trod*. David Langford (b. 1953), is a British writer of science fiction, fantasy and technology. He caused something of a stir with *An Account of a Meeting with Denizens of Another World, 1871*, a purported account of a Victorian close encounter recorded by William Robert Loosley, which ufologists zealously leaped on as further proof. He has written a humorous science-fiction novel, *The Leaky Establishment*, and compiled *The Unseen University Challenge*, based on Terry Pratchett's Discworld. He has won many awards for his writings in the science-fiction fan magazines and for his own news and gossip magazine *Ansible*. Some of his fan writings have been collected as *The Dragonhiker's Guide to Battlefield Covenant at Dune's Edge: Odyssey Two* (1988) and *The Silence of the Langford* (1996).

Jeffrey Marks, *Stolen Affections* with Lawrence Schimel. Jeffrey Marks (b. 1960) is an American writer and engineer from Cincinnatti. Ohio. He is the editor of the mystery anthology *Canine Crimes* and the author of a biography of mystery writer Craig Rice.

Edward Marston, *War Hath Made All Friends*. Edward Marston is the best known pseudonym of author and playwright Keith Miles. A former lecturer in Modern History, Miles has written over forty original plays for radio, television and the theatre, plus some six hundred episodes of radio and television drama series. He has written over twenty-five novels. Of most interest in the historical mystery field are his two series. The first featuring Nicholas Bracewell and his company of Elizabethan actors which began with *The Queen's Head* in 1988; the second featuring Ralph Delchard and Gervase Bret who resolve crimes as they travel the country helping compile *The Domesday Book* in 1086 – this series began with *The Wolves of Savernake* in 1993.

Amy Myers, *Footsteps in the Snow*. Amy Myers is best known for her books featuring the Victorian/Edwardian master-chef with the remarkable deductive powers, Auguste Didier, who first appeared in *Murder in Pug's Parlour* in 1987. She was previously an editor for the publisher William Kimber for whom she compiled the *After Midnight Stories* series of anthologies. She has also written a series of novels under the name Harriet Hudson, including *The Wooing of Katie May, The Sun in Glory* and *Look for Me by Moonlight*. She contributed *Who Killed Mamillius*, based on *The Winter's Tale* to the first volume.

Stan Nicholls, *We are for the Dark*. Over the years Stan Nicholls (b. 1949) has been an editor, manager of a book-shop, proof-reader, literary advisor and columnist, and, since 1981, full-time writer. He is perhaps best known for his interviews and biographies which include *Wordsmiths of Wonder*, about writers of SF and fantasy, *Ken and Me* about William Roache and *Gerry Anderson*. He has also produced several series of horror and fantasy novels for the teenage market, including the crime novel *Fade to Black*.

Tina and **Tony Rath,** *Conspiracy Theory*. Tina and Tony are a husband-and-wife writing team who have produced several stories both together and individually. Tony is currently working on an historical novel set during the Napoleonic Wars – history being one of his specialities; Tina is working on her PhD thesis on 'The Vampire in Popular Fiction,' vampires being one of her specialities. Tony tends to provide the ideas and historical detail and Tina develops the plot and characters.

Mary Reed and **Eric Mayer,** *Fortune's Other Steward*. Mary Reed and Eric Mayer are another husband-and-wife writing team whose short stories include a series about John the Eunuch who investigates crimes in the early days of the Byzantine Empire, and a series about Inspector Dorj of the Mongolian Police. In their own right they have each written a number of books and articles on a remarkable assortment of esoteric subjects, ranging from Mary's items on weather lore and fruits and nuts, to Eric's articles on marathon running. They contributed *A Shadow That Dies*, based on *Richard III*, to the first volume, *Shakespearean Whodunnits*.

Lawrence Schimel, *Stolen Affections*, with Jeffrey Marks. Lawrence Schimel (b. 1971) is a prolific American writer with many story sales in the fields of fantasy, science fiction, horror and erotica. His first story collection was *The Drag Queen of Elfland* and he has edited the anthologies *Tarot Fantastic* and *Camelot Fantastic.*

Darrell Schweitzer, *Murdered by Love.* Darrell Schweitzer (b. 1952) is a prolific American critic, editor and writer, mostly of fantasy, including the novels *The Shattered Goddess, The White Isle* and *The Mask of the Sorcerer*, and the short story volumes *We Are All Legends, Tom O'Bedlam's Night Out* and *Transients and Other Disquieting Stories.* He contributed *The Death of Falstaff*, from *Henry V*, to the companion volume.

Peter Valentine Timlett, *Beneath Which Hour?.* Peter Timlett (b. 1934) is best known as the author of *The Seedbearers* trilogy tracing the adventures of survivors from Atlantis in early Britain. He has produced several short horror stories and is also a noted expert on the occult.

Ron Tiner, *A Kind of Wild Justice.* Ron Tiner (b. 1940) is a comic-book artist with a penchant for fantasy illustration and the co-author of *The Encyclopedia of Fantasy and Science Fiction Art Techniques.*

Peter Tremayne, *Methought You Saw a Serpent.* Peter Tremayne (b. 1943) is the pseudonym of Celtic scholar and historian Peter Berresford Ellis who, under his own name, has written many books tracing the history and myth of the Celts, including *The Celtic Empire, Celt and Saxon, Celt and Greek* and *Celt and Roman.* In the fiction field he established a reputation for his Dracula series collected in the omnibus *Dracula Lives!*, and the Lan-Kern series based on Cornish mythology, which began with *The Fires of Lan-Kern.* He is perhaps now best known for his series of historical mysteries featuring the seventh-century Irish Advocate, Sister Fidelma, which began with *Absolution by Murder.* He contributed *An Ensuing Evil* to *Shakespearean Whodunnits.*

Robert Weinberg, *Three Meetings and a Funeral* with Lois Gresh. Robert Weinberg (b. 1946) is an American bookdealer, collector and author who has written a number of novels of fantastic fiction. He has produced several featuring occult detective Alex Werner, starting with *The Devil's Auction*, plus a sequence of humorous fantasy novels which began with *A Logical Magician.*